For: alpha —

I hope

novel worthy of your *time*.

Stafford Chenevert

AMBER
WAVES
OF GRAIN

MW01483292

AMBER WAVES OF GRAIN

STAFFORD O. CHENEVERT

Copyright © 2010 by Stafford O. Chenevert.

Library of Congress Control Number: 2009912078
ISBN: Hardcover   978-1-4415-8957-6
               Softcover   978-1-4415-8956-9

All rights reserved. No part of this book may be reproduced or transmitted in
any form or by any means, electronic or mechanical, including photocopying,
recording, or by any information storage and retrieval system, without permission
in writing from the copyright owner.

This is a work of fiction. Names, characters, places and incidents either are the
product of the author's imagination or are used fictitiously, and any resemblance
to any actual persons, living or dead, events, or locales is entirely coincidental.

This book was printed in the United States of America.

To order additional copies of this book, contact:
Xlibris Corporation
1-888-795-4274
www.Xlibris.com
Orders@Xlibris.com
69151

Acknowledgments

Without the support of my wife, Phyllis, and children, Sharon Gaude and Stephen Chenevert, and assistance from people like Adrien Ardoin, Rosemarie Chenevert and my daughter-in-law Nikki Chenevert the realization of this dream would not have been possible.

A debt of gratitude goes to the staff of the Pointe Coupee Library for their assistance in my research. To Bobby Underwood, Charles Ransome, Paul Averitt and others who shared their Air Force experiences with me, you have become a part of "Amber Waves of Grain." The prayer in Chapter 10 is the creation of my late brother, John Chenevert, except for the last line. I secured his permission to use the poem before his death in February 2006.

To the great city of Amarillo, Texas, I dedicate this novel, on behalf of the many young men who served at Amarillo Army Air Field and later Amarillo Air Force Base. You will always be a part of our lives.

Chapter 1

A hot scorching Texas wind blew unobstructed across the open prairie as I stood on the shoulder of U.S. Highway 287 just a short distance from the gate leading to Amarillo Air Force Base. Turning from the stinging dust, I reached for a handkerchief to hold over my mouth and nose. The dust cloud became thicker, obscuring my view of a B-52 bomber making a slow descent onto the distant runway.

With the suddenness, the dust cloud engulfed the Panhandle, so did it disappear, allowing my attention to return skyward to a distant silvery spot now appearing against the clear blue sky far to my right. Assuming a 'parade rest' stance before my secondhand 1959 Ford Fairlane, I continued to watch as the dot grew into a recognizable shape. An adrenaline rush began to fill my fatigued body, dispelling the ill effects of the twelve-hour drive from my home in south Louisiana.

Once more, a besieging gust claimed my attention. Believing its purpose was to fill every orifice of my body with dust, I mentally attempted to accept the violation of my body as a welcoming gesture from Texas. Adding to my discomfort was the annoying way the wind whipped the legs and shirt sleeves of my well-starched and neatly pressed khaki uniform. Countering the relentless pushing of the wind at the back of my uniform cap, I tightly grasped the bill and pulled it down for a more snug fit.

Through the thin veil of dust, I watched as the second bomber made a slow languorous descent onto the runway. Because of the great distance separating us, only the low-muffled roar of the powerful jet engines signaled the bomber's safe arrival. A hubristic smile temporarily transformed my frowning face. An Air Policeman watching from outside the nearby Guard shack offered the only resistance to my desire to commemorate my first sighting of these magnificent planes with a shout of pride.

Thinking the last of the bombers had landed, I stepped away from the car with the intention of driving the short distance to my first-duty station. Another gust of wind succeeded in stealing my cap, causing it to tumble in the gravel and dust like an uprooted tumbleweed. With something of a slight disconcerted smile, I mumbled, "Dead-gum wind!" before giving chase.

As a new recruit and still fastidious about my uniform, a well-placed spray of saliva delivered to the scuffed area of the bill received a good buffing with the once-more-retrieved handkerchief. For the benefit of the Air Policeman's watchful eyes, I returned the cap to my head and adjusted it according to Air Force regulations by using two fingers to gauge the proper position above the eyes.

In the process of chasing the cap, my highly polished shoes became dusty, triggering an automatic response, every recruit learns early on in Basic Training as a final point of readiness before inspection. The toe of the right shoe received several swipes on the backside of the left pants leg followed by the reverse treatment of the left toe on the back of the right pants leg.

Distracted by the brief dust storm and the landing of the bombers, the open countryside surrounding the base had momentarily escaped my attention. In Childress, Texas, where I changed from my preferred traveling attire of blue jeans and polo shirt to the required Air Force khaki uniform, I began noticing a difference in this new *terra firma,* in which I found myself. Being from the bayou country of south Louisiana where water and trees are a part of the everyday surroundings, this alien, open land with no bounds, on which to focus, began to play tricks on my senses.

After returning to the car, I made the short drive to the gate with as much pride as I could bring to bear, given the humiliation visited upon me by the wind. Stepping in front of my car with an uplifted hand, the Air Policeman signaled me to stop.

"Welcome to Amarillo Air Force Base," said the square-jaw Staff Sergeant with a taunting grin. "Copy of your transfer orders," he ordered while bending down to the driver's side window.

"Does the wind blow this way all the time?" I asked offering up a copy of my transfer orders.

"No," replied the Sergeant with a sardonic smirk. "Sometimes, it blows the other way."

Accepting the gibe as a local joke, I took no offense.

With a small map of the base, I found my way to the Headquarters Squadron of the 3320th Technical Training School Squadron while giving the sprawling base a careful study. After a two-day ordeal of "processing in" and repeating my Cajun, tongue twisting name a hundred times, I received an assignment to the Administration Office in Hangar 4000, home of the Jet Engine Mechanic School. With primary clerical responsibilities in the office to a civilian psychologist who counseled students having difficulty with their studies, I soon learned reading "Doc's" handwriting was as much a task for me as my name was for the office staff.

The barracks on Amarillo Air Force Base, all designed the same, were divided into four bays consisting of several rooms. A dayroom equipped with a small television and pool table separated the upper and lower bays.

Settling into the communal life of a barrack is less formal than an office environment and the continuing difficulty presented to those trying to pronounce my family name quickly earned me the nickname of Yogi. I accepted the appellation, offered up by my roommate once I attempted to pronounce his Hungarian name.

Dubbed "Tank," because his body appeared as thick as it was wide, the Airman First Class from Pennsylvania, whose father owned a coal mine, of which he talked incessantly, calling it the "hole," was one of those Neanderthal guys with hair all over his body. Tank had a reputation around the barrack as being a scrapper, but contrary to his virile appearance, he had a weak stomach, subjecting him to a number of disgusting practical jokes.

Tank owned two things out of character for a person of his physical stature and skill in the art of pugilism; a collection of classical records and a parakeet named Pete. At first, Tank's "unwinding sessions of classical music" after work while stretched out on his bunk reading his mail or looking at a Playboy magazine drove me from the room, since I was still into rock 'n roll.

While trying to maintain some semblance of my former civilian life, as well as maintaining my sanity, in the "alien environment" of the Panhandle and barracks life, I found attending Sunday services at the beautiful white chapel on base as a means of coping. As a teenager, I didn't particularly enjoy Sunday school, but desiring some connection with my former life, even this point of reference became enjoyable.

In addition to the Jet Engine School, there was also an Administration School on the base in Building 5105 located between my barrack and Hangar 4000. It took several discussions with "Doc" about the "career advantages" such a school would offer, before my request for enrollment came through. In addition to exciting new things . . . like proper filing procedures, letter writing and office management techniques, I found myself the only Airman in a typing class with twenty-five WAFs.

Following graduation, a gung ho attitude possessed my body and spirit while trying to revamp the office to the theoretical world of academia. Most of the offered suggestions went unheeded, causing me to realize the world of 'Administration School' and the 'Day-to-Day World' of a real office is realms apart.

However, my newly acquired organizational skills became useful as I assumed the responsibility of reorganizing the main reference library of Technical Orders on the various jet engines taught in the school.

After several weeks, numerical designations such as J-57, J-79, and J-85 became as familiar to my brain as the keyboard on my manual Underwood typewriter.

Several months after my arrival in Amarillo, a new Airman named James Kaiser from Arab, Alabama, reported for duty one morning in the Hangar office. A friendship between us developed immediately since we were the only two Southern boys in the office and our slow drawl presented no language barrier. Our mutual fondness for such things as "greens, grits, pigs' feet and hominy" cemented further the friendship.

James was of small stature, about five feet, seven inches and weighed approximately 165 pounds. For the most part, he was an amiable person except when "tight," which took a considerable amount of beer to accomplish. He wasn't one who quaffed his beers, but slowly savored every sip as if contemplating the complex process that went into making the brew.

Another of James' passions was tobacco. He had learned, beginning at the age of twelve, to take the simple pleasure of the leaf to an art form. After each meal in the Mess Hall, while leaning back in the chair, he passed the time by leisurely creating a circuit of smoke by discharging a small trail from his nostrils, while slowly pulling it back into his mouth. James also had a fondness for country music and his soft crooning of Kitty Wells or Skeeter Davis' most recent hits while sitting at his desk, irritated our civilian secretary, a buxom grandmotherly type named Mrs. Milo.

Another person to come into my life that summer was Airman Third Class Paul Schlebecker, a farm boy from the Midwest. Standing about the same height as James, Paul was more muscular and wore his thick wavy brown hair an inch or two longer than Air Force regulations prescribed, much to the irritation of the Squadron's First Sergeant who bore the designation of "Sausage Sam" because of his peddling of homemade Italian sausage on base. Paul had a baby-smooth complexion, for which he received some ragging since at the great age of eighteen and nineteen, facial hair was proudly seen as a sign of masculinity. To stifle his critics, Paul in his characteristic jocular manner boasted with a great grin, which seemed to further enlarge his prodigious mouth that he shaved once a month if he needed it or not. Paul too was a smoker, and when in uniform he carried his cigarettes in his right sock. When in civilian clothes, his pack of Lucky Strikes rested as an enlarged epaulet on his left shoulder joint in a double fold of his T-shirt sleeve.

Paul had one flaw in his character. His ebullient spirit sometimes took on a gauche nature and expressed itself in such crude forms as expelling gas in public or putting plastic dog poop on Tank's tray in the Mess Hall, just to watch the *big man's face turn green*.

Paul's roommate was a tall good-looking blond boy from Chicago by the name of John Richardson, who wore his uniform cap on the back of his head in a cocky jaunty manner. John didn't just walk down the hall; he swaggered in an effort to imitate his favorite movie star, Troy Donahue. John usually reeked of Old Spice, and in keeping with his teenage rebel image, John carried a small comb in his shirt pocket. When most likely to impress members of the opposite sex, John slowly removed the comb and dragged it through his Vitalis laden crew cut.

In spite of his good looks, perfect physique, and attractive cleft in his chin, John had one physical flaw; a diastema, large enough, through which a dime could be passed.

The friendship created with these three boys who came into my life that summer expressed itself in our youthful lust for life, generated by a form of freedom unknown before in each of our lives. Gallivanting was the only purpose to our lives away from the base and the occasional "gas wars," which drove the prices down to fifteen or twenty cents a gallon accommodated well, our low pay and resolve to live fast and for the moment. Metaphorically, we drove a stake in the center of Amarillo, claiming the city as our own.

Amarillo, like most military towns had three business establishments, which appealed most to young single GIs. On the main business street of the city, named after President Polk, were several pawn shops, a tattoo parlor located in the bus terminal at 4th and Fillmore and of course a bordello. The latter, an old hotel, built sometime during the early 1900s, had long since seen its glory days.

With the old hotel in the middle of Polk Street as the main source of attraction for the GIs who received liberty only on Saturday afternoons, two other points on opposite ends of the street held different attractions for those of us who were mobile. At the corner of Route 66 and Polk Street was St. Anthony's Hospital and Nursing College, which meant plenty young single girls. On the opposite end of the street was The Double Dip, an ice cream and burger stand where young locals and single Airmen hung out after football games and movies. After such occasions, the parking lot took on the appearance of a carousel as cars crept by in a tumultuous mixture of music, enthusiastic greetings and the ever present smell of greasy burgers and French fries.

Cruising up and down Polk Street on Friday or Saturday evenings became a ritual; we understood and shared with other kindred spirits. One of the high lights of such journeys always occurred at the railroad crossing on Polk Street in the vicinity of several old brick warehouses. Seeking to heighten our hilarity attempts to become airborne were made without regarded to the damage being inflicted to the brick street or the frame of our cars.

John's car, given the affectionate nickname, *The Iron Lung*, because of its habitual nature to smoke was an imposing1955 Chrysler New Yorker C-300 with a Hemi V-8. Its 300 hp engine, equipped with a four-barrel carburetor could do every bit of the 140 mph marked on the speedometer in spite of its smoking capabilities. Decked out with heavy chrome-plated bumpers, "Twin Tower" taillights and a gold medallion bearing the number 300 on each hubcap, *The Lung*'s massive black body seemed exaggerated by the six-inch wide red stripe running its full length.

That first summer of my tour in Amarillo quickly turned into fall, followed by an unforgiving winter, which blew into the Panhandle with the fury of a mad longhorn. Being from South Louisiana and yet to see my first significant snowfall, I awaited the climatic change with some apprehension. For weeks the north wind maintained its ancient custom of blowing frozen tumble weeds down Polk Street, crashing them into passing cars with the sound of shattering glass. The snow accumulation that first winter wasn't much, but the thing to catch my attention was how it drifted around the quadrangle. The biting cold, to, which I wasn't accustomed, only increased my dislike for the region and the city.

The Venetian blinds hanging before the windows in my room moved with a slight rhythm as the cold blistering wind forced its way past the loose fitting windows of the barrack. This same cold draft, which had been pushing its way through the windows all night caused a shudder to travel across my body as I adjusted my necktie for the final time before the locker door mirror. After slipping on the heavy Air Force overcoat I looked with contempt across the room at the small radiator below the windows, thinking how useless it was against the blistering wind and swirling snowflakes dancing against the window panes.

After an agonizing week of suffering as a result of the drafty barrack, apparently built during the early days of the base, my three friends and I discussed our common plight and agreed to a solution of sorts. Setting out on a "heater hunting" expedition we headed for the Tascosa Drive-In Theater.

The acquisition was quite simple. A slammed car door on the heater cord and a short drive to the next pole completed the transaction. With the procurement of four heaters we returned to the base where each received a new plug; recently obtained by Paul from Base Supply. Soon a wave of somnolent warmth in each of our rooms began to fight back the winter chill.

The other boys in the bay soon became aware of our torrid living conditions, but the secret managed to escape Sausage Sam's attention until Paul failed to put away his heater one morning before leaving for duty. During an unannounced "shake down inspection" the following Saturday morning, the remaining three heaters became the property of the First Sergeant and the CQ Runner who accompanied him.

As a just castigation for our thievery, the snowfall the following night came down in what I imagined to be a blizzard driving the temperature in my room to the freezing point. In desperation to save my life and that of Pete, I removed the mattress from my bunk and threw it down the stairwell. Trudging down the stairs with my pillow, two blankets and Pete's cage, I decided to take up residence in the boiler room, the warmest spot in the entire building.

Awaken the following morning by someone kicking my leg; I stirred sluggishly before having the blanket jerked from over my face. Staring up at Sausage Sam with a degree of defiance, I let the First Sergeant know the boiler room would be my sleeping quarters until the winter winds subsided. Without saying anything, Sam started for the door where he paused to look back. In a gruff voice to demonstrate his authority, Sausage Sam ordered that I haul all my crap back to my room. "And clean the bird shit out of that cage!" he shouted before stepping through the door.

With the coming of winter, we sought a respite from the bleakness of the weather by attending professional wrestling matches each Thursday night at the Amarillo Sports Arena. Our little motley group wasn't really wrestling fans; we just enjoyed the violent and psychotic surrealism taking place in the ring and the arena. As the large auditorium erupted into a din of hysteria, a barrage of tomatoes or eggs were sent flying toward the ring from the cheap bleachers where most GIs were required to sit, since they were admitted for half-price. Our group's greatest enjoyment, however, came from taunting the local fans who idolized two of Amarillo's favorites, Dory Funk and Ricky Romero. By cheering for such 'bad boys' as the Dalton Brothers, Sputnik Monroe or Wahoo McDaniel, an Indian chief who wore a war bonnet into the ring, our small pack of renegades drew threatening remarks from the nearby irritated fans.

That first winter dragged on interminably, taking a toll on animals, people, and car batteries throughout the Panhandle. During the long miserable days and nights spent sleeping in the boiler room, I developed a longing for summer and the blowing dust.

Chapter 2

Tepid living conditions for everyone in the barracks came as the blistering winds of winter slowly turned into gentle spring breezes. Pete and I said a fond *adieu* to the boiler room and began spending more nights in my room as the radiator seemed now able to hold its own against the occasional winds seeping past the windows.

The huge snow drifts against the barracks continued to melt away in the warming sun, leaving only a few splotches to remind us of the misery they had brought into our lives. Sparsely blades of grass sprang forth in their wake, indicating Mother Earth *enceinte* with life was approaching her time of delivery.

With the coming of spring, something more than just green grass and the sweet sounds of song birds came to the Panhandle. It signaled the renewing of two traditions at Amarillo Air Force Base. What we, in the 3320th School Squadron, dubbed "Sausage Duty," ranked slightly below the occasional Mickey Mouse parades on Saturday mornings to honor visiting dignitaries.

As the weather warmed and the final vestige of snow melted away, the First Sergeant required the boys of our barrack to muster in front of the Orderly Room one beautiful Saturday morning. With an orotund voice, Sausage Sam's call for his troops to stand at attention brought the sound of bootheels slamming together as the deep furrows in each of our foreheads faded. Standing as rigid cadavers in our well-starched and seldom worn fatigue uniforms, we feigned our *combat readiness* to do our duty with the awaiting *artillery* and other *arms of combat* lying on the ground at our brogans. The military objective was to take from the 3340th School Squadron what rightly belonged to "our man Sam," the annual Base Beautification Award. With rakes, shovels, wheel barrows, fertilizer-seed spreaders, and other hand weapons at our disposal, the battle lines in the sands of Amarillo Air Force Base were drawn.

Growing grass of any significance on the base, fell right below the parting of the Red Sea in the scheme of great events, so in order to prepare the quadrangle, the entire area was raked and cleared of all gravel, discarded cigarette butts, or any other infinitesimal debris capable of escaping the eyes of anyone except a First Sergeant. Under his watchful eyes, a row of boxwood plants, carefully measured and equally spaced before the Orderly Room, became the first line of attack.

The greatest challenge of the day came when a dump truck showed up with a load of broken concrete. Our anguish soared to new heights when commanded to sort through the pile for only those about the size of a cantaloupe. The pieces not meeting the Sergeant's specifications went through a modification at the hands of John and me, each wielding a sledge hammer. Each selected stone then received a coat of white paint and carefully placed in a line at the corners of the sidewalks and along the walkway leading to each set of steps before the barracks.

When Sausage Sam dismissed his troops at 16:00 hours, we were all in agreement that Bacchanalia time was nearing. Following a refreshing shower and shave, four very tired veterans of Sam's War managed to walk to the Chow Hall in a spirit of blitheness, knowing we had mounted a significant first attack in overcoming the enemy. During the return trip to the barrack, we decided to spend the evening at the Airmen's Club since our desk jobs as Administrative Clerks hadn't conditioned our bodies for Sam's form of combat.

The Airmen's Club covered about the same floor area as that of an average High School gym, but with a ceiling height of only ten feet, a cloud of cigarette smoke four feet thick hovered throughout the place.

On Friday and Saturday nights, thousands of teenage recruits filled the Club to capacity, with the intention of living up to Hollywood's image of war heroes, who always got drunk and fought their way to fame and glory. To control this truculent crowd of John Wayne imitators, a number of NCOs patrolled the Club in an effort to keep a throttle on the 'beer-inspired' testosterone level.

Wanting to distinguish ourselves from the recruits, my three friends and I wore civilian clothes. James, who was attempting to adapt to the cowboy culture of the Panhandle, wore a western style shirt with pearl snaps, a new pair of khaki pants, and penny loafers. John, who had become the quintessential cow town, 'Dapper Dan,' strutted down the sidewalk besides James in a new western outfit, including an ostentatious white hat, while leaving behind an Old Spice vapor trail through, which Paul and I walked.

After finding what we considered a safe table in a back corner, out of the usual line of flying beer bottles, a regular hazard in the Club, we settled down and ordered each a beer. The fact that two WAFs were sitting at the next table with several young recruits, became a source agitation for Paul and John, which they were determined to correct. The consumption of several beers intensified, not only their disapproval, but Paul's ribald character who shared several unsolicited lewd jokes with the girls.

Paul's dirty jokes and an invitation for the girls to visit a secret submarine location on the base with him and John, failed to accomplish the desired reaction. With the consumption of several more beers, their machismo began to ramp up, dragging James into their scheme. I continued nursing my first beer.

A loud caterwaul erupted above the noise of the Club, when one of the recruits at the next table suddenly stood, knocked over his chair, and challenged the Airman next to him with a running string of vulgarity. After being laughed down by his friends, the recruit wiped the beer dripping from his ear before picking up his chair.

Attempting to hide our snickering behind the quart bottles of Lone Star, we watched as John filled his mouth once more, before firing a second salvo through his diastema at the recruit's ear. Through years of practice, he had 'fine tuned' the art of spewing beer or any other liquid with such perfection, he could hit an ear at twelve feet in the darkest of barrooms.

As the resulting fight at the next table exploded and spread throughout the Club, the burly chested, NCOs bearing shotguns and swinging night sticks rushed in, seeking revenge for having to 'baby sit' a bunch of drunken teenagers. The distinctive sound of ratcheting shotguns caused a rush for every exit.

Escaping through an emergency exit with the two WAFs, Paul and John invited them to take a ride in *The Iron Lung* to visit the secret submarine installation located on the far side of the Base near the Test Cells. James and I just stood aside and watched the uncontrolled exodus produced by the continuing ratcheting of shotguns.

As the tumultuous crowd continued fleeing, a stern voice of authority distinguished itself above the clamor.

"Okay, Airman! Turn if off!" Turning in the direction of the voice, I saw a flashlight beaming down on James' penis as he delivered a golden flow of urine against a young sapling.

"I'm not finished peeing," James slurred with an elfin smile and a slight sway from side to side.

"I said, 'Turn it off . . . Airman!' And put that thing in your pants!" yelled the Air Policeman as he pushed his night stick against James' hand attempting to break his grip.

Turning his body slightly toward the Air Policeman, James unintentionally urinated on the man's night stick. A sharp jab to the stomach brought about an immediate interruption in the flow, but not a retraction of the spigot.

Taken to the Air Police Headquarters and dragged before the Desk Sergeant, we both stood on a painted line on the floor; all the while, James maintained a death grip on his penis that he had refused to put away while in the crew cab pickup truck.

"You have a live one tonight, Brew!" said the arresting officer to the Desk Sergeant busily searching through some filing cabinets with his back toward us. "The little son-of-a-bitch pissed on my stick," continued the Policeman as he entered another room.

While the Sergeant was busying himself with the files, I noticed the name plate on his desk, that read 'Staff Sergeant, Broussard'. *"Ah . . . a fellow Cajun,"* I thought.

Trying to ingratiate myself with the good Sergeant on behalf of James, I gave a loud harrumph hoping to draw his attention away from the filing cabinet. In a cheerful tone, I hailed my Cajun brother with a highfalutin, *Bon soir cousin.* (Good evening cousin).

Without turning to face me, Sergeant Broussard replied in a gruff voice, "That won't help you, Airman."

I could see this guy had been away from Louisiana too long and had forgotten what it meant to be a Cajun. In desperation, I looked over at James hoping to dissuade him from his present course of holding onto things. To my surprise, he was now gripping with his left hand and saluting with his right hand while weaving in a small circle.

"Put that thing in your pants before the Sarge turns around," I whispered in his ear, while trying not to laugh.

"Yogi, I haven't finishing peeing," James replied grinding his teeth. A shudder then seemed to shake his whole body.

Without looking at either of us, the Sergeant sat down at his desk on a slightly raised platform and routinely fed a form into his typewriter. After adjusting the form in the proper position and hitting the space bar to bring the carriage to its proper starting position, he spoke in a perfunctory manner without really facing us.

"All right, cousin," give me your last name first, your first name second, and your middle initial last." The Sergeant's voice was mechanical and dry.

James failed to respond while maintaining his grip, but no longer saluting.

"Look, numskull! Give me your last name first!" yelled the Sergeant as he turned to face us.

The Sergeant's eyes immediately focused on James' left hand and his neck hyperextended like that of a chicken reaching for something through a fence.

"Airman! Are you holding yourself?" shouted Sergeant Broussard in a boisterous tone.

"I wasn't finished peeing, Sir," replied James still holding on and trying to control his balance.

Taking the night stick from the right edge of his desk, Sergeant Broussard reached forward and landed a solid blow to James' left upper arm. James flinched but maintained his grip.

"Don't Sir me, Airman! Do you see any bars on my collar?" rejoined the Sergeant in an agitated tone while pointing the night stick at James' face. Turning his anger and night stick on me, the Sergeant yelled, "You! Stable that pony, or I'll throw both of you into the Guard House!"

"Me?" I asked befuddled.

"Do it!" commanded Sergeant Broussard.

Looking at James, I could tell he was in great pain. Not wanting to see him spend the night in the Guard House, or myself, I pulled opened his *braguette* with my left hand while taking my handkerchief in the right hand to *stable the pony.*

After leaning next to James' ear, in a very calm voice, I said, "You little Alabama Red Neck if you tell anyone I touched your dick, I'll knock so many teeth down your throat you'll be able to bite an apple with your butt!"

Returning to his chair, Sergeant Broussard began again by clearing his throat and readjusting his typewriter, somewhat angrily.

"All right, Airman, give me your last name first, your first name . . ."

A very long "ahhhhhh" interrupted the Sergeant. The most delightful smile I had ever seen transformed James' face. As the Sarge and I looked down at James' crotch, a large wet spot began to develop on his khaki pants and rapidly made its way down the left leg toward his penny loafers. In silent dismay, I watched as the left shoe began to overflow, sending a stream of urine toward the Sergeant's desk.

Very slowly, Sergeant Broussard lifted himself from his chair and leaned across the desk to watch the stream flowing in his direction. Resting his bulky upper body on his hairy arms, he stared up at James as his face went through a series of contortions and changed several shades of red, declaring his choleric disposition. In a fit of Cajun anger, he yelled in French, *Jette ce cochon au dehors* (Throw out this pig).

Without waiting to see whom the angry Sergeant was addressing, I took James by the arm and lead him from the office. With each step, the urine-filled loafer left a small track on the floor and made a sloshing sound, as distinctive as the ratcheting shotguns in the Club.

With the advancement of spring and Sausage Sam's war for the Base Beautification Award now involving the boys of the neighboring barracks for a couple of weekends, my three friends and I discovered a wonder of nature south of Amarillo; Palo Duro Canyon.

According to a brochure picked up at the tourist center, Palo Duro Canyon was the site of the last major battle of the famous Red River Indian Wars, which finally brought the Comanches and Kiowas under control and returned them to the reservation. This battle fought in a drenching thunderstorm, led the Indians to call it the "Wrinkled-hand Chase."

On a beautiful Sunday afternoon, as my friends and I each rented a horse at the corral in the canyon, the exploits of young Captain Charles Hatfield of E Troop of the 4th Cavalry or those of Charles Goodnight who followed him as the first rancher to settle the canyon, were the furthest things from our minds. Blazing our own trail through the beautiful canyon as fast as we could, once out of sight of the guys running the corral was the only thoughts we shared. Driven by the innate nature possessed by all males to demonstrate their masculinity, we sought further to show off our equestrian skills by racing lengthy ways through a small creek, trying to wet the lagging riders. After a short run and all four horses and riders were sufficiently wet, the "run" came to an end with no clear winner.

Walking the horses at a leisurely pace, John and I rode side by side in front of James and Paul. In Paul's usual gauche manner, he entertained us with a tale about a girl he knew in High School, whose rump resembled that of John's horse. The story was reaching a point of outlandishness when two horses galloped past us, carrying two screaming *damsels in distress.*

Without thinking, John and I buried our boots into the flanks of our horses, causing them to dig their hoofs into the rocky ground of the canyon floor. With the pounding of thundering hoofs, we were off to the rescue in true cowboy fashion and possible romance from the grateful girls for our heroic deeds. Leaning forward in the saddle, I disregarded the horse's long smelly mane flying in my face as I encouraged him to even greater speed by whipping his neck with the reigns. The increased efforts of my gallant steed caused him to draw great gulps of air through his distended nostrils.

John Wayne or Gary Cooper could not have executed a more perfect rescue. Hanging precariously from the saddle, I grabbed the reins of the runaway horse with one hand before pulling back on the reins of my own horse. My brave charger dug his hind hoofs into the loose sand and stones of the stream, which in my mind was now a dangerous torrent, threatening to drown me and the frightened maiden. The temperamental runaway horse pranced around wildly in the water for what seemed an interminable time, preventing me from gazing upon the face of my "would be grateful ladylove."

Regrouping with John, who had rescued a beautiful girl with shoulder-length blonde hair and blue eyes named Casey Duff, I presented to him Dracula's daughter whose name I learned was Opal. With more hair on her legs than I reasoned on mine and the sweaty black locks protruding from under her armpits brought a bewildering stare to John's face, before a slight snicker parted his lips. A pair of shower thongs rounded out Opal's wardrobe of knee-length jeans, apparently cut with a cane knife, and a grungy yellow tank top. My heart sank in further disappointment as Opal reached for the reins while smiling. She had a diastema that would put John's to shame. *Why couldn't John have saved this broad,* I thought scornfully. *Then they could get married and had sons who could learn to spew beer like a cobra.*

Once reunited with James and Paul, I suggested the girls could now ride off together. The horses, upon which Paul and James were riding, appeared to have a less stunned expression on their faces than their riders when they rejoined our little party. I knew then, the badgering coming my way from those two knuckleheads for not saving the horse and losing the "hound's tooth" would be unbearable.

As the ride through the canyon resumed, John and Casey led the way while James and Paul once more brought up the rear behind Opal and me. The snickering from the rearguard caused me to occasionally reach my right hand to my side, away from Opal's view, and give them the finger. The gesture only served to spur on their buffoonery with an adaptation of "Home on the Range." With his legs crossed over the horse's neck in front of the saddle, Paul strummed an imaginary guitar as he and James worked out the words to a tune they called "Homely on the Range." Opal remarked that she enjoyed their singing.

While left unscathed by the rescue, except for my wounded pride, the rest of the Sunday afternoon was spent in a state of mortification while riding beside my "little dogie," whose infatuation with her champion appeared to be growing by the minute; much to the delight of the Texas troubadours trailing behind us. I left Palo Duro Canyon, feeling as anguished as I imagined the Indians must have felt on the morning of September 28, 1874, as they watched the U.S. Army destroy more than one thousand of their ponies in the canyon, their one-time sanctuary.

Chapter 3

The month of May, named after the Italic goddess Maia, meaning "good mother or nurse," brought a climatic healing to the Panhandle and my life, as James and Paul laid to rest, temporarily, their opus, "Homely on the Range." Through the combined efforts of Mother Nature and the virility of the First Sergeant, recapturing the Base Beautification Award was just a matter of time, as water sprinklers located throughout the quadrangle worked their magic. As our bodies acclimated to the rigors of "Sausage Duty," our tour of duty in May was less fatiguing as it had been when the war began. The number of troops appearing on the "sick roster" and declared *hors de combat* from sore muscles and other *lies* lessened in time.

On that first Saturday afternoon in May, when Sam dismissed his troops, he assigned John and me the responsibility of taking up all the hoses and sprinklers once the grass was sufficiently watered. This extra duty, which killed another two hours threw, a kink into our plans for taking a couple of girls to the Tascosa Drive-in via *The Iron Lung*, since in a moment of blind G.I. camaraderie I agreed to let James and Paul use my car for the night.

The Pink Elephant, a true Texas honky-tonk of mudsill height and corrugated tin outer walls on Route 66, was our first stop of the evening, where we hoped to hookup with Paul and James. Since they were not there, we each took a Lone Star beer 'to go' and headed for the Double Dip.

Cruising into the rear entrance to the Double Dip with as much grace as possible, given its bad shocks, *The Iron Lung* emitted a faint blue smoke trail. After backing into a parking spot, we got out leaving the headlights on, the usual signal to the Car Hops of our desire to order. While waiting, we nursed the remainder of our beers.

As usual for a Saturday night, the parking lot was a menagerie of foregathered young people, energized to a point of wild hilarity by the loud music blaring from several car radios. The carefree atmosphere that comes with such a youthful gathering seemed fueled by the honking horns of parading jalopies and hot rods. These cars, reflective of their owner's personality, appeared as hermaphroditic beasts of metal outer shells and human inners. Like *The Iron Lung*, they too belched out their own offensive fumes as they slowly traversed the parking lot as prowling carnivores looking for something to devour. Each beast upon entering the parking lot demonstrated its prowess by issuing forth a wild call, vocally, glass pack, or otherwise. An occasional backfire caused by nimble fingers, quickly switching "off," and then "on" again, the ignition would usually cause a stampede among the other animals.

Among the macho beasts prowling the parking lot, appeared a shiny new red VW Beetle, which seemed as out of place as a Panda in Africa. When the VW, occupied by two High School age girls, made its first run through the parking lot, John stood away from *The Iron Lung* and slowly raised the longneck bottle to his lips. Paul and James pulled into the parking lot behind the Beetle.

The VW, now temporarily halted by the traffic jam, gave John an opportunity to try out his Troy Donahue routine. After giving a loud harrumph, throwing back his shoulders and running his pocket comb through his Vitalis enriched hair, he sauntered toward the car with his small finger jammed into the neck of his beer bottle. Before reaching the VW, it moved forward several feet with the traffic, spoiling his efforts.

"Hey . . . beautiful," John shouted in a low desperate pleading voice as the VW continued to move slowly away from him toward Polk Street.

While left standing in the line of traffic with his arm reaching out and the beer bottle dangling from his finger, he called out, "Where you've been all my life . . . babe?"

"In Grade School," yelled back the passenger who then flipped him the bird.

The finger gesture and resulting blaring car horns and laughter didn't deter John. Standing on his toes and yelling through his cupped hands while trying to hang onto his beer bottle, John called out, "Hey, sweet thing . . . I don't have your phone number."

"And further more . . . you won't get it lover boy," yelled back the girl who had now turned around in the seat and was hanging out the window. "Try calling the whore who brought your sorry ass into the world."

The roar of laughter raised by the surrounding spectators left the Master of "come-on-lines" standing humiliated in the parking lot. James and Paul even joined in the taunting.

Spinning around to face us, John hurled his beer bottle against the pavement near the front tire of *The Lung*. Deadpan expressions replaced the smiles on Paul and James' faces as they jumped back from the splashing beer.

"That bitch's got no right to call my mother a whore," shouted John thrusting his finger in the direction of Polk Street.

"Forget it John," I injected attempting to sound supportive. "What the hell she knows about you or any of us? She's just a high school kid."

Moving toward *The Lung*, John eased up onto the fender without saying anything. The expression on his face signaled he needed to be alone. My beer now seemed flat, so I put it on the pavement to the rear of *The Lung*.

After what seemed an interminable long and quiet time, which was unusual among us, our burgers and fries having been consumed, we were about to leave, when the VW made a second run through the parking lot. The girl who had occupied the passenger seat was now driving.

Once more, the Beetle became stuck in the stalled traffic. John's quick pace toward the front of the car indicated he had something on his mind other than adding a name to his little black book. My friends and I looked at each other, unsure what this lanky Chicago kid was up to. With all the macho finesse he could muster, John stood in front of the VW with his left foot on the bumper and his right foot stretched out a few feet to the rear. His stance reminded me of runners poised in the starting blocks at a High School trackmeet. The high pitch sound of the VW's horn agitated him, so he shifted his weight to the car bumper causing it to bounce.

"You're not a very friendly little elementary brat," John said in a gruff tone while pointing at the driver and continuing to pump on the car bumper with his foot, causing it to rock.

After giving the horn a long blast, the driver yelled out in a tart tone. "Get your foot off my car . . . you Air Force trash . . . or I'll run you over like a bug!"

With this stinging insult, the unflappable John leaped on the front bumper with both feet and began jumping up and down. His wild antics began to attract a crowd including Paul, James, and I, who ran over to the VW. While the little VW rebounded under his rhythmic moves, it appeared to gain in elevation with each bounce as did the screams from within.

"You think I'm Air Force trash and my mother's a whore?" shouted John as he rested momentarily from his bouncing to catch a breath. "You're gonna smash me like a bug?" he yelled pointing to his chest as the crowd of GIs gathering around the red VW grew. "Hell . . . bitch, you're riding in a bug." Before continuing his desultory "boil over" John planted his left shoe in the center of the shiny red trunk and pointed his finger at the windshield. "I think my trashy Air Force friends and I will roll *this bug* over on its back like a turd tumbler!"

"Come on down, John," I pleaded while taking hold of his pants leg, "let it go! It's no big deal what this broad thinks of us, the Air Force or your mother. She's just some snotty nosed kid."

"Damn it . . . Yogi, she owes us an apology," snapped John as he stared down at me. Pounding on his chest, John shouted in a boisterous voice as he stood in the center of the VW's trunk, "She owes me an apology for calling my mother a whore!"

John's rage in defense of his mother seemed out of place, given the fact he often said, as a child he hated her, because of the many sailor friends she had when they lived in San Diego. John's line about "all girls being chicks and all chicks made for frying" had developed in his adolescent mind as a result of his mother's sending *him to the movies while she and her friend fried some chicken.* Scornfully John said, *The chicken was never there when I returned.* The anger showing in John's face indicated, the girl unknowingly awakened a truth hidden for many years, transforming the carefree handsome boy who wanted to be Troy Donahue, into someone I no longer recognized, but felt empathy for, because he was my friend.

After receiving a resounding endorsement from the crowd, John jumped to the ground with his arms raised in the air as a conquering hero. Like wild beasts of the jungle turning against one of its own, the young boys, mostly Airmen, followed John's command to grab the front bumper of the VW. In the excitement of the moment, I too, took hold of the car and became a part of the crazed pack. With each bounce of the VW, the frightful screams of the two girls increased until the front end came off the ground.

With the VW in a vertical position on its rear bumper, John extracted from the driver an apology, for his mother and the "Air Force trash" present. Satisfied with the apology, John ordered the grinning faces around him to lower the car. At about three feet from the pavement, all hands released the bumper.

After bouncing several times, the VW shot from the parking lot with the thrust of a jet fighter. While driving off into the night, the driver assailed John with a wake of vulgarity, to which he responded with his own invective charges while grasping his crouch.

"Yogi, do you want to ride over to Casey's place?" asked John as we walked back to *The Lung.*

"Thanks, but I'm not up to seeing Opal's hairy armpits. I think the three of us will go back to the Pink Elephant."

Breaking the monotony of my administrative job in the Jet Engine School was a daily detail, which I enjoyed, thanks to the most punctual civilian employee on the Base; a man named Mr. Joe Mahoney. Promptly each morning at 09:00 hours, a blue Air Force pickup truck from the Motor Pool sounded its horn at the large doors of the hangar signaling me that it was time for the morning mail run.

While sorting through the mail one morning after such a run, I noticed a set of transfer orders for a Technical Sergeant Davy Crockett from Andrews Air Force Base in Maryland. The unusual name struck me funny, and I called it to James' attention, who shared my interest in the name. We were wondering why ole Davy Crockett hadn't joined the Army and followed in the footsteps of other great mountain heroes like Daniel Boone and Sergeant York, when a phone call from the Orderly Room cut short our pleasurable speculating. Airman Zuccarello, always the bearer of bad news, said, "Sausage Sam wanted to see me ASAP."

Ten minutes later I was standing at parade rest before the First Sergeant's desk, gripping with white knuckles the Flight's Guidon. A sickening feeling turned my stomach, as Sausage Sam explained in graphic details an assortment of ancient War Stories about men who sacrificed their lives carrying forward various Regimental flags, *never allowing them to touch the ground or be captured.* Grinding his teeth in my left ear for emphasis, I expected he would spit forth yellow dental aggregate at the conclusion of this course in *"gung hoism."* Pacing about me and the emblem so dear to his heart, the blustering Italian Sergeant, for a while, had me believing, I, like Private Henry Fleming, from Red Badge of Courage, would eventually find the courage to charge the very *mouths of the cannons of Amarillo.*

This entire stratagem was a prelude to show the importance of the new assignment, for which I was "volunteering," as the Flight's Guidon Bearer in the upcoming base parade. It appeared, the war for the Base Beautification Award was nearing an end, and I would be the one to plant the flag in the heart, or some other place, of the First Sergeant from the 3340th School Squadron.

To celebrate my new ennobling position, I agreed to purchase one beer each for my three friends at a bar near the base on U.S. Highway 287. Sarge's Place, owned and operated by Master Sergeant Jankowski, an instructor at the Jet Engine School, and his American Indian wife whom we called "Pocahontas," became our destination.

Frequented mostly by older NCOs, Sarge's Place, housed in an oversized Quonset hut had a reputation for being rough. Sergeant Jankowski, who stood about 6'6" and weighed three hundred pounds, all of which were muscles, also had a reputation of being the proud owner of a sawed-off baseball bat, which he didn't mind using.

Suspended from the ceiling, were a multitude of propellers from various aircrafts dating back to World War I, including a propeller spinner supposedly from a Hawker Tempest Mark V fighter, c. 1945? A collection of pistons, flywheels, and other parts from older aircraft engines, hung haphazardly along the front sloping wall among an assortment of damaged rotary blades representing a variety of jet engines. Against the far wall of the building hung part of a small aircraft wing, apparently from a trainer that showed considerable damage.

Sergeant Jankowski, a POW of the Japanese during World War II, had no love for our Asian allies and demonstrated his odious feelings in the form of the bar's most unusual ornament. Displayed in the center of the bar's mirror, among the liquor bottles was a chamber pot, from which draped a Japanese flag looking like the wick of a "bitch lamp." If you had $20.00, the gall, the pressure, and the equipment, one could stand on the bar and *shoot for the Jap flag.*

Pocahontas was behind the bar talking to several NCOs, when we came through the door. She hardly looked our way. John swaggered his way to the bar. We followed. After stepping upon the foot railing, he placed a ten-dollar bill on the bar, which Paul surreptitiously thumped, driving it to the duckboards.

"Hey, butt hole!" shouted John with an angry face as he grabbed Paul by the shirt collar.

"Now, boys . . . there'll be none of that in here!" demanded Pocahontas while easing over in our direction. "What's the ruckus all about?"

"This fool threw my ten spot on the floor," protested John while pointing to the bill on the duckboards.

The prearranged subterfuge accomplished its intended goal, as the barmaid bent over to retrieve John's money. Once standing, Pocahontas' face reflected she too had accomplished her goal. After giving her short skirt a readjusting tug, the low-cut neckline of her blouse received the attention of eight well manicured finger nails, which lifted her buxom breast, causing a slight bounce. The voluptuous feminine tease caused the middle aged NCOs at the bar to raise their longnecks in rhythmic fashion, one after the other, as a drill team manipulating rifles on a parade field. A minxish smile from an experienced barmaid fired the ardor of four sex starved boys, who took their beers with laughter and a surge of testosterone to a table at the rear of the barroom, unaware that they had been "sandbagged."

In the process of making our way to a table near the damaged air craft wing, we walked passed a strange-looking "cowboy" sitting alone at a table in the center of the room. We all gave him a causal stare. The stranger had long uncombed red hair, which protruded from all sides of his hat while his Rip Van Winkle beard hung well below his chin. His steeple-shaped straw hat, which was incongruous for Amarillo, became an object of our conversation during the first few rounds of beers. Sitting on the table before this "cowboy," were ten or fifteen empty beer mugs, each containing a whiskey shot glass. The tall thin stranger hovered over his brood of empty containers as a mother chicken guarding her young, while his hat rested on the crown of his wiry head.

"Who's the stranger?" John asked Pocahontas as she sat a fresh round of beers on the table before my friends.

"Dern, if I know," replied the Barmaid with a shrug, while looking over her shoulder at the stranger. After picking up the bills from the table, she stuffed them between her breasts. "Been drinking them, head busters all afternoon," she continued as she gathered up three empty bottles. After lifting my bottle and realizing it wasn't empty she returned it to the table. "You gonna need another?"

"Later," I replied.

"What's he doing in this place?" Paul asked Pocahontas who walked off without answering his question. Turning to John, he continued with a slur, "Ain't this an Airman's Bar?"

"You're damn tooting it is," replied John with some resolution. He and Paul toasted each other and then guzzled down their beers in a show of masculinity. James and I glanced at each other, as if sharing the same ideas about the brewing Kamikaze mission.

After several more beers to our table, and several more boilermakers to the cowboy's table, James too became irritated with his presence and began to empathize with John and Paul's displeasure with a cowboy drinking in a bar patronized by GIs. Holding to my customary two beer limit, irritated Pocahontas.

Slamming down a fresh bottle of beer on the table, John declared, "And furthermore . . . I don't like his dead-blasted cowboy hat." Cool froth oozed forth from the bottle onto his hands, which he then wiped on Paul's shirt.

"Hey, bastard," Paul protested as he pushed John's hand away.

"Don't think that's a cowboy hat," injected James while resting one elbow on the table and pointing at the stranger. "That looks more like a hillbilly's hat. Kin Turkey or West Virginia, I'd say."

"What the hell, you know . . . about Kentucky . . . you little Red Neck peckerwood?" John asked in a scornful tone. "You've never even been outside the city limits of Saudi Arabia, Alabama."

"That shows what you know," James fired back in anger, while sitting up in his chair, "you damn Yankee. It's Arab, Alabama, you fool!"

Following by a loud belch, Paul demanded in a gruff voice, "I think we should . . . ask the puny hillbilly to leave this Airman's Bar."

"I think we should leave the man alone," I suggested, hoping to dissuade the triad from turning the place into an *abattoir* for the sake of establishing the "watering rights."

"I think someone should take that silly hat off his head," John countered.

"Why don't you do it? Seems . . . it's bothering you . . . more than *Us!*" I fired back.

"Let's flip quarters for the honors," suggested Paul with a smile, which appeared more prodigious than usual.

Reluctantly I joined in this foolhardy game and flipped a quarter in the air as a visceral cramp claimed my body. Four hands quickly covered the quarters as they hit the table among the empty bottles of courage. We stared dubiously for a moment at each other before revealing our destiny. James, the smallest man in our group, was the odd man out. For some reason, John seemed to derive a great deal of pleasure at James' misfortune.

Pushing back his chair, James rose to the challenge, finished off his beer in an outward show of bravery and marched off to honor his comrades, teetering in the process. A feeling of commiseration engulfed me as I watched my friend march off to a battle that I knew wasn't his doing, and I felt deep down in his inebriated body, if possible, he was experiencing the same body-wrenching fear that must have gripped Private Henry Fleming before the battle of Chancellorsville.

In a moment of insanity, James removed the stranger's straw hat and placed it on his own head. The tall stranger slowly stood and retrieved the hat. With it securely pressed in place with the right hand, a long left arm reached across the table seizing James by the collar. Empty beer mugs and shot glasses crashed to the floor, as James landed on the table facing up: kicking as a child refusing a diaper change. The cowboy delivered a quick double salvo to James' face.

"Damn you, John!" I shouted and ran to rescue my friend.

Charging headlong into the long arms of the tall thin stranger was equivalent to charging into the main rotor blades of a helicopter. The explosion in my right eye, which reached the deep recesses of my brain, sent me writhing to the floor. Someone's bootheel moved back and forth on my right hand as I lay wounded in a state of disorientation. The crashing sounds of battle raged all around me, as I struggled to free my hand. A sharp blow to the back of my head produced a dark, yet obscure peace to my mind, shutting out the world.

A form of strabismus, caused by the blow on my head affected my sight, for all I could see was a beautiful full-breasted cherubim shrouded by a brilliant nebulous, assisting me to a chair. Her lovely white arms waved off an angry, furious demon standing before my friends and me with a firry baseball bat in his hand.

"That's enough, Jan," said this angel of mercy, as she lowered me into a chair before the tall stranger lying on the floor. "Now!" this angel shouted. "You go . . . on," she said while waving her hands at Sergeant Jankowski, "go put that bat behind the bar."

Sergeant Jankowski invited us to leave his fine establishment once we were able to walk. Too groggy to drive and a feeling of blindness still lingering, I decided to let Paul drive us back to the Base. En route, we licked our wounds and plotted our strategy for the next time we met the tall redheaded stranger. *His hat and everything else would be ours,* we lamented.

Standing before the lavatory in my boxer shorts and shower thongs, I endured the excruciating pain as long as possible, before abandoning the early morning ritual of brushing my teeth. After laying aside the tooth brush and rinsing my mouth a couple of times, several lower teeth were gently touched to determine the source of pain. Several were loose. The thought of losing my teeth before reaching twenty-one wasn't a pleasant thought, as I continued the self-examination. Shaving I would have to do; that I couldn't forgo.

Since James had latrine duty that morning, it was almost 10:00 hours before he reported to the office. His late arrival, coupled with his physical condition, caused Sergeant Black to be suspicious of his tardiness. Bearing two black eyes and a badly swollen lower lip, James skulked about the office digging through filing cabinets and hiding behind propped up binders of Technical Orders, which he normally would not touch, trying to avoid the hawkish eyes and prying questions of Mrs. Milo. Later in the morning, we both decided to "bite the bullet," suffer the ridicule, and go down to the coffee bar on the far end of the catwalk.

Growing up in South Louisiana, I had had *café noir* New Orleans style, *café au lait* Avoyelles style, and plain ole Creole Belle Lafayette style, but never coffee with a touch of salt until coming to Amarillo Air Force Base. In my estimation, only a Yankee would come up with such a concoction. On this particular morning, someone added an extra amount of salt to the urn, which was readily apparent. James' face went through a series of contortions, but he remained silent. I, on the other hand, figured the extra salt would help heal my aching teeth and gums, so with each sip, I held the coffee in my mouth before swallowing. While lamenting over our "sins" of the previous night, for which John received the blame, we struggled through the bitter preparation.

Around 14:00 hours, Mrs. Milo and I were the only two in the outer office. Since it was tea time for her, Mrs. Milo removed from her desk drawer the small electric probe used in heating the cup of water sitting on her desk. When a tall skinny Technical Sergeant walked into the office wearing a well-starched khaki uniform, which appeared to have a leathery finish, she removed her cat-style eye glasses, allowing them to rest on her breast, before gently touching her crown of gray hair held in place by a multitude of pins and silver filigree clips.

The Sergeant's khaki shirt had two military creases splitting each of the front pockets, while equally sharp creases split the new stripes on the sleeves. His pants legs, also creased to a razor's edge, came to a prefect length above his highly polished black military shoes. The slow deliberate removal of his blue uniform cap revealed a fresh GI style flat top. A wisp of talc filled the office. Enhancing the Sergeant's appearance was a thin kept military mustache. With the cap securely tucked high under his left arm, he paused momentarily before the closed door with the seriousness normally associated with a visit by the Inspector General.

"May I help you Sergeant?" I asked, turning from my typewriter to look up at the tall redheaded stranger.

"Technical Sergeant Davy Crockett," he answered with a heavy Southern drawl. As he offered me a copy of his transfer orders, I stood up.

"Welcome to Amarillo, Sergeant," I answered, after accepting the paper with my left hand and foolishly offering him my swollen right hand, which he mercilessly crushed.

"B'jiminy, Airman, where the blazes is everybody?" asked Sergeant Crockett whose eyes appeared to be forced wide open, while maintaining his rigid posture.

While introducing Sergeant Crockett to Mrs. Milo, James entered the office. A sudden change came over Sergeant Crockett's face as he stared at James and then turned for a closer look at me. He turned back to James over whom he towered like a red rooster over a bug.

"Gaud, a mighty boy," Sergeant Crockett said with a short chuckle, "if you don't make a jim-dandy of a raccoon." The embarrassing gibe caused James' face to turn to a deep red.

"They had a slight altercation with a cowboy last night at Sarge's Place," added Mrs. Milo while dipping a tea bag in the cup of steaming water.

"Did this here fisticuff take place on Roadway 287 outside the base?" asked Sergeant Crockett in a firm voice.

James and I glanced at each other and forced a bland smile. A shudder traveled down my back as the pain in my face and teeth intensified at the stranger's question. Staring at the Sergeant, I knew he would, from now on, be a daily reminder of the most terrible Wednesday night in my life.

"At a juke joint run by a brute with a bludgeon?" continued the wide-eyed Davy Crockett with a quizzical stare at James.

"Yes, sir," gulped James as his Adam's apple did a spasmodic run. A pallid complexion came to James' face, which highlighted the bruised flesh around his eyes.

Stepping back toward my desk, I interrupted with a friendly, "Hey, Sarge!" Trying to draw his attention from James, I quickly picked up some papers from the desk and added nonchalantly, "No harm done . . . except to us."

"'Cepting for this here lump on my head," added Sergeant Crockett whose eyes were still wide open, as he touched a spot on his scalp. "Ever . . . I see that there big lug again without his bludgeon, I'll learn him a thing or two."

"You'll see him everyday," Mrs. Milo said with a whimsical smile while sweetening her tea with two heaping spoons of sugar. "You'll be working for Master Sergeant Jankowski."

"You mean to say that bastard." Crockett paused for a second and looked somewhat embarrassed at Mrs. Milo. "Excuse, my French madam," the sergeant said with his head slightly bowed. "You mean to say that hoss is in the Air Force?" asked Crockett with a delightful look on his face while holding his eyes wide open.

"Thhhat's right," replied three voices in what sounded like a musical chorus.

"Well, by cracky, there be days you get peed on 'n there be days you do the peeing," averred Sergeant Crockett with a grin.

Startled by Sergeant Crockett's colorful expression, Mrs. Milo spilled her cup of tea onto the top of her desk ruining several reports she had been working on all morning. After helping Mrs. Milo clean her desktop, Technical Sergeant Crockett decided to wait for Sergeant Jankowski in the office. For a couple of hours, he regaled the three of us with wild tales from his youth as a "shine runner out of Devil's Holler, Kinnntucky." Before coming to Amarillo, Sergeant Crockett enjoyed the distinction of being a member of the Air Force One crew.

While working on the President's plane, then housed at National Airport in DC, he decided to see what kind of "mash" the "Big Wigs" were drinking while flying. Crockett claimed, "Kennedy's people drank more and ate less" than any other previous administration and a man with his fondness for the "mash" couldn't pass up the temptation to sample what the President was drinking. At his court martial he complained of the inequities of military life, claiming that Pushinka, the white puppy given Kennedy by Khrushchev, had the right to crap on Air Force One, while he, a member of the Air Force, didn't even have the right to have one drink aboard the same *Gaud-dern plane.*

Sergeant Crockett's departure from the office was a memorial event, which almost caused Mrs. Milo to faint. Before exiting the door, the tall redheaded Sergeant turned and invited James and me to join him one night for *an evening of sho nuff funneling, fighting, and fornicating.* As Mrs. Milo struggled, first for a breath and then for her oversized glasses still resting on her large bosom, apparently hoping they would hide the deep sanguine color creeping across her face like a rash. The hillbilly Sergeant apologized again for his French and marched out the door with his glassy eyes still wide open. The three of us, left in a laconic vacuum of silence, looked at each other and wondered where this "tornado came from!" Settling down in my swivel chair, I made a mental note that some day when things were slow in the office; I'll have to go sit through one of Sergeant Crockett's classes.

The usual Friday evening hubbub at the Double Dip was not yet in full swing as I sat cross-legged on the front fender of my car, enjoying the combined delights of a beautiful spring evening, a cherry coke and the cute Car Hops. Leaning forward slightly, to make contact with the soda straw, since lifting my right elbow from its resting place on my right knee required a greater effort, a long slow sip was taken, as a watchful eye was focused on the few early prowlers.

At some point during a second cherry-coke, I came to an erect position as an unfamiliar car with a base sticker on the windshield left the line of traffic and pulled over next to me. The driver, leaning over the girl next to him, yelled out the window to me.

"Hey, buddy! You're from the Air Base?"

"Yeah. The 3320th School Squadron," I answered while jumping down from the fender.

"Look . . . we're going to a movie at the Paramount, and we have an extra girl in back without a date," the driver said, still leaning over the girl next to him. Pausing for a second and pointing to the backseat with his thumb, he added, "How about coming along with us?"

While trying to steal a glance at the backseat without being too obvious, I shrugged and answered, "I'm sorry, but I'm waiting for someone."

As the car drove away, I resumed my perch on the fender.

Twenty minutes must have passed before the car reentered the parking lot, causing a slight lurching within my heart, as I once more dismounted the fender. Meeting the car almost before it came to a stop, offered undeniable proof that I was now willing to be this yet unseen girl's escort for the evening.

After squeezing into the backseat, I shook hands with Brenda Blackwell, my date for the evening. A better than average-looking girl, Brenda had shoulder-length brown hair and a nice smile. She didn't appear to be frightened of this skinny Cajun, with a black eye, as she introduced the couple sitting in the front seat.

Sitting next to Brenda was a very beautiful girl with short, light red hair, named Allie Sailhamer. Her mesmerizing smile and blue eyes caused me to hold her hand longer than customary during an introduction. The boy sitting next to Allie said his name, while extending his hand. Realizing a moment of awkwardness had developed, the soft hand of this goddess was released with a demurely, "What?"

"Scott Young," repeated the boy with a tart sound in his voice.

"Oh! Yeah . . . sure. Nice to meet yeh, Scott." Scott and I exchanged handshakes.

"What's your name?" asked Scott with a quizzical expression as he jerked my hand as if offering a challenge.

"Yogi will do," I answered with a friendly snigger.

"How'd you get . . . ?" Allie started to ask, but was interrupted by Scott.

"Look, if we're going to the movie, let's go!"

The Boot Hill Bar and Dance Hall was our first destination following the movie. Scott, who was in a disgruntled mood most of the evening, started quaffing Lone Stars with a sense of urgency almost immediately after we settled at a table. Allie sat quietly almost tranquil, except for a nervous finger nail working surreptitiously at the label on the beer bottle before her. Brenda and I danced several times while Allie and Scott sat silently at the table. Seeing she was clearly agitated with Scott's behavior, I asked her to dance when the band began to play a song called "It's Only Make Believe."

"Your boyfriend seems to be in a foul mood," I said as we moved into each other's arms.

"He's always in a foul mood," answered Allie as she moved closer to me. "What about you, Yogi? Is that shiner the result of a bad mood?"

"No," I answered with a chuckle. "Just . . . a misunderstanding over a hat."

For a moment, Allie paused. While I stared down at her, she came to her toes and kissed me on my swollen eye. The blank, but pleased expression on my face caused Allie to smile.

"That's an old family remedy," Allie said with a minxish smile. "It dates back to the time my brother got his first black eye in the fifth grade."

"I like your family's remedy for pain," I answered.

As we started dancing again, our bodies touched, only slightly, with a rhythmic tease. The childlike softness of her hand in mine and the flowery perfume of her hair coupled with a radiant energy from her body incited a strange sensation deep within my spirit, unknown before. I could sense a fusion of our spirits taking place as I pulled this goddess like form even closer, desiring the completion of the oneness I felt taking place. For the remainder of our time on the dance floor, we didn't speak for I feared that the magic of this special occasion was just a time of make-believe.

Chapter 4

Mused in a state of near mental paralysis, my mind replayed the magic moments of the previous evening, as a gentle morning breeze stirred the small guidon above my head. The soft ruffling sound generated by the emblem representing the Headquarter Squadron, seemed to express in its waving, a shared sense of glory that the prize, for which we had strove was ours. As we stood at parade rest, awaiting the hubristic Sergeant's descent from the Orderly Room, Paul relayed to me by word of mouth that James wasn't in the formation.

Leaving the guidon with Paul, I ran back to the barracks, up the stairs and down the hall toward James' room. Grasping the door frame with my left hand prevented me from sliding on the highly polished hardwood floor past the room. Standing in the doorway, gasping for a breath, I tugged at my tie, and looked down at the slacker sitting on the edge of his bunk. With his face buried in both palms and elbows resting on his knees, James' attempt at dressing hadn't gotten past his white GI boxer shorts.

"Man . . . the entire Flight is standing in formation," I grumbled from the doorway. After pausing for a breath, I pleaded, "Come on, James . . . get a move on it!"

"I can't make it, Yogi," James answered, turning his face in my direction. The discoloration around his eyes, like my own was darker, giving credence to Sergeant Crockett's description of his appearance.

"Damn, man! You look awful!" Without meaning to gloat over my friend's pathetic condition, a small snicker managed to escape my lips. "Where'd you find that Mexican broad who was in the parking lot last night?"

"Crockett found them," James replied while burying his face in his hands again.

"I can't believe you went drinking with that nut," I declared while placing a pair of shoes before him, not realizing I had them crisscrossed. From a partially opened drawer in the closet, I retrieved an undershirt and offered it to James who languidly placed it across his legs.

The thumping sound of heavy shoes rapidly climbing the wooden stairs echoed down the quiet empty hallway of the barrack. A sense of urgency caused me to snatch a pair of uniform pants from a hanger and thrust them before the sluggish urchin. A blue uniform slid past the door with a shout of "whoaaaa." A head soon appeared at the door from the direction, in which the uniform had rocketed. Standing back from the door before entering the room, John's face, like the two gawking back at him, showed more confirming evidence of our eventful encounter with Sergeant Crockett.

"Yogi! You had better . . . get down there!" declared John, manifesting evidence of the stair's toll. "Sausage . . . Sam . . . is yelling blue blazes." He coughed a couple of times while staring at James.

"See . . . if you can get him dressed," I said, offering the uniform pants to John.

"I ain't dressing that little Red Neck!" John shouted after coughing a couple more times. Stepping into the hall with the pants in his hands, John called to me, "What's wrong with him?"

"Too much tequila and . . . too many chicken fajitas . . . I guess!" I yelled back while running down the hall toward the stairs.

"That little Red Neck . . . he wouldn't know what to do with a chicken dinner, fried or otherwise. And, I ain't dressing him!" shouted John.

In order to assume my position in front of the Flight as guidon bearer, a short romp across the dew-covered grass was necessary to bypass the column of disgruntled men, who were expressing in muffled tones, their dissatisfaction with the Air Force's "Mickey Mouse" parades on Saturday mornings.

The First Sergeant paced feverishly before the formation with his hands interlocked against his buttock. Paul was bearing a Cheshire cat's grin when I resumed my position ahead of the formation and accepted the guidon. Upon detecting a movement within the ranks, the First Sergeant immediately spun around, locking his black eyeballs upon me in a hawkish fashion. My supposedly late arrival was a source of agitation for the First Sergeant, who apparently had planned that nothing, let alone a peon Airman, was going to ruin "his big day." Being the person nearest him, I became the sole target of his haranguing and Italian gesticulating, expressing verbs not needing translation. During a brief hiatus in his denunciation of "lowlives" I attempted to remove the dew from my shoes by wiping them on the back of my pants legs. This move further angered the sergeant who moved to my left and began shouting in my left ear.

"When you salute the Colonel, I want to hear that Flag pop on the other end of the flight line." He grimaced and pointed in the direction of Hangar 4000 before barking, "Do you h-e-e-e-ear me, Airman!"

"Yes, sir, I hear you!" echoed across the quadrangle along with some snickering.

Sausage Sam finally called his troops to attention. In a warm-up maneuver, he marched us around the quadrangle while calling cadence in a gruff voice reminiscent of Basic Training. As we marched passed our barrack a glimpse of two heads peeping from the lower part of the heavy glass window of the door was detected as John and James tried escaping Sam's attention. Walking beside me, in crablike fashion, Sam continued his arm waving while demanding "the rag to be popped" with more snap as I executed the movement several times during the circuit. James and John ducked from the building and joined the formation as we passed the barrack following our third trip around the quadrangle.

A slight breeze blew across the freshly mowed grass beyond the taxiway near Hangar 4000 and Base Operations, which separated the ATC side of the Base from that of SAC and the city airport. While standing in formation, at parade rest, a meaningless discussion developed among several of us about the city's tallest buildings, which were clearly visible because of the clear morning sky. As the crowd filled the bleachers setup for dependants and visitors from the city, the Baseband added to the festive spirit of the morning with lively selections from John Philip Sousa.

The Base Commander's long black car, equipped with emblems of his rank, soon drove onto the tarmac near the far end of the formation. A rippling call for *"Ten-hut"* flowed down the flight line as the commander's car drove by.

After speeches by the City's Mayor and a visiting Congressman, Lieutenant Colonel Henry W. Waldmire walked onto the flight line to present the Base Beautification Award to the winning School Squadron. My knees almost gave way as Sausage Sam and I stepped from the ranks. A flawless left-face maneuver was followed by a short trek before a right face was executed, thus beginning a long march across the open tarmac to a designated point before a bank of microphones.

I was oblivious to what was being said, mused only in the thought of "popping the rag" to Sam's satisfaction. Caught unaware that the Colonel was waiting to attach the rosette to the guidon, I snapped the staff with the skill of a veteran of many years, hoping to bring it to a parallel position even with the Colonel's hand. The adroitness and force, with which the guidon came down, sent the decorative wooden ball on top of the staff flying through the air, straight for the Colonel's face. A dull, almost faint cry of exasperation came from Sausage Sam.

A quick shifting of the Colonel's head saved his life, but my current status in Sausage Sam's outfit, I knew, was dubious at best, once he finished "ripping me a new one." Like Private Henry Fleming who fled the battlefield during his initial testing at Chancellorsville, I too wanted to flee, but unlike the Private's situation, there were no trees on the flight line to skulk behind. Adding to my humiliation, a photographer from the Jet Journal, the base's newspaper was present and recorded the mishap for all ages.

The First Sergeant hoping to take advantage of this auspicious day by grabbing for every bit of glory coming his way invited Colonel Waldmire to review *his troops*. With an about face, the little wooden ball was left, like an unexploded cannon ball in the morning sun, on the flight line. Marching back to the formation, I too, like Private Fleming desired a little red badge of courage in my hour of shame.

Beginning at the rear of the column, Colonel Waldmire attempted to make a quick walk-by inspection, until he reached James about midway the formation. A "rubberneck" glance at James's face brought the Colonel to an unexpected stop. The raccoon face under scrutiny focused on a point in the far distance, as the Colonel studied its features for a few seconds before allowing his eyes to drift downward across the ruffled uniform. The crisscrossed shoes on this creature's feet caused the Colonel and Sausage Sam to hold their downward stare for several moments.

"What happened to you, Airman?" asked Colonel Waldmire in a dry tone, raising his head slowly to stare James in the face.

"Had a fight with Davy Crockett, Sir!" replied James with a slight weaving as if unstable.

With a hand gesture from the unhappy First Sergeant, the Colonel was encouraged to move down the line. Sausage Sam purposely sidestepped Colonel Waldmire to give James a stern glance.

The inspection continued until the Colonel stopped before Paul. A brief study of the youthful smiling face produced a similar question.

"What happened to your face, Airman?"

"Had a fight with Davy Crockett, Sir!" replied Paul with a sarcastic smile.

Feeling he had been "put up on," the Colonel moved down the ranks.

Standing, at long last, before the tall redhead Technical Sergeant, the Colonel now showed signs of agitation. Pressing downward on his hips, with both hands, he carefully studied Crockett's swollen lip and cheek. A morose face possessed the First Sergeant as he anticipated Sergeant Crockett's story.

"Did you, *Also*, have a fight with Davy Crockett, Sergeant?"

"No, Sir!" sounded Sergeant Crockett in true military fashion without flinching. "I am . . . Davy Crockett. Sir!" A deadpan expression swept across the Colonel's face.

The inspection of the Squadron came to an abrupt ending as Colonel Waldmire turned to Sausage Sam with a revolting sneer.

"Sergeant! You might have the best damn gardeners in the Air Force, but they are without a doubt the most undisciplined, incorrigible men I have ever encountered!"

As the Colonel walked away from the Flight shaking his head, Sausage Sam strutted back down the line of men in a stooped position as if his knees were giving way. Standing about five feet from the formation, he yelled at James as his face writhed.

"Airman Kaiser!"

From the rear of the formation, a weak *Yes sir* was heard.

"Fall out and retrieve that ball!" shouted the First Sergeant.

With some difficulty, James darted across the flight line, scooped up the wooden ball, and delivered it to Sam before rejoining the formation.

"The Aviators" by John Philip Sousa as performed by the Baseband, putting a touch of Achilles' spirit in each of our feet, as we marched past the review platform on the way back to the squadron area. Our hubris spirit for having won the annual war for the Base Beautification Award was however about to take a temporary setback.

The First Sergeant's refusal to dismiss us immediately upon returning to the squadron area, made evident his displeasure with our performance during the inspection. Pacing back and forth on the wide wooden platform fronting the Orderly Room, he went beyond his usual creative capabilities of stringing vulgar expletives together while frantically gesticulating. Adding to my humiliation, the angry Sergeant threatened to have the wooden ball implanted in my scrotum as he hurled it to me. The last such vulgar philippic to grace my ears came from a barefoot Atchafalaya swamp fishwife standing in a pirogue. The "butt reaming" administered by this crone, who caught my cousin and me running her catfish lines, caused me to suffer a near allergic reaction to catfish for many years.

After dismissing the entire Flight except for Crockett, my three friends and I, the First Sergeant marched us around the quadrangle for the better part of an hour while calling cadence. Mocking faces peering from the windows of the barracks worsened our mortification. At the end of this exercise in military discipline, James had two blisters on his feet, and I knew how to "pop the rag" with moderation.

After coming to a final halt before the Orderly Room, the First Sergeant dismissed us in a gruff tone and then turned in disgust for the steps. Our bodies slumped with weariness as we stared at each other, knowing the war was over, but there would be more difficult days ahead defending our position as Amarillo's top Gardeners. Not anxious to return the guidon to it resting place behind the Sergeant's desk while he was still in the Orderly Room, I hesitated outside for a few seconds examining the wooden ball and staff. Each bore a peculiar hole.

"Yo . . . Yogi!"

Paul's wide mouth, manifesting a smile, which reached from ear to ear, caused an uneasy feeling in the pit of my stomach as he reached into his pocket.

"You might need this screw to hold your new testicle in place."

The little screw tumbled through the bright morning sun, like a brilliant star and landed in my open hand. A feverish sensation careened through my body as it dawned upon me that the morning's mishap was the result of a practical joke.

"Paul! You little fart," I yelled as the prankster walked off laughing. "Your foolishness almost caused me to kill an Air Force Lieutenant Colonel with a damn wooden ball!"

A familiar sound from many years past caused my eyes to shift away from the car on my left to the two riders on bicycles darting in and out of the snail-like traffic. The fluttering sound of playing cards vibrating against the spokes of the bicycles demanded a longer look as I waited impatiently for a car to back from the parking slot under the canopy. The two young boys continued working their way parallel with the slow-moving vehicles, as if looking for an opportunity to cross the parking lot of the Double Dip Drive-In. The bicycles, decked out with coca-cola bottle tops fastened to the spokes of both wheels, streams on the ends of the handlebars and a car radio antenna attached to the back fenders, didn't appear completely out of place, since they too reflected the personality of their owners, as did the other vehicles traversing the parking lot during the early evening hours.

An anxious driver behind me lightly touched his horn when I hesitated before moving into the vacant parking slot. After parking next to a green-and-white 1957 Chevy Bel Air convertible equipped with a continental kit, I glanced at the driver. We exchanged smiles. By way of the rearview mirror, I could see the bicyclists had swung around and attempted to pull in behind my car. A long, loud blast from a car horn caught the attention of the obstreperous crowd, bringing an immediate tranquil stillness to the parking lot. Simultaneously, my car rocked with a crashing sound and a muffled moan.

"You little wetback!" yelled the agitated driver while leaning out his car window. "Why the hell don't you look where you're going?"

While exiting the car to see what had happened, a youthful voice assaulted my ears with an angry outcry directed at the driver. The only two words I caught from this scathing denunciation in Spanish were "gringo" and "perro" (dog).

"You run into my car like that, you little fart, I'll break your dirty Mexican neck," yelled the agitated driver.

The young Mexican boy who had plowed into the back bumper of my car was lying on the pavement holding his badly skinned right knee. The crashing sound attracted several onlookers who gathered around the car. The expression on the young boy's face reflected a mixture of fear, pain and embarrassment, all symptoms I had suffered earlier during the day.

"Are you okay?" I asked while bending over to look at his knee.

An almost inaudible response came through a constricted throat, "Si."

"You Mexican kids got no right riding around here."

The cruel reprimand drew my attention to the starkly stare of a Car Hop whose akimbo position demonstrated her disgust with the situation.

"That's beside the point right now," I answered with a defiant frown. "How about bringing a cup of water and some paper napkins so I can clean his knee?"

The Car Hop demurred for a moment while vigorously working her chewing gum before turning and walking toward the pickup window. After helping the young boy to his feet, I assisted him to a table under the canopy. While we waited for the water and napkins, the other boy moved both bikes under the canopy near the far end of the table.

The injured bicyclist appeared to be about twelve years old. Several minutes passed, and still the water and napkins hadn't arrived. A sense of fear was still evident on the boy's face as I again checked his knee and then looked up into his dark moistened eyes.

"What's your name, amigo?" I asked, while, gently ruffling his hair with my right hand.

A dry voice with a small whimper answered, "Benito."

"And your name is?" I asked turning to his friend.

"Pablo." With a small dirty hand, he raked his long hair away from his face as he studied my black eye.

"My boss said that you Mexican kids gotta get away from here, just as soon as he cleans your leg," announced the unsympathetic Car Hop as she held out the cup of water and paper napkins before me.

"Maybe they would like something to eat before leaving!"

"We don't serve their kind," replied the girl shifting her weight from one hip to the other.

"You serve my kind . . . don't you?" I snapped in an agitated tone. Without intending the crass tone, I felt abashed.

She demurred before answering. "Yes. Of course, we do."

"Well . . . I'll take three hot dogs, three orders of fries, and three cherry cokes. Thank-you!"

The Car Hop gave me an inimical stare for several moments while habitually popping her chewing gum. As she walked off, the boys glanced at each other and said something to each other in Spanish.

"Hope you guys like hot dogs?" I asked with a slight chuckle.

Two dark brown faces smiled at me while their heads moved in the affirmative.

With something of a bland smile, I encouraged Benito to hold his leg straight out and away from the table, while I poured the water over his knee. A short exchange in Spanish between the boys caused a worried expression to cover Benito's face.

A slight whimper coincided with a flinching action as the cold water slowly ran across Benito's knee. Another dialogue in Spanish took place between the boys as I sponged off his leg with the napkins. Because of the cheerfulness in their voices, I looked up from the task at hand.

Before I could turn to see the source of their delight, a soft voice called my name.

"Yogi, is that you?"

While holding the wet napkin on Benito's knee I turned in the direction of the voice. It seemed an interminable age passed before I could respond to the figure standing before me. She was even more beautiful, to the point of being voluptuous, than I remembered from the previous evening and a frisson shot through my body like an electrical charge. She was wearing a man's long sleeve shirt, which appeared to be a couple of sizes too big, with the sleeves rolled up to a point between the wrist and elbow. Cinching the shirt tail tightly around her waist was a large knot, which served the added purpose of concealing her navel. The frayed edges of her cutoff blue jeans extended just a few inches below the cheeks of her buttocks. The incessant whispering of Benito and Pablo amplified my momentary speechlessness.

"Could I be of some help?" Allie asked, moving closer to the table with a small first aid kit.

"Yeah . . . sure . . . you're a nurse, right?" Without realizing it, I squeezed Benito's knee causing him to let out a little whimper.

"Maybe a little iodine would be better than plain water," Allie said with an alluring smile directed at me and then Benito.

Sitting on the table next to Benito while his knee was being attended, I desired a wound of my own.

"How's the eye?" asked Allie with a teasing smile while looking up from Benito's knee.

"It's okay." A slight touch to the eye caused Pablo and Benito to converse once more in Spanish. "The treatment you administered last night while we were dancing was very therapeutic." With a slight snicker, I added, "For a while . . . I was sorry, both eyes didn't need attention."

After applying a Band-Aid to Benito's wound, Allie gave him a reassuring pat on the side of the leg before closing the first aid kit.

The arrival of the hot dogs and fries seemed to be skimpy in comparison to the mysterious nourishment my spirit seemed to be receiving from Allie's gentle laughter. Judging by the stares directed toward her by the two boys, I could tell they too were enjoying her presence.

"Would you care for something to eat?" I asked Allie while distributing the food on the table.

"Thanks, but . . . no. I should be going." With a hand gesture, Allie turned and pointed at the Chevy Bel Air. "My friend has to be going."

"That's a pretty classy item," I replied.

With a chuckle, Allie gave me an askance stare. "Somehow, I never thought of Crystal as classy." She laughed once more, this time holding her fingers before her mouth.

"No . . . no I mean your friend's car. It's pretty classy." A flushed feeling came over me while trying to correct the situation my tongue had gotten me into, by saying what my mind was actually processing.

"I know what you meant, Yogi," Allie said gaily as she took my arm. "Come on. I want you to meet this classy gal."

Being dragged toward, the Bel Air caused me to recall what it felt like, as an unwilling preteenager, being forced to attend parties where dancing with girls was required. While standing beside the door on the driver's side, I could tell, Crystal was perhaps a couple of years older than Allie and possessed a totally different personality. Her heavy mascara and fiery red lips were too ostentatious for my taste. However, her full bosom amply exposed by a low 'V' neck blouse became a magnetic field for my eyes. I could feel my face turning red as I nervously glanced, occasionally at Allie standing next to me, knowing she could read my mind.

Before saying good night, I walked around the car with Allie and opened the door for her. Leaning forward on both hands, gripping the passenger side door, I said good night while fighting an urge to lean over into the car and claim for myself a small dose of her family's remedy for black eyes and other pains. Crystal said good night with a coquettish smile while giving the neckline of her blouse a slight forward tug.

After the Bel Air backed from the parking slot, I stood frozen for several minutes before walking back to the table to rejoin the two boys. They each had another cherry coke, much to the dissatisfaction of the Car Hop and her boss, while I forced down the cold dog and fries. Before saying good night to them, I made a final inquiry about Benito's knee, coupled with another gentle ruffling of his hair. After straddling their bikes, they rode off into the night toward the 14th Street, leaving me with the thought that this would be the last time our paths would cross.

A warm refreshing shower managed to wash away some of the weariness of my long day. The illuminated numbers of the electric clock on the floor next to my bunk stood out like the eyes of an owl in the dark room, revealing the lateness of the hour. It was 23:00 hours. My familiarity with Tank's record player allowed me to switch it on in the dark after discarding the damp towel wrapped around my lower body. The sound of the record dropping onto the turn table caused Pete to chirp. To antagonize him further, I ran one finger across the wires of his cage before walking to my locker for a clean pair of boxer shorts.

As the mellifluous sounds, I had hoped would lull me to sleep filled the room, I stretched out on the bunk and exhaled a low sigh, declaring my appreciation that the day was coming to a close. Gazing up through the Venetian blinds, a full moon, which hung in the clear night sky, as a giant heavenly streetlight, had a titillating effect upon me as if its beams touched my body. The thought of seeing Allie again, caused a strange quivering to move within my heart. The embers ignited within my spirit by our initial meeting, now became a raging fire of desire within my bones as her seductive appearance replayed itself in my mind. Pete began to voice his apparent disapproval of my late night concert by increasing the tempo of his chirping. As my blissful feeling increased, I wondered how much his singing would increase if he could experience the erotic feelings possessing my body.

It had been a long day and still mental images of its beginning were painfully fresh in my mind, especially the wooden ball bouncing across the flight line. Given my present state of ecstasy, Sam's reaction to the incident now became humorous, as well as Paul's buffoonery. With my arms folded back under my head, I continued to gaze at the heavenly luminary as my favorite opus from Tank's collection entitled, "Firebird" deepened the strange phenomenon possessing my soul.

Long before the record player clicked off, mental and physical fatigue put to rest my lustful rumination.

My eyes appeared stuck as I struggled to open them in response to the hand gripping my arm. An unfamiliar male voice roused me to a semiconscious state.

"Are you . . . the guy they call Yogi?" asked the immature male voice.

Still somewhat dazed, I started incoherently at the inquisitor. "What? What?"

After what must have seemed an interminable period to my nocturnal visitor, I propped up on one elbow.

"Must have been one helluva night?" the young Airman quipped.

"What's the problem?" I asked after sitting up. To hasten my recovery, I gave a loud harrumph and shook my head.

"You've got an emergency phone call in the Orderly Room," the boy said with a slight wince.

"Who is it?" I asked, while trying to stand. The deep sleep left me somewhat groggy. "Do you know?"

"Some broad . . . name's Opal . . . I believe."

While searching for my pants, my brain was doing acrobatic moves, trying to figure out Opal's reason for calling me at this time of night. In spite of my foggy condition, the brief search led to the jeans at the end of my bunk under the discarded dust cover. The young inexperienced CQ Runner stood guard as I dressed. After locating my shower thongs, I teetered out the door behind my suspicious guardian.

Opal was incoherent when I answered the phone. In a state of near panic, her hysterical shrieking was unclear and all I could make out was that Casey was extremely ill and needed to go to the hospital. Not meaning to sound crass or escape her plea for help, I foolishly asked why she hadn't called John. Disregarding my question, her pitiful gabbling continued amid a fit of sobs.

I returned to the barrack after agreeing to drive into town. I went immediately to John's room. Paul was awakening; but he knew nothing about John's whereabouts. Upon returning to my room, I hurriedly donned the wrinkled shirt from the previous evening and slipped on a pair of tennis shoes.

After running up the outside stairs leading to the girls' garage apartment, a ghostlike face, moistened with tears, confronted me as the door swung open. Opal was incoherent and crying uncontrollably while dragging me by the hand through the apartment to Casey's room. Lying on a blood-soaked bed was a lethargic half-naked female body not resembling the beautiful Casey, I remembered from Palo Duro Canyon. A bloody coat hanger was lying beside her. More out of reflex than skill I tried to check Casey's pulse amid Opal's hysteria and cries, for action. While continuing to hold Casey's hand, I demanded an explanation after angrily shouting for Opal to shut up.

The revulsion of Casey's act caused a temporary paralysis to grip my whole being. In a calm voice, which expressed my shock more than my ability to handle the situation, I ordered Opal to get a fresh sheet.

In a moment of clarity, Opal and I gently rolled Casey's body from the pool of coagulating blood. With Opal's help, I wrapped Casey in the clean sheet before carrying her downstairs to my car. The drive across town to St. Anthony's was fast and reckless, as Opal sat in the backseat cradling Casey in her arms.

The emergency room burst into a beehive of activity, when I carried Casey through the doors. A couple of nurses hurriedly ushered me into a small treatment room. A tall thin nurse, with prodigious, almost masculine hands, began wrestling the tangled sheet from Casey's body after I placed her on the bed. A shocked expression rolled across her face as she glanced in my direction with an inimical gaze. Opal and I backed away and stood frozen near the door, while other nurses crowded into the small room, which was coming alive with urgent commands and calls directed at no one in particular. The tall thin nurse finally vented her displeasure with me, by loudly demanding that I leave the room.

For some time Opal and I sat in the waiting room, while a steady flow of doctors and nurses scurried in and out of the treatment room. Before long, the tall nurse called us back into the room to answer more questions. Amid a steady flow of instructions to the nurses, the doctor continued his flippant inquiry as if he already knew the answers to his well-phrased questions. Mortified by the consequences of Casey's action and the doctor's endless interrogation, Opal finally revealed that her friend tried aborting her unwanted fetus with a coat hanger. In a gruff tone and the wave of his hand, the doctor ordered us out once more, after directing an unfriendly stare in my direction.

Returning to the waiting area, I was too anxious to sit and began pacing. Opal sat in silence with downcast eyes, anxiously wringing the now, tear-soaked handkerchief I had offered her earlier. A deep sigh from Opal caused me to turn. She buried her face in the moistened handkerchief as the gurney being pushed by two orderlies paused momentarily, before entering the treatment room. In an act of kindness, I stood beside Opal. As the stoical-faced doctor approached us, Opal raked her fingers through an unmanageable head of frizzy black hair and pulled me close to her side. The doctor's tone was cold and accusatorial as he looked at me, while explaining Casey's need for emergency surgery. Opal and I sat down beside each other in silence, with long expressionless faces as the gurney moved down the hall away from us. At the moment, I wanted to kill John.

Some time passed, before I remembered leaving my car near the emergency room entrance. Excusing myself, I stood and walked out of the hospital. After moving the car to a designated parking area, I walked back toward the building, but something prevented me from going inside. A secluded bench, over shadowed by a small tree, offered a tempting hideaway.

Sitting alone in the darkness, the horrifying images of Casey's bloody body and the coat hanger tormented my mind. A great feeling of loneliness came over me and for a moment, I wished smoking had been an acquired habit, since it always seemed so therapeutic in times of crisis. In desperation to relieve my mind of the sight, I started counting the seconds between the lonely barks of a dog crying in the night across town. The sound of a speeding car, trying to beat the signal light at a nearby intersection disturbed the stillness and my counting of the dog's barks.

"Sir . . . we have some news about your friend," said a gentle, familiar voice coming from the doorway.

"Thanks," I answered while standing. Without turning to face the messenger, I asked, "Will she be okay?"

"The doctor will come down in a little while to speak with you." The white uniform moved in my direction.

"Yogi," Allie said with a light laughter in her voice, "is that you?"

"Yes . . . it is," I replied. The gloomy spirit encapsulating my mind wasted away, as Allie moved toward me in the shadow of the small tree.

"What are you doing out here?" Allie asked smiling.

"Just needed . . . some fresh air."

"She'll be okay, Yogi," Allie said while touching my upper arm in a show of support. "Why don't you come back inside?"

After giving my shoulders a shrug I replied, "Thanks." As we walked toward the doors, I was feeling more comfortable and asked in a jovial tone, "Is there any coffee around this place?"

"I think there may be some in the nurses' lounge," Allie said with a grin. "Maybe your friend inside would like a cup as well."

The clock on the wall in the emergency room showed the time as 04:00 hours. Because of the quietness of the early morning hour, all the nurses sitting around the station in the emergency room were busying themselves with medical charts or catching up on shift reports. While Opal was napping in a chair, Allie and I sat across the room, each nursing a cup of coffee that would put New Orleans style, chicory enhanced *café noir* to shame. As she spoke, my eyes traced with deep concentration, every lovely feature of her face. I didn't mean to stare, but for some reason, I felt my body was drawing its very life sustaining energy from her presence. Allie, apparently feeling uncomfortable by my intense gaze, stared down into her cup of coffee for a moment, before offering up a smile and a blush. I wanted to apologize, but couldn't find the words so for a moment I looked in Opal's direction.

"This girl you brought in tonight," asked Allie, drawing my fixation back to her angelic face, "is she the girl you were supposed to meet Friday night at the Double Dip, when we picked you up?"

"No!" I answered, giving my head a quick twisting motion in the negative. "Casey . . . no . . . she's dating a friend of mine . . . John." After downing a shot of coffee, I added, "Whom I would like to choke right about now."

"Is she the one?" asked Allie with a slight gesture with her head toward Opal.

"My goodness! No!" I declared with a chuckle. "I made the mistake of rescuing her a few months back in Palo Duro, but that's the extent of my involvement with her." Realizing my comment about Opal was unkind, I stumbled through an apology, which made Allie laugh.

"It seems you have a habit of rescuing people, Yogi," Allie said, touching my hand. "What you did for those two boys tonight at the Double Dip was very kind."

"That's me," I answered with a smile, "Yogi . . . the gentle bear. Rescuer of the underdogs and misfits."

Allie and I both laughed. For several moments, we sat in silence while finishing off the coffee.

"Have you seen Brenda since the other night?" Allie asked while placing her empty cup on a nearby table.

Thinking her question was a subterfuge, designed to seek more than a casual knowledge about the relationship between Brenda and me, I answered her question with a question.

"And you . . . are you still seeing Scott?"

"When he's not in one of his moods," responded Allie, while offering to take my empty cup. "I wasn't being nosy . . . I mean about you and Brenda."

"Yeah . . . I know," I answered with a smile. "And, yes I have seen her since then. In fact we had a date last night. I mean tonight . . . Saturday night."

Allie tried to refrain from laughing. She was as confused as I was, about the day of the week. After agreeing upon the day she insisted on hearing the whole story behind my daring rescue of Opal. I never felt as comfortable around a girl as I did with Allie that night and wished this portion of the night would never end. Her contagious charm, free laughter, while holding her fingers against her lightly colored lips, drove my heroic tale to new heights of embellishment.

The doctor's arrival brought an end to my talkativeness. He explained to Opal and me that the injuries done to Casey's body by the coat hanger necessitated a complete hysterectomy and her stay in the ICU would be for several days. Opal's emotional reaction to the news became almost unbearable. After assisting her to a chair, the doctor quietly mumbled an order to one of the nurses.

Saying good night to Allie twice in one night, was more of a fantasy than even I could have dreamed up. As before, I longed for another of her family remedies for my eye, but that too, was only a dream. The return trip to Opal's place was silent, except for a few moans of grief expressed by my anguished passenger as she reclined against the passenger side door. The shot given her by the nurse before we left the hospital was beginning to take effect when we reached her apartment. While removing Opal's shoes and assisting her into the bed, fully clothed, she tearfully pleaded for me to stay with her.

The lumpy foldout sofa was torturous, but after some time, fatigue overtook my body, bringing to a close the longest day of my life. Before dozing off, Benito and Pablo once more popped into my mind. I realized my mishap on the parade field was minor in comparison to the ramparts of discrimination such Mexican kids would face in life. The visceral pain encountered upon first seeing Casey, returned with the awareness that the bloody mattress still existed in the next room. This too, seemed trivial after a while in comparison to the many difficult days facing her; as she would have to cope with a mistake that would haunt her for the rest of her life.

Chapter 5

The smell of frying bacon wafted through the apartment, awakening my olfactory senses while revivifying my aching body. After rolling onto my back, the events of the previous evening began to unfold, as my eyes and mind adjusted to the strange environment. A sliver of sunlight penetrating a small hole in the heavy drapes covering the only window in the room revealed it was daylight. A protruding object from the sofa bed caused me to swear under my breath before propping up on one elbow. Half awake, I scanned the room for my jeans.

The sheets hastily tucked at each end of the sofa bed the night before, were now a jumbled mess, which I pulled forward and wrapped around my lower body while moving to the edge of the mattress. Cognizant of Opal's presence in the kitchen, I stood to retrieve my jeans draped across a black Naugahyde chair, while still holding a portion of one sheet around my body. After ambling to the chair and picking up the pants, a struggle with an inside-out pant leg ensued, causing some loose change to fall to the floor as well as the sheet. While kneeling on the floor to recover a quarter near the wall behind the chair, a light whisper of perfume caused me to look over my shoulder.

"Good morning," Opal announced attempting an alluring smile. "Thought you were going to sleep all day."

An automatic reaction caused me to place the contrary pant leg over the fly of my boxer shorts as I stood. The provocative aroma of Opal's perfume intensified, as well as the feverish sensation in my face as she stepped toward me, wearing a pink peignoir, opened in the front, over a short gossamer nightgown. Her well-combed hair and slight red lips made it obvious she had been up for some time.

"Breakfast is almost ready," Opal said as I turned from her to slip on the jeans.

"You didn't have to go through all that trouble," I answered after turning to greet her with a blush.

"It's no trouble, Yogi," Opal remarked with a shrug, before closing her robe and tying the sash. "I enjoy cooking." After bending down and reaching for something on the floor beside the bed, she held out my shirt with one hand while offering up a carefree smile. "Is this . . . what you're looking for?"

"Yeah . . . thanks." I accepted the shirt at arm's length.

Realizing her flirtatious stare, caused me to hold the shirt before my bare chest Opal finally turned her eyes from my upper body, while pointing in the direction of a nearby door. "You have time to washup before the biscuits are done."

A breakfast, more appetizing than anything served in the Mess Hall, complete with flowers on the table, greeted me after returning from the bathroom. During breakfast, Opal made an attempt to force upon me more scrambled eggs, hash browns, bacon, hot biscuits, and fruit cocktail while I tried to ignore her minxish grins.

Opal's attempted coquettish come-on, coupled with a tantalizing show of cleavage, caused me to forget about the plans Brenda and I had for the afternoon, until she asked what I was doing later. Surreptitiously I checked my watch a couple of times knowing there wouldn't be enough time to return to the base in order to change clothes. Opal's detection of my third, more noticeable glance at the watch brought an ashen color to her cheeks. With a doleful upward glance while toying with the bit of eggs remaining on her plate, Opal hinted she could use a ride back to the hospital, *if I had the time.* The tartness in her voice, even if not intended, succeeded in causing me to feel like an ungrateful jerk.

Before leaving the apartment, Opal asked one more favor of me. Between the two of us, we managed to carry Casey's bloody mattress downstairs to a trash hopper.

A number of young GIs were already sitting on the steps and buttress before the student nurses' entrance at St. Anthony's, as I climbed the long flight of steps, by taking two at a time. Unfamiliar with the rules of the place, I waited near the door after the stoic nurse behind a small desk scribbled down my name and Brenda's. Her inimical stare brought on by my tarrying, drove me from the building, feeling chagrined, as if my *braguette* was open.

My wait in the hot afternoon sun came to an end, as the glass doors opened, bringing an adrenaline rush to my body. My heart palpitated as I stood to greet the beautiful image walking in my direction. Allie was the last person I expected to see.

She was wearing a pair of white shorts, less provocative than the ones of the previous evening at the Double Dip, and an oversized man's shirt, tied in a knot at the waist. The blue ribbon holding back her hair accentuated her blue eyes, leaving me as enchanted as the evening before.

"Good Allie, morning." The gabbled phrase caused me to blush. My second attempt, with a slight chuckle was more coherent. "Good morning, Allie."

"Good afternoon, Yogi," Allie said with a slight giggle. "Apparently you didn't get much sleep last night."

"A little," I replied succinctly. I couldn't understand why my mind was so dysfunctional after our voluble time together in the emergency room the previous night.

"Yogi! Brenda has to work," Allie said in something of an apologetic tone. "She asked me to come down and tell you."

"Well, that shoots the shit out of my afternoon!" Embarrassed by the developing foible in my character, which caused such an outburst, I quickly apologized before standing.

"I'm not doing anything this afternoon, Yogi if you would like some company," Allie said with a slight movement of both arms.

"We were . . . just going to Thompson Park," I answered still feeling somewhat uncomfortable.

"It's been sometime since . . . since I've been to the park," Allie said tightening the knot in her shirt.

A knot developed in my throat. Realizing Lady Luck had smiled upon me, my embarrassment subsided with a smile I couldn't hide.

Our afternoon was filled with jovial small talk while strolling through the park, or sitting on the grass along the edge of the small lake. So much lush green grass was too inviting to pass up and Allie laughed freely as I stretched out on the acclivity of a hill beneath a small oak. As I lay there, the beauty of the surrounding elms, cottonwoods and willows, washed over me like a gentle breeze filling the void within my soul, created by the drab openness of the Panhandle, to which I still hadn't adjusted. While sitting next to me, Allie tickled my forehead with a blade of grass as I lay with my arms folded behind my head, staring up at the beautiful blue sky. At some point, I pretended to fight off the blade of grass by grabbing her wrist. A wry face, expressing fright more than pain, transformed Allie's countenance. A clinched fist delivered a blow to my ribs, causing me to release her arm. As the panicky expression left Allie's face, she jumped up and ran to a willow tree near the water's edge. For a while, I remained sitting, stunned by her strange reaction. With some apprehensiveness, I stood and walked to the tree, stopping just a few feet behind her. For a second, Allie glanced in my direction, wiped her eyes, and offered up a halfhearted smile. I apologized for hurting her.

"I'm sorry Yogi," Allie said. "I shouldn't have hit you."

The carnival music of nearby Wonderland caused Allie to smile.

"How long has it been since you rode the flying horses?" I asked, extending my hand to her.

Taking my hand, Allie started running toward the amusement park. The gaieties of our laughter as we ran up the hill permeated this beautiful island of green in the midst of a city I was starting to love.

The afternoon, Allie and I shared in the park, occupied every waking moment of my life for several weeks. My job became repetitious and I lost all desire for food. Brenda and I continued seeing each other, mostly on weekends for a movie at the Paramount on Polk Street, and slowly I began to realize my real purpose for seeing her, was a means of maintaining a connection with the hospital in hopes of seeing Allie occasionally

.

After attending church service one Sunday morning at the First Baptist Church, I drove the short distance to the Double Dip where I was to meet my three friends for an afternoon of horseback riding in Palo Duro. After eating a burger and fries, I changed into a pair of jeans and polo shirt in the backseat of my car, while hoping like hell that one of the Car Hops wouldn't walk upon me.

My friends were running late, so to kill time I sat on the front fender of my car scanning an old copy of Playboy, while sipping on a cherry coke. Engrossed with the centerfold, a long horn blast caused me to jerk up my feet, when a car whipped into the vacant parking slot next to me. A good case of the *cul rouge* would have developed over the scare, had someone else other than Allie been driving. She and Crystal were still laughing, when I stepped down and squeezed my way between the two cars to toss the magazine on the backseat of my car.

Kneeling in the driver's seat, facing the rear of Crystal's convertible, Allie asked, "If you can tear yourself away from the magazine, how about a ride?"

"Only if I can drive," I answered.

After making several drags up and down the Polk Street in the snazziest car in Amarillo, with two of the prettiest girls in Texas, my macho desire to see what the Chevy would do on the open road caused me to turn onto Route 66 and head toward the base. Two hundred and eighty-three horses came alive under the hood, as the Ramjet fuel injection carburetor answered the demand of my right foot. Jubilant and approving shouts from my passengers, who were holding their arms in the air as if riding a roller coaster, competed for my attention with the rushing wind deflected above my head by the panoramic windshield. As the Bel Air rocketed down the highway beyond the Air Base, the open country seemed endless, except for the fence posts, which began to blend together.

Upon returning to the Double Dip, I offered Allie a ride back to the hospital, which she gladly accepted. Crystal felt slighted, but seemed to understand we wanted to be alone. Before returning to the hospital, I drove to The Leaning Tower of Pisa on North 8th Street, so Allie and I could spend a little more time together. The kitchen portion of the restaurant extended out into the dining room, so the customers could watch the chef work the dough by tossing it into air. We both wondered while laughing if he had ever dropped one.

The drive back to St. Anthony's was intentionally slow. At the bottom of the long flight of steps, we repeatedly said good night while an awkward paralysis prevented me from taking her into my arms. After saying good night for about the fifth time, Allie came to her toes and lightly kissed me on the cheek. She quickly turned and ran up the flight of steps, leaving me more bewitched than ever.

Wearing a necktie each day was a requirement of my office job. A habitual preemptive loosening of the tie and collar button took place several feet from the steps of my barrack. Walking past the outside phone booths, I thought of giving Allie a quick call for our parting the night before continued to plague my mind. The desire to rid myself of the nuisance around my neck prevented me from doing so.

With equal eagerness, the uniform jacket came off upon reaching the sanctity of the barracks. In a few moments, the exuberant sounds, which always punctuated the end of our day began to fill the hall with the arrival of several other boys. Stripped down to my boxers, I greeted Pete with a slight teasing as I dragged my finger nail across his wire cage before checking his water container. He acknowledged my antagonizing with an attempted peck at my finger and a few chirps. Hoping to unwind for a short time before going to chow, I switched on the Tank's record player and stretched out on my bunk. As a wave of soft relaxing strings of some unidentified opus filled the room, so did Pete's chirping, until I became annoyed and pulled off one sock and hurled it at him. The fluttering of his wings disturbed the loose feathers and bird seeds at the bottom of the cage. I watched annoyed as it settled to the floor.

After relaxing for a while, I decided to walk down the hall to James' room. He wasn't in. Thinking he may be in Paul and John's room, I walked to the far end of the barrack.

John was sitting on his bunk with a disgusting frown on his face, while Paul sat on his bunk, bearing a full face grin. I pretended to ignore the foul odor in the room while pulling one of the chairs from under the table. James entered the room a minute after me, carrying a shoe box. His jovial face soon writhed.

"Damn Paul!" declared James fanning the air. "Can't you go to the latrine if you have to fart?"

"I'm gonna put a cork in his butt, if he doesn't stop," lambasted John with a frown.

What's in the box, Red Neck?" asked Paul moving to the edge of his bunk.

James opened the shoe box revealing an assortment of homemade cookies.

"What's the occasion, Red Neck?" asked John as his face changed to a smile.

"This week I'll be eighteen," As the shoe box made a trip around the room, James explained how his mother had to sign so he could join the Air Force.

In keeping with John's constant ribbing of James, he asked, "Did she do that so you could get your first pair of shoes?"

"I salute you James," said Paul as he leaned over to fart.

"Paul, you're a damn animal!" chided John while taking the box of cookies from him.

News of the arrival of such "Care Package" from home had a way of filtering through the bay, and soon the room became crowded with guys all dressed in white boxer shorts.

"Somebody strike a damn match!" one of the new arrivals to the party exclaimed. "It smells like crap in here."

Reaching in his pocket, James extracted his cigarette lighter. The roar of laughter and belittling remarks leveled against the Alabama Red Neck for not understanding the reason for lighting a match caused James to extinguish the lighter and returned it to his pocket.

The laughter soon died as the shoe box made another trip around the room. Since a couple of boys standing in the hallway were smoking, Paul's request to barrow James' lighter didn't seem unusual. After lying back on his bunk, Paul flipped open the lighter. An adroit movement of his thumb across the striker brought forth the expected small flame. With a sweeping move, the lighter found its way to the proper position just as Paul expelled what must have been his greatest burst of gas, sending a long blue flame across his bunk. For a moment, we all maintained our positions in quiet disbelief; before an explosion of laughter filled the room.

"You, son-of-a-bitch!" James shouted while jumping from his chair and straddled Paul. Trying to wrestle the lighter from Paul's hand, James continued his castigation, "You 'maphrodite' . . . ya farted on my lighter."

Once in control of his lighter, James wiped it on Paul's blanket. An automatic reflex to sniff the lighter caused a guffaw to erupt in the room producing tears and stomach cramps. A couple of witnesses to the fiery spectacle demanded an encore, but James refused to donate his lighter as a source of ignition.

During noon chow, the following day, Paul's fireworks dominated our conversation until James brought up John's lecherous capabilities as well as his "fried chicken" philosophy about girls. By nature, John wasn't a taciturn individual, but he had a way with both words and girls. His apparent lack of concern for Casey's well being still disturbed me, and while I visited her twice after her discharge I withheld my thoughts on the subject since John and I were friends.

Our noon time dialogue about John's "luck with girls" prompted James to reveal a personal secret, which most GIs wouldn't divulge even if threatened with death. The fact that he was now an eighteen-year-old virgin, come out with such ease, that Paul and I just sat there with faces of stone. We almost felt sorry for him because of his despondent look and the fact that he didn't realize that most stories told in the barracks, about "some ole girl back home," were generally fabrications to maintain a certain macho facade. During James' third trip to the milk canteen, Paul and I almost simultaneously had the same thought. *John could remedy James' predicament.* Paul even suggested that Opal might be available for the big event.

Two hours later, John called my office stating he had a solution to James' problem. "Our birthday gift" to James would cost each of us five dollars. I wondered how he had arranged this in so short a time, but knowing John, I figured he had girls on stand-by for such occasions.

Our celebration began at the Pink Elephant, which had become one of our favorite places since our encounter with Sergeant Crockett at Sarge's Place. I nursed one beer for the duration of our stay while John and Paul treated James to several high balls in preparation for the coronation. In amazement, I was thinking there wouldn't be enough liquor in Texas to get him drunk enough to escape Opal's hairy legs and armpits. When the birthday boy was feeling up to the main event of the evening, John decided we move on.

In his usual disjointed fashion, John headed up our obstreperous troop through the parking lot beside the old brick hotel on Polk Street. The solution to James' predicament became obvious.

The décor of the old hotel lobby appeared trapped in a time warp, when patronizing cowboys, railroaders, and wildcatters sought the pleasures of an older generation of working girls. Along the dark wood paneled walls were several large paintings of cowboys, Indians, and solitary windmills all depicting an earlier period of the Panhandle's history. Hanging from a lofty ceiling, adorned with elaborate tiles was a massive chandelier whose many burned-out bulbs bespoke of a glory that once was.

Rising from the sofas and love seats located throughout the dimly lighted lobby to greet us was a menagerie of sultry working girls in every shape, size, and hair color, in a rainbow of negligees and matching heels.

"Hold on, my little chickadees!" John said flippantly as several girls started our way. The three of us stood behind his outstretched arms as if cowing from the onslaught of hungry wolves. With wanton pride and a broad smile John averred, "Ladies . . . the best damn rooster in the U.S. Air Force has arrived to do some crowing."

The lobby came alive with snickering as a woman appearing to be in her mid-forties stepped forward to greet us. Several silver filigree clips held in place a doughnut sized bun of bright red hair on the back of her head. She wore a long flowing pink peignoir over a matching diaphanous gown, which revealed that her ample bosom was once as charming as that of the younger women. The fluffy pink boa draped around her neck was skillful flip over one shoulder as she approached us. After removing the long plastic cigarette holder from her mouth, she stood before John and blew a coquettish stream of smoke to the side of his head.

"Well, young rooster," she said before pausing for another drag on her cigarette. "Just how much crowing are you up to?"

"Lady, I can crow all night," John averred facetiously as if undeterred by the virago. "But, our most pressing problem tonight is this little Alabama rooster. It's his birthday, and this is his first trip to the hen house."

Amid a burst of giggles, several of the more eager girls moved closer causing James' face to turn blood red.

When James moved backward from the hungry beasts, John took him by the arm and while grimacing clipped, "Come here, boy!"

As John continued his malarkey, Paul and I became willing captives of two eager girls who appeared more interested in obtaining a client rather than listening to John.

"Now, what we need . . . . is a beautiful young girl with caring ways and gentle hands to lead this young lad across the threshold into manhood."

James appeared to be suffering from rigor mortis as the Madam escorted him forward by the elbow to select a girl to fulfill John's requirements. The vampish touches of several girls caused James' Adam's apple to bob, creating a slight movement of his bolo tie.

"There's the chicken for you . . . James ole boy!" John averred in a brash voice. Paul and I turned our attention from the girls working at cranking our motors.

Startled at the sight of Crystal, who entered the lobby from a small side room, caused me to shove away the eager hands of my enthusiastic Cyprian. Standing with my mouth agape Crystal and I stared at each other in silent for a few moments as her chagrin face appeared to be a mirror reflection of my own. Her full bosom added a more décolleté effect to her red negligee, more so than that of the other girls. Her matching red heels reminded me of the shoes worn by Marilyn Monroe in the movie "River of No Return." From a red velvet ribbon fitted lightly around her neck was attached a small silver butterfly.

Without acknowledging John's intended union of herself and James, Crystal spoke in an abash tone.

"Hi . . . Yogi."

With a quizzical expression directed at me, John asked, "Damn, boy you been holding out on me?"

"I don't have to account to you for all my moves," I bristled.

While nervously interlocking her fingers together into a single fist, Crystal took a few steps back toward a door leading to the room, from which she came. After a momentary glance toward the room, she beckoned someone to the lobby with a busy left forefinger and a teasing timbre.

"Come, see who is here, Allie."

The name reverberated in my ears. Temporary paralyses sieged my body as I waited. Allie's minxish smile quickly disappeared when she turned to face me. A cold numb feeling traversed my body. The noisy chatter of the girls overpowered the signal to my immovable feet to flee the building. For a moment, my mind tried to convince my senses that the apparition in the hot pink negligee, high heels, and heavy makeup only resembled the girl I knew.

"Hi, Yogi," Allie said with downcast eyes. When she spoke, my heart attempted to reject the unwanted realization.

I failed to respond immediately. For some reason, a dolorous expression momentarily transformed Allie's face as she quickly diverted her eyes toward James for several moments. Unconsciously, I glanced at James before returning my gaze to Allie.

Before I could acknowledge Allie's greeting, John stepped in front of me. In his usual bullish manner he declared: "That's the chicken for me!"

John's lack of concern for Casey coupled with his self-assured personality and condescending attitude toward all girls brought to the surface the resentment that I still harbored toward him.

"You're not frying this chicken, John!" I said in an agitated tone while taking him by the arm and pulling him around.

Sensing a potential problem for her establishment, the Madam quickly moved between us.

"Calm down boys! There's plenty to go around." Taking John by the arm, she added, "Here, you go big boy; if your crowing is all you claim, you'll need Dixie. She'll give you something to crow about."

Taking James by the elbow, the Madam guided him toward Crystal, which seemed to please him. Paul's broad grin demonstrated that he was satisfied with his own selection; a girl named Angel. In an uneasy manner, I walked toward Allie and greeted her with a tepid smile.

John, Paul, and I, each contributed five dollars toward James' birthday gift as agreed upon beforehand. With the tab settled a rapturous hubbub echoed through the lobby as we headed for the elevator. Allie and I stood beside each other, but aloof to the lewd exchanges taking place around us as the companions of my three friends began stoking the fires of youthful desires.

The old elevator came to a jerky stop. With a feeling of apprehension and embarrassment, I stepped from the elevator before Allie who reached out and took my hand. With jollity, my three friends walked down the hall in one direction to their place of anticipated bliss while Allie escorted me in the opposite direction to room 210.

The musky odor of dampness, melted wax, and pine sol meant to disguise the smell of urine that filled the room like a thick darkness as I walked pass Allie who held open the door. As she mechanistically lit a single candle positioned on an antique dresser with a round mirror, I surveyed the room while leaning back against the door. The only other light in the room came from a night light emanating through a small opening in the bathroom door. In certain places, the walls, bare of fading wallpaper, as well as a large water spot on the ceiling, offered proof that the ancient hotel had long outlived its original purpose. The wrought iron bed, made up with a well-worn pink spread, had four tall posts with what appeared to be removal caps. The only other furniture in the room were a chest of drawers, upon which sat an old record player, and a floor lamp, both of which appeared as antique as the hotel.

Feeling awkward and unprepared for the occasion, I remained by the door as Allie moved around the bed to fold back the spread and sheet. Nervously my hands searched the door knob for a key.

After fluffing the pillows Allie held her head askance and asked, "Don't you think you should get undressed?"

"There's no lock on the door." I retorted with an uneasy tremble in my voice.

"No. There isn't," Allie answered in a calm matter of fact way. "It's that way for the safety of the girls. Would you like some music, Yogi? Some guys do."

"What the hell you're doing in this place!" Realizing my question sounded like something from an old movie I moving away from the door.

"What's a nice boy, like you, doing in a place like this?" Allie countered with a smile intended to rebuff my hostile tone.

"I am not trying to be funny!" I answered in a gruff voice while moving to the foot of the bed. "You look cheap . . . you know it?" I countered brusquely. "You're not the same girl . . . the one I spent the afternoon with in Thompson Park just a few . . ."

"I am the same girl!" Allie snapped, cutting me off. Her voice sounded agitated as she backed away from the bed and stood in a corner near the chest of drawers. "And what gives you the right to question me about what I do and where I go?"

"Hell, I mean, you were different then . . . You were a beautiful sweet . . ." My tongue refused to move further as a constriction closed my throat. For a moment, I desired John's volubility.

"If you would prefer another girl, Yogi . . . I'll understand." Allie's voice laden with a sense of rejection caused me to look down at the floor before responding.

"No. I don't want another," I answered quietly while resting against the foot end of the bed.

Before me hung a set of heavy drapes pined together in the middle preventing the light from the outside street lamps from penetrating the world of darkness, into which I had stepped. Feeling as if the drapes covering the windows also covered my face I had trouble breathing until Allie spoke again with an unrelated question, which at first didn't register.

"What's your friend's name?" asked Allie while moving to a position near the window to my left. "The one . . . having the birthday?"

"What?" I asked turning my face toward her.

With a slight shrug, Allie repeated the question. "Your friend's name? The birthday boy."

"James. His name is James," I answered laconically without moving. "You know him?" I asked, looking in her direction with an accusing stare. "I noticed you staring at him."

"No," Allie answered while turning and walking back to the record player. "He just looks like someone I once knew."

An uneasy hiatus transpired between us as Allie sorted through the LP's before putting one on the turntable. The poor quality of the record indicated, it too had outlived its usefulness like everything else in the hotel. With an almost apologetic tone, Allie spoke once more while wrapping her arms around her chest.

"Yogi, about that day . . . in the Park . . . I just thought you could use the company. That's all!" After pausing for a second or two, her voice became softer as she continued, "That afternoon, I pretended to be what you thought I was."

"You pretended . . . ?" My voice raised a notch or two. "I thought you said you enjoyed the afternoon?" After pausing for a moment, I angrily added, "I suppose you're just pretending now with your smiles and sexy pink negligee."

"Yes! I pretended then," Allie averred in a slightly angry tone before turning her face toward the candle, "and I pretend . . . like everyone else who enters that door. Just as you would be doing now if some other girl was here. Would you believe it? Some of the guys who come in here even ask if they can call me by their girlfriend's name!"

"This is one lousy damn business you're in. You know it!"

"Grow up, Yogi, this is life!" Allie snapped back in an angry voice. She paused for several moments before replying with a short smirk, "Damn boy. You're as green as wheat in the spring time."

Angrily reacting to the belittling insult I grasped my shirt at the waist with both hands and pulled it free from my pants. "I'll show you who is green as wheat," I answered kicking off my penny loafers.

The commercial transaction accomplished with much pretending on both our parts, left me feeling forlorn and unfulfilled. The fantasies I had had of such an evening with Allie were now a distorted picture, which I wanted to erase from my brain. While Allie went to the bathroom, I lay on my back looking up at the water-stained ceiling wishing I was any place by there. To me, Allie no longer appeared desirable. I no longer wanted to touch her body or have her touch mine.

A loud banging on the door caused me to quickly jump from the bed.

"Come on Yogi," shouted John. "If you need some help . . ."

"Go to hell, John!" I yelled back as Allie came out the bathroom wearing a terry cloth robe.

Wearing only my sock I walked naked to my clothes draped over a chair near the window. I no longer felt any respect for the girl I once thought estimable. Allie sat on the bed in silence while watching me dress. Once fully dressed, I started for the door after offering a quiet meaningless 'thanks.'

"Yogi, will I see you again?" asked Allie with a somber face.

"I don't think so," I answered reaching for the door knob.

The trip back to the Air Base included a stop at the Pink Elephant as the clamorous celebration of James' birthday came to a close. The birthday boy, now a man in every right, proclaimed this day his greatest and boasted exuberantly of Crystal's capabilities. Paul found release for his ecstasy by offering up catcalls into the Texas night while sitting in the window of *The Lung* pounding a rhythm on the roof in time with the blaring radio. John was strangely quiet. For me, the ride was a lonely desperate one as I slumped down in the backseat trying to find relief for my mind in a bottle of Lone Star.

After reaching the barrack, I immediately went to my room and stripped as quickly as I could, in the belief that my clothes were contaminated. After retrieving a clean towel from the locker, I walked naked to the latrine, something I had never done before.

The warm water showering down upon my body felt refreshing and purifying. Several times I lathered my entire body and scrubbed to the point of abrading the skin. No amount of water seemed sufficient to purge the filth and perceived stench from my body as well as the anguish tearing at my insides. After sometime, I leaned against the wall opposite the shower head and rested my forehead against my folded arms as the warm pulsating water pelted my back. I wanted the shower to last forever, but the purgation came to an end when someone else entered the latrine.

As the water came on in the other shower stall, I turned mine off and stepped out to dry myself. A quick glance was give to the latrine duty roster taped to the hallway wall before returning to my room, as naked as when I left it. Before stretching out on the wool blankets of my bunk, a clean pair of boxer shorts was donned after loading a couple of LPs onto Tank's record player. A strange mixture of emotions came over me as I gazed up at a full moon through the open blinds, which for some reason didn't seem as bright as the one seen before from this same position.

Chapter 6

The large trees near the Administration School took on a new beauty for me as I made my way to the hangar the following morning. They represented a continuity needed in my life at the time. In comparing them to the massive, ageless live oaks of south Louisiana, I thought about how trees are different from people in that their lives are never deceptive. Oaks always produce acorns, and pecan trees always produce pecans. The lives of humans are not so ordained.

Because of latrine duty, it was several minutes past 09:00 hours, when I arrived at the office, thus requiring one of the other boys to make the morning mail run. After removing my jacket and hanging it on a coat tree a group of well-arranged, handwritten notes, obviously placed there by Doc, and a familiar sealed folder greeted me. Of all mornings, I wasn't up to facing Doc's awful handwriting or Colonel O'Quinn.

Sergeant Black's first orders of the day concerning a certain Airman Payton Bridgewater having to be in Colonel O'Quinn's office at 10:00 hours, failed to draw a response from me. My obtuseness caused him to repeat himself before walking into Doc's office and closing the door. My gesture to James, expressing my desire for a cup of coffee, caused him to reach for a pack of cigarettes on his desk before standing.

James was still bubbling with euphoria over his birthday gift. As we made our way down the catwalk, he walked ahead of me with a slight turn of his body toward me as he talked continuously about Crystal. His inquiry into my acquaintance with her, and Allie drove away the ebullient spirit I shared for a moment. Following the coffee break, I went downstairs to Sergeant Crockett's class to meet Airman Bridgewater.

Sergeant Crockett wasn't one to interrupt a lecture just because a visitor walked in, so I patiently stood just inside the room as he continued a long narrative about the importance of keeping track of one's tools while working on the flight line. The story he shared to illustrate his point concerned an incident at an Air Base in California where a strange discoloration on the wing of a jet fighter caused the aircraft to be grounded for some time. As it turned out, a flashlight belonging to the Crew Chief left inside the wing above the jet engine was the culprit. The melted evidence produced to confirm the tale and the veraciousness of its bearer brought forth a roar of laughter from the students.

As the tale concluded, Sergeant Crockett's attention turned to me along with fifteen adolescent faces. A young boy on the far side of the room stood after my purpose for the interruption was stated.

Airman Bridgewater appeared to be about eighteen. He was tall and lanky with handsome features. Like the other boys in the room, he was dressed in fatigues, which were leathery from an ample application of starch. A small plastic accouterment containing his ear plugs hung from the top button hole of his shirt. His fresh GI style haircut seemed to highlight his smooth youthful face that caused me to wonder if this kid was yet old enough to shave.

Before beginning our trek to the Colonel's office, I introduced myself to Airman Bridgewater hoping that the small gesture of friendship would put him at ease. Like the other fifty or so boys with whom I make this same trip, Airman Bridgewater was edgy for he knew such meetings often resulted in some form of "washing back" in the training. In the course of our conversation, Bridgewater from Allentown, Pennsylvania, stated that he had joined the Air Force to be an Air Policeman as was his father. He didn't like the jet engine school and had no desire to be a mechanic.

Colonel O'Quinn was a tall man, in his early fifties, of lean stature with a sharp face, which bore a slight scar from the ala of his left nostril running across both lips down to his chin. The Colonel's thick graying hair, well groomed and split with a deep part high above his left ear, appeared in sharp contrast with his bushy eyebrows, which always needed trimming.

Bridgewater and I saluted Colonel O'Quinn and remained at attention before his desk until ordered to stand at ease. In a clear military manner, I greeted the Colonel with a strong *Good morning, Sir* and handed over Bridgewater's file.

The slashing sound generated by the letter opener as it ripped through the paper seal broke the silence of the office. A quick glance toward Bridgewater, intended to reassure him, revealed a small bead of perspiration running down the side of his stony face. After flipping through several pages and a few muffled grunts, the Colonel looked up at Bridgewater.

"You have an explanation for this report, Airman?" asked Colonel O'Quinn while placing the open folder on the desk.

"No Sir," Bridgewater answered in an almost inaudible tone.

"Speak up, Airman!" the Colonel countered in a raised voice.

"No Sir!" responded Bridgewater in almost a shout. "I have no explanation, Sir!"

"Your aptitude test shows, you have the capability to complete this course of study," the Colonel replied in almost a sedate tone.

A *Yes sir* blurred forth even though there wasn't a question.

"This report is recommending, you be 'washed-back' three weeks."

Once more, a stentorian *Yes sir* echoed through the office cutting short the Colonel's sentence.

For some reason, Colonel O'Quinn departed from his customary "peptalk" to a long harangue about devotion to country, Air Force, and family. Airman Bridgewater's face bore a deadpan expression as his body seemed to stiffen and for a while I thought he had stopped breathing. When the Colonel glanced down at the folder again, I foolishly took advantage of the pause and requested to speak.

The Colonel looked at me with a strange, almost disfigured expression for this was the first time I had intervened on behalf of a student.

"You have something to add, Airman?" asked the Colonel with a sour tone as his bushy eyebrows appeared to rise to the middle of his forehead.

The Colonel's acerbity caused me to wonder what happened to his usual benign grandfatherly personality. At this moment in his life, Bridgewater, like me needed the support of a friend, and since my foot was already in the "cow pile," with no way of shaking it free, I pursued the unwise decision to intervene.

"Sir," I continued while staring at a picture of a jet fighter on the wall behind the Colonel's desk, "Airman Bridgewater has expressed a desire to be an Air Policeman and feels he would be of greater value to the Air Force in that capacity."

The room was silent for several moments. Finally, my eyes were lowered enough to see the Colonel staring down at the report. I glanced at Bridgewater. His entire body seemed frozen until his Adam's apple moved indicating there was still life in the statue. When the Colonel looked up, his bushy eyebrows settled on the top rim of his glasses causing my heart to palpitate. I had transgressed one of the basic rules of survival in the military . . . *speak when spoken to and offer no opinions.*

The Colonel removed his glasses and slung them on the desk while maintaining a scowl face intended for my detriment. After dismissing Airman Bridgewater, who offered a snappy salute and quickly left the office, Colonel O' Quinn walked around the desk. I was as petrified as James was, the previous evening. The Colonel's inimical gaze immediately suggested permanent latrine duty and scatology would be my new MOS (Military Occupational Specialty).

The office door had barely closed behind Bridgewater before a barrage of words enfiladed my right ear. My place in the chain of command, equated to *whale crap and the other things at the bottom of the ocean,* didn't entitle me to an opinion in such matters as this recruit's education. Upon accepting the Colonel's assessment with approbation, and enthusiasm, I exited the office with as much speed as I could without appearing on the run.

The following Friday evening, our weekend of carousing began at the Red Garter, an impromptu looking honky-tonk, made of plywood painted bright red. As we entered the door, the smoke cloud hovering two feet below the ceiling seemed to pulsate with the country music. Two things about the Red Garter immediately caught every first-time visitor's attention; the large ornate mirror, running the full length of the bar, and the chicken wire barricade surrounding the bandstand.

While waiting at the bar for a beer, a familiar female voice calling my name caused all of us to turn. Brenda's tepid greeting brought on an equally halfhearted smile from me.

"We have a table back there . . . if you guys would like to join us," Brenda announced in a raised voice attempting to be heard over the music."

"How many is 'us'!" Paul blurted out.

"Three, besides me," answered Brenda while leading the way.

After a round of introductions, a form of natural pairing off took place. Brenda and I stood behind two chairs next to each other, while James was attracted to a cute dirty blonde named Coco. Paul and John didn't appear to be interested in becoming so formal so the names of the other two girls went unnoticed.

Brenda and I were still standing when the band began to play "It's Only Make Believe." The song, which once held such sweet memories of Allie for me had became an abhorrent tune in my mind and in a crude fashion, I dragged Brenda to the dance floor hoping to drive from my memory any remaining thoughts of Allie. Apparently Brenda misunderstood my eagerness and placed a strangle hold around my neck. After several moments, she permitted me to breathe by backing away for a subtle, but probing question about my afternoon with Allie in the park. I felt her apology for having to work was duplicitous so I lied and pulled her back into my arms.

As the night wore on, the party became livelier and James' interest in the large mirror seemed to escalate with each beer. The reason for the chicken wire became obvious as the crowd expressed its dislike for the band by throwing beer bottles toward the stage. In the middle of their feeble attempt at Patsy Cline's 'I Fall to Pieces' the band and building was brought to a dead silence by the shrill cry of a woman's voice.

James was standing on the bar holding his cowboy boots, one in each hand, and threatening to crash the enormous mirror. The barmaid, a corpulent middle-aged woman, demanded in a boisterous voice that he should come down or face the police. A couple of guys who apparently misunderstood the meaning of Coco's uplifted arms pleading with James to come down hoisted her to the bar adding to the frustration of the barmaid.

Shoving my way through the clamorous crowd, I joined Paul and his date at the bar where my efforts to entice James from the bar were overpowered by the cheering audience demanding that James remove more of his clothing.

"Get that bastard off my bar!" the woman screamed vociferously as she slammed a large open hand on the bar.

"Damn it, lady! I'm trying!" I shouted back before yelling up to James. "Hey! You little Alabama Red Neck . . . come down before she calls the law!"

"I'm gonna . . . bust it . . . Yogi," James yelled teetering while raising one boot in a threatening manner.

"Don't you dare!" shouted the barmaid with both arms raised.

Hoping to prevent James from throwing his boots, I instruct Coco to wrap her arms around him. The attempt caused James to stagger back a few steps before regaining his balance. A clamorous roar of sighs and cheers resounded throughout the bar. With one finger of each hand looped through the mule ears of the boots, James lowered his arms, and Coco stood back. Leaning forward, he tried to address the barmaid with a heavy tongue.

"I haaaate . . . that loooousy band," James said while allowing his boots to hang free at the end of each arm. He staggered forward one or two steps while maintaining his bent-over position before Coco stopped him with one hand against each shoulder. Without straightening up, James dropped the boots to the bar before turning to the barmaid and loudly declared, "That lousy band hadn't played one song by Kitty Wells."

"Get him off my bar!" the wretched barmaid screamed once more before signaling the band members to assist her.

"Hang on, lady," I counter in a louder tone. "Tell the band to play something by Kitty Wells."

"What song?" she asked with a disgust look on her face.

"Hell! I don't know . . . anything," I screamed back.

The Barmaid waved the band members back behind their wire barricade with instructions to play something by Kitty Wells. Paul and I assisted James and Coco from the bar.

As the band began playing, "It Wasn't God Who Made Honky-Tonk Angels," James placed one arm around my neck and pulled my face close to his. With a fetid breath and stiff finger poking in my chest, he mumbled, "You're a good friend, Yogi."

The barmaid refused to sell any more drinks to James and threatened to kick us out if we gave him any. The restriction appeared not to bother James, since he was becoming intoxicated with Coco, his first real connection since coming to Amarillo. The rest of the night, James danced in his socks and for some reason, the band seemed to recall more songs by Kitty Wells.

Because the student nurses had a 9:00 p.m., curfew on Sunday evenings, James and I took Brenda and Coco to an early movie at the Paramount downtown. They didn't care as much for the 'Time Machine' with Rod Taylor, as did James and I. Following the movie, we made a couple of runs up and down the Polk Street between St. Anthony's and the Double Dip just to kill a little time. As we sat at a red light near the old hotel during one run, my mind, eyes and heart searched for the one person I wanted most or dreaded to see. When the light turned green, I drove on after Brenda elbowed me.

Brenda's displeasure with my distraction in front of the hotel was more fully expressed when we returned to the Double Dip. She quickly got out the car on the opposite side from me and slammed the door. To demonstrate further her annoyance, she refused to order, which caused me to limit my request to a cherry coke. After James and Coco ordered, he assisted her to the trunk of the car opposite Brenda and me. For his efforts, he received a gently arm around his neck as he stood beside Coco. I didn't appreciate someone sitting on my car, but when Brenda asked me to boost her onto the trunk, I agreed hoping this would change her petulant mood.

In an effort to change Brenda's frigid mood, I attempted to engage everyone in a discussion of the movie. During our conversation something going on in the parking lot a short distance from us caught James' attention causing him to step away from the car.

"Hey, Yogi, isn't that *The Lung* down there?" James asked with a worried look on his face while moving almost in the line of traffic.

Stepping away from Brenda's side, I looked in the direction of Polk Street.

"Looks like John trying for some Mexican fried chicken," I added with a chuckle.

"They don't serve fried chicken here," Coco said with a puzzled look on her face.

James tried mimicking John's philosophy with a Mexican accent. The crashing sound of breaking glass and the fearful scream of a Carhop brought our blithesomeness to an abrupt ending.

"Damn, Yogi," James called out, "I believe that Mexican broad is gonna gut the chicken man."

James and I broke into a full stride toward *The Iron Lung* leaving the girls behind. A Mexican girl armed with a broken beer bottle was holding John at bay when I reached his side. An expression of panic and fright disfigured her brown face as she stood trembling in front of three young boys as if protecting them.

"What the hell's going on, John?" I inquired after catching my breath.

"Hell, I don't know," John replied while gesturing with his right hand toward the girl. "This crazy Mexican bitch . . . threatened to cut me."

With a face of defiance, one of the boys moved beside the Mexican girl and pointed his finger at John.

"That bastard gringo touched my sister on the teta . . ."

I then recognized Benito, the young boy, Allie, and I had assisted sometime back.

An abdominous man with a large tattoo on his massive deltoid waddled toward us with a spatula in one hand. Hair from his neck and back protruded all around the collar of his badly stained T-shirt, which clung tightly to his sweaty body. A dirty dishcloth hung from his apron string while another served as a sweat band around his head.

"You Mexican kids, get the hell out of here," the man angrily announced while waving the spatula at the Mexican girl. "You aren't anything but trouble. Go back to the barrio where you belong."

"Look mister! She's not the one who started this crap," I avowed while stepping toward him. At this point, John disassociated himself of the skirmish by easing back toward *The Lung*.

"Hey! I don't need some Air Base trash telling me how to run my place!" the man retaliated while violently shaking the spatula in my direction.

"You had better look around, Mister," I snapped back. "Most of the cars here have Air Base stickers on the windshields. And, if you're not careful who you're calling trash, we'll put out the word on the base to boycott this place."

As the wry expression left the big man's face, the spatula came to rest near his right thigh. "I still don't serve their kind," he replied with a mean askance stare toward the girl.

My attention and question turned to the girl. "Did you and the boys order something?"

"Si," she replied with a tremor in her voice.

"Bring them their food," I said forcefully to the man as several Carhops began to move closer. "Then . . . they'll leave."

As the grizzly man turned and started toward the building, he mumbled something under his breath to one of the Car Hops while pointing the spatula back toward the girl. A slight annoyance caused by Brenda's demanding voice lanced my brain as she called my name amid the resuming din of the parking lot. Even my momentary glance in her direction didn't require the skills of a physiognomist to see that my involvement had only added to her growing displeasure with me.

"Hey, Yogi," John said after swaggering back toward me and waving his hand in front of the girl. "I don't know why she's so uptight."

"John! Shut up and go back to your car!" I answered in an agitated voice.

After he walked off, I turned to the girl once more.

"Look. I'm sorry, for what my friend did," I said in a soft voice, trying to let her know that everything was all right.

"You have a *perro* for a friend," she angrily answered back while pointing the broken beer bottle in John's direction. Her accent was captivating even when expressing anger.

"Why don't you give that to me?" I asked nodding toward the broken bottle.

"My boss said for you to leave as soon as you're done." The Carhop's pretentious tone caused the girl and me to look in her direction.

Benito said something in Spanish as the Carhop walked off. The Mexican girl pointed the broken bottle toward him while giving him what I understood to be a Spanish scolding. Once more, I requested the bottle.

"You're not from Amarillo, are you?" the girl asked while relinquishing the bottle with a relaxed, transformed face.

"No," I answered. "I'm stationed at the Air Base."

"Yogi!" Brenda called from a position near John's car.

A quick backward glance at Brenda revealed her dissatisfaction with me, and the whole evening was mounting.

"You had better go," the girl said, "your girlfriend is getting angry."

Benito said something in Spanish while shaking their fingers as if touching something hot. The other boys snickered.

"My brother said that your other girlfriend, the "chilli pepper," with the red hair is prettier than this one."

Brenda's voice interrupted our conversation once more.

After a short pause, I shrugged and added with a grin, "Well, I had better go." Not knowing how to say "good night" in Spanish, my best attempt was a simple "adios."

Before leaving, I told the girl my name. Her name was Caridad. After shaking hand, she walked toward the table and sat next to Benito, whose garrulous nature produced a steady flow of words. Brenda made no effort to hide her indignation when I reached *The Lung* while John tried to recover his lost pride by proclaiming his innocence. I was in no mood for Brenda's bitching and John's hypocritical ratiocination.

"Damn it, John, you beat everything. You know it," I lashed out. "That Mexican girl came close to turning the barnyard rooster into a capon."

James and Paul enjoyed the farcical sarcasm and gave a great belly laugh as the girls looked on in confusion. James took advantage of the opportunity to taunt John for a change by clucking as a chicken as we walked away from *The Iron Lung*.

"Hey Yogi! You guys wanta go for a beer?" John called out trying to put the shine back on his image.

"I've seen enough beer bottles for one night, John," I called out without turning in his direction.

The ride back to St. Anthony's was long, silent, and frigid for the occupants of the front seat. A secretive glance in the rearview mirror revealed that James and Coco were enjoying a more amiable environment. After parking along the curb, on the opposite side of the street from the hospital, James and Coco made a fast exit and dashed, hand in hand, across the street in front of an oncoming car. Their euphoric laughter expressed a youthful wiliness to court danger. Brenda rejected my subtle attempt at reconciliation by refusing my hand as we walked across the street.

The long flight of steps and buttresses were dotted with a dozen or more couples enjoying their final intimate moments of the evening together. The trees surrounding the building, as always, blocked most of the illumination from the nearby streetlights creating a serene romantic spot for such an occasion. James and Coco quickly found a secluded spot while still laughing over their brush with death. Brenda, now walking several feet ahead of me, sidestepped a couple sitting in the shadows of the left buttress. A familiar voice spoke my name from the darkness.

Stopping two steps above the couple, I turned to face Allie who was now standing in the light. I moved back down to her level and accepted her extended hand. The gesture seemed incongruous given our familiarity with each other. Yet, its warmth, coupled with a friendly smile awakened a feeling within my spirit I thought disposed. My grasp reluctantly came to an end when Scott stood and reintroduced himself with an extended hand.

Brenda was obviously piqued when I sat next to her, several steps above Allie and Scott. My mind swirled in a whirlpool of anguish as I stared at Allie's back while resting my chin on my folded arms across my knees. I no longer knew what to believe about her.

The conversation between Brenda and I, while seated bordered on the edge of antagonism until the double glass doors opened, illuminating the steps. A tall nurse in a white uniform announced it was time for the girls to come in.

We remained seated for several minutes as most of the other girls made their way to the doors. A slight, almost nonconnecting kiss, while seated, preceded our tepid good night before Brenda stood and ran up the steps, leaving me to believe that continuing such a relationship was a dalliance. James and Coco enjoyed a protracted embrace until the impatient nurse pulled them apart with a loud harrumphing sound. Before releasing each other, they tenderly shared a kiss of infatuation and desire.

The Iron Lung, parked in front the Pink Elephant, caused me to slow down, but my aggravation with John hadn't subsided enough to face him again. The fence mending with John would be unnecessary, come sunrise, but with Brenda however, that would require more time. In a matter of several days, my friendship with Allie had been lost, and now the shaky relationship with Brenda appeared bogged in a morass of suspicion and distrust. The only bright spot in my life at the time appeared to be the alliance I had created with Airman Bridgewater, which I knew wouldn't last long because of his temporary status as a student.

Chapter 7

With the passing of twelve hours and a shared breakfast with my friends on Monday, John's beer bottle debacle became comical as we ragged him about his failure to obtain the desired chicken fajita dinner at the Double Dip.

Once at the office, the thought of possibly running into Colonel O'Quinn while making the morning mail run, caused me to ask James to take the trip for me once we returned from our first coffee break. Since he agreed, I made a reconnaissance trip downstairs when the students had their first morning break to see if Airman Bridgewater had heard anything about our own debacle in the Colonel's office. A negative response on his part brought some comfort to my mind.

Upon returning to the barracks that afternoon, I attempted to call Brenda before going up to my room. She wasn't in, so once more, I left a message for her to call. Heading up the stairs anticipating a few relaxing moments with Hank's classical records before going to chow, I loosened my necktie and unbuttoned the uniform jacket while on the run. After turning on the record player, I checked Pete's water container while teasing him by dragging a finger nail across the wires of his cage.

A light knock on the open door brought to an end, my harassment of Pete. John swaggered into the room, his body, smelling as if he had been drenched with Old Spice. In his characteristic, blasé manner, he jerked the chair from under the table and straddled it, before asking if I would do a favor for him. Since *The Iron Lung* could no longer bury the speedometer needle, John had made arrangements with one of the Sergeants in his Department to rectify this problem with a tune-up. With the promise of a beer, I considered, the drive into town would further mend our differences from the previous evening.

After leaving *The Lung* at the Sergeant's house on North Mirror Street, John asked if I would mind running by Casey's apartment *for just a little while*. I knew they were seeing each other again, but couldn't understand Casey's willingness, given John's attitude while she was in the hospital. The only compensation to reward my deference to John's request was a home-cooked meal prepared by Opal. During the meal, she did most of the talking, since the tension between John and Casey was obvious. Occasionally, while maintaining a lowered head, Opal looked up at me with a flirtatious smile, which I tried to ignore.

John and Casey retreated to her bedroom after supper. I became Opal's prisoner in one corner of the couch, while trying to ignore her hairy armpits and legs by pretending to be interested in Gun Smoke. The thin walls of the apartment managed to muffle some of the strident voices emanating from the other room, but it was clear, Casey was attempting to rid John of his narcissistic attitude.

Since the feared phone call from Colonel O'Quinn's office or the Orderly Room hadn't materialized by the end of the workday on Thursday, I reasoned, *Whatever happens, will happen and worrying over it wouldn't change things.* Before going up to my room, I tried calling Brenda as I had done twice each night since she expressed her dissatisfaction with my friendliness toward Caridad. Agitated by her obvious attempts to avoid me, I slammed the telephone receiver on the hook and kicked open the door.

John was pestering Pete when I walked through the door of my room. The devilish grin on his face before walking to the straight chair and assuming his favorite position left me suspicious. In his smooth characteristic manner, John attempted to state his reason for waiting on me. Interrupting him, I shouted, *No*! and irefully tossing my uniform jacket across the bunk.

"Come on, Maaan," John pleaded. I attempted to ignore him by pretending to search for a coat hanger in my locker. "You know *The Lung* isn't ready. Besides it's just to a drive-in movie."

Roiled by John's proposal, I hurriedly hung the unbuttoned shirt in the locker, disregarding the regulation spacing.

"John! I said, 'no.' I don't care if you're going to sit in a cave. I won't be seen in public with Opal as a date!"

"If I ask you . . . pretty please," John said sarcastically. A stark stare negated his smile. "Come on, Yogi, Casey won't go unless Opal goes with us . . . and you . . . she thinks a lot of you . . ."

"And, I'm the only sucker with a car," I retaliated while slipping off my pant.

"You know that's not what I meant."

"John, I'm not dating a girl who has more hair on her legs than me," I answered with a penetrating stare. After hanging the pants in the locker, I pointed to one armpit for emphasis. "And, on top of that . . . the broad has more hair under her arms than me."

"And her biceps are bigger than yours," John quipped with a short chortle before lowering his forehead to his folded arms across the back of the chair.

"You're a funny person. You know it," I fired back sounding tart.

"Look man, this broad got the hots for you. I know what I'm talking about."

"If she's so hot, tell her to go sit on an iceberg with the other hairy creatures," I retaliated.

"I'll make you a deal, Yogi; I'll pay for the movie . . . for the four of us," John stuttered nervously.

"What about popcorn and peanuts for the hairy monkey?" I asked sardonically.

"Popcorn and peanuts for you and the monkey," John answered while attempting to hold back a smile.

Stretching out on the bunk, I figured the "chicken man" would turn "chicken" and abandon the idea if I drove up the price for the evening.

"And gas money," I demanded raising my head from the pillow. "A full tank."

"Damn, boy! That will wipe out what little money I have until payday." The expression on John's face as he stood from the chair indicated he was losing his usual aplomb demeanor.

Awaiting the results of his ruminations, I attempted a Paul size grin while putting both hands behind my head. "That's the deal. Take it or leave it."

I flinched when John looked down at me and said, "Allll . . . right. It's a deal."

In the back of my mind, I reasoned that Opal's reluctance to shaving, was a religious thing. Maybe she was a Jehovah Witness or a member of some group who didn't believe in shaving and would reject a hairless guy like myself in favor of some grizzly Neanderthal like Tank. Furthermore, Friday night was a long ways off, and Brenda could still forgive me and call before the bewitching hours.

"There's one more thing . . . John," I said trying to wiggle my way out of the socially distasteful trap, into which I had fallen.

"What now?" John scowled.

"Before this deal flies, that hairy broad will have to shave . . . cleaner than a scalded *cochon de lait,* or the deal is off." I answered resolutely.

"I don't know what that is, but I'll shave the bitch myself, if necessary," John answered with a fatuous expression.

"And one more thing, two certain . . . knuckleheads are not to know about this. You hear!"

Purposely, my shower Friday evening dragged on for as long as possible, hoping a reprieve from the social death sentence facing me would come, even if from Brenda. While I dressed, John's arrival was preceded by his odoriferous shaving lotion, annoying little whistle and jaunty stride on the hardwood floors. As he walked through the open door, his cocky demeanor manifested itself as he pulled the straight chair from under the table and gave it a quick spin before straddling it. With his arms folded on the back of the chair, he glanced at his watch several times while coaxing me to put on some speed.

A slight snicker from John caused me to step from behind the locker door, where I had been for several moments trying to decide, which shirt to wear.

"Damn it, John!" I shouted with a morose stare before turning to James and Paul.

"We're here to send you off with a little song . . . called, 'Homely on the range'?" declared Paul while trying to maintain a straight face.

"I told you, these two blockheads were not to know about this!" My inimical gaze directed at John wiped the smile from his face. "I ought to leave you sitting high and dry . . . right now!"

"I couldn't help it, Yogi," protested John while standing. "I didn't know what to tell them . . ."

"Since when you gave up lying?" I replied angrily.

"Hey, Yogi," James interrupted with a smile, "the evening won't be a total waste. While ole John's doing his thing in the backseat, you and Opal can sit in the front seat discussing your favorite razors now that she's shaven cleaner than a hound's tooth."

The mocking guffaw, which followed filled the room scaring Pete who began raising a ruckus. As if rehearsed, Paul began to strum a make-believe guitar, while he and James leaned their heads together for a revised rendition of "Homely on the Range."

Homely, homely on the range, where the deer and the hairy do roam,
Where the buffalo play and the ole Yogi will pay . . .

My anger fueled by James's remark about John's activities in the backseat, produced one more restriction for the "chicken man," which caused me to interrupt the balladeers.

"There's one more thing, blabbermouth," I said looking at John.

"Now . . . what?" asked John with a morose glance.

"None of your usual drive-in movie activities in the backseat of *My* car," I answered in a matter-of-fact way, while poking him the chest with my finger.

"Damn man! You're going too far, Yogi."

John's protest against the bridle put on his usual lecherous backseat activities ignited Paul and James' lewd creativity that produced an obscene ditty called "Horny on the Range." The joke was now on John, who demonstrated his lack of appreciation for the new restriction by heading out the room with a boisterous command that we were running late.

Only a portion of my brain, while suffering the clamping pressure of a vice, was functioning enough to realize the sheets and soft mattress, upon which I lay were not that of my bunk. For a moment, I refused to move, even though the same damaged brain was telling me that someone's arm was across my chest. My left eyelid appeared to be stuck, as the eyeball rolled around within the sockets trying to force it open. Upon accomplishing this laborious task, a brilliant ray of sunlight shinning through a small hole in the window shade shot through the pupil of my eye, lancing my brain with great pain. Automatically the eyelid slammed shut, revealing for the first time its capacity to make noise. The foul taste in my mouth suggested I must have drunk from Sergeant Jankowski's chamber pot sometime during the night.

As my eyeballs rolled around in the sockets like steel balls in a pinball machine, I forced open my left eye once more. Again, the same bright light pierced my brain, charging it with the realization that it was daylight. I gasped while springing to a sitting position.

The arm across my chest fell away, causing the body, totally hidden under the sheet, to groan. While wondering if this succubus had contributed to my present condition, a frizzy head slowly emerged from under the sheet. For a moment, Opal and I stared at each other before I evacuated the bed in a backward move similar to that of a crawfish. Opal pulled the sheet over the upper part of her body, as a blush washed across her face. With a grin, she lay there looking at me . . . looking at her, before I slowly looked downward, discovering my nakedness.

As quick as I had left the bed, I returned.

"Where . . . am I?" I asked in a muffled voice while holding the sheet over my head.

"You're right here," Opal replied in a ding bat sort of way. Her voice seemed to pierce my ears with the same sharpness the sunlight had inflicted on my left eye.

"Where is here?" I asked with my face buried in the pillow.

"My apartment," Opal answered with an upswing in her voice.

"How did I get here?" I asked, realizing that my brain and tongue were now capable of forming sentences with more than three words.

"You drove." Opal answered succinctly. I was starting to think a sentence of two words was the most she could put together.

"Where's John?" I asked spreading out my legs to prevent the bed from moving.

"With Casey." She continued with the two word sentences.

"What day is this?" I asked, still hiding under the sheet.

"It's Saturday."

"Saturday!" I repeated, while lifting my face from the pillow. With this move, Opal peeled the sheet from my head. While propped up on my forearms, I said in a rueful tone, "Damn, today is Sausage Day." In anguish, my face fell back to the pillow.

"You want sausage for breakfast, Yogi?" Opal asked in a squeaky voice.

"Hellll . . . !" I caught myself and then continued with a polite, "no." "Today is Sausage Day at the Base. John and I were supposed to have yard duty."

After rolling over onto my back, I raised the sheet above my head in a reconnaissance move. Opal, apparently misunderstanding my action, slammed her arm down on the sheet next to her body, bringing the sheet back down over my face. After rolling onto my stomach, I extended my head, still covered by the sheet, over the edge of the bed.

"What are you doing?" demanded Opal in her second sentence with more than two words.

"I'm looking for my shorts!" I answered while hanging over the edge of the bed.

"They're up there." Opal replied with a slight giggle.

"Up where?" I asked, pulling my upper body back onto the bed.

"On the light fixture," answered Opal, while pointing toward the ceiling.

Looking up, I spotted my boxer shorts gracefully hanging from one of the pointed edges of the light fixture. Opal anticipated the question my brain was trying to formulate.

"You . . . threw them there last night!" Opal answered, smiling.

Still with just my head exposed, I tried stretching my neck to focus on some black object hanging next to my shorts.

"What's that black thing?"

"That's my panties," Opal answered with a giggle. "Don't you remember throwing them up there?" My failure to respond caused Opal to giggle once more. "You . . . pulled them off with your teeth."

My snappy glance of disbelief in her direction negated the felicity covering Opal's face.

"Boooy, you're some crazy guy when you get tight," answered Opal, while smiling at me. A feverish sensation warmed the back of my neck.

After a few moments of rumination, I muddled aloud my confused thoughts, "Two beers have never affected me this way before."

"It wasn't just the two beers," Opal added gaily. "It was the six Irish coffees you had . . . after the beers."

"Irish coffees!" I solicited befuddled.

"Yeah," Opal answered while dragging out the word, "John bought them for you."

"That lowlife!" I declared, trying to sit up. "I'm gonna kill that son-of-a . . ." My throbbing head drove me back to the pillow.

I felt Opal was reading my thoughts as I stared up at the light fixture, wondering how to retrieve my shorts.

"I'll cover my face, if you want to get your shorts," Opal said pulling the sheet over her head. The bed moved as I stood, causing Opal to ask from under the sheet with a titter, "You'll get my panties, too?"

"Yeah," I answered, "but keep your face covered."

Opal and I dressed on opposite sides of the bed with our backs toward each other. Once dressed, Opal walked around the bed and stood for a moment near the tall bedpost, as if trying to decide if I appealed more to her in my shorts or naked. While Opal went into the bathroom, I walked to Casey's room and gave a loud military style knock on the door.

"What?" John's voice indicated a sense of pain.

Opening the door, I walked in and stared at John and Casey for a moment before demanding, "Get up, John! We have to get back to the base. We have Sausage Duty."

"Crap!" John answered while struggling to sit. "What time is it?"

"I don't know, but its daylight," I answered. "Sam's gonna grind our butts into *boudin rouge.*"

"What's that?" asked Casey.

"Cajun blood sausage. Which we will be if you don't get up, John."

"You eat blood?" asked Casey with a frown.

The thought was more than John's stomach could handle, and he gagged a couple of times before I reached for a small wicker trash basket near the bed. With the first heave of vomit, Casey jumped from the bed and headed out of the room. After several more heaves, long thin rivulets of mucus began leaking from the trash basket onto the floor.

"I hope you die, bastard," I said to John as Casey reentered the room with a wet washcloth.

"What's eating you?" John asked wiping his face.

"The six Irish coffees . . . that's what?" I answered feeling petulant.

"Didn't you enjoy the aftermath? Go back to bed, Yogi," John answered, holding his head over the trash basket. After several dry heaves, he wiped his face once more and said, "We're already AWOL so what the hell, go to bed."

After handing the dripping trash basket to Casey, John fell back onto the pillow. He looked as if he would be out for several more hours. Walking back to Opal's room, the forthcoming consequences of being AWOL wouldn't have seemed so bad, had I spent the night with Sandra Dee or some other Hollywood starlet.

The bedroom light fixture became my focal point, until Opal returned from the bathroom. A faint scent of lilac drifted through the room as she walked round the bed, disheveled the robe, raised the sheet, and softly settled in. As if rigor mortis possessed our bodies, we both lay there for several minutes without speaking while staring up at the light fixture. For some depraved reason, I was glad about John's condition, since he was the reason I ended up sleeping with Dracula's Daughter. Contrary to his question, I couldn't remember if I enjoyed the consequence of the Irish Coffees and felt thankful for the amnesia.

After some time, Opal broke the silence with a question while turning her face toward me.

"Yogi. Who's Allie?" Her voice sounded different. It was soft and expressed a sense of concern.

"Who?" I solicited, while rolling my head in her direction.

"Allie?" she stated in the form of a question. "Is she your girlfriend back home?"

"Why . . . you're asking?"

"Last night while we were . . . you know," Opal answered, as if afraid to speak of the event. "You kept calling me by her name."

Feeling chagrin, I didn't know how to respond. I thought of Allie and the pretending she said was required of her with the patrons of the House. The Irish coffees were the only excuse I could think of, to explain my rudeness.

"It's okay," Opal answered, rolling onto her side to look at me. "You must love her very much." Her pause seemed interminable, while my attention turned once more to the light fixture.

"You said some really nice things, Yogi. I sort of enjoyed them . . . even though I knew you really meant them for her."

Opal's dejected spirit and gloomy plea for acceptance caused me to turn my head in her direction.

"She's a lucky girl to have someone like you to love her." Opal offered up a twisted smile while running her forefinger down the center of my chest. "I hope, someday, I will have someone to say such nice things about me."

"You will," I quipped nervously, as her open hand moved down my abdomen. The light fixture became a cynosure in an effort to combat the responses of my body.

"Yogi, if you want to pretend again that I'm Allie . . . I won't mind," said Opal while moving closer to me.

Once more, I turned my face toward Opal. Choking back a short burst of laughter, I said, "Bet, I can throw my shorts on that light fixture as well sober as I did drink last night."

A burst of giggles and a violent disturbance under the sheet caused it to appear suspended over the bed, as we both eagerly disrobed before flinging our underwear at the light fixture. Allie's statement about pretending with the boys who visited the old Hotel flashed once more through my mind, causing me to realize my present pretending with Dracula's Daughter to fulfill her need to be wanted, was equally deceitful.

Chapter 8

The stillness of the hot Texas afternoon caused a heavy mixture of perspiration and coconut-scented vapors to linger over the quadrangle. Into this miasma, a multitude of transistor radios pumped a din of musical sounds occasionally distorted by a roar of laughter. Beside each of the twenty-five or so, pale bodies baking in the sun, similarly clothed in tan P.T. shorts and military style sunglasses, was an assortment of paraphernalia ranging from the common shower thongs, towels, and various size bottles of suntan lotion. Throughout the quadrangle, amber-colored Lone Star bottles, showing evidence of being "worked on," precariously sat like so many prairie dogs on flat stomachs, as if declaring metaphorically that their contents would soon be inside.

Our motley little gang of four rested in quietness, in a haphazard arrangement, on our own wool blankets, among the other venturesome fools who dared tread on Sergeant Sam's lush green grass. While pretending to escape the noxious atmosphere and verbal chastisements leveled against Paul by some of the guys unaccustomed to his pastime of farting, I rolled over to a procumbent position and rested my forehead on my arms. Opal's words concerning my drunken disclosure about Allie resounded in my head, blocking out the occasional taunting remarks by my friends for having spent the night with Dracula's Daughter.

While trying to isolate myself from the others, an amalgamation of thoughts concerning Colonel O'Quinn, Sausage Sam, Opal, and a possible Article XV rambled through my mind. Staring across the quadrangle at the heat waves rising from the surrounding sidewalks and parking lot, caused a mental picture of a shady-tree lined, gravel road to move stealthily into my mind. For a while, the jovial voices of two youthful barefooted boys, riding stripped down bicycles on such a road, brought some peace to my troubled spirit. Those carefree journeys on Sunday afternoons, appearing now to have taken place in someone else's life, seemed always to bring my brother and me to the same resting spot before a small wooden frame Negro church. While lying on the acclivity of the large ditch in the refreshing shade of a massive live oak, our tired bodies seemed always revivified by the lively rendition of "Bless That Wonderful Name," which traveled unabated through the quietness of the summer afternoons.

The openness of the Panhandle, still alien to me, mocked my spirit with the same maliciousness meted out by my friends, as I longed for the simple beauty of a "real tree."

"Know what this quadrangle needs?"

My question brought a pause to the schmoozing of my three friends.

"One WAF for each guy out here." John answered with a Cheshire cat grin.

Rolling over and sitting up for a more complete visualization of the idea, I answered, "No!" After realizing John's suggestion would be nice, I added: "Yeah, that would be nice, but I was thinking of a live oak tree."

"Don't think Sausage Sam would tolerate a dead one." Paul averred with a characteristic jocular tone.

"That's not what I meant, knucklehead," I answered sounding petulant. "You guy from up north can't imagine how beautiful a large live oak can be."

"I thought you Cajuns lived in the swamp surrounded by cypress trees."

"John, what the hell you know about a cypress tree," I retaliated, "you've never been outside Chicago until you joined the Air Force."

"If you're thinking what I think you're thinking," Paul interrupted while coming to a sitting position, "I'd suggest you get out of the sun."

"I know we'll never see such a tree grow to any size, but this Air Base will be here for many years, and someone else might get to enjoy it. Back home . . . there are some live oaks that are twenty-eight feet or more in circumference and their branches spread out as much as hundred feet on each side of the trunk."

"Damn, boy!" Paul exclaimed as if doubting my description. "What size acorns these trees put out?"

"The size of a cantaloupe," answered John with laughter of derision.

"Yeah, it takes four squirrels to carry one acorn," added Paul with a smirk.

"Yogi's right," answered James coming to my defense. "We have some of the same trees in Alabama." James paused as if considering the idea. "Where in the hell we gonna find a live oak in Amarillo?"

"Who pulled your string, you little Red Neck?" John asked, taunting James. "You wouldn't know an oak from a pussy willow."

Paul and I both remarked at the same time, "He does now, since his birthday party."

It took John a few moments to catch the humorous connection, Paul and I saw in his choice of words. James didn't appreciate the pun and attempted to squirt some tanning lotion on John for his crass remarks. As our laughter died, so did the idea. Our love affair with the sun continued for several more hours amid the rising vapors and noisy radios.

The wooden ball on top of the Squadron's guidon behind Sausage Sam's desk became my focal point as the indignant First Sergeant catechized John and me about our whereabouts Saturday morning. The sergeant, standing akimbo, with bulging eyes, was in marked contrast to our relaxed parade rest position and deadpan faces. Since John's tongue seemed indefatigable and more adroit in matters of skirting the truth, I remained silent unless questioned personally.

When we emerged from the Orderly Room some twenty minutes later, we were definitely not suffering from a harmful case of steatopygia. I was feeling somewhat pleased at Sam's decision to forgo a formal Article XV, in exchange for our "volunteering" to pulling two weekends of KP in the Mess Hall used by the students, in addition to confining ourselves to the Base. John felt defiant, since this inconvenience would put a strain on his renewed relationship with Casey.

In a lusty tone outside the Orderly Room, John expressed his desire to transplant one of Sam's bushes to a location that would be anatomically unpleasant for the First Sergeant. As I turned to walk away, he reached out and took me by the arm. His facial expressions telegraphed a devilish idea was taking shape concerning the First Sergeant's bodily modification.

"Whatever you're thinking, John, just forget it!"

"What were you saying yesterday about a tree, Yogi?"

"Hey! I was just thinking aloud," I answered feeling agitated.

"I think a tree would enhance the green area," John countered with a slow nodding of his head while staring across the quadrangle. "Yep . . . a tree is what the area needs." Turning back to face me, John smiled and added, "If we planted a tree in the middle of Sam's precious green area . . . that would chap his ass raw."

"Forget it John! It's not worth it."

"Are you saying ole Opal wasn't worth it?"

"I'm not saying anything, blabbermouth." Feeling piqued by John's grin at my discomfort, I retaliated by repeating James' question. "Besides, where are we going to find an oak tree? And furthermore, how are we going to pay for it?"

"Boy, haven't you ever heard of a "recon" mission?" asked John with smugness.

"Yeah . . . the Army does it all the time," I answered with the acerbity of the First Sergeant, "but we're in the Air Force . . . knucklehead!"

Even for a rooster, 04:00 hours, is early. John and I tried to remain inconspicuous by taking a position to the rear of the small contingent of slick sleeve recruits standing on the loading dock outside the Mess Hall. The smell of old grease permeating the area seemed to hold my attention more closely than did the pot-bellied Mess Sergeant, who randomly assigned different tasks to a list of faceless names on his clipboard. With everyone dismissed to their respective responsibilities, John and I stood before the Sergeant with confident smiles that a clerical error had omitted our names from his list.

"You two birds from Sam's outfit?" asked the rotund Sergeant, glancing at his clipboard while stepping in our direction.

"We're here just for the breakfast hours, Sergeant," John answered with an air of confidence.

"You're here all day!" The biting reply of the Sergeant wiped the smiles from our faces. "Since you like to talk, big boy, you'll work the clipper." With a taunting twist to his mouth, the Sergeant moved his face within inches of John's and snarled: "You can discuss the menu with each person returning their tray; if you have time!"

Seeing what John's facile tongue had earned him, I decided to remain silent, thinking the petulant Sergeant would further vent his frustrations by assigning me the job of trucking garbage cans or cleaning out grease traps.

The roiled Sergeant pointed his clipboard in my direction. "And you!

You'll man the milk canteens on both sides of the Mess Hall."

The morose expression on my face changed to an impish grin. *"Today is my lucky day,"* I thought.

"Follow me," demanded the Sergeant while using the clipboard as a semaphore, just in case we had trouble understanding words.

As the Sergeant waddled ahead of us, John made an obscene gesture intended for our eyes only toward the back of the man's head. The Sergeant quickly stopped and with the grace of a ballerina executed a pirouette, bringing his face next to John's raised finger. The blissfulness of John's face melted like wax, as his finger slowly folded back into a raised fist, which seems to hang in the air until the Sergeant whacked it with his clipboard.

"By the way . . . a milk truck will be arriving . . . shortly," said the Sergeant whose voice seem to drift into space. While glancing at John, the Sergeant added with some asperity, "Get the clown here to help you unload it."

While being instructed in the delicate art of loading and maintaining a clean milk canteen, the unmistakable sound of an air horn echoed through the early morning stillness. The little milk truck I had envisioned turned out to be an eighteen wheeler. Standing agape before the double doors of the refrigerated trailer, the hundreds of stainless steel containers awaiting John and I seemed an insurmountable task, until a vehement voice drove us into action.

With the opening of the Mess Hall doors, keeping up with the demand for the white liquid nourishment became a vicious battle. For the first time, the laborious effort of the poor cows on the other end of this supply line crossed my mind. During the reloading of one canteen, the small rubber spout on the bottom of the stainless steel container ruptured, spewing milk all over my fatigue uniform and the dining room floor. Before the breakfast hours were half through, the job I thought would be a breeze, turned out to be a nightmare, leaving me with a desire for the solitude of the garbage cans and grease traps.

For a short while, the demand for milk by starved teenagers subsided, and I was able to check with John to see how his morning was going. While standing beside him, a disgruntled Airman apparently not satisfied with his breakfast, threw his steel tray across the counter with a quick spin causing a blob of SOS to fly in my direction. With a quick evasive move, the blob landed on the floor missing my already fetid uniform, which was starting to smell like sour milk. In an agitated tone, John slammed the tray back toward the recruit with a philippic outburst. In doing so, he knocked the tray from another young boy's hand, causing the remains of a runny fried egg to splash onto his sleeve. Being fastidious about his uniform and personal appearance, John went into a momentary rage and began throwing steel trays until the Mess Sergeant walked up behind him.

Still steaming after, the Sergeant walked off, John began laying out his retaliation plan to the other guys working the clipper. Unconsumed milk was to be collected in a tall glass and laid aside as a just punishment for the next recruit who foolishly mishandled his tray.

The demand for the cold white substance soon picked up with the arrival of another flight of ravenous juveniles. I resumed my "milk run," putting John and his malicious idea out of my mind, until a series of crashing sounds drew everyone's attention toward the doorway leading to the clipper. A mental picture of John delivering a cannonade of milk to the wrong recruit flashed through my mind. The steel container of milk I was attempting to lift into the canteen was lowered to the concrete floor where it bounced generating a sharp metallic sound.

When I ran through the swinging door leading to the clipper, a feisty young Airman with milk dripping from his face had John pinned down behind a large stainless steel cooking pot by hurling steel trays in his direction. As each tray sailed across the Mess Hall, ricocheting off the cement floor or some kitchen appliance, a barrage of curses flowed from the familiar face grimaced with anger. The Mess Sergeant bulldozed his way through the throng of spectators, bringing to an end, the barrage of steel. The rhythmic rising and collapsing of the urchin's chest began to slow, as his anger and breathing came under control. For a minute or two, his young body continued to shudder before he wiped his shirt sleeve across his face, revealing his natural color.

Airman Bridgewater maintained a pit-bull stare at his adversary, who cautiously emerged from behind a large cooking pot with a chagrined expression. With a boisterous voice and gesticulation compatible to Sausage Sam's best efforts, the Mess Sergeant cleared the little room before beginning his short inquiry. Bridgewater wiped his face on the opposite shirt sleeve before angrily telling his side of the story while pointing a threatening finger at John. Before leaving, Bridgewater picked up his cap from the floor and exited the room through one swinging door, slamming it with force against the wall. Hoping to avoid the Mess Sergeant, I departed through the other door.

Airman Bridgewater was wiping his face and khaki shirt with a paper napkin, as I approached him cautiously from the side and cleared my throat to get his attention.

"Hey . . . look, I'm sorry about what John did," I said, while awkwardly extending my hand and offering a friendly smile.

"You know that bastard?" asked Bridgewater while continuing to abrade his shirt with the dry napkin.

"Yeah, his name is John," I answered with a shrug, while hesitating to pull back my hand. "He's really not a bad guy . . ."

"I ever come across him in the Airmen's Club, I'll show him who's bad."

"Trying wetting the napkin," I suggested, while pointing to a glass of water on a nearby table. "Ask the guys if you can use some of the water in those glasses."

After dipping several paper napkins into a glass of water, Bridgewater wiped his face and then began working on the shirt.

"Have you heard from Colonel O'Quinn's office?" I inquired while Bridgewater took another unused napkin from the table and dipped it into a glass of water.

"No. You?"

"No."

"I know I won't be returning to class next week," answered Bridgewater, "because I'm the only one in my flight scheduled for KP."

"Hey . . . Dipstick! Get that milk container off the floor!" shouted the abdominous Mess Sergeant as he exited the clipper area and waddled in my direction.

Bridgewater and I said a speedy good-bye and shook hands. Dragging me by one arm toward the milk container, still sitting on the floor, the irate Sergeant continued to vent his displeasure with John's performance and mine very loudly in my right ear.

It was a beautiful Saturday morning, my first trip into town since spending the night with Opal, whom I hoped never to see again. During my two-week restriction to the Base, I managed to talk with Brenda several times on the phone. With each succeeding phone call, her attitude left me with the idea that the incident with Caridad at the Double Dip no longer bothered her.

While sitting on the buttress left of the glass doors, I became engaged in a meaningless conversation with a couple of other GIs who were also waiting in the warm summer sun for their dates. Before long, I was left sitting alone checking my watch occasionally in nervous anticipation of our reunion. Once more, I was about to give up, when the door opened drawing my attention from my watch. A sense of déjà vu crisscrossed my mind when Allie stepped outside and walked toward me.

The sight of her, in a pair of white shorts and an oversized man's shirt, the tail of which was gathered to the front and tied in a knot at the waist, caused a shiver to flicker through my body. The shirt collar slightly turned up, added to the coquettish image she intended by leaving the two top buttons of her shirt undone. Something was different about her demeanor and the heavy makeup and mascara, so uncharacteristic of the girl I remembered, seemed intended to disguise what appeared as a large bruise under her right eye.

Initially, our conversation was a desultory inane rambling about each other's welfare as I pretended to ignore the bruise. Several times, I glanced at the glass doors, hoping Brenda would rescue me from my jumbled emotions brought on by the lingering memories of James' birthday celebration at the House.

"What did you and Brenda have planned for this afternoon?" asked Allie while looking toward the street to avoid my stare.

"Horseback riding in Palo Duro," I answered, sounding edgy.

To avoid Allie's intoxicating perfume, I walked over to the buttress and sat down without inviting her to join me. After several moments of uneasy silence, Allie sat on one of the steps several feet from me and stared toward the street. In a moment of exasperation, I blurted out my frustration with Brenda's dallying, which brought a response from Allie as she briefly looked in my direction.

"Yogi, Brenda wanted me to tell you she had to work this afternoon."

"Is this going to be a replay of our Sunday in the park?" I snapped back while standing.

"No," Allie answered with an abashed expression. "The truth is . . . she's seeing someone."

"Lying and pretending must be a course requirement at St. Anthony's." I vehemently stated while starting down the steps.

"No! It isn't." Allie's tone duplicated mine as she stood.

"Since you're so damn good at delivering messages, tell that bitch to go to hell!" I shot back in an incisive tone.

As I started down the steps, Allie called my name in a pleading tone. For a second, I stopped before turning to look up at her. While nervously wringing her hands, Allie took a couple of steps in my direction before stopping.

"Yogi . . . I'm . . . not much of a cowgirl . . . but if you would like some company . . ."

With a fervid, hateful tone, I shot back, "I don't date whores . . . okay!"

The image of Allie's anguished face and sobbing retreat up the steps plagued my mind for weeks, in spite of my attempted beer purgation. John's lingering desire to alter Sausage Sam's body with an oak tree, gained my acceptance with each night of overindulgence. It seemed the more I toyed with the idea, the more intoxicating its grip became to my soused mind and body, as a means of forgetting Allie's painful face. During an intoxicated "recon" mission one Saturday afternoon, John achieved new heights in his ability to weave tall tales to satisfy the quizzical stares of the nursery owners who seemed to question the unlikely interest of four young GIs in a live oak tree.

Our reconnoitering finally paid off at a nursery just outside of town on U.S. Highway 287. A preplanned diversion concocted by Paul and John to get the nursery employee to leave the tree outside the fence became so realistic, James and I had to step in before fists began to fly. Over their loud vulgar exchange and shoving each other, I waved to the befuddled young boy to leave the five-foot tree in front of the building. We would return later.

A roar of laughter brought on by the success of the ploy-filled *The Iron Lung*, as it accelerated unto the highway leaving the young employee in a miasma of smoke and the smell of burning rubber. An idea born in a moment of desperation and nurtured by revenge and beer was about to take root.

A flushed feeling traversed my body as I anxiously sat in quietness on a high back damask chair in the lobby of the old Hotel. My nervous fidgeting with the red bow on top of the small gift box in my lap caught the attention of an unoccupied girl sitting across the lobby. Toying with the ribbons on her negligee as if imitating my restlessness, coupled with her coquettish smile was beginning to erode my pretended lack of interest, until a woman wearing a soft pink robe over a long diaphanous nightgown entered the room. I recognized her as being the same woman who had stood between John and me the night of our first visit.

While strolling through the lobby, she teasingly touched the faces of several young boys with a soft open right hand while holding a long plastic cigarette holder in her left hand. With a certain amount of curiosity I followed her trek around the lobby counting the number of time the long boa around her neck received a flip across her left shoulder, only to have it fall forward again. My solitary position seemed to concern her, for several times our eyes met, until the muscular upper arms of a tall blond-haired boy became the focus of her lecherous touches.

As she worked her way through the lobby toward me, I stood, out of politeness or acquiescence to her libidinous hand. Her inquiry about my three friends caused me to suspect the politeness was nothing more than a subterfuge, since her eyes glanced down at the gift box several times as we spoke. After taking a slow, leisurely drag on her cigarette and blowing the smoke to the right of my face, a languid right hand preceded the name, Rose as a means of introduction. I thought the appellation was appropriate, given her flaming red hair.

With an askance glance, Rose pointed to the gift box with her plastic-encased cigarette, trapped between her index and middle fingers. "Which one, of my girls, deserves such a reward?"

My response was tepid. "She's not here, yet."

"You're waiting for Allie," responded Rose dryly while slowly bringing her cigarette before her mouth. "Why didn't you bring your rooster friend?"

"Allie said she's here every Wednesday evening."

"She's late," replied Rose in a tart tone. "There are plenty of other girls."

"No . . . thanks. I'll wait for Allie."

My visit to the hotel wasn't to satisfy a physical need, but instead an attempted resolution to the anguish I had been suffering since my last visit. In recent weeks, my woebegone condition had became noticeable to several people in the office, but only Mr. Joe Mahoney the civilian truck driver who picked me up each morning for the daily mail run, tried to explain that the direction my life was heading, would only take a toll on my life, my wallet, and job performance. This I had already come to realize. I felt guilty about lying to Mr. Joe about my real feelings for Allie and her secret life, but somehow I felt he would forgive me and her if he knew the truth.

Rose must have sensed I wasn't in a mood for conversation, so, after taking another long drag on her cigarette and holding it, she gazed into my face as if attempting to stare me down. The crumpling sound of heavy shopping bags, incongruous to the environment of the hotel, finally drew our attention toward the door. Allie's rushed entrance into the lobby came to a quick stop for a moment, as Rose loudly inquired into her tardiness after blowing a plume of smoke toward the ceiling. For a moment, Allie and I both seemed oblivious to Rose's harsh tone and stared at each other in quiet apprehension before Allie offered an uneasy smile. Rose's voluptuous desire to touch the bodies of young men caused me to reject her cold nefarious hand when it squeezed my upper arm with a slight tug, as if pulling me toward Allie.

The large shopping bags from Fedway's Department Store on Polk Street appeared as awkward in Allie's hands, as the small box in mine, which I tried to hide by moving it to the side of my body. She was dressed in a nice soft chiffon blouse with matching slacks and low heels. With crass remarks about patrons who come bearing gifts, Angel and Crystal sashayed to a position between us, disrupting our silent discourse.

"The poor boy's been waiting for twenty minutes," Dixie said in a boisterous voice. "Better take him upstairs before he busts a blood vessel."

The ensuing laughter and crude remarks caused me to blush. Allie appeared unscathed by the gibe.

"Give me a few minutes to change into something more comfortable," Allie said in an apologetic tone, while lifting the shopping bags slightly.

"You look fine . . . the way you are," I answered, meekly.

"The boy's in a hurry, Allie," answered Angel in a sardonic tone.

The wave of laughter that followed us to the elevator appeared to heat the back of my neck as the summer sun had the day my friends and I lay on the blankets in the quadrangle. Sam, the elderly black man who operated the elevator, offered up a broad, but silent smile as the doors closed behind us. Briefly I glanced over at Allie and quietly offered to take her bags. An almost imperceptible movement of her head in the negative drove my eyes to the back of Sam's neck as he stood silently facing forward. The uncomfortable silence in the old elevator, disturbed only by the slight crumpling of the shopping bags shifting against Allie's legs, came to an abrupt ending with a harsh grinding mechanical sound as the elevator came to a jerking stop.

Allie's mood became almost cheerful as she escorted me down the hall to room 210, while my feeble attempt at some meaningful questions about her purchases only betrayed my attempts to conceal the uncomfortable feeling overcoming me. As I held open the door, Allie offered up a vampish smile and quietly said *thank-you* as she brushed slightly against me while entering the room. In what seemed a mechanical motion, Allie placed the shopping bags on the bed while slipping off her shoes before reaching for a match to light the single candle on the antique dresser. Being back in the room intensified my uneasiness, as recollections of my first visit came rushing back into my mind. As Allie walked over to the record player on the chest of drawers and began sorting through several LPs, I closed the door before stepping toward the bed. The silence of the room became as suffocating as the musky odor.

"I think you'll like my new negligee," Allie said in a tone barely audible over the scratchy voice of Dean Martin.

"That's not why I'm here," I answered, while tightness closed my throat. "I brought this for you . . ." I said holding out the gift box. After clearing my throat, I continued with an apologetic tone and shrug. "It's not much . . . just a peace offering."

My brain seemed incapable of communicating to my tongue the thoughts I wanted to express.

"I want to apologize for the way I spoke to you the other day on the steps at the hospital." My tongue seemed thick and incapable of moving. "What I said, I mean . . . the name I called you. That's not the way I think of you, Allie."

"You needn't apologize, Yogi," Allie said while continuing to face the record player. "I've been called that before, in fact . . ." Unconsciously, her hand found its way to her swollen eye.

"The black eye you're trying to cover with all that makeup, is it . . . ?" I asked in a commiserating tone while moving toward the foot of the bed, which I saw as a protective barrier, shielding me from my own emotions and desires.

"Yes," replied Allie with some tartness after turning to face me. Immediately, her eyes turned toward the floor. "A gift from Scott . . . another . . . disappointed friend."

An interminable period of silence filled the room as we both appeared searching for something to say. Allie lightly touched her eyes with the back of her hand before looking up at me.

"Again . . . I'm sorry," I said once more, while holding out the gift toward Allie.

"Thanks, Yogi, but I can't accept it."

"Please take it," I said with a jerking motion of my hand. "Let's call it a token of the friendship we once had."

Allie accepted the small gift box with some apparent reluctance, after gingerly touching her eyes once more with the back of her hand.

"Thanks," Allie said as she leaned forward and kissed me on the cheek. With a smile, preceded by a small sniffle, she added, "And, your apology is accepted."

The momentary touch of her lips against my face, coupled with the refreshing scent of her hair sent a frisson of sexual excitement through my body. Within my being, the natural desires of my body wrestled with the lingering memories of my previous visit to the room.

With trembling hands, Allie slowly slipped the ribbon from the box after sitting on the bed, where I joined her. We both laughed quietly as she struggled with the excessive Scotch tape I had used. A truly beautiful smile transformed her countenance as she removed the water globe from the box and held before her face. After shaking it several times, the small glass-spherical containing a small angel came alive with floating imitation snowflakes as Allie held it to her face again.

Once more, Allie leaned forward to kiss me on the cheek. Several moments of silence transpired as I stared into her beautiful eyes before standing to resist the desires rising within my body.

"If you're in the mood, Yogi," Allie said, after standing and giving me a gentle embrace.

"Maybe some other time," I answered. Before moving away from the tempting warmth of her body, I gently kissed her eye. With a smile, I added, "That's an old family remedy for black eyes and sundry pains a friend of sometime back, told me about."

The life force within my body seemed to die as I stepped away and started toward the door. For several moments, I gripped the knob incapable of turning it, because deep down inside, I knew my intended purpose for coming to the hotel wasn't complete.

"Allie," I said while standing only inches from the door while gripping the knob, "the first time I came here . . ."

"Please, Yogi, let's forget about that night. We both said some mean things." With this plea, I felt Allie's hand touch my shoulder.

Without turning to face her, I began to speak in a quiet voice.

"Ever since I first saw you in the backseat of that car, I dreamed of making love to you someday, but not like that night." I swallowed hard and paused for a few moments. "What we shared that night was cheap . . . meaningless . . . and for that, I hated you and . . . and myself. When I returned to the Base . . . I felt a stench covered my body, which I couldn't wash off. I tried and tried and tried. Over and over my whole body was soaped and scrubbed repeatedly; still this awful feeling wouldn't leave my body and my mind."

A low humph cleared my throat.

"It was several days before I realized the stench surrounding me, hadn't come from this place as I thought." Once more, I stopped and after leaning my forehead against the door in shame, the most difficult part of my confession began to find expression.

"I hated myself . . . because of what I felt while making love to you. I could never hit you or any girl, but . . . but, I wanted to hurt you that night . . . the way you had hurt me . . . and . . . and after it was over . . . I was left with this awful feeling . . . that I had raped . . . the most beautiful girl . . . I have ever known."

Allie breathed a deep sigh and slowly put her arms around my waist while resting her head on my back. For several moments, I stood motionless squeezing the door knob. Having freed myself of the demon possessing my mind for so many weeks, I opened the door and left without turning around to say good-bye or asking for Allie's forgiveness. As I stood waiting for the elevator, my whole body seemed to tremble until a gentle voice from down the hall called my name.

Turning, I watched as Allie hesitated at the door before walking in my direction.

"Yogi," Allie said in a contrite tone as she approached me. "Look, I'm no angel in a water globe, but if you wouldn't mind taking a fallen angel horseback riding some afternoon . . . I'm still willing to go. Maybe we can make a new start. Just as friends. No secrets. No more pretending."

The pleading in her eyes caused me to answer with a slight chuckle. "Only, if your armpits and legs are shaven."

The opening of the elevator doors confronted me with a dilemma. I wanted to go with Sam and leave behind Allie's secret world, but her offer of a new beginning in our friendship seemed appealing.

"Is the young man taking the elevator, Ms. Allie?" asked Sam from the open elevator door.

"Not yet, Sam," Allie said signaling him to close the elevator door. "We need to talk more about this horseback riding trip."

Chapter 9

Running up the flight of steps at St. Anthony's, hand in hand, Allie and I weaved our way through a gauntlet of criticism expressed by the other couples sitting in the soft glow of a distant streetlight. Our laughter and passage went unimpeded. Adding to my jubilance, was a combination of lust and a youthful foible, which led me to believe the "spider web" beyond the door of room 210, through which I had stepped willingly, one week before, could be trodden without harm. Allie's reasons for going to the House became an entanglement, temporarily put aside as a result of the intoxicating passion ignited in my soul by our first truly intimate meeting.

The pungent mixture of odors emanating from our soiled clothes was the reason behind our self-imposed isolation on the far end of the left buttress facing Polk Street. Because my clothes were already dirty and smelling like saddle leather after a long day of horseback riding in Palo Duro Canyon, I decided to lie down on the cool buttress and rest my head on Allie's folded legs. The dancing shadows across her face, no longer covered with the ostentatious mascara, seemed to restore the energy drained from my body. While laying there our banter conversation punctuated with flirtatious smiles, led me to playfully tease her about how quickly she had taken to horseback riding with so few instructions. Allie countered, by gently pulling my hair and poking fun at the deadpan expression, which crossed my face at the sight of several combines, working their way, in a sawtooth formation through a wheat field outside of Canyon. Such a wonder had long been a part of her childhood, but for me, coming from south Louisiana, where there were no combines or wheat fields, this beautiful sight in the setting evening sun was reason enough to pull off the road and watch.

Amid our laughter, Allie began telling a story about her childhood on such a wheat farm, during which her thoughts seemed to become tangled, leaving her in a melancholy mood. Allie became strangely quiet while staring down into my face and her hand ceased its gentle caressing of my hair. I misunderstood her gaze as amorous and attempted to sit up to kiss her. A gruff voice and an increase of light to the outside area, as the doors of the building, came open spoiling the tenderness of the moment.

Sitting up and propping myself across Allie's legs by placing my right hand on the opposite side of her body, I once more attempted to satisfy the hunger upwelling within my body. Our lips barely touched before she turned away. In a calm, almost impassive tone, Allie thanked me for a wonderful afternoon before giving me a slight kiss on the lips. I desired a more passionate ending to such a wonderful day, but Allie's response brought the evening to a disappointing end.

Because of its bad shocks, *The Iron Lung* sat close to the ground under the weight of the heavy dirt-filled black plastic container, while the better part of a five-foot oak tree jutted out the trunk on the passenger's side. Sitting in the darkness along U.S. Highway 287, with the lights out, the irregular staccato of *The Lung* became humorous to everyone except John, who lambasted the mechanic who had "tuned up" the beast. As we sat there, watching the movement of the two Air Policemen at the small gate, *The Lung* belched out a noxious fog, which soon became life threatening not only to us, but also to the oak tree. With the use of a few choice words, we encouraged John to drive-on, less we should all die from carbon monoxide.

Fate was on our side and after several minutes, one Air Policeman drove from the gate in a pickup truck.

Cautiously John left the roadside and drove toward the guard shack without turning on the car lights. Paul encouraged him to correct this suspicious maneuver by punching him on right shoulder, while adding to the long list of names already attributed to his credit. With the speed of a turtle, *The Iron Lung* struggled across a speed bump causing its overstressed frame and springs to produce a torturous sound. The little Hawaiian girl figurine on the dashboard swayed with a salacious rhythm.

A young Airman Third Class stepped out of the small shack and foolishly stood in the path of the car with a raised left hand. A green military style flashlight, producing a saber-sharp beam, quickly scanned the inside of *The Lung* before focusing on John's face.

"Got some identification, Sir?" the immature voice asked under the stress of trying to sound authoritarian.

"I got a damn Base sticker on my windshield," John replied in a defiant tone, as he extended his head partially out the window. A distressing, quiet, "*Ohhhhh crap*," followed.

A familiar voice spoken with an icy tone confronted John with a question.

"You're the milk thrower, aren't you?"

"Bridgewater! What the hell you're doing pulling Gate duty?" I asked after recognizing the face partially obscured by the steel helmet.

A beam of light blinded me for several seconds.

"Yogi, is that you?" asked Bridgewater in a friendlier tone.

"Get that light out of my eyes . . . boy!" I answered in a rough tone. "Yes, it's me."

"What you guys got in the trunk?" Bridgewater asked in a voice, which sounded feminine.

"It's a tree . . . fool!" John averred. "What the hell does it look like?"

"I know it's a tree, but what are you doing hauling it around at this time of the night?"

"It's a surprise birthday gift for our First Sergeant," answered Paul as he leaned over to look out the driver side window.

"I'm sorry, guys, but I can't let you bring that on the Base, without a pass," Bridgewater scowled, trying to regain his authoritarian tone.

"Bridge, are you a real Air Policeman or just playing some kind of Air Force Mickey Mouse game?" I asked.

"I was transferred this week," answered Bridgewater with a proud expression.

"One week! And they got your green ass on the Gate already," asked Paul with a smirk.

"This is my first night on the Gate! I'm on OJT . . . and the sergeant . . . he had to go take a crap."

"Look, Marshal Dillon," Paul replied in a sardonic tone cutting short Bridgewater's nervous explanation, "if this is your first night, then how the hell they expect you to know what requires a pass or not?"

"Look, Bridge," I injected, picking up on Paul's thought. "I'm sure, you'll learn, as you get more experience on the job that the real Air Force operates best without passes and regulations . . . and all that other junk. And, a smart fellow like you will soon learn, that the best Air Policemen are those who know when to look the other way . . . and when . . . not to."

"I get the feeling, you guys are trying to con me," stated Bridgewater with a puzzled look on his face.

"Look, Bridge, you owe me one . . . remember?" I said in a pleading tone. "Or, have you forgotten already about Colonel O'Quinn?"

Several moments of silence and a scowling face indicated the young Policeman was wresting with his first real law enforcement problem.

After slightly pushing back his steel helmet Bridgewater pointed a finger in my direction. "This makes us even, Yogi . . . you hear!"

"You got it, Marshal Dillon," answered John as he stepped down on the accelerator. *The Iron Lung* sputtered away from the gate, leaving Bridgewater in a thick atmosphere of choking smoke.

Just as the tree took root in the center of the quadrangle, the clandestine affair between Allie and me continued to develop into a web of intrigue, which separated my friends and me for a while. Not only did a change occur in my life as a result of the amatory entanglement, but a side of Allie, began to emerge, which offered proof that her life was also a spider's web, from which she couldn't break free. This entanglement manifested itself in an unexpected way one evening, as I turned off the road to the Twin Drive-in on the Canyon Highway.

As we progressed in line toward the ticket booth, Allie became talkative, expressing a dislike for drive-ins and complaining that I should have told her of my plans for the evening. The closer we came to the ticket booth, the more intense her pleading became, until out of frustration I shouted for her to be quiet. Her whole body began to tremble as she turned away from me and began to make gasping sounds as if struggling for a breath. While trying to calm her down and apologizing for shouting, I failed to notice when the car ahead of me pulled past the ticket booth. A long blast of a car horn behind me drew my attention away from Allie.

Because of her gasping sounds, I decided to leave the line and head back to the highway amid a barrage of honking horns and verbal assaults. Just a short distance from the theater, I pulled to the roadside and slammed on the brakes. Before the cloud of dust could settle, Allie exited the car and found a resting spot against the front bumper. Still baffled by her peculiar behavior, I remained in the car for several minutes while trying to bring my own temper under control.

A stiff arm and open palm extended over the hood in my direction halted my cautious advance toward her. Strange nonhuman sounds issued from her mouth, as she stood trying desperately to breathe. Not knowing how to respond, I stood against the left fender of the car and watched her for several minutes before turning away. On the ground before me was an orange side clump of dirt, which I moved around with my cowboy boot.

My anguished mind could not tolerate the silence and after what seemed an infinite period, I turned in her direction. With both hands resting on the hood of the car, I asked in frustration, "What the hell's wrong with you?"

"You should have told me . . . Yogi! I don't like drive-in movies!" Allie retorted.

"It's just a damn drive-in!" I shouted angrily before kicking the lump of dirt, sending it into the road.

After a period of uneasy silence, I moved to Allie's side and leaned against the hood of the car. Several moments passed before I could feel Allie's fingers groping for my hand. As our hands came together, I gave hers a slight squeeze, which produced a slight smile. As Allie began speaking in almost a whisper, her grip tightened and her voice cracked as she explained in a jumbled fashion "some guidelines" that were to govern our relationship. At first I chuckled at the idea, released her hand, and walked away in disbelief. In silence, I listened to her incoherent pleading, while my foot became busy with another clump of dirt.

Drive-in movies were totally out of bounds; we were not to fall in love with each other, and there would be no sex in our relationship, away from "the House." After listening to Allie's complex rules, I stepped away from the clump and angrily declared her plan neurotic, insane, and as crazy as she was. A stinging slap across my face silenced my tongue.

My protest to her ridiculous "guidelines" continued in silence, as I resumed toying with the clump on the ground before giving it a swift kick. A sharp pain shot through my big toe as the apple size stone went tumbling across the highway. My hopping around and yelling was a disguise to overshadow my sudden outburst of a single expletive, manifesting an evolving fault in my personality. A slight giggle behind my back caused me to turn with a limp toward Allie who was holding the tips of her right hand fingers over her mouth as if protesting my neurotic, insane, and crazy action. We both began to laugh.

"I thought it was a clump of dirt," I said while limping toward Allie.

Hoping to take advantage of her more cheerful demeanor, I suggested she agree to one slight adjustment to her "ridiculous guidelines." I would be able to say I love her on Christmas Day, 4th of July, our birthdays, and certain special occasions. With an asquint stare, Allie didn't fully agree.

"I don't want you to fall in love with me, Yogi. I want us to be friends . . . only."

Turning away from her once more and looking into the darkness, I answered, "Allie, what's already in my heart can't be changed by your rules."

Summer soon gave way to autumn, a more pleasant season in the Panhandle, bringing with it an end to a period of adjustment for Allie and me. Our Wednesday afternoon rendezvous at the House became an accepted routine in our lives, although never monotonous. With the passage of time, the entanglements of our unconventional relationship began to manifest a building-jealousy within my mind, which slowly ate away my spirit.

Room 210 in the old hotel, became something of a retreat for me from the hectic environment of barracks life. For Allie, the room became a means of confronting the darkness behind her secret life. The afternoons we spent together in our "own little world" weren't always about sex. Often we would simply lie together on the bed and talk about my day at the Base or the things she was learning in nursing school. Talking to

Allie was easy, but she shared little information about her life as a farm girl and after a while, I realized that was a part of her life she wanted to keep private.

As a result of my weekly visits to the House, Rose deeply resented the relationship developing between Allie and me and expressed her displeasure, at first in an amiable way before the other girls in the lobby. My feelings that her real intentions were to reinforce her rules against such entanglements became a reality one evening as I rushed through the door, knowing that I was running late.

"Where's Allie?" I asked Crystal as she approached me.

The remains of what appeared to be a birthday cake, two bottles of champagne and several glasses sitting on a small table in the center of the lobby soon caught my attention. The smile on my face disappeared as it dawned upon me that the usual festive mood connected with such items was missing.

"Where's Allie?" I asked again while several of the girls looked in my direction.

"In the office with Rose," answered Crystal placing her wine glass on a nearby table.

Rose's office was small and dark. Like the rest of the old hotel, its decor appeared to have survived the years since its construction. Adding to the gloom and darkness of the office was a dark paneling made of knotty pine boards, from which hung several massive painting depicting the Panhandle's history as the cattle country that it once was. The new swivel chair of white fabric seemed incongruous behind Rose's dark wooden desk, with its numerous upholstery tacks holding in place the leathery texture covering. The two high back leather chairs before the desk, appeared to have been at, sometime in their long life the same shade of black, but like everything else in the building time had taken its toll.

When I entered the office, Allie was sitting on a large black overstuffed sofa against the right wall. She wiped her eyes before standing.

"What the hell's going on Rose?" I barked while walking toward Allie.

"Yogi, please don't say anything," Allie said, holding her hand out as if attempting to stop me.

"I've cautioned you two before about this ongoing affair," grimaced Rose.

"What we do away from this hell hole is none of your damned business, Rose," I shouted, while reaching for Allie's hand.

"She is my business!" Rose snapped back in an indignant tone. "I have a rule against these girls becoming personally involved with the patrons. It'll come to no good."

"If you really care about her," I countered with a vengeful tone, while moving behind one of the large chairs and banging my fist on it, "then help her get out of this life!"

"You're a damned fool boy!" Rose screamed back while pointing her well-polished forefinger nail at me. "She's here because she wants to be here."

"Please, Yogi, would you just leave," pleaded Allie as she took me by the arm.

With one quick jerk, I freed my arm from Allie's hand, as I lashed out once more at Rose.

"I don't know what drives Allie to this place, but I love her, and your damn rules won't change that or our seeing each other."

Rose pushed forward, the large office chair, behind which she stood, before walking over to one of the windows. Without turning, she ordered us out the office in a vindictive tone.

"Even a bitch like you must have been in love . . . once in your life," I answered sardonically while taking Allie by the hand, hoping to leave the office.

"You may not believe this boy, but I was once as beautiful as any of those girls out there and yes . . . I was in love once." Rose's voice was doleful causing me to stop at the office door. Released the curtain, through which she was looking, Rose waited for several moments before turning and walking to her desk where she picked up a pack of cigarettes.

After lighting a cigarette and taking a long drag, Rose continued with a pensive glance, while maintaining a lowered head. "You remind me of the bastard in some ways," Rose said after exhaling the smoke. "He too was pigheaded . . . and in love! Mostly he was horny and naïve about life . . . hell, we both were . . . like most young fools. Yeah, and he too promised . . . to love me forever."

After pulling the chair from the desk, Rose tried staring me down by adding, "Men . . . you're all born with the same line of crap and dead feelings from the belt buckle up. He loved me, all right . . . until I got pregnant, and he left town in one direction and my old man sent me packing in the other." After sitting in the chair, Rose stubbed out her cigarette in an overfilled ash tray and dismissed us with a wave of her hand. "Go on; get the hell out of here . . . both of you. No broad should have to work in a hell-hole like this on her birthday."

While I stared at Allie with a bland smile for keeping her birthday a secret, Rose pulled open a desk drawer and offered up an envelope without lifting her head.

"So you won't think . . . I'm a total bitch," Rose said with a smirk. "Here . . . I have four gift certificates for you to Little Italy."

With some awkwardness I walked toward the desk.

"You tell that old dago, he had better treat you right. You hear!" Rose said while hold up the envelope without looking at me.

The argument left me in a mood of ambivalence toward Rose, which I sensed Allie shared, so we left the House taking with us the remainder of the champagne and birthday cake as suggested by Crystal and several of the other girls. In the car I tried to cheer up Allie by proposing we go to Thompson Park and spend the rest of the evening eating cake, getting drunk and making love. Allie suggested I take her back to the hospital.

Upon reaching St. Anthony's, Allie carried the cake box up the steps with the intention of sharing it later with the other student nurses. The bottles of champagne, I left in my car hoping to share them with my friends at the base. After placing the cake on the top step to her right, Allie sat down and pulled her knees close to her body and rested her chin on her folded arms. In the months we had been seeing each other, I had become familiar with Allie's body language.

As her melancholy mood deepened, Allie began revealing in a quiet despondent tone, the tragic story of a young patient admitted to the hospital during her shift the previous day. In an ironic twist of fate, the child, severely beaten by her drunken father, had celebrated her tenth birthday the same afternoon. As we sat there Allie became extremely quiet and kept her face turned away from me. I realized she was crying, so I leaned my body against hers and held her until she freed herself from my embrace.

Our good-night kiss, while seated, wasn't passionate, but I felt there was more love and tenderness in the heart of this girl than any I had known. I attempted to apologize for not knowing it was her birthday and asked if I could express my love for her even if it violated our road side agreement. Allie just shook her head, "no." After standing, I walked down the steps a short ways before turning back and suggesting she take the cake to the little girl in the pediatric ward. From her seated position Allie agreed and offered a languid wave. Her raised hand gave me an idea, which would accomplish my desire to express my love for her without her knowing I was breaking our road side agreement. While lifting my right hand high above my head I signed the international sign for *I love you*. As I walked away into the shadows of the trees, I felt Allie's reaction to her young patient was revealing something about her own life, which she was not yet willing to share.

Chapter 10

The vastness of the Base seemed magnified by the absence of traffic and the rhythmic pounding of bootheels keeping time with the stentorian voices of Drill Instructors calling cadence. The large open area that lay between my barrack and the Mess Hall became an inviting short cut as I began the sunrise trek to breakfast. In the distance, a lone jack rabbit sat motionless in the sparse grass, as if determined to hold his ground against my invasion of his sandy terra firma. Feeling especially blithesome, I picked up a small stone and hurled it in the rabbit's direction. Apparently, my throwing arm had lost some of its adroitness since my night with Opal, for the stone landed two feet to his right. The rabbit's speedy retreat was short-lived before he returned to his haunches to give me another stare. Perhaps he, just as I, wanted nothing more than to enjoy the early morning stillness; so without further hostilities, I crossed his domain under watchful eyes.

When James and I made our first trip to the coffee urn, there was a sense of electricity in the room among the instructors. They were discussing this 'new and wonderful plan' the Air Force and Army had concocted, which would allow those men in the Air Force who could fly small aircrafts or helicopters to transfer to the Army with a commission as Warrant Officers. As part of the deal they would have to extend their enlistments and be willing to go as 'advisors' at a later date to a place called Viet Nam. After work James and I tried finding Vietnam on an old globe, but were unsuccessful.

In addition to names like Nikita Khrushchev and Fidel Castro, which I vaguely remembered from high school, Vietnam became a new name added to my vocabulary in the fall of 1962. The news media was still talking about the Bay of Pigs incident of the previous year, calling it the first 'black eye' for the new Kennedy administration, which was of no concern to my friends and me. The periphery of our world extended from the Base to the Pink Elephant or perhaps the Red Garter and there were no communists in these places to worry about. We were content with leaving politics to men like Kennedy, McNamara, and Dean Rusk.

At noon, James and I joined Paul and John at the Mess Hall, during which time we joked around about this faraway place with a funny sounding name. Airman Bridgewater's approach to our table later during the meal produced a few cutting remarks about his Air Policeman's uniform, complete with silk ascot, bloused pants legs, white lanyard, black pistol holster, and white parachute cord boot lacing. After taking a seat, he inquired about "our tree" with a sarcastic grin.

"Darn, I believe, everyone on the Base is concerned about that damn tree," snapped John.

"I should be concerned!" stated Bridgewater with an expression causing his eyes to go wide open. "You guys put my career in jeopardy by driving through the gate . . . with a tree sticking out of your car trunk."

Our recollection of Bridgewater's deadpan expression that night caused us to laugh. The conversation about the tree gave way temporarily to the subject of a break-in at one of the Base warehouses, before Bridgewater raised another subject.

"Did you guys hear that one of the B-52s over at SAC was disabled by a jack rabbit yesterday?"

"What they gonna do . . . court martial the furry little bastard?" sallied James.

Paul being quick to pickup on the thoughts of others, rapped his fork on the table and announced, "Airman Jack Rabbit, guilty of damaging government property and sentenced to a four-year hitch at Amarillo."

"I think Airman Jack Rabbit's fate is more serious than that!" announced Bridgewater after the laughter died down. "How would you guys like to make a rabbit hunt tonight?"

"Are you serious?" asked John incisively. "How the hell you gonna arrange that?"

"Yes. I'm serious," answered Bridgewater, "they were asking for volunteers, and since some of the other guys have something else to do tonight."

"Hell yes, I'm for it," I answered, looking around the table for the response of my friends.

"How many of the furry little bastards can we shoot?" asked Paul in a jocular tone.

"As many as we can," replied the young policeman in a voice of authority, "or, until the shells run out."

After pausing for a while and taking a few more bites, Bridgewater offered a bland smile and added, "There's one little catch to this hunt . . ."

"Like what?" demanded James as he sat up more erect.

"We have to bury everything we kill," Bridgewater replied as if taunting us.

"Hell, that ain't a problem," declared Paul. His full grin revealed another of his wise cracks was coming. "We don't have to say Mass over them, eh?"

"These are Texas rabbits, jack assssss," John faltered as he slapped Paul on the back of the head. "They're most likely Presbyterians."

John's action produced a brief guffaw and a pronouncement of blessings upon us by Paul including the sign of the cross. For the next several minutes, a jumbled foolishness enjoyed only by young boys our age enveloped our table, as Vietnam, rabbits, and communists became lost in a noisy schmoosing. For us, at the time, life consisted of eating, gallivanting, and working, without much seriousness about it, and going to the local bars in town. There was never a serious thought in our lives about what tomorrow would bring; for us there was no tomorrow, only today, only this hour.

True to his word, Bridgewater, now dressed in his fatigues, as were my three friends and I, arrived at our barracks at 20:00 hours, with four shotguns, shells, and four headlights and a shovel. In Louisiana, such accouterments constituted a Cajun's hunting outfit.

The hunt was concentrated mostly around the SAC area of the Base, but well within the perimeter of the ATC command. The fellows at SAC were jealous of their property, a fact we knew about, since a story had circulated about how they "abused" an intruder who wandered onto their turf while riding a motor scooter.

By 23:00 hours, we had almost a hundred dead jack rabbits in the back of Bridgewater's crew cab pickup. James' assessment of the evening, putting it on a par with that of his birthday celebration drew mixed reviews from Paul and John. I enjoyed the hunt, but silently rejected James' assessment since my disappointment with Allie that night still plagued my mind.

While burying the rabbits in an open area at the end of the taxiway on the training side of the Base, we were met by several trucks, each carrying a number of APs, who were staking out what they called "guard posts" along the perimeter of the Base. We jokingly questioned them about what kind of games the Air Force was up to, but the Staff Sergeant heading up the group only said, *They were following orders.* After a few minutes of speculating, they moved on into the night.

The Base was awash with rumors the following day, ranging from war with Russia to just military drills. Our belief that these Air Force Mickey Mouse war games wouldn't involve us became shattered wishes when a duty roster from Base Headquarters arrived in the morning mail. James and I, in spite of having to pull guard duty on the swing shift, would still be required to pull our regular day jobs at the jet engine school.

Standing at parade rest in fatigues and brogans before the Air Police Headquarters, James and I, along with approximately fifty other Airmen, endured a briefing about a crisis taking place in Cuban over some Russian missiles. The whole thing didn't make much sense to any of us, because the Captain trying to explain it seemed like he didn't understand it himself. The only point made clear was that *we were defending America against Communism and that Our Commander In Chief was doing all that was necessary to protect our national interest.*

Armed with old carbines, which I was sure wouldn't fire, even if we wanted them to, and couldn't, since we were not issued any ammo, I alone with the other 'defenders of America' were dropped off at various points along the perimeter of the Base. My post was near the end of SAC's runway, but at a respectable distance. The guys at SAC were trigger-happy and unlike us had live rounds. In addition to an empty carbine, my equipment included a full canteen of water, which was to last all evening, a GI flashlight and an apple taken from the fruit tray at the Mess Hall.

James' post was next to mine, about three hundred yards down, so while it was still daylight, we could see each other as we walked between the designated pickets. While walking my post with "old faithful" slung over my right shoulder, I considered how the previous night we were better armed against the Texas jack rabbits than we were this night against the communist threat to Amarillo.

As darkness set in on the panhandle, the runway lights at SAC became visible, giving a certain beauty to the evening that I had not seen before since I was never in the area at night. There appeared to be a great deal of activity going on, for trucks were running in all directions, all with flashing red lights. A few planes made a landing, which I took to be commercial airliners, since the city airport shared the runway with the Air Force.

After several hours of walking my post in true military fashion as required, I decided it was time for a drink of water and perhaps a snack. After all, I felt an invasion of Amarillo wasn't imminent. A small knoll in the sea of knee-high grass that I had been walking over all evening became my selected spot of repose. From this vantage point, I could watch the activity taking place at the SAC Base in one direction and a silhouette of James, against the lights of the ATC Base, in the other direction.

After mashing down some of the grass to form a sitting spot, I sat cross-legged with the carbine across my lap. While lifting my head to drink from the canteen, the purple dome of heaven seemed dotted with myriads of stars dwarfing the beauty of the runway lights. For a moment, I held my upward gaze, until water began running down each side of my chin. A single profane expletive sounded forth as I quickly lowered my head and wiped away the water with my shirt sleeve. After screwing the top back onto the canteen, I removed my fatigue cap and placed it on the ground beside my right thigh.

Once more my eyes turned toward the wonders of heaven, as my right hand automatically reached into the pocket of my field jacket. A crisp sound broke the stillness of the night as I bit into the firm apple. When I lowered my eyes, there sat before me another of God's wonders: a young Texas jack rabbit, as if evaluating the nocturnal invader of his home turf.

Frozen with the unchewed bite of apple in my mouth, the rabbit and I stared at each other for an immeasurable time, as children playing "flinch." The object being . . . the first to move . . . loses. About to choke on the accumulating saliva, as if it was a quid of tobacco, I thought it best to swallow. Mr. Rabbit won.

Slowly, I lowered the saddled bitten apple to my fatigue cap. Even more slowly, my unloaded weapon found its way to my shoulder, putting the young rabbit in harm's way.

While maintaining a deadly bead on the rabbit, I softly pronounced him dead, before shifting the chunk of apple to the inside of my cheek. Mr. Rabbit defied my pronouncement and continued sitting on his haunches.

"You're a lucky rabbit," I said easing the weapon to its original position across my legs. "My friends and I put one hell of a hurt on you guys last night! It was open war between man and *les lapins de garenne*. And you guys lost big time."

The rabbit continued to sit still, looking as if he understood the meaning of my boastful words. Carefully, I reached for the apple on my cap. After biting off a small piece, I pitched it to him, causing it to fall short by several inches. Slowly his powerful hind legs pushed him forward to claim the boon.

"You know one thing . . . a rabbit with fine looking legs like yours, had better never go to Louisiana or you'd end up in some Cajun's gumbo pot." A thought hit me, producing a slight chuckle. "Bet, a fine looking rabbit like you must have plenty girlfriends, I mean, rabbits having the reputation of being sex machines 'n all."

After receiving another small bit of apple, the rabbit shook his head from side to side while his long ears pointed forward.

"I believe you're the damnedest liar I've ever met, except for maybe my friend John, whom I believe is part rabbit," I said with a slight chuckle. "If you want more of this apple, you'll have to tell me about some of your sexual exploits."

Mr. Rabbit didn't move, except for his ears, which seemed to move in different directions.

"Okay! If that's the way you want it, I'll go first with one story, but you had better not back out on me," I said, pointing my finger at him as he sat up on his haunches.

After taking a sip of water from the canteen, I lifted the fatigue cap by the bill and placed it backward on my head.

"You see . . . when I was fifteen years old, I took a job at a cotton gin making twenty-five cents an hour. For a boy my age, back then, that was good money, and it beat the hell out of planting sweet potato slips. That was my first real job, I mean working for wages. My job at the gin was operating this big vacuum hose, which sucked the cotton out of the wagons. It was hot work, so often I worked without a shirt like most of the men did in the gin. My mama cut the legs off my overalls, which helped some in the heat, but I didn't like the way she cut them. Shoot . . . they looked like she used a hatchet and since she didn't hem them; they were always unraveling, leaving these long threads hanging. I hated that . . . and swore if ever I'd become a grown man, I'd never wear another pair of short pants again.

"Well, anyway, this mulatto girl, about two years older than me, came by the gin everyday on her old bike. She'd always have her right pant leg rolled up because she didn't have a chain guard on her bike. You'd have to be a human to understand that . . . I mean getting your pants leg caught in a bicycle chain meant a busted ass every time. I had seen her around the gin several times before, because her daddy, a white man, worked on the press upstairs. She wasn't a bad looking girl for a mulatto, because her mama was what we call a "high yellow" and her daddy being white . . . well to be truthful about it, she was cute. Boy . . . my ole man would have skinned me like a rabbit had he known that I even looked at that girl.

"Everyday, she'd come around wearing this same old T-shirt that had a hole in it right over her left breast. When she'd come walking around, her nipple would occasionally stick through the hole, like a bird's head poking out of a bird house.

"I know you don't understand what I'm talking about, but . . . I mean a lot of white boys in the South fooled around with black girls when I was coming up. I wasn't the only one. Well anyway, this mulatto girl, Floralee was her name, came to the gin one day while I was vacuuming the cotton from this old black man's wagon.

"Hey, white boy," Floralee called up to me after propping her bike against a nearby pole and giving her shirt a downward tug. "How much do they pay you to do dat?"

"Twenty-five cents an hour if it's any of your business, Floralee," I answered while wiping the sweat from my forehead with a handful of cotton.

"Best, git the devil from dis here place gal," said the old black man sitting on the seat of the wagon.

"I'm gonna climb up there with you white boy," Floralee said while giving her shirt another tug causing her nipple to briefly poke through the hole in her shirt.

"Don't you be uh climbing up here gal," said the old black man. "Yo Popper be done took a willow branch to you for put'n the devil to dis here white boy's heels."

"Shut your fool mouth, Ruffin'," Floralee answered scornfully. Looking up at me, she asked in a coquettish tone, "Kin, I climb up there boy and watch you work?"

"I don't care," I answered watching carefully the hole in her shirt. "It ain't my wagon."

Looking over to my right, I could see James' silhouette against the lights of the Base as he continued to walk his post. Perhaps his faith in the imminence of a Russian invasion was stronger than that of Mr. Rabbit and me. Pausing long enough to take a sip of water from my canteen, I noticed a few cumulus clouds had moved into the night sky during my hubris rambling.

"One day as Floralee and I sat side by side on a board between two poles where I would rest between wagons loads, she caught me looking at her breast through the hole in her shirt. "White boy, how much you give me fur a show nuf, look-see?" she asked.

"That depends on how long I can look," I said.

"For one dollar, you kin look from the first whistle to the second whistle," she answered.

"One dollar!" I answered in almost a shout. "Whyyyy, you must be the craziest *negress* in the parish. Why that's worth four hours pay! Hell, Floralee, white girls won't charge that much."

"Aren't no white girls 'round here gonna sho you what I am gonna sho you," Floralee answered as she twisted her shoulders.

"What about twenty-five cents?" I asked.

"You got a hard quarter?"

"Yeah."

"Leave me to see it," Floralee said holding out her hand.

"Well, Mr. Rabbit, I just reached into the pocket of my overalls and pulled out the quarter and one nickel."

"What that nickel fur?"

"Buy me a Dr. Pepper . . . from that machine inside the gin . . . to go with my lunch," I said.

"Kin, I have the quarter now?" Floralee asked.

"No!" I answered shoving it back into my pocket. "Not 'til I see the goods."

"Believe me Mr. Rabbit when that dinner whistle blew, Floralee and I ran like two jack rabbits to the seed house where I had my sandwiches and Dr. Pepper, while staring at the prettiest brown boobs you ever wanted to see for one delightful half hour."

As if interested in my juvenile nonsense, the rabbit slowly moved forward before once more sitting on his haunches.

"That's pretty much the end of my story, except to say that I was sorry to see ginning season come to an end that year."

A loud roar from the jet engines of a B-52 moving onto the runway caught my attention, causing me to look to my left. Apparently, accustomed to the noise, the rabbit maintained his position. Before I resumed my confabulation, the rabbit stretched out his neck as if begging for another small bite of apple. His reward once more fell short of his position.

The B-52s at SAC began taking off, at regular intervals, each leaving behind multiple streams of black smoke made visible in the night sky by the runway lights. As they climbed over my head, the powerful thrust of the jet engines caused me to speculate about the time required to reach their destination, which was unknown to me and Mr. Jack Rabbit.

"I guess you know one of your friends disabled a bomber a few days ago?" I asked in a bristling tone.

Mr. Rabbit's long ears aimed in my direction seemed more threatening than my empty weapon.

"Say, you and all your cousins we killed last night wouldn't be communist saboteurs, now would you?" I asked scornfully. After pausing for a while, I continued with a firmer voice. "If you are, I'll have to blow your furry little butt to hell . . . like that of your cousins. I'll do it too . . . whenever the Air Force gives me some bullets."

After biting off another piece of apple, I tossed it to the rabbit.

"Mind if I call you Hopper?" I asked the rabbit as he sat on his haunches. "You know . . . if the Russians could train you rabbits to sabotage our B-52s by jumping into the jet engine that would be one hell of a secret weapon." Then with a chuckle, I added, "Hey, they could call you long ear, little farts 'kamikaze rabbits.'"

The rabbit shook his head violently from side to side as if disagreeing with my idea. After placing the remaining bit of apple in my field jacket pocket, I slowly stood so as not to scare him off.

"You stay here, Hopper," I said, "I have to make a round. The whole damn panhandle might be crawling with Cubans. From what I understand, they are worse than Cajuns when it comes to eating rabbits."

As I slung my weapon over my right shoulder, Hopper dashed into the grass. I walked to the far end of my post and waited for James to complete his circuit. Upon his arrival, he lit a small smelly cigar, which I hoped wasn't Cuban, and we stood there for a while, talking about the absurdity of guarding a military installation with empty weapons.

It wasn't long before Bridgewater, of all people, dropped off our relief and drove us to the Mess Hall for a half-hour break, where James and I enjoyed a steaming cup of coffee and a piece of pie. During our break, we watched the news on a T.V. that someone had set up in the Mess Hall. We, as well as several other guys, watched in silence as a very excited news reporter explained how his *unnamed, but highly placed source stated there were in Cuba, sixteen missiles with a range of one thousand miles. The death toll would be in the millions if such missiles were to be launched against America.*

For the first time, the reality of so horrendous a possibility raised a disquieting fear in each of our minds, evident by our faces, as we sat in silent disbelief. A vision of my mother sitting on the front porch reading her Bible and my father kneeling before a rocking chair in the darkness of our home brought a momentary tranquility to my spirit.

Upon returning to my post, I made several rounds, as a faithful trooper to ascertain that Hopper's world was secure from any communist insurgents. Feeling dejected and forlorn, I craved his companionship and hoped to share with him another apple, should he return during the evening. From my lofty, however small rampart of Texas soil, I watched the traffic moving about the SAC Base with great anxiety. The stately bombers moving around in the soft glow of the runway lights failed to offer the same sense of arrogant security they had earlier.

The sea of grass surrounding me seemed to close in, losing its redolent sweetness, as a desire for Allie's perfumed hair against my face caused me to wonder what she was doing and how long it would be before we could see each other, if ever. With the growing stillness at SAC to my left and the absence of traffic on Route 66 in the far distance, my despondency deepened until I detected a movement in the grass.

It was Hopper. Only his head emerged from the camouflaging grass.

"Hey, Hopper," I said in a comradely spirit, while taking the apple from my field jacket pocket, "I brought you another apple." After biting off a small piece, I pitched it to him hoping to draw him from the tall grass. For several minutes, I watched in silence as he maintained his position.

"Look, Hopper, what I said earlier about killing a hundred of your relatives . . . I . . . I didn't mean to be so boastful."

I paused for a few moments, as Hopper eased from the tall grass to claim his reward.

"Hopper, you know what I miss most about my home?—Mom's homemade bread and something that we poor Cajuns called calas. Avoyelles Parish calas is what Mom called them. They're similar to what the rich folks in N'awlins call beignets. One time, some of my friends and I went down there, for Mardi Gras, and like "country fools come to town" we went to Café Du Monde in the French Quarter and ordered café au lait and beignets. Hell, Hopper, that wasn't nothing but plain ole coffee milk and calas, which I've had every day of my life for breakfast."

As I thought of my family back home, I remained silent for a while as Hopper stared at me as if sharing my pain. After a moment of seriousness . . . as serious as a boy my age could be, my nervous garrulousness reasserted itself.

"I don't see what all the fuss is about Hopper, I mean going to war, so Castro can be 'head massa' on his own sugarcane plantation. You, Hopper . . . you've never been on a sugarcane farm, but I have . . . and believe me, it's no fun. Down in South Louisiana, we have sugarcane farms everywhere and each one means nothing but pure hardwork from daylight to dark. Hell, at the end of the day, your hands hurt so much, you can't even hold your pecker to take a leak. And your whole body is racked with so much pain . . . you even have charley horses in your eyelids."

Hopper wagged his head from side to side in disbelief. I threw another piece of apple this time with the intention of hitting him for not agreeing with my assessment of farm life and the political issue of the day.

Hopper fled back into the tall grass. When he reappeared moments later, I threw to him another piece of apple hoping to draw him from the tall grass.

"You know Hopper, you and your family should consider moving across Route 66, over yonder, away from the Base. If there's another incident involving one of your cousins . . . I'm sure, there will be more hunts."

My soliloquy came to a halt long enough for a sip of water.

"You may not be so lucky next time. You know Hopper, a man should look after those who are special to him." Thinking of Allie, I took another sip of water to palliate my deepening wistful mood. "Hey, Hopper, you suppose somewhere in Russia, there's a boy . . . maybe my age, sitting in a field like this . . . thinking about his family . . . and . . . his girlfriend."

"There's this . . . girl in Amarillo," I soliloquized while swallowing hard, " . . . her name's Allie. As my mama would put it, 'she's pretty enough to make a jack rabbit hug a hound dog.'" I laughed a bit out loud. "Anyway, she has beautiful blue eyes and short auburn hair, which she brushes back and sometime holds it back with one of those things called a bandanna, I think. When I think of her, Hopper, I always think of the line from this poem called 'Ligeia' by this guy named Edgar Allan Poe. To be honest, the guy was a nut, but he wrote really nice poems. Anyway, in this poem, he describes his girlfriend's face and in one line he says, "In beauty of face, no maiden ever equaled her." That's the way I feel about Allie, Hopper.

"I suppose if we go to war with Russia, I'll be out here every night for the rest of my life, and never see her again. You know Hopper, something else that would be awful about such a war; I mean other than losing my family . . . not being with the one I love most . . . when the end comes. I never thought of this before, Hopper, but I guess growing old with the one you truly love is a unique kind of love."

I paused for a while and stared down at the ground. With my shirt sleeve, I wiped my eyes before tossing one of the apple cores to Hopper.

"Hopper, you can't possibly know how much I loved this girl, before I discovered something about her that almost shattered my life." The thought of that night was painful, so I took a moment to clear my throat before going on. "There's this place in town . . . Allie and the other girls . . . call *The House.* Anyway, Allie refuses to discuss her reasons for going there. All she says is that 'I don't understand or I wouldn't understand.'"

Once more I adjusted my cap on my head. Hopper sat still.

"To be honest, Hopper, my Wednesday afternoons wouldn't be nearly as wonderful, if Allie and I couldn't see each other there, but I would accept it, gladly."

"My friends think I'm just some . . . well I'm not gonna use the words they use, but I didn't fall in love with the first girl I had . . . like they think." At this point, my legs were uncrossed, and my knees pulled close to my body as I sat slumped over. "See Hopper, I didn't tell you everything about that summer. Before ginning season was over, Floralee and I were sharing lots more than sandwiches and Dr. Peppers. And it was costing me a hell of a lot more than twenty-five cents, too."

As my one-sided colloquy continued, the butt of my rifle was placed on the ground between my feet. With both hands gripping the rifle barrel and my head resting on my arms, I continued to pour out my heart to Hopper about a subject I was unable to share with anyone else.

Still looking down at the ground, I paused long enough to wipe my eyes before glancing up at my silent confessor. His condemning eyes caused me to pull my knees closer to my chest, as I nervously began plowing the rifle butt into the sandy dirt.

"Hopper, I know you rabbits don't believe in God, nor can you read the Bible, but . . . in the Bible there's a story about a preacher's name Hosea who married a whore named Gomer. I guess that's pretty much like Allie and me, except I ain't a preacher. See Hopper, in this story, this preacher loved this woman very much in spite of the fact that she couldn't give up the trade. One time she ran off . . . and Hosea went looking for her. He found her . . . in the slave market standing on the auction block, naked, as on the day she was born. Because he was a preacher 'n all, you know . . . the people made fun of him for bidding on such a woman."

"Hopper, if Allie was on an auction block naked, like that, I would do the same thing for her that Hosea did for Gomer, even if all my friends laughed at me. That's how much I love her. I love her that much, Hopper. I really do. I really do, Hopper. And I don't give a damn about how many people say, it's wrong . . . my friends, these fancy-talking preachers . . . and even, God. I don't care!"

The anger and self-condemning feelings bottled up in my heart for so many months finally came out. As I sat there crying before my only friend who would listen without offering a chastising opinion, the tears ran down my face and onto my hands as my body experienced a time of paroxysm and my soul, a period of purgation.

How long I sat there crying in the solitude of the night, holding on to the rifle barrel for support, I don't know, but my new friend with whom I shared my heart and apple remained with me. What I had said about God, I said in anger, for I knew he cared for Allie, and I, just as he cared for Hosea and Gomer. It had been a long time since he and I last spoke, and I wonder if he would still remember my voice. With a contrite spirit and breaking voice, I tried to renew the relationship I had severed, as Hopper sat on his haunches before me as if in prayer.

The bright stars of the Texas night and the runway lights of the SAC Base now appeared as candles of a church, as I gazed into God's celestial abode to offer a prayer in the only way I knew.

"Can you see me, Lord, sitting alone and broken in the night?
"So small, I must seem, with all the wonders in sight.
"Below the cover of darkness as white clouds roll by
"Can you see me, Lord, as this lonely man cries?
"Can you see me, looking up from this spot where I am?

"Can you see me, Dear Lord, as just one little man?
"Can you see what I feel and what I need to say?
"Can you see me tonight as if it were day?
"Can you hear my heart as I sit and pray?
"Can you forgive me Lord for the words, I've spoken this day?

In the distance, I could see the headlights of the pickup truck bringing my relief. I stood to say good night to Hopper. "I don't know if I'll be back tomorrow evening Hopper, but if I am, I'll bring you another apple or two."

Hopper dashed into the tall grass as the pickup truck approached. After climbing into the back of the truck with the other guys and it began to pull away, I cupped my hands and yelled back to my friend.

"Hopperrrr, you should be a psychiatrist!"

Several suspicious glances in my direction caused me to turn from the other men. The runway lights at SAC became obscure specks in the sea of grass, as the first of thirteen long nights came to an end.

Chapter 11

My nocturnal vigil with Hopper became a lonely ad infinitum ordeal against communism as my duty on the grassy knoll approached the thirteenth evening. Each evening as I sat in the quietness of the Texas night, the activity and lights on the SAC side of the Base to my left, continued to captivate my imagination. My speculations over the destination of the bombers must have sounded as the ramblings of a pettifogger to Hopper, who nibbled away at the bits of apple thrown to him. In the distance, across the openness of the Panhandle, the lights of the city only served as painful reminders that Allie was somewhere among the tiny specks of illumination.

Hopper grew accustomed to my presence and with each passing evening, he ventured closer as we shared apples and colloquies on politics and females of both species. Each evening, as the truck bringing my relief approached, I expressed my appreciation for his companionship and reluctantly encouraged him to move to a safer location across Route 66.

It also became a matter of habit to call St. Anthony's upon returning to the barracks, only to hear the same mechanical voice that reminded me of the lateness of the hour.

On Sunday evening, October 28, which was to be our last night of guard duty for several days, I decided to bring Hopper a special treat, several raw carrots, which I finagled from the Mess Sergeant. When Hopper failed to show at our knoll, my disappointment and desire for his companionship caused me to walk my designated post with more diligence, seeking a friend rather than a would-be enemy. At some point in the lonely evening, driven by an apathetic spirit, I removed one of the carrots from my field jacket pocket, wiped away the fuzz and ate it. My forlorn spirit found some comfort in the thought that perhaps Hopper had taken my advice and moved on to a safer location, out of range of the Base Rod and Gun Club, which usually sponsored the rabbit hunts. Toward the end of the shift, I realized my friend wouldn't show up. As the pickup truck bringing my relief drove through the open field, I flung the remaining carrots into the distant grass.

When James and I returned to the barrack that night, the entire quadrangle was flooded with light from the surrounding barracks, signaling something was afoot. The dayroom, filled with boys sitting on every available chair as well as the pool table and floor, had an eerie stillness when we entered. After weaving our way through the crowd, we stood against the windows and assumed the same "arms folded" position as the others staring at the television. The murmuring between groups of boys scattered throughout the room soon turned into wild shouts of jubilation as the reality of the historic moment unfolded. Nikita Khrushchev had "flinched," losing to Kennedy, just as I had lost to Hopper on that first night.

The next morning at 04:00 hours, the CQ runner awakened me and James with orders for us to report to the Orderly Room. The war initiative on the Base had shifted from fighting a distant threat from Russia and Cuba to a local threat: thieves on the Base.

The days were long and boring as we walked a continuous almost tardigrade pace around several large buildings, again with empty carbines. What I missed most of all during this monotonous routine was the companionship I once shared with Hopper.

October 31, was our last day of such duty. It was a Wednesday and Halloween. All during the day, as the hours dragged on, I could think of nothing else but Allie. After more than twenty-one days we would, at last, be together.

After stopping by the mail room, I rushed to the barrack for a quick shave and shower, which took priority over my one letter.

James entered the latrine shortly after me and placed his shaving kit on the metal shelf above the lavatory. His boxer shorts, as usual hung low on his narrow hips and after folding the waistband, one turn to take up the slack he asked, what seemed to me, a rhetorical question.

"You're going into town, Yogi?"

While shaving my neck with my head tilted back, my response came in the form of a grunt. My Wednesday evening trips into town were no secret, so I knew his question was not merely to determine my destination.

Attempting to appear blasé, James wiped the condensation from a small area in the center of his mirror and asked, "Mind if I ride in with you?"

With a shrug to disguise my curiosity, I answered, "I don't mind."

"That girl . . . what's her name?" James solicited, while hiding his face in a steaming washcloth.

A quick glance toward James preceded my question. "Crystal?"

"Is she still . . . ?" James' unfinished question caused me to turn in his direction once more. Quickly, he turned back toward his mirror.

"She surrrre is," I said in a jocular manner. "And, I'm sure she'll be glad to see the birthday boy. Hell, she might even give you a bonus, for being such a brave defender of freedom and the American way."

"I could use a bonus after all this time," James calmly replied, while giving the waistband of his boxer shorts another roll.

Determined to unveil his hidden curiosity, I scooped a handful of water from my lavatory and threw it against his face causing him to retreat to a spot near the window. As the bombardment of water kept James at bay, I lambasted him for keeping secret, his interest in Crystal. Soon his boxer shorts became waterlogged and began to slip on his hips as he tried fighting off the hydraulic onslaught. A friendly execration concerning my birth and Cajun heritage brought the barrage to an end. To keep his waterlogged shorts from slipping further, James gave the waistband an extra roll.

The House, decorated for the occasion with imitation black cats, artificial spider webs, jack-o-lanterns, and other Halloween ornaments took James and me by surprise as we entered the lobby. In keeping with the theme of the evening, the girls were all wearing black negligees, matching high heels, and carnival type masks resembling a variety of cats. The very sight of so many young, beautiful felines, eager to be of service, caused James to harrumph a couple of times while tugging at his bolo tie. With a snicker, I glanced toward him and softly suggested that he loosen the damn thing as a tigress sashayed in our direction.

"Where's Allie," I asked the tigress, whose lecherous hands and flirtatious body contact with James caused him to blush.

Removing the tiger mask, Crystal replied, "She's in the office."

The stolid expression worn temporarily by James paled in comparison to mine, as I made my way toward Rose's office through a gauntlet of lascivious hands. Allie and I surprised each other at the open door of Rose's office. The moment I once thought would never occur was upon me and I greeted it with a physical and mental paralysis. The image before me was even more beautiful than I remembered, more desirable than I was capable of describing to Hopper. As the surprise wore off, we simultaneously and quietly spoke each other's name before embracing each other. The warmth of her soft body and enticing perfumed hair revivified feelings, I once thought dead while on guard duty. Our gentle greeting soon developed into a clinching embrace, filled with joyful laughter and giggles as I lifted Allie from the floor and swirled her around several times.

"You're getting me dizzy, Yogi!" Allie said cheerfully, tightening her grip around my neck.

"Being away from you has made me dizzy," I retorted, holding her off the floor. While trying to ignore the barrage of ribald remarks hurled at us by the other girls, I attempted to tell Allie, how much I missed her.

Rose exited her office and sidestepped Allie and I after acknowledging my presence with an inimical, but silence glare. Her Halloween outfit consisted of a long black diaphanous *peignoir,* matching heels, and black boa. She fluttered her artificial eyelashes ostentatiously while greeting various patrons with amorous touches and palls of smoke streams blown above their heads.

"I've missed you too, Yogi," Allie answered with a gaily laughter.

Rose momentarily turned and looked at Allie and me with a scornful face before greeting James with a loud but friendly voice.

"Well, if it ain't the birthday boy!"

"You have a good memory for an old broad, Rose," I said sardonically, trying to force her to at least verbally acknowledge my presence.

After blowing a stream of smoke above James' head, Rose softly touched his left cheek with a coquettish openhand and added softly, "You boys go on upstairs now. Tonight we're having a two for the price of one special for all, you brave defenders of Amarillo."

James', Adam's apple made a quick up-and-down motion as Crystal pulled his body against her.

Upon entering room 210, hand in hand, I stood for a moment with my back against the door and pulled Allie from the darkness into my arms. Rising from the odoriferous suprasternal notch of her neck was a bewitching fragrance, which excited every fiber of my body, as I indulged myself in an *aperitif* of things to come.

Teasingly, Allie cautioned me to save my energy and pulled away from my arms. Methodically, she moved as a shadow through the darkness of the room, lighting the strategically placed candles. As the illumination increased, the Halloween decorations carefully placed around the room became evident, adding a sense of mystery and wonderment to the familiar surroundings. Fastened over the head of the bed with several thumb tacks, were a pair of large black cats made of heavy paper, while a large rubber spider hung suspended over the bed from the ceiling. A small jack-o-lantern, made from a real pumpkin, sat on the old chest of drawers near the record player.

Abandoning my position against the door, I remarked gleefully, "This old room is beautiful." Walking past the bed, I tapped the rubber spider, causing it to swing. "Hope this is not a female black widow," I said with a touch of witticism.

"You have been gone long, if you think this old room looks good," Allie rejoined, with an exquisite smile as she glanced back at me. While she sorted through a stack of LPs, I walked up behind her and hugged her.

"I've missed you Allie," I said softly, while kissing her on the side of the neck.

"I've missed you too, Yogi," Allie muttered with a subtle smile, after turning to face me and wrapping her arms around me.

The clicking sound made by the record player dropping an LP onto the turntable, triggered a reaction in my body as if programmed to the stretchy sound coming from the well-worn record. Allie's response to my eagerness was warm, but not effusive. After pushing back from my arms, she suggested that I go to the bathroom to clean myself and then take off my boots.

When I exited the bathroom a few minutes later carrying a towel, Allie was sitting in the bed in her favorite Oriental position.

"I know it's been a while since you were last here, but the House rule is still one raincoat per customer . . . and you have to use it," Allie said offering me a condom.

Looping the towel around her neck and pulling her toward me, I kissed her on the neck and said, "You had better get two more."

"Three . . . ?" Allie asked, with an ogle while slowly dragging her finger down the center of my chest. "Rose said one free one. What's the occasion?"

"One, to honor President Kennedy for standing his ground," I said, with a smirk while allowing the towel to fall over her shoulders. Toying with the ribbon on her negligee, I whispered, "and another, to salute this new friend of mine with big ears and then there's ole Khrushchev . . . for being the man who caused me to realize how much I need you."

"Yogi . . . you shouldn't make fun of your friend just because his ears are big," Allie said with a smile.

While coming to my knees and leaned forward to kiss her, my body seemed to shiver in anticipation as I whispered, "Someday I'll tell you about our nights together on guard duty."

As Allie came to her knees, in response to my fervid desire, my trembling hands pulled free the bow on her negligee, which she gently disheveled. The passion within our bodies erupted into a consuming flame, causing us to fall over onto the bed. Like the wax, of which the candles were made and transformed by the flame, so were our spirits infused by the ardor, which welded our beings together into a union of gentle oneness.

The wave of tranquil relief, ending the desire, which had possessed my mind and body for so many days, left me feeling exhausted, but fulfilled and elated. While staring down into Allie's intoxicating eyes, I realized my description of her beauty to Hopper on that first night of guard duty fell short of the goddess lying before me, in the soft glow of the dancing candlelight. My goddess, unlike the famous Venus de Milo, had arms, arms made of flesh and blood, warm and tender, eager and willing to express their affection for me.

Leaning forward to kiss Allie on the neck, the fresh scent of her perfume filled my brain with floral pictures of the honeysuckles, which grew wild near my childhood home, and the four-o-clocks that bloomed in our yard in the cool of the evening. *All of these simple pleasures of life,* I thought, *could have been lost in one moment of madness, had someone decided to plunge the world into a nuclear war. But most of all, Allie and I would have been denied these beautiful moments together.*

Walking from the bathroom for the third time, I felt the least I could do to ingratiate myself with Rose would be to express my appreciation for the "two for one special." Allie sat silently on the bed, watching as I slipped on my pants. Her warm, tantalizing smile only reinforced my own suspicions that my feelings for her had reached a point, beyond which I thought they would go. Without saying anything, I sat on the bed and placed my boots at my feet. Allie got up and blew out the candle on the chest of drawers.

While leaning back, pulling on the inside straps of the right boot, Allie teasingly pushed me backward onto the bed and fell upon my body.

"You still owe me one pony ride. The one for Khrushchev," she said while tickling me in the ribs.

"I'll have to owe you," I said lifting my head to reach her mouth for a kiss.

"You wouldn't want it to be said you're a weakling?" Allie replied tickling me under the arms.

Trying to restrain her hands, I laughingly replied, "Right now . . . . I . . . I don't care."

A wrestling match soon ensued, as Allie continued to tickle me.

"We had better cut this out," I muttered, rolling over on top of her, "or I'll have to undress again."

A knock on the door, accompanied by Dixie's voice, interrupted our frolicsome play, and for several moments we lay there staring into each other's eyes.

"Allie?" I asked while lowering my head next to hers.

Her name seemed to stick in my throat, causing me to roll over and lie beside her. I lay there for several moments looking up at the ceiling before speaking again.

"Allie, I would like it . . . if you didn't go back downstairs with me when I leave," I said with some hesitation before turning my face toward her.

"I have to, Yogi," Allie protested with incisiveness. After pausing for a while, Allie sat up and turned away from me. "It's the House rules. It's for our protection."

"I know the damn reason! Another of Rose's rules," I countered in a gruff tone. When she failed to turn back toward me, I continued in a softer tone. "It's just . . . after this evening . . . Allie . . . I couldn't bear to see the face of some other guy downstairs looking at you."

"Yogi, have you forgotten?" Allie asked, sounding piqued as she reached for a bathrobe. "We made a deal . . ."

"No. I haven't forgotten . . . *Your* roadside stipulations," I retorted from my position on the bed. "Allie . . . I can no longer deny with my lips what my heart is feeling."

"I don't need . . . and don't want another jealous boy in my life, Yogi!" Allie answered resolutely, while tightening the sash of her bathrobe. An uneasy expression transformed her face as she turned to face me. "Go on . . . finish dressing."

As Allie extinguished two additional candles, I moved to the edge of the bed to put on my left boot. Mastering this simple task, I leaned forward and rested my forearms on my legs. Allie walked back to the foot of the bed and stood beside me. I felt she was sharing my thoughts as she reached over and kissed me slightly on the cheek before speaking.

"Yogi, when we agreed to start seeing each other . . ." There appeared to be a short pause in her thoughts. "You agreed . . . to accept this place as a part of my life, because it is. You agreed we would just be friends . . . just for fun . . . and an occasional roll in the sack . . . here, and that's all."

"After all these months . . . is that all I mean to you . . . an occasional roll in the sack?"

"Of course not!" Allie snapped, before walking toward the window and pulling apart the heavy drapes to look out. "Yogi, I like you . . . you're a nice guy 'n all, but . . ." Once more Allie paused before continuing in a strange wearisome tone. "Maybe Rose is right about our relationship."

"To hell with Rose," I shouted, coming to my feet. "She still doesn't like the idea that we're seeing each other away from this place."

The stillness in the room made our momentary emotional distance from each other seem greater than the limits of the small room. For some time, we both appeared at a loss for words, and I assumed, both hoping this wonderful evening wouldn't end on a sour note.

"You're becoming too serious, Yogi," Allie countered in a quiet tone. "That wasn't a part of our agreement! I told you I didn't want you to fall in love with me! And . . . I can't fall in love with you."

I remained standing in torturous pain, looking at Allie's back.

"Allie, why don't you leave this place?" I asked, moving against the foot of the bed. My hands gripped the wrought iron with such force I felt sure my finger would leave an indention in the railing.

"Please, Yogi. Not tonight," Allie pleaded as she reached out and grasped the heavy drapes with one hand. Her voice changed as she added, "Tonight . . . has been much too wonderful to end this way."

"Is it for the money?" I asked, fearing her answer.

"No! Yogi, it's not about that." Allie said in a melancholy tone. Her toying with the drapes told me she was wrestling with something she couldn't bring herself to reveal. Several moments of silence passed before Allie lowered her head and pleaded, "Yogi . . . please . . . hold me?"

As my arms surrounded her waist, Allie turned and placed her head on my shoulder. "Someday, Yogi, I promise . . . I'll try to explain."

Allie's morose tone seemed to amplify the stillness and darkness in the room, which had gone undetected before. Perhaps for the first time, my heart heard her promise as a plea for support.

"We had better go down," I said giving her a slight kiss on the neck.

After wiping her eyes and giving a slight sniffle, Allie kissed me on the cheek and said, "I'll do it . . . this one time, Yogi. I'll stand by the window until you reach your car." With an almost silent laughter she added, "Rose is not going to like this."

"So, who gives a damn?" I asked with a smile.

Our good night at the door, inside the room, reignited the passion, which began the evening, dispelling briefly the incident, which almost destroyed an evening of bliss. After several passionate kisses, which made our parting more difficult, Allie escorted me to the elevator where we joined James and Crystal. Allie and I smiled at each other as we noticed Crystal wearing James' bolo tie.

When I exited the elevator without Allie, the expected confrontation with Rose materialized.

"Where's Allie?" Rose asked in a boisterous voice, which seemed almost masculine.

"She'll be down in a minute," I answered, abandoning my earlier thoughts of expressing my appreciation for the "two for one special."

"She's supposed to come down with you," Rose shouted, waving her finger at me. "That's the rules, Mr. Big Shot. Who the hell you think you are . . . a damn . . . General or something? You had better learn the rules around here, boy!"

"I have a new rule of my own, Rose! And I don't give a damn if you like it or not," I shouted, walking toward the front door. "Come on, James let's get the hell out of here."

James, unperturbed by the confrontation between Rose and me, took his time saying good night to Crystal. After kissing the silver-tipped strings of the bolo tie, he cautiously pulled the neckline of her negligee forward and released them to a place of obscurity between her buxom breasts.

"One thing more Rose," I called to her while holding open the door for James, "you need to get a thicker outfit! Your old sagging *derriere* is showing through that thing."

As the girls and patrons in the lobby laughed, Rose was determined to have the final word.

"Someday buster boy, you're gonna sag in a place where you won't think it's so damn funny," Rose shouted back in a boisterous voice.

As James and I walked to my car, his exuberance didn't measure up to the night of his birthday party, but for no apparent reason, everything around us was a source of great amusement. As if infected with tarantism, our poking and shoving on each other in jest, was an expression of the prowess we felt for having stood before the communist threat to Amarillo, as well as fulfilling our youthful virility of lust.

Before getting into the car, I turned around and looked at the second floor of the old Hotel trying to locate room 210. As promised, Allie was standing at the dimly lit window from where she blew me a kiss. Before she closed the drapes, my hand went up, high above my head, offering a silent expression of my love for her in the form of the international sign for "I love you."

Chapter 12

Sitting on my bunk in the dark, I swore at the knotted shoelace before wrestling off the shoe and throwing it to the floor hitting the electric clock. The illuminated numbers showed the time as 03:00 hours. As I struggled with the other shoe, the clock produced a grinding sound as the numbers rolled over to three-o-one. A feeling of nausea accompanied by muscle spasms, wrenched my stomach and throat causing a pause in my effort to pull the polo shirt over my head. Pausing briefly with my head encased in the outstretched shirt, I waited for the retching to pass before pulling my arms free from the sleeves and falling backward onto the pillow.

The excruciating pain in my face and head drove me back to the pillow after attempting to sit; responding to the reverberating voice calling my name. Fighting to remove the rough hand pushing at my shoulder, I moaned a long angry, "Whaaat?"

"You have an emergency phone call in the Orderly Room," replied the silhouette.

"Who are you?" I asked, rubbing my face while attempting once more to sit.

"You have a phone call in the Orderly Room," the perturbed voice repeated. "Some broad . . . Brenda. She says it's important."

"What time is it?" I asked, trying to focus on the unfamiliar face.

"05:00 hours."

"Who did you say the call was from?" I asked trying to untangle the polo shirt still looped around my neck.

"Some broad . . . Brenda . . . I believe!" he answered gruffly. "Come on, now. I don't have all day."

The short drive into town seemed to take forever, as Brenda's jumbled words and incoherent pleading replayed itself in my semiconscious mind. My right eye, bruised and turning purple, had found some relief from the warm washcloth placed over it after returning to the barrack from the Orderly Room.

Two city police cars parked near the ER entrance at St. Anthony's, caused a chill to run the length of my back as I hastily walked toward the glass doors. Upon entering the ER, my eyes automatically turned to the two officers speaking with a woman to my left. Brenda came from behind the nurse's station to meet me. Our rocky, short relationship accounted for our tolerant exchange of smiles.

"Where's Allie?" I asked, looking around.

"She's in room six," Brenda answered, as she turned and hurriedly walked in the direction of the treatment room.

Upon entering the room, which contained several beds separated by privacy curtains, Brenda pulled back the curtain surrounding Allie's bed. She was dressed in her white uniform and lying in a fetal position. Approaching the bed, I noticed her body quivered as if cold. Softly, I called her name twice before she looked up at me with swollen eyes. Slowly she raised her right hand, which I accepted with a gentle squeeze. Without speaking, Brenda and I looked at each other as she pulled forward a small metal stool for me to sit on.

"Hey," I said to Allie in a soft voice after sitting. A gentle kiss to her hand caused her to squint to keep from crying.

Allie tried speaking several times, but her words were only whispered sibilants without meaning. When Brenda left the room, Allie gestured that she wanted to sit up. For what seemed an interminable period, I sat on the bed holding her around the shoulders until the sniffling and body shivers subsided. Accepting my handkerchief, Allie wiped her eyes before speaking in a broken tone, while staring down at the floor.

"She's dead, Yogi," Allie mumbled, while squeezing the handkerchief into a small moist ball.

"Who's dead?" I asked while a kaleidoscope of thoughts filled my mind.

"The little girl I told you about."

"What happened?" I asked drawing Allie closer.

"Her father was drunk and . . ." Allie paused to take a breath, which seemed to come with irregular jerks. "He beat her." At this point, she began to weep uncontrollably with her head on my shoulder.

Allie's tears flowed with such freedom a wet spot became visible on my shirt.

The dragging sound made by the curtain being pulled back, caused Allie and me to give the intruder an askance stare. A doctor in gray scrubs and white coat wearing a stethoscope around his neck extended his hand.

"I'm Doctor Cavanaugh."

I stood, shook his hands and introduced myself as Allie's friend.

Doctor Cavanaugh was a middle-aged man with a goatee, handle-bar mustache, and long narrow sideburns. He reminded me of a riverboat gambler from the movies. His thick glasses appeared to have slipped to the end of his nose.

"May I see you . . . ?" asked Doctor Cavanaugh, peering over the rim of his glasses while giving his head a slight motion.

"Sure." Turning to Allie, I said, "I'll be right back."

In the hallway, Doctor Cavanaugh removed the stethoscope from around his neck, pushed it into his coat pocket and pushed his glasses back on his nose. While we spoke, my attention seemed focused on his eye glasses as they slowly slid forward again.

"Many of these student nurses react this way, when they lose their first patient," stated Dr. Cavanaugh in a 'matter of fact' way. After pushing his glasses back with his middle right finger he added, "I've ordered a mild sedative for now, but before you take her to your house, one of the nurses will give her something stronger to help her sleep."

"My house?"

"She requested, you take her to your house," answered Doctor Cavanaugh.

Realized the Doctor wasn't aware of Allie's true meaning, I went along with his misunderstanding. Reaching into his coat pocket Dr. Cavanaugh pulled out a prescription pad. "Get this filled sometimes today." Once more, his glasses began to slide. "The shot should help her to sleep for several hours, but if she should need one of these . . . give her only one . . . every four hours."

"Okay," I replied taking the prescription from his hand.

"One other thing," said Doctor Cavanaugh, as I started to return to Allie's room. "Tell Nurse Sailhamer that she is to see Doctor Tully, Monday morning before returning to class."

"Who's Doctor Tully?" I asked, pausing to look at him.

"He's a Psychiatrist on staff," answered Doctor Cavanaugh, once more pushing his glasses up higher on his nose before walking away.

After folding the prescription and placing it in my shirt pocket, I returned to Allie's bed side and held her hand.

"Yogi, you didn't do something foolish last night, did you?" Allie asked while reaching out to touch my face, but stopped when a nurse entered the room carrying a hypodermic needle.

The nurse and I gave each other an uneasy stare while she gave Allie the injection.

Feeling ashamed, since I couldn't remember most of the previous evening, I didn't answer Allie's question, but said, "Come on . . . we have to be going."

"Yogi, I want to see her before we leave," Allie asked gripping my hand.

"That may not be possible," I answered, placing my arm around her waist. "I'm sure her body must be in the morgue by now."

"No, she's in the next bed," Allie countered, stepping away from the bed. "They're waiting for the Coroner."

My legs became weak at the thought of seeing a dead child's body. The face of a battered child wasn't something I wanted to see.

"Allie . . . I don't think this is a good idea."

"Please, Yogi," Allie begged as she moved in the direction of the other bed.

"Perhaps it would be best if you remembered her as she was."

"Please, Yogi. Let me see her?"

Allie moved inertly through the opening in the curtain before the sheet-draped bed. The child's tiny body appeared to cause a very slight ascending slope in the sheet covering her body. With some hesitation, I slowly pulled back the sheet, exposing her face. In a strange way, the child appeared to be smiling, as if frolicking in the beauty of the fall afternoon.

Allie squeezed my hands very hard. As a form of paroxysm overtook her, she spoke in a broken voice.

"He . . . raped . . . her, Yogi. That bastard raped her."

This unsolicited bit of information about the girl's death fell upon me as a mighty stone, which seemed to squeeze the breath from my body. Once more, Allie broke down into heavy sobbing, as we both stood there clinging to each other.

Brenda entered the room after a minute or two and reminded me that I should take Allie home, since the shot would be taking effect. With a very gentle touch, Allie stroked the little girl's hair and tearfully said good-bye. As Brenda pulled the sheet back over the child's face, I whispered Rose's phone number to her and asked if she would call her.

A faint odor of fresh paint lingered in Rose's three-room apartment as I carried Allie through the door. The living room, about half the size of the bedroom, contained a large black leather sofa, a swivel recliner and a small television set with rabbit ears, which sat on a small table in the far corner near a window. An oval area rug, which appeared too large for the room, covered just about the entire floor. The lower part of the walls in all three rooms were finished in a dark wainscot paneling, while the upper parts were covered with wallpapers of different designs to accentuate each room. Holding back the heavy drapery bordering each window, was a cord tieback, each designed with a nice tassel, permitting sunlight through a thin sheer curtain. A bookcase, also of dark finish, with glass doors, stood near the entrance door to the apartment.

Separating the living room from the bedroom was an archway, which supported a heavy filet crochet portiere designed with swans of various sizes. While holding Allie in my arms, I hesitated upon entering the bedroom, to stare at a true masterpiece of furniture carpentry. The huge bed made in the shape of a swan, with the tail serving as the headboard and the swan's breast and neck serving as the foot, caused me to stand frozen for a moment before ordered by Rose to put Allie on the bed.

On each side of the bed was a small mahogany night stand with tapered legs, upon which sat a table lamp. Near the double windows, two high back damask chairs flanked a large pedestal table, with a starburst design on top. Against the wall nearest the bathroom was a chiffonier.

As I walked under the swan's head, even though it rose to a height of about seven feet, an automatic reflex caused me to duck my head. Crystal and Rose hurriedly pulled back the heavy comforter and sheet on the bed, in addition to removing the many pillows and bolster. Allie was almost asleep as I sat her on the bed.

"You, go look in the top drawer of the chiffonier, there's a pair of silk pajamas. Bring them here," Rose said to me, while starting to work at the many buttons on Allie's uniform.

After finding the pajamas, I returned to the bed and told Rose, I would take over.

"Are you sure?" Rose asked, giving me a peculiar look.

"Yes. I can do it." A slight movement of my head accompanied my mild insistence.

"If you need any help with anything," Rose said, as she and Crystal walked away from the bed, "I'll be downstairs." Before leaving the bedroom, Rose gave me a sardonic stare while shaking her head. "Boy, looks like you rode through hell last night."

"I feel like it."

"Could you use something to eat?"

"I would appreciate it," I answered. "And, some coffee, if you don't mind."

"I'll send up an ice pack for that eye, too," said Rose as she parted the portiere to leave the room.

After Rose and Crystal left the room, I began working at the buttons on Allie's uniform, while she tried fighting me off and pleading for me to stop.

"C'mon Allie," I said. "You can't sleep in your uniform."

"Please . . . Yogi . . . don't . . ."

Allie's body finally gave way to the medication. Gently I laid her over onto the bed and managed to finish removing her uniform and bra. With some difficulty, I was able to put the pajama top on her by rolling her over on one side and then over onto the other side.

In the process of pulling the pajama bottoms to her hips, I noticed two large jagged scars on the inside of her thighs, which seemed to extend upward beyond the hem of her panties. Another similar scar on her left side extended downward from her pelvis to below her panty line. With one finger, I pulled down the elastic waistband to better see the scar. During the many months of our relationship, I had never seen this most private part of Allie's body and for a while I felt ashamed for taking such limited liberties, while she slept. Knowing how vain girls are about their bodies, I thought perhaps these scars were the reason Allie didn't want me to undress her. I pulled the elastic waistband back up and finished pulling the pajama bottoms over her hips.

With the sheet and comforter pulled over Allie, I moved one of the large chairs from the table near the window and positioned it near the bed. Allie's body moved in sporadic jerks and her face twitched, indicating even while sleeping, her mind was troubled. Reaching across the bed I took her hand gently, so as not to awaken her. For the longest time, I sat there thinking how beautiful she was and how much I had come to love her.

My body was tired from lack of sleep, so I pulled the bolster toward me and rested my head on it. How long I slept clutching Allie's hand, I wasn't certain.

"Wake up, boy."

My body gave a start, as Rose pushed on my shoulder. "Your breakfast's on the table over there," Rose said, looking down at me. "And there's an ice pack for that eye."

For a moment or two, the surroundings had me confused. My arm felt heavy for having fallen asleep on it. While rubbing it to get the blood circulating again, I looked over at Allie. She had not moved.

Rose had placed the tray of food on the round table near the window. So I moved to the table and sat down as she smoothed out the comforter and sheet, covering Allie. The breakfast of eggs, toast, juice, and ham was delicious, and I ate quickly as Rose moved about the room, making a fuss about things that didn't seem to matter.

"Where'd you get that bed?" I asked, while finishing off the last bite of toast.

"Had it made by a local carpenter," answered Rose, rubbing the neck of the swan with a sense of pride showing on her face.

"That's the damnedest bed, I've ever seen," I said with a chuckle. "Hope you're not offended Rose, but that thing looks like it belongs in a whore house."

After joining me in a short burst of laughter, Rose added, "Saw one like it in a museum in Richmond some years back, so I had a local carpenter make this one." As Rose rubbed the swan's neck once more, she added with a grin, "Bet, Ladybird Johnson never slept in anything this elegant."

"I bet Ladybird Johnson never saw the action that this bed has seen," I added laughing derisively.

"You damn right, honey," Rose answered, moving away from the bed toward the table where I was sitting.

After picking up the tray of empty dishes, Rose started out the room. As she went through the portiere, I called to her while standing. "Rose! I appreciate this kindness . . . I mean what you're doing for Allie."

"No problem, Yogi," Rose said, standing on the other side of the portiere. "Now . . . you put that ice pack on that eye. And try to get some sleep." There was a motherly sound in her voice.

"Hey, Rose." I stepped through the portiere, while removing the prescription from my shirt pocket. "Could you get this filled?"

Rose took the prescription and placed it on the tray. "I'll have Sam take it down the street to Skaggs Drug Center soon as they open. And . . . I'll send up a pot of coffee for you."

With Rose's departure, the room became quiet once more, so I sat down in the chair next to the bed and watched Allie sleep, while holding the ice pack against my eye. With one elbow propped on the bolster, supporting my head in my hand, I almost dozed off, as part of the previous night painfully flashed through my mind.

My head continued to hurt. Laying aside the ice pack, I trudged to the bathroom hoping to find something to ease the pain. All I could find that resembled pain pills was a bottle of Midol. I figured two should be enough. No glass or paper cups were in the bathroom, so with the pills in hand, I walked across the apartment to the small kitchenette next to the living room.

The kitchenette, small but very neat, didn't even have a dirty fork or glass in the sink, leaving me with the impression that it wasn't used. After finding a glass in the cabinet, I opened the small refrigerator and found a container of orange juice, from which I helped myself. With the downing of the two Midols, I hoped nothing more about my body would change, except the elimination of the pain in my head.

While walking back to the bedroom, I paused at the bookcase. Hoping to find something to pass the time, I opened the glass doors and quickly scanned the volumes. The Good Earth was the first to catch my eye. Flipping through the pages, I couldn't imagine Rose reading such a classic. On the same shelf next to each other were *Pilgrim's Progress* and *Tobacco Road*. Feeling those two books shouldn't be together, I moved the latter to a lower shelf. *Great Expectations, Soldier's Pay, Of Mice and Men*, and *The Catcher in the Rye* were others I looked over.

Returning this last book to the shelf, I recalled how much I disliked
Holden, the first time I read the book in high school. He was a wimp,
always depressed about everything, and by the time I had finished
reading the book, I was depressed, because he never called the girl he
talked about calling throughout the whole book. I was impressed with
Rose's collection, but after finding nothing to read, I returned to the
chair near the window and sat down at the round table.

Allie moved and moaned several times, causing me to walk to the
foot of the bed to check on her. Her face twitched as if in pain, and I
stood at the bed holding on to the neck of the swan for support. Gripping
the swan's neck with both hands, I placed my face against my hands and
stood watching her sleep, wondering what was going through her mind
and wishing I could remove the pain . . . she was suffering. Allie settled
down once more, so I returned to the chair near the window. I hadn't
noticed before, but there was a Bible on the table. At first, I sat there
gazing at it, as a strange force pulled my hand toward it. I retracted my
hand and placed it in my lap. Then once more, my hand went forward
and picked it up. This book, which had been so much a part of my early
childhood seemed strange in my hand, perhaps because it had been so
long absent from my life.

As I opened the cover, there was a note, which read: *To my daughter,
Rose, from your father, Elihu Houston.* Such a superscription brought a
hundred and one questions to my mind and a smirk to my face. Without
intending to, I opened the Bible to the book of Hosea and held it for a
moment, before starting to read. In doing so, Hopper came to my mind
and the conversation that he and I had that first night on guard duty. In
a matter of minutes, I became so engrossed in the tragic love story of
Hosea and Gomer; I failed to hear Rose enter the room.

"You find something to read?" asked Rose standing before me with
a coffee pot, two cups, and a sugar bowl on a tray. "Make some room . . .
there on the table, and I'll put this down."

After closing the Bible, I placed it on the floor near my chair. Rose
placed the tray on the table once I pushed back the table lamp. After
plugging in the coffee pot, I poured myself a cup and offered to do the
same for Rose.

"No thanks. I've had enough," answered Rose, turning around to look at Allie. "How's she doing?"

"She's not having a restful sleep," I answered, sitting down in the chair.

"You have yourself a good girl there, boy," answered Rose pointing her finger at me. For the first time, I understood Rose's tone, as maybe she now approved of the relationship between Allie and me.

"I know it, Rose," I answered. "I just wish I could make her understand how much she means to me."

"Loving a man doesn't come easy for girls like Allie . . . and the others in this place," answered Rose, as she walked to the window and looked out. I continued sipping the coffee. Rose prolonged her stay at the window, looking out. "What are you reading in the Bible?" Rose finally asked without turning from the window.

"The book of Hosea," I answered. "Have you ever read it? It's about a preacher in ancient Israel, who falls in love with a working girl named Gomer."

"Don't believe I ever read that one," answered Rose, turning away from the window. "And you can bet old . . . Elihu Houston never used that story as a sermon text."

"He was your father?" I asked, attempting to hide behind the coffee cup.

"Yeah. Around the Big Bend country, they called him the 'horse trough preacher,'" answered Rose, as she picked up the Bible from the floor and placed it on the round table near the coffee pot. "They say he baptized more people in horse troughs than any preacher in Texas . . . hell I guess in any other damn place, too."

"I can't imagine your father being a preacher." I laughed a short brittle laugh.

Rose paced nervously between the bed and the window, as I poured myself another cup of coffee.

"Mind if I ask a personal question?" Rose stopped and took hold of the swan's neck.

With a wave of her hand she replied, "What the hell . . . go ahead?"

"Sometime back, during one of our more friendly discussions," I began, trying to sound 'friendly' and not nosey, "you said your father ran you off because you got pregnant when you were in high school. What happened to the child?"

"I went to Waco . . . lived there with an aunt and uncle, who took the child as their own after he was born."

"Have you seen him since then?"

"I used to see him each year at Christmas." Rose turned, her hands gripping the swan's neck slightly above her head; she leaned forward for a moment, before continuing. "He was told I was his old maid aunt from Amarillo."

"Didn't you ever want to tell him the truth?" I asked.

"No. He has a Mama and Daddy . . . and that's all I wanted for him." There was sadness in her voice, which I could almost feel. As she turned from the bed, she continued, "Now, he has a family of his own . . . and I'm satisfied knowing he's happy." Trying to bring a more jovial mood to the conversation, Rose added, "He's some big shot Assistant D. A. in Dallas. Hell . . . if he knew his ole lady was running a whore house, he'd probably have my ass locked up."

We both laughed.

"What about your father, Rose . . . have you seen him since you left home?"

"Once or twice," answered Rose, nervously walking to the side of the bed to look at Allie. "My ole man was a hellfire and brimstone kind of preacher . . . there wasn't much room for loving and forgiving in his kind of preaching." Rose adjusted the sheet covering Allie. "Believe me, Yogi, had he been there, when the adulteress was brought before Jesus, she would have been a dead bitch."

The hostility in Rose's voice caused me to lower my cup to the table with a thump.

"I'm a hard bitch, Yogi. You know that," Rose said, glancing at me as she walked toward the portiere. "In this line of work you have to be." Pausing at the portiere, I assumed to judge my reaction, Rose added, "But, even a bitch like me needs to be loved, and that was something my ole man couldn't or wouldn't do."

As Rose walked toward the door and reached for the knob, I jokingly spoke aloud, "Rose, you are a bitch . . . at times. But, for what it's worth, right now, I love you."

Rose left the room without challenging my declaration, which disappointed me since she usually had the last word in our debates. I moved back to the chair near the bed. As I settled down, Allie moved and moaned several times, while trying to sit. I walked around the bed to help her.

"Hey . . . how are you feeling?" I asked, helping her to sit up. "Would you like something to eat?" I asked.

"I'm not hungry." she replied in a drowsy manner.

"There's some juice in the refrigerator," I said in an insisting tone. "You should try some."

I gave her my best pleading face, which brought forth a soft 'Okay' followed by a thank-you kiss. Her hand softly touched my face.

I was desperate for a smile and tried my best to get her to talk about anything that would take her mind off the little girl. As I made my way to the kitchen, I asked what she thought of the swan bed and told her what Rose said about Ladybird Johnson. From the kitchenette, I detected a small smile on Allie's lips.

Taking the glass of juice with both hands and resting her arms on her knees, Allie took several sips before reaching out with one hand to touch my face.

"Yogi, you didn't do something foolish last night?"

I figured the medication had caused her to forget that she had already asked me that question.

Not knowing how to answer her question and not wanting to lie, I just answered, "Yes, I did. I hit some guy at the Airmen's Club."

With a slight smile Allie replied, "Judging by your eye . . . looks like he hit back."

"He was bigger up close than I thought from where I was standing, when he threw the bottle," I answered with a smile, while holding my hand over my eye.

Handing me the glass, Allie slid under the comforter and sheet before turning her back toward me. For the longest time, I lay next to her with my arm over her body. In the silence of the room, it was as if we could hear each other's hearts beating. Allie took my hand and kissed it before holding it to her breast.

"Had she survived the rape . . . do you think she would have been a respectable girl?" Allie asked, clinching my hand.

"I can't answer that, Allie. No one knows how such a thing impacts a girl's life," I said softly.

I propped myself up with one arm to look down at her, as she continued to gaze in the direction of the kitchenette.

"Why did she die, and not me, Yogi?"

"I don't know Allie, life doesn't give us such choices," I answered leaning over her to see her face.

"Do you think she was ever told she was loved?" Allie asked, as she once more took my hand and pulled it close to her breast.

"I hope the kindness you showed her in the hospital was understood by her as a sign of your caring for her."

Allie rolled onto her back and looked up at me. As she placed my hand to her mouth and kissed my fingers softly she asked, "Yogi, would you please say, you love me?"

A moment of disbelief rushed over me at such a request, for this was the first time Allie had asked me to express my love for her. During the many months we had been dating, I was always the one who initiated such expressions of affection, and had done so only with her permission according to our roadside agreement.

With an amorous stare, I looked down into Allie's eyes and whispered, "Allie, I love you. I've loved you from the very first moment I saw you that night in the backseat of that car."

Reaching up Allie put her arms around my neck and pulled my face to hers. In a moment of tenderness, she kissed my sore eye, which I understood as her way of expressing her love. We laid there in the big swan bed, wrapped in each other's arms, until I felt Allie's arms relax, indicating she was once more sleeping. I slowly removed her arms from around my neck and carefully got up from the bed. After readjusting the comforter and sheet over her, I moved back to the chair on the opposite side of the bed.

As the afternoon turned to evening, the city seemed to come alive, as lights began to illuminate the metropolitan area. I stood by the window looking out, watching the cars move up and down Polk Street. The shrieking sound of an ambulance, with its lights flashing, racing down the street toward St. Anthony's held my attention, until it disappeared beyond the old warehouses near the railroad tracks. Allie groaned, causing me to look back at her. In doing so, I realized that this place and the hospital, in the distance, were both a part of her world and if I were to remain a part of her life, then I would have to accept her and the worlds, in which she lived.

After settling in the big chair by the bed once more, and taking hold of Allie's hand, I thought of something Rose had said about the adulteress in the story from the Bible. As best as I could remember the story, the men, beginning with the eldest, dropped the stones and walked away realizing their sins was as reprehensible as that of the adulteress. Thinking back on my own behavior, the previous evening, I came to realize I had no right to judge Allie.

Chapter 13

A gentle knocking caused me to stir. A feeling of grogginess, coupled with the sheets and blanket entangling my body hampered my efforts to move to the edge of the foldout couch. As my senses acclimated to the surroundings, I recognized the familiar pattern of tapping.

Just as I grumbled for the early morning intruder to come in, the door came open as Crystal bumped it with her buttocks. In a cheerful tone, which seemed to exaggerate her Texas drawl, she cheerfully asked, "Y'all ready for breakfast?" The plates, cups, and flatware on the small cart made an annoying clinking sound, while being pulled across the threshold.

"I could use some coffee," I answered groggily, watching her sashaying through the portiere with a teasing movement of her *derriere*.

"You spent the night on that sofa?" asked Crystal, with a coquettish stare from the other side of the portiere.

"Yes, I did. Allie needed the rest."

Without standing, I leaned over one arm of the couch while attempting to keep my lower body covered with part of the sheet.

"You're looking for something?" asked Crystal with a benign smile, while placing the covered plates and coffee pot on the round table near the bedroom window.

"My brains . . . and my pants," I answered, resting my elbows on my knees. Pulling down my head by grasping the back of my neck, I continued with a chuckle, "I believe, I lost them both."

Sitting there holding my throbbing head, an uneasy felling came over me as I felt the presence of someone standing near me. As my eyes slowly came open, I could see Crystal's open-toe slippers were only inches from my bare feet.

Looping the pants around my neck, Crystal slowly pulled my face toward her abdomen. "Besides a new brain and breakfast, is there anything else you could use?"

"The breakfast will do," I answered, staring forward at her navel.

With the satisfaction that I had been sufficiently aroused, Crystal let the pants fall across my shoulders and stepped back. Once more she sashayed through the portiere and moved the cart away from the round table near the window. I quickly stood, turned toward the kitchenette, and slipped on the pants. Without a shirt, I walked to the bed and lightly touched Allie's shoulder.

An angelic smile slowly brightened Allie's face before she stretched both arms above her head. "Good morning, sleepy head," I said, bending down to gently kiss her on the lips.

Reaching up, Allie pulled my face next to hers, preventing me from standing. The closeness, by which she held my face against hers, signaled the crisis connected with the little girl's death had not passed.

Crystal's high pitch tone while saying *"Good morning"* caused Allie to break her hold around my neck.

"I didn't know we had company!" Allie said raising her head slightly to greet Crystal, now leaning against the swan's neck.

Glancing toward Crystal, I said, "She brought breakfast . . . among other things not normally found on the menu."

"Well, since you don't want anything else, I go back downstairs," answered Crystal with a minxish twist of her hips before starting for the living room.

"Please, stay and have a cup of coffee, Crystal," Allie pleaded, swinging her legs over the edge of the bed.

Pausing at the apartment door, Crystal answered, "Y'all need to be alone. If you change your mind about dessert, handsome, I'll be downstairs."

"What's that all about?" asked Allie, after Crystal pulled the door close.

"Nothing. She . . . enjoys teasing me." I patted Allie on the legs. "Come on lazy bones, breakfast is getting cold." While escorting Allie to the table, I asked, "How would you like to ride to Canyon this afternoon? The museum's open."

"Thanks, Yogi, but I really need to study."

Allie's mood remained somber, as she silently picked at her food for a while, before returning to the bed and covered with the sheet. Realizing I hadn't had a shower in two days, I decided to indulge myself in a bath, since such a luxury didn't exist in the barracks. Not having any clean clothes to change into, I would have to wear the same pants and shirt, but at least my body would be clean.

Hoping to dispel Allie's gloomy mood, I walked to the side of the bed and sat beside her. Leaning forward for a kiss, I asked, "How would you like to join me in a bath?"

My proposal brought a strange expression to Allie's face.

"Come on . . . you can scrub my back, and I'll scrub yours," I pleaded, while leaning forward once more to kiss her.

The slight movement of Allie's head in the negative wiped the cajoling smile from my face. Without pressing the issue, I walked to the bathroom leaving the door open.

From a shelf over the end of the tub, I used in liberal portions some of Rose's bath oils, beads, and perfumes while filling the tub. Returning to the bedroom, I walked to the double windows and opened the heavy drapes, allowing the early morning sun to bathe the room with a soft warm glow. Allie watched quietly from her position in the bed as I removed my pants and draped them over the chair near the window.

Lying in the warm bath with only my head showing above the heavy bubbly froth, I repeatedly call for Allie to come scrub my back. After several minutes, she appeared at the bathroom door. To tease her, I disappeared under the bubbles.

Reappearing with a crown of suds on my head, I once more attempted to entice Allie to join me by reaching out my hand toward her. The melancholy expression on her face while sitting on the floor just beyond the doorway, left me feeling she wanted to join me, but for some reason couldn't. As a teasing gesture, I threw some suds in her direction, but that too failed to bring a smile to her face.

Feeling desperate for a smile, I raised one leg above the suds and remarked, "I bet ole Opal wishes she had as much hair on her legs."

Allie finally smiled.

After drying myself and donning the same dirty shorts, I walked back into the bedroom, feeling refreshed, clean, and smelling like cheap perfume. Allie was once more sitting in the bed; her dolorous expression made me wonder if her young patient was still on her mind.

"Hey! You need to get dressed." I jauntily said, after removing a hair brush from the top drawer of the chiffonier and returning to the bathroom.

"Yogi," Allie asked in a pleading tone, "did you undress me yesterday, when we got here?"

"Yeah! I did!" I called out nonchalantly, while continuing to brush my hair.

"Why . . . you?" Allie asked with a morose tone. "Why not Rose or Crystal?"

Stepping in the doorway, I answered, "Because . . . I knew how much you were hurting and . . . I wanted to be the one to help." After placing the brush on the chiffonier, I walked over to the bed and sat down beside her. Hoping to bring a smile to her face I jokingly asked, "What difference does it make? I've seen your breasts before."

With both hands Allie gripped the pajama top and pulled it tight around her body, as if wrapping herself in it. Turning her face from me, she asked, "Did you remove my panties?"

"Of course not!" I shot back with a chortle before standing and walked to the chair to retrieve my pants.

"Yogi, did you see my scars?"

Allie's question caused me to pause before turning to face her.

"Is that what you're worried about?" I asked with a short chuckle, taking hold of my pants.

The gloomy expression on Allie's face triggered a devilish idea in my mind. Holding out both arms, I allowed my jeans to fall to the floor while scowling. Creeping around the bed stiff-legged with both arms extended I said, "I believe . . . my beautiful creation . . . I'll take a look at your scars."

Unable to restrain my laughter at my own poor imitation of Frankenstein's monster, I jumped into the bed, straddling Allie. My attempt to deliver a vampirish kiss to her neck resulted in a vigorous tussle. Amid our tossing around, I laughed wildly, while working at the sheet between us and attempting to kiss her on the neck.

Allie threw me from her body with a great deal of strength. For a moment, I lay there laughing.

"No . . . Yogi!" shouted Allie, while rigidly extending her right arm toward me. "Please don't look at me, Yogi. Please don't."

The fear in Allie's face, as she retreated to the headboard immediately reminded me of her outburst of emotions during our first trip to a drive-in theatre. Remembering that night, I immediately backed off.

As tears began streaming down Allie's face, I sat up, my mouth agape, with both hands partially extended toward her.

"Allie . . . please . . . please stop crying," I pleaded.

A strange loneliness gripped my heart as I continued pleading with Allie. We sat apart for a while, before her trembling hand slowly reached for mine. Our fingers lightly touched each other as if groping in the dark.

"Hey, look I was just joking around." I said apologetically, as our fingers became interlocked. "I'm sorry. I didn't know you were so sensitive . . . about a little scar." As the fear in Allie's face began to subside, she pulled my hand to her lips.

Slowly I moved closer to Allie. As her head came to rest on my shoulder I begged her forgiveness. While holding each other, I began wondering if her scar was the reason she refused to share a bath with me. Some time passed before I suggested we should get dressed. While shaking her head in agreement, Allie asked me to close the drapes.

With our backs toward each other we dressed in silence, and then went downstairs to say good-bye to Rose and the girls. At the backdoor of the House, a drop in the temperature became noticeable, as Crystal and several of the other girls all said good-bye to Allie with a show of affection, I thought unknown in their world.

"You take care of yourself, now, you hear," said Rose after taking a long drag on her cigarette encased in a long plastic holder. "And, I don't want you returning to this place for three or four weeks."

After assisting Allie into the car and closing the door, I thanked Rose for her hospitality.

"Yogi," Rose called as I walked around to the driver side. Pausing long enough to take a drag on her cigarette, Rose stared at me and said, "I may have misjudged you. Maybe you are good enough for one of my girls."

Coming from Rose, I took this as a great compliment. With something of a jaunty wave, I thanked Rose once more, before driving off.

Seeking some protection from the wind, Allie and I sat huddled in the sun on a low-level step against the left buttress after arriving at St. Anthony's. Sitting between my legs, Allie leaned back against my chest, while I wrapped both arms around her upper body.

Turning her face toward mine Allie said pensively, "Yogi, thanks for being with me this weekend."

"There's no need to thank me, Allie. I'd gone AWOL if necessary to be with you," I answered before kissing her on the neck. "Oh! By the way, the E. R. doctor says you are to see Doctor Tully before returning to class tomorrow."

"Who is he?" asked Allie with a surprise look on her face.

"Doctor Cavanaugh said he's a Psychiatrist." I hesitated before continuing. "Allie, please, don't get angry, but . . . maybe he can help you . . . not only with that little girl's death, but severing your ties with the House . . . and Rose even said she didn't want you to come back for several weeks."

"Yogi, let's not discuss this now," Allie said turning to look toward the street.

Allie pulled my hands to her mouth, which I took to mean she didn't want to talk further about this matter or the events of the past two days. The wind grew colder, so I suggested she go in, since neither of us had a jacket.

Before getting up, Allie breathed into my hands once more and then kissed the tips of my fingers. We stood. After a tender kiss and a hug, we said good-bye. Our fingers slowly slipped apart, as I stepped away and started down the steps. About midway down, I turned to see if Allie was still there. She was. I raised my right hand and offered up the international sign for "I love you," which was still a mystery to her. Allie smiled and gave me a languid wave. Skipping down the flight of steps, my arms became rigid as I shoved my hands deep into my pants pockets to keep them warm.

Chapter 14

The time, Allie and I spent together following her banishment from the House, proved more disappointing for me than anticipated. We spent most of our time at the Double Dip or just riding through the downtown area with no particular destination in mind. We discussed the upcoming Thanksgiving dinner on base, which she agreed to attend if I wore my uniform, since she had not seen me in it. The idea didn't go over very well with me and I felt the only way out was to request she wear her nurses' uniform. She totally disagreed. Since I refused to wear my uniform, Allie insisted we go shopping one Saturday, for me, a '*Thanksgiving outfit*' as she called it.

The week before Thanksgiving, Airman Bridgewater, received a TDY assignment to an Air Base in Kansas, as part of an EOD (explosive ordinance disposal) team. Tank, my roommate, and his collection of classical records departed for an Air Base in California. Since the Air Force wouldn't ship his parakeet, Pete became mine. Now that he was my property I decided to do something about his "lonely bachelorhood." Mrs. Milo suggested the "Bird Man" of Amarillo could solve "the lonely bird's problem."

James and I managed to find the Bird Man's place, after driving around for some time. We were both amazed at the number and color of parakeets in the large bird house in his backyard. The first thing to be decided was, of course, to determine if indeed Pete was a 'Pete,' which the man pointed out could be determined by the color of the cere, just above the beak. Pete's was blue, meaning he was a male. We looked at females of every color, yellow ones, . . . whites, . . . blues, . . . and multicolored ones. Then I noticed a pretty red one. The color of her feathers reminded me of Allie's hair. The solution to Pete's loneliness was about to be accomplished with the purchase of a Crimson Rosella. The names, Pete and Rosella sounded good together.

The tumbleweeds rolling their way to Lubbock, as Dan True would put it, were a mass of ice crystals crashing into my vehicle, as Allie and I rode in silence down the Polk Street toward the bus station. The Thanksgiving dinner we shared with my friends and their dates earlier during the day was enjoyable, even though I was the only one with a tie, a part of my Thanksgiving wardrobe selected by Allie at Levine's Department Store.

After parking along the curb across from the bus station, I removed my heavy parka from the backseat and put it on before taking Allie's suitcase from the car trunk. While saying good-bye, I pulled her into the parka while she wrapped her arms around me. For several minutes we stood there, clinging to each other, knowing such a moment wouldn't be ours again until December 30, since Allie was returning to her home for Christmas.

The disapproving stare and muttered rebuke of a passing elderly woman caused Allie and me to pull apart with a slight chuckle. From the parka pocket, I pulled out a small gift, wrapped in red paper, and handed it to Allie. A surprised look came to her face. After opening the gift, an oval watch with a telescope expansion band, purchased from Sears for $9.99, she rewarded me with a slight kiss and said I would have to wait until she returned from Indian Ridge with my gift. This prompted me to pull her back against my body, while asking if expressing my love for her would violate our roadside agreement. Allie didn't answer, but just placed her head on my shoulder deep within the parka.

Allie's arms tightened around my body, and we stood there for several more minutes in the blistering wind, until a final boarding call ended our embrace. I reached for Allie's suitcase on the sidewalk, but she took it from my hand, saying she would prefer to walk across the street alone. Watching her walk away, I felt as if the icy wind was driving from my life, the very essence of my soul.

Each night during Allie's absence, I'd marked off another unfulfilled day on the calendar inside my locker, before turning in. The days were cold and even lonelier than those spent on guard duty during the Cuban Missile crisis. During Christmas week, someone put a silver star in the top of Sausage Sam's oak tree as it stood a lonely vigil in the snow-blanketed quadrangle. That was the only Christmas tree in my life that year.

On the afternoon of December 30, a large column in the bus terminal became my refuge from the wind as I checked my watch. Realizing only five minutes had passed since the last time check, I returned to the lobby and asked the ticket agent if the bus would be arriving soon. After resuming my position beside the column, another five minutes dragged by before the sound of a diesel engine caused me to peer around the column in anticipation. As the passengers exited the bus one by one, the long needed surge of energy—my craving spirit caused me to step away from the column. Not wanting Allie to see me right off, I stood behind the crowd gathering around the open door of the bus.

Standing beside the luggage compartment of the bus, Allie rose to her toes several times, attempting to see over the crowd while occasionally glancing back at the man unloading the suitcases.

When I stepped into her view, we paused for a moment. Smiles transformed our faces as we slowly began walking toward each other. Our paces quickened until we met in an embrace of laughter and hungry kisses, which brought to an end for me a long and difficult December.

New Year's Eve fell on a Monday, resulting in an extra long weekend for all military personnel. Allie and I, as well as James and Coco, attended a party that evening in Canyon, hosted by a student nurse in her mid-thirties, who decided to start a career following her husband's industrial accident at a local helium plant.

The party was a casual affair, so we all wore jeans and boots. Allie wore a pair of tight jeans, a pretty western shirt with rhinestone snaps, a red scarf around her neck and a leather coat, which she had brought from home. She explained, it once belonged to her brother, who had died while in high school.

The coat made of Elk hide with a sheep skin liner and collar, was very heavy and appeared to swallow Allie. It had one small pocket on the upper right side of the chest while two larger pockets, fitted with flaps, graced the lower part of the coat. On the left side across from the small pocket was a horse's head made from an assortment of small colored beads. On the left sleeve, at the shoulder cap, was a buffalo head made from the same size and assortment of beads as the horse's head. On the right shoulder cap was a Thunder Bird of similar design. Each shoulder had crossing it from back to front a narrow band of multiple-colored beads in a beautiful display of Indian art work. A row of narrow leather fringes approximately five inches long, some studded with small blue stones ran the full length of the outside seams of each sleeve, from the shoulder to the wrist.

Stitched into the back of the coat was the profile of an Indian, wearing a war bonnet, encircled by turquoise stones. At the end of each feather in the bonnet were several threads of various colors. A type of whip stitching bordered the edges of the coat, which was fitted with buttons fashioned by hand from deer antlers.

Everyone at the party admired the coat and took turns trying it on. James, who was more into cowboy fashion than I, fell in love with it. The coat was slightly large for him, but fit me perfectly.

Throughout the evening, a gentle but heavy snowfall blanketed the little town of Canyon, which for me, being from south Louisiana, turned the world into a Winter Wonderland. When the party broke up at about one a.m., the hostess suggested we spend the night saying we could sleep on the floor or wherever we could find a place. Quietly in the presence of others, Allie asked me to please drive back to Amarillo.

Just a few miles outside Canyon, the snowfall became extremely heavy and the hazardous driving conditions began taking away the beauty I saw in the snow earlier. Silently, I knew we had made a mistake by deciding to return to Amarillo. James and Coco insisted we turn back, but Allie wanted to continue, so we did. Driving was difficult at best, yet I continued very slowly, taking notice of the overturned eighteen wheelers in the ditches.

I was becoming very concerned, when in the distance a dim light from a small tourist court became a welcome beacon. James suggested we pull in to see if any rooms were available. Allie was against the idea and wanted to try going on. In frustration, I gruffly retorted, *No! We can't!,* and cautiously pulled off the highway. Coco remained silent on the subject.

The Palo Duro Inn consisted of a long horseshoe configuration of brick cabins with an office building in the middle toward the front. The front of the office building protruded outward in the form of a room, with multisides made up of large windows.

James and I dashed thorough the office door and while laughingly dusted the snow from our shoulders, requested two rooms. The old man behind the desk looked us over for a while, before stating that the rooms were ten bucks apiece.

As we took turns signing the registry, the old man tightened the cord on his bathrobe and then pointed over his right shoulder.

"The rooms are over that way. The sheets are fresh, and the rooms should be warm."

After each taking a key, we returned to the car. The rooms were near each other, but separated by a small garage, which was too small for my car, so I parked in front of one unit. James and Coco immediately jumped out and dashed to the door with shouts and laughter of alacrity. Allie hesitated and held my hand, asking once more if we could *please go on.*

"It's too dangerous, Allie," I protested with some restraint. "We have to stay here for the night!"

With some reluctance, Allie followed me to the door, where I struggled to find the key hole, while the snow blew down the neck of my coat. Once unlocked, the door blew open, filling the small room with a blast of cold air. For a moment, Allie and I stood beside each other looking around the room, before I removed my parka and hung it on a hook left of the door.

The furniture in the room seemed to cover every square inch of floor space and consisted of a regular size bed, an old chest of drawers and a high backed chair to the left of the bed with a floor lamp behind it. The bed itself was an old brass bed with tall corner posts, each crowned with a large brass ball. It appeared to be extra high and covered with a bedspread, which must have been as old as the tourist court itself.

For a moment, a chill shot through my body causing me to tremble. After moving before the gas space heater, I looked at Allie still standing near the door, wrapped in the leather coat. With a gentle voice, hoping to palliate her apparent dissatisfaction, I encouraged her to remove the coat and join me near the heater.

When she didn't answer, I gestured with one hand toward the bathroom and asked her to excuse me.

Allie was sitting in the high back chair with her feet drawn up on the seat holding the leather coat tight around her body when I reentered to the bedroom.

"Are you cold?" I asked from the opposite side of the bed in something of an agitated tone.

With her chin resting on her knees she answered, "No" without looking at me.

"Then . . . what?" I asked with a tone of impatience in my voice.

"Yogi, please . . . I can't stay in this room," Allie pleaded, with a tremor in her voice.

The sadness in her voice was the same I had heard that morning in Rose's apartment and the night she became so afraid at the drive-in movie. Feeling guilty for my reaction, I walked around the bed and stood before her not knowing how to respond to her mood. Slowly her hand reached up for mine, which I accepted before sitting on the bed beside her.

"Yogi, can't we leave?" Allie pleaded.

"No!" I retorted without wanting to. Only after she withdrew her hand from mine, did I realize my tone was harsh. "Look . . . you can sleep in the bed . . . by yourself . . . and I'll pull the chair around to the foot and put my feet up . . . and sleep in the chair."

Without saying anything, she just shook her head "No." I was becoming more irritated by the moment, because I felt she was being unreasonable, and in my anger I lost control of my tongue once more.

"This is the worst damn storm in years, and we can't leave." I said sitting more erect on the bed.

"I can't stay here tonight. Don't you understand?" Allie yelled back.

"No, I don't understand!" I snapped back. "Would you stay if I put ten dollars on the bed?"

Anger writhed Allie's face as her open hand struck my face. Immediately she gasped and turned her face away from me. For some time we both sat in silence, before I stood, kissed her on the side of the face and whispered an apology. As I turned to walk away, Allie's hand reached out for mine. She stood and placed her arms around me. My disappointment in the way the evening was going, caused me to not respond in kind.

"Allie, what's wrong with us?" I asked, stepping away from her slightly. "While you were gone, my life wasn't worth living. And, now that you're back . . . we're fighting. Of all nights, we should be making love tonight . . . not fighting."

Allie's downcast eyes caused me to take her into my arms. Even through the thick leather coat, I could feel her body tremble. After a short time, I broke our embrace and walked toward my parka.

"Where are you going?" Allie asked taking a few steps away from the chair.

"I have an idea," I said, reaching for the door knob. "Come on."

As we headed out the door into the blinding snow, Allie gripped my hand and followed my lead toward the office. The adventurous romp through the accumulating snow and cutting wind made my laughter appear as a mocking cry, defying the forces of Mother Nature.

Our rushed entrance into the little office caught the old man by surprise. He gave us a strange stare, as we stood there with melting snow running down onto our faces.

"Is there something wrong?" the old man asked, adjusting the sash to his bathrobe.

"No, sir," I answered with a sight chuckle before glancing at Allie. "The room's okay . . . but, we have a problem." I hesitated and unconsciously gesticulated toward Allie with one hand. "You see . . . my girlfriend doesn't . . ."

As I stumbled around, looking for an explanation, the old man raised his hand and asked, "You two not married?"

"No, sir . . . we're not." I answered.

Looking at Allie, he said, "Young lady, your parents should be real proud of you." He pointed his long skinny finger at us and while winking at Allie he added, "Too many young folks these days are sleeping together before getting married. It ain't right, you know." Moving his head up and down with a slight nodding, the old man repeated, "Your parents should be real proud."

"I was thinking maybe we could spend the night here in the office on the sofa or maybe on a chair," I said looking around.

As he came from around the desk, the old man tightened the cord of his bathrobe and said, "Follow me."

With some skepticism, we followed the old man into a small room behind the office, where a badly sagging army cot caused us to turn toward each other with contrasting expressions.

"The young lady can sleep here," said the old man, standing before the cot with a sense of pride. "I'll get the wife to fetch some fresh sheets and a pillow slip. And, you can sleep yonder in the office in that old recliner." A boney finger with a slight curve pointed back toward the office.

Looking at Allie, I asked, "Will this be okay?"

"Ye . . . yeah!" Allie replied with a slight motion of her head. The expression in her voice didn't match the one on her face. Allie and I both took off our coats and placed them on a nearby chair.

The old man walked toward the back of the room and after opening a door, called out to his wife to bring out some fresh sheets and a clean pillow slip. We all walked back to the office and stood around waiting for the old lady to appear with the needed linens. I stood, looking around the office, which was a museum of family photos and whatnots, apparently collected over the years.

"You and your friend from the Air Base?" the old man asked, in a tone that told me he already knew the answer.

"Yes, sir," I answered.

"Me," he said pointing to a picture of a young sailor on the wall, "I was in the Navy during the war. When I got discharged, I wanted to move as far from the ocean as possible, so I moved to Amarillo . . . first, and then came here in 1952 and built this place."

The old man paused for a while and then continued as if thinking of something else to say. "They planted the wheat fields across the road some ten years ago and here in back. Sometimes when the wheat gets up and the wind gets a blowing . . . it reminds me of the Pacific." He paused once more and after wiping a picture of a battleship with a handkerchief from his robe, he added, "I don't ever want to see the ocean or a Jap fighter again as long as I live."

The old man's wife, a very stout lady, finally appeared with the linen and suggested he make up the cot.

"Mr. Wheeler been sleeping on that thing almost every night since we opened this place," said the old lady as we made our way back into the little room. Allie assisted the old man in making up the bed while Mrs. Wheeler gave us an unsolicited history of the cot, which included the $3.00 purchase price.

"Mama," interrupted Mr. Wheeler, "maybe these young folks would like a cup of hot cocoa before turning in for the night."

"No, that won't be necessary," I injected hastily. "We've put you folks through enough trouble already."

"That'll be no trouble," said Mrs. Wheeler as she turned to leave the room.

"Mama, bring this young girl something comfortable to sleep in," called out Mr. Wheeler.

Grins transformed Allie's face and mine as we glanced toward each other, both wondering what would Mrs. Wheeler have that would possibly fit Allie.

Once the cot was made-up, Mr. Wheeler left the room. When Allie sat in the sunken middle of the cot, which caused her knees to appear unusually high, we both laughed.

Sitting on the floor before Allie, I rested my head on her knees. With my head tilted back, I looked up at her and said, "The only good feature about this cot is you can't roll out once you lie down."

"I'm sorry Yogi; your year isn't ending the way you would have liked," Allie apologized while kissing me on the ear.

"It's okay," I said tilting my head back in her direction. "Just so it ends with you." Allie leaned forward to give me an upside-down kiss, which Mr. Wheeler and his wife interrupted. "The wife" as Mr. Wheeler called her, was carrying a tray with two cups of hot cocoa while he carried what appeared to be a nightgown and a lady's robe on extended forearms as if carrying a flag.

"This nightgown here may be a little loose on you sweetie," Mr. Wheeler said to Allie as he place the items on the cot beside her.

"But it'll keep you warm," injected Mrs. Wheeler setting the tray on a small table near the cot. "Its heavy flannel."

"I remember the time the wife was as small at this here little girl," chuckled Mr. Wheeler, looking at me while putting his arm around his wife.

"And I remember the time you were as handsome as this young man," countered Mrs. Wheeler, with an admiring smile at her husband.

"Everybody's handsome and pretty when they're young," offered Mr. Wheeler as an antidote to his wife's statement.

With a slap to his wife's broad buttocks, which caused Mrs. Wheeler to feign disapproval by slapping at his hand, Mr. Wheeler suggested they *leave so the young folks could say good night.*

After the old couple departed, I returned to the office, taking one cup of cocoa with me, so Allie could change into her borrowed nightgown. After flipping off the office lights, I walked to one of the windows to watch the falling snow. The streetlight outside the office showed that the snow was now coming down even harder than when we first arrived. I stood before the windows, enjoying the hot beverage and watching the snow as it blew past the window in what appeared to be sheets of pure white. I had never seen so much snow before, and the sight once more took on the beauty of a Christmas postcard. The wind was blowing by what I imagined to be a gale force by this time, and the snowflakes swirling around the tires of my car and the doors of the cabins appeared busily searching for their own resting spot for the night.

The sound of an opening door caused me to turn from the window and my musing. Allie stood before me in the doorway, with a pleading smile in a very large, full length, flannel nightgown. I wanted to laugh, for the contrast between this granny gown and her usual décolleté negligees at the House seemed humorous. Yet, in the filtered light from the street lamp she radiated an innocence, which I thought was very beautiful.

"Well, how do I look, Mr. Yogi?" Allie asked holding out each side of the large gown. I got the impression she was trying to mimic Mrs. Wheeler.

Walking toward Allie, I tried mimicking Mr. Wheeler by saying, "The wife looks very sexy."

With a kiss, we wished each other a Happy New Year, before walking over to the window to watch the swirling snow perform Terpsichore acts against the window pane. While we each were enjoying our cup of cocoa, Allie leaned against my chest. I placed one arm around her waist and held her tight against my body craving her affection. When the light in the cabin shared by James and Coco went out, I felt we were both sharing the same thoughts.

Musing aloud, Allie wondered if Coco would be wearing James' bolo tie tomorrow. The jealousy I felt, prevented me from responding. Allie lowered her head and softly apologized once more for the way our year was coming to an end. Once more she promised to someday explain her fears, before turning and placing her head on my shoulder. Her attempt to keep silent her sniffles caused me to pull her body closer to mine. Several minutes passed before I took her into my arms and carried her into the next room.

After placing her on the cot, I pulled the covers to her neck and kissed her once. Allie's hand reached out and took mine as I started to leave her side. She asked that I stay with her for a little while. After sitting on the floor beside the cot, I took Allie's hand. In a coy kind of way, she kissed my folded fingers before placing our coupled hands against her breast.

"What do you think of the leather coat?" Allie asked with an impish grin.

"It's a little big on you, but I love it. It's very nice," I replied with an air of witticism.

"I'm glad you like, Yogi," answered Allie with a minxish smile. "It's the Christmas gift I promised you."

"My what!" I responded sitting up.

"That's why I went home for the holiday," answered Allie, showing forth a gentle smile. "I had hoped to give it to you when we returned to Amarillo, tonight."

"Allie . . . I can't accept that coat . . . it's too expensive and besides you said it once belonged to your brother."

"My brother's . . . dead, Yogi," Allie answered with a somber face. "I'm sure he wouldn't mind if you had it."

"What about your parents?" I asked. "Did they agree to this?"

Trying to add a spirit of gaiety to the moment, Allie squeezed my hand while offering up a short chortle. "They both agreed, Yogi. There's one stipulation, however."

With a serious face, I questioned, "What's that?"

"They both insist you come up to the farm this summer."

"It's a deal," I answered, before bending over to kiss her. "Hey, your old man isn't the kind of jealous daddy who likes grinding up young boys, who come calling on his precious little daughter, is he?"

"In Indian Ridge, he has a reputation as a jealous father," answered Allie with a chuckle. "Now go on . . . try on the coat again."

After retrieving the coat from the chair and putting it on, a great swell of pride washed over me. My face reflected the joy this beautiful gift had brought me. It seemed to fit even better, now that it was mine. I had never been given a more precious gift, one I knew carried the memories of someone who was loved and missed very much. Never, did I feel more unworthy to receive such a gift. Allie had never mentioned her brother or his death and while I strutted around the room, the blitheness in her face slowly changed, causing me to feel ashamed of my selfish pride. After removing the jacket, I returned to the cot, knelt down beside Allie and gave her a kiss. Taking hold of my hand, Allie once again asked me not to leave her.

Several times, I dozed off while sitting on the floor beside the cot, before realizing I needed to get up and go to the recliner in the office. Coming to my knees, I leaned over and kissed Allie once more. I knew, in her sleep, she couldn't deny me this opportunity to express my love for her, so softly I whispered, *Allie, I love you more than anything in this world. I have since the first moment I saw you in the backseat of that car. I will love you . . . until my eyes close in death.*

The swirling snow around the streetlight once more drew me to the window upon returning to the office. Now collected in a pile on the trunk and roof of my car, as well as in great depths around the tires, the snow no longer appeared to be a threat, but almost as a friend, for it was keeping me and Allie from a world that had brought so much pain in our lives during the last few months. The endless coat of pure-white stretching into the distance beyond the range of my eyes left me with the desire that its purity would purge the world of all its evils.

I thought of Allie sleeping in the little room behind the office. We knew each other so intimately, yet I knew so little of the darkness, which seemed never to leave her mind. After exhaling against the window pane, I drew a heart in the condensation and wished the New Year would bring us closer in more than a physical way.

As I continued watching the snow coming down in such great quantity, considering that each snowflake is different, I couldn't help but think if there was even an argument for the existence of a supreme being, then these little wonders would be it. The whistling of the wind around the corner of the building broke my concentration. I then became aware of how tired I was. I walked over to the old recliner and lay back for a moment, before pulling the blanket to my neck.

Before dozing off, I looked about the little office and while watching the broken illumination from the outside light dance across the ceiling, I whispered, "Happy New Year, Yogi. It's 1963."

Chapter 15

The winter storm that blew into the Panhandle on New Year's Eve lingered for several more weeks with only an occasional break from the blistering wind and snow. Both men and beast were at its mercy, as were the tumble weeds rolling across the plains from as far away as Kansas. Along U.S. Highway 287 outside the Base, their frozen entangled masses in barbed wire fences created a natural barrier, where half-frozen cattle gathered for some relief from the howling wind. Standing motionless, with their backs toward the wind and heads hung low, they appeared to be creations of chalk. Seeing them, one could sense that they just as the humans, desired an end to winter's death grip upon the Panhandle.

Slowly, the spring thaw came with the March winds, bringing a welcome relief both to mankind and the creatures of the area. The small trees on the Base began to show forth some new shoots of green, and slowly, the blades of grass began appearing in the quadrangle before the barracks. As the few remaining patches of snow melted away, Sam's oak tree, having survived its first winter, proudly offered its branches to the birds.

The coming of spring meant a renewal of the First Sergeant's favorite Saturday pastime for the "lowlives," meaning anyone less than an NCO. The renewed battle for the Base Beautification Award began with the boys from my barracks. The fourth weekend of March was a pleasant one and since my three friends were exempt from "Sausage Duty," they teamed up with three guys from Air Frame Repair for a camping trip on the Canadian River, north of a dam under construction. Allie and I had planned to go out of town with a couple of her friends, so I had to pass on the outing. On Friday afternoon, while helping them load the camping equipment into *The Lung* outside the Base gym, they gave me the business for letting some "dame run my life."

Later that evening, when I returned from chow, one of the guys from down the hall informed me that Allie had called. After hanging up the phone, I relieved my anger by kicking the phone booth. Our trip had to be cancelled.

For some reason, I woke up early Saturday morning. While lying on my bunk listening to Pete and Rosella sing to each other, the drabness of my room became more noticeable. Since the room was mine alone, now that Tank shipped out, I felt some improvements were in order.

Before returning to the barrack from breakfast, I picked up one gallon of Air Force blue paint for the walls, one gallon of white paint for the ceiling, locker, and door and window frames from Base Supply. Without taking a break, except to explain my gung ho spirit to an occasional visitor, who wasn't happy with my project, fearing Sausage Sam would require they do the same, the work continued until late Saturday night.

Still I didn't allow the criticisms and innuendos; that I would become the barrack's pariah, deter me from the task. By Sunday afternoon, the job was completed. Pete and Rosella seemed to appreciate my efforts, if no one else did. After moving my bunk and table back into the room and cleaning up the mess, I treat myself to a burger and one beer at the Airmen's Club before doing my laundry and writing a letter to the folks back home.

I had just walked into my room from the shower, when the three campers showed-up. They had heard the news about my room. They stopped by to inspect the job and question my sanity. Paul and John saw my efforts as demoralizing to the whole barracks. Before leaving the room, John wondered why I couldn't have found something to do with my free time that *wouldn't bite them in the butt.*

With the arrival of spring, the Headquarters Squadron also saw the arrival of a new commander in the form of one, Captain Francis Ford. Captain Ford was a tall, skinny, frail looking man with a very thin mustache and big ears. The collar of his shirts always appeared to be one size, too large.

The Captain's first mission, it seemed, was to whip the barracks into shape, an idea we knew he received from the First Sergeant. Each evening after work, for the entire last week of March, we cleaned windows inside and out, painted the fire escapes, the front doors to the barracks and even the white elephants (trash dumpsters) in preparation for a squadron inspection.

Our barracks were as clean and ready as we could possibly get it by 08:00 hours, the following Saturday, as Sam and Captain Ford made their way toward the building. Each man dressed in fatigues, assumed a relaxed position in the hallway beside the door of his room awaiting the call to attention. As Sam's boisterous voice called the lower bay to attention, we glanced at each other in fearful anticipation.

The sound of heavy boots running on the hardwood floor caused everyone to look toward the Dayroom. John came to a sliding stop before me on the highly polished floor.

"Yogi, you gotta go downstairs," John uttered, while gasping for a breath. "Paul . . . Paul's locked himself in *The Iron Lung.*"

"What? What the hell's he doing in the car?" I asked, looking around expecting Sam and Captain Ford to appear at any minute.

"I think he's drunk." replied John with a sense of urgency. "You have to go get him."

"How . . . the hell he got drunk so early in the morning?" I argued, looking around again. "Besides, that's the best place for him, maybe he won't be seen by Sam and the Captain."

"That's a good idea, Yogi," John said, as if he was considering my suggestion. "Run down the fire escape, and tell him to stay there until they're gone."

"Hell! I won't have time, John! The inspection team will be coming upstairs any minute," I replied in a desperate tone.

"Yeah, you will," answered John, walking away from me toward the other end of the barrack. "They're still downstairs on the far end."

John darted back down the hall and through the dayroom toward his room as I made a dash for the fire escape.

Paul was in *The Iron Lung,* all right, with the remains of a quart bottle of beer. My efforts to have him roll down the window resulted in a mouth full of beer spewed against the window at my peering face. A rigid middle finger pressed against the window through the rivulets of beer indicated my efforts were a waste of time.

In frustration I shouted, "Paul! You little son-of-a-bitch, you had better stay here until Sam and Captain Ford leaves the barracks."

Sergeant Sam and Captain Ford were coming through the dayroom as I came running down the hallway back toward my room. The inspection team approached my room; their faces grimaced while I tried to control my breathing. Captain Ford gave me a momentary glare before entering the room.

"You had some other business to attend to, Airman?" Sam growled, moving his face only inches away from mine.

"No sir, Sergeant," I answered in a choking voice, trying to hold my breathing down to a normal rate.

Grunting sounds from inside the room caused my eyes to momentarily shift from the First Sergeant's inimical stare.

"Sergeant! Come here!" called Captain Ford from the room.

Sausage Sam walked into the room. With my face turned slightly toward the door, I could hear the locker doors open and close amid mumbled voices.

"First Sergeant, make a note of this man's room," the Captain said to Sam, as they exited my room.

"Are you trying to start a damn bird hatchery in this barracks?" Sam barked at me, with his face only inches away from mine. I could smell the garlic on his breath.

"No sir, First Sergeant! Just thought the male could use some female companionship!" I barked back.

Sausage Sam stood back. My eyes took a downward glance at his clipboard while he scribbled something on his tablet.

"Those damn pictures had better be back in the Orderly Room before the day is out!" shouted the First Sergeant into my right ear. "Do you hear me, Airman?"

"What pictures, Sergeant?" I asked with a puzzled look on my face.

Sergeant Sam's neck hyperextended toward my face as he shouted, "You know damn well what pictures, Airman!"

Captain Ford completed his inspection of the other rooms as well as the latrine, before returning to my room. I was beginning to think, an Article 15 would be my reward for painting the room without authorization from someone up the chain of command.

As soon as the inspection team started down the stairs, I darted into my room. Above the head of my bunk, was an Air Force flag thumb tacked to the wall. Hanging on the wall above the table were four pictures—one each of President Kennedy, Robert McNamara, Secretary of Defense, General Curtis Le May, the Air Force Chief of Staff and General Charles H. Pottenger the Base Commander. I immediately recognized these items as being from Sausage Sam's office.

Knowing I had been 'haded' caused a fever to wash across my body. As it turned out, Paul's feign condition served as the bait to get me out the barracks. The boys on the bay felt Sam's cherished military icons would complement my redecorating efforts.

The phone call I feared from Captain Ford seeking some retribution against me for painting my room without proper authorization came on Thursday around 10:00 hours. As it turned out, an Article 15 wasn't my reward, but rather a three-day pass with unrestricted travel miles.

Since the pass had no travel restrictions, I asked Allie if she would like to go home for the upcoming Easter holidays. Of course she did. We made plans that weekend to leave early Wednesday morning and return late Easter Sunday evening. This trip would be my opportunity to thank her parents for the leather coat.

During the trip, Allie talked almost nonstop about the farm, Indian Ridge, her home town, and her family, as if attempting to build in my mind a mental picture, which I would accept. Still I was somewhat nervous about meeting her parents and hoped they wouldn't be disappointed in this skinny Cajun.

The further we drove from the city, the more obvious the openness of the Panhandle became with wheat fields moving gracefully in the morning breeze as an ocean of green on each side of the highway. I recalled Mr. Wheeler's parallel between the fields and the Pacific and smiled as I saw the similarity for the first time. My thoughts returned to the snowstorm of New Year's Eve, when the earth lay beneath a blanket of white and wondered how dead and forsaken these open fields must have appeared under such conditions. Now that the earth was green and full of life once more, I realized nature had completed its annual cycle and the promise of a bountiful crop was showing forth.

After driving for about an hour and a half, we turned onto a farm road and traveled for a while longer before approaching a small bridge with a steel superstructure. A teenage couple, standing on the bridge looking down at the narrow stream below, turned to acknowledge my casual wave. In the rearview mirror, I watched as they tossed something into the water below.

As we continued to drive, Allie stated the farm would be recognizable by the large trees in the yard. It seemed her great-grandmother, also from the South and a lover of trees as well, had planted them when she moved to the treeless plains as a new bride to start a family. Allie knew how much I missed the trees of Louisiana, and how often I had expressed the thought that the openness of the Panhandle was something I still hadn't adjusted to.

From the top of a ridge, the trees appeared as giant monuments on the *qui vive* over an ocean of swaying wheat. Approached the driveway, I slowed down to savor the beauty of these majestic creations, which on judging by their size and gnarled condition appeared to have existed since the beginning of time.

After stopping the car a short distance from the house, I slowly stepped out and stood beside the open door, mesmerized by the beauty surrounding me. Allie slammed the car door and ran toward the house leaving me alone to bask in the unexpected beauty.

The large white two-story clapboard farmhouse was as majestic a country home as Allie had described. The front porch graced by several square wooden columns, accommodated well the extra-wide swing suspended from the ceiling by two large chains, several sturdy white rockers, and a hammock on the far end. Two equally spaced dormers with curtains in the windows, adorned the sloping metal roof over the porch.

To the left of the house was a large barn and barnyard, or corral, as they would say in Texas, but I didn't see any horses at the time. Inside the corral was a windmill slowly turning in the midmorning breeze in front, of which sat a round aluminum water trough. Outside the corral and further to the left were several grain bins, a large equipment building, under which were parked an old tractor, a combine and a very old Ford pickup. The rustling leaves of the cottonwood trees intermittently broke the quietness and serenity of the place, causing me to glance upward.

Allie escorted her mother out to greet me. Mrs. Natty, a big-framed woman of German descent, wore her hair in a bun held in place by an ample supply of hair pins. With her colorful homemade apron, simple black shoes with low heels, she appeared the quintessential farmwife, who had long before abandoned cosmetics since such a thing was incongruous with her simple lifestyle.

Stepping away from the car door, I moved forward to greet Mrs. Natty, while she finished wiping her hands on the apron.

"Mama, I would like for you to meet my friend . . . Yogi." said Allie, standing beside her mother.

Mrs. Natty's face displayed a warm friendly smile as she clinched my hand with a firm grip, causing me to feel there was nothing genteel about this woman.

"That's your real name, son?" Mrs. Natty asked with a heavy Texas accent, while still holding my hand.

"No, ma'am," I answered apologetically with a blush, while attempting to gently pull free my hand. "It's a nickname. The guys at the Base hung it on me."

"Mama, where's Daddy?" asked Allie looking around.

"Ohhhhh . . . Henry left before daylight for Dalhart, said he needed some part for Maude," answered Mrs. Natty, nervously toying with her apron.

"Daddy will never get rid of that old combine . . . will he?" countered Allie.

"Daughter, you know your Daddy," answered Mrs. Natty shaking out her apron. "He's not one to replace a piece of farm machinery so long as it has one minute's life in it." After giving me a hardy slap on the shoulder, Mrs. Natty remarked: "Well, you two fetch your bags and bring them on into the house."

Two sets of steps on the left side of the house offered different entrances into the home. The door nearest the front of the house led to a large dining room dominated by a massive antique table, a hutch, and other matching pieces. The interior walls of the dining room were made of beadboard, as was the rest of the house, I discovered later. Descending into this room was a darkly stained staircase leading to the second floor. On the wall above the hutch was a large set of horns, a reminder of the days when Longhorns were the cattle of choice of Texas ranchers.

Near the other outside steps leading to a very large kitchen, was what I had known as a child as a plantation bell mounted on a pole. To the rear of the kitchen was a veranda running the full length of the house.

Upon reaching the dining room, I placed the suitcases on the floor near the hutch as Mrs. Natty apologized for the untidy condition of the house, which wasn't noticeable to me.

"I reckon, you could sleep in the spare bedroom down here," Mrs. Natty said, pointing to a door to the right of the dining room.

"Mama, why don't you let him use Robert Earl's room?" asked Allie, looking at her mother with something of a plea in her eyes. "It has a private bath."

Mrs. Natty stood motionless for a few moments before wiping the table with her apron. Her delay made me uncomfortable.

"No," I injected. "The room down here will be all right."

"Mama," Allie pleaded, while giving me a quick glance before looking toward her mother. "It'll be all right."

Mrs. Natty was nervously adjusting a chair before the table while considering Allie's suggestion. With an expression of apprehension, Mrs. Natty looked at me and said, "Allie's right. Robert Earl's room has a private bath."

Allie glanced at me with a reassuring smile as I followed her and Mrs. Natty up the stairs. As we approached one bedroom door, Allie put her suitcase on the floor in the hallway and gestured for me to follow her mother to the adjoining room. At some point before Robert's room, I stepped on a squeaky board, which caused me to unconsciously step aside.

"Mama?" Allie asked in a demanding tone. "When will Daddy get around to fixing that board?"

"Daughter, your Daddy's been promising to do something about this floor since you and . . . Robert were kids," said Mrs. Natty, pausing at the bedroom door.

Robert's room was a typical boy's room. Several football trophies on a chest of drawers were crowded among pictures of him spanning several years of his life in football uniforms. A high school football jacket hung on a hook near the bed against the back wall adorned with several pictures of the same pretty girl. Besides a poster of an Indian chief above the bed, a school pennant bearing the same colors of the jacket was pinned with the word "Indians" in descending letters. Inside a ceramic washbasin, to the right of the door, sat a football as if awaiting the youthful hands, which once took pleasure in its existence. An old cowboy hat sat beside the washbasin.

While placing my suitcase on the bed, I noticed Mrs. Natty took up the cowboy hat and after gently holding it for a few moments, hung it on a nail to the right of an oval mirror. When Mrs. Natty turned back toward me, I quickly glanced toward Allie who opened the bedroom closet, revealing a large sexy picture of Sophia Loren on the closet door, which she and her mother pretended to ignore. With a cautious glance at her mother, Allie pushed aside what I assumed were Robert's clothes, before offering me the newly created space. Mrs. Natty announced she would fix us something to eat and quickly left the room, leaving me with the feeling that my intrusion into this locked away shrine wasn't such a good idea.

"Hope this won't keep you awake all night," Allie said with a smile, nodding at the picture.

"Perhaps it would be best if I moved downstairs," I said with a shrug.

"No! You stay here," Allie answered, offering me a couple of coat hangers. "Mama will be okay. It's just this is the first time any outsider has come into this room since Robert's death."

"Is this a picture of Robert?" I asked, walking over to a picture on the chest.

"Yeah," Allie answered with a downward glance. "It was taken a few months before he died."

"Hope you're not offended, but he looks like James," I answered gaily, while taking hold of the picture for a better look. "He's a little stouter than James, but they look alike."

"I think so too," Allie said soberly, while coming around the bed. "The first time the four of you came to the House . . . when I . . . saw James, a strange feeling came over me. It was as if I was seeing Robert." Looking at my suitcase, Allie asked, "Want me to unpack your things?"

"No. I'll do that." I answered, returning the picture to its enshrined position. "I need to freshen up too."

"When you're ready . . . come to my room, and we'll go downstairs for something to eat." Allie quickly kissed me on the cheek and left.

The squeaky board in the hallway sounded shortly after Allie left Robert's room. Her muffled anathema directed at the troublesome board caused me to smile. After unpacking, I walked to Allie's room by way of the same squeaky board. Her bedroom was quite different from Robert's and reflected everything a girl's room should be. Pink was everywhere. The most beautiful piece of furniture in the room was the canopy bed with very large posts. The extra thick mattress and many decorative pillows caused me to think of Rose's swan bed among other things.

On a bookcase against one wall were several trophies, which caught my attention because of the horse and rider on top. Allie's face went blank when I walked over to the bookcase and picked up one trophy for a closer look. Engraved on the trophy was, "Awarded to Allie Sailhamer—1st Place Winner—Barrel Racing Competition—1957."

"What's this?" I asked, holding up the trophy. "I thought you told me you didn't know much about riding horses! You let me make a fool of myself that day in Palo Duro Canyon. I was supposed to be giving you riding instructions!"

"Yogi, you seemed to be enjoying yourself so much, I hated to burst your bubble." Hoping to appease my wounded pride, Allie gave me a hug. "Come on; let's go, get something to eat. Later, I'll show *You* how to ride."

"Little girl, you need your tail feathers plucked for lying to me," I said taking Allie into my arms. With this, I thought of Pete and Rosella still in the car. As we held each other, Mrs. Natty entered the room and cleared her throat.

"I have some sandwiches for you in the kitchen," she said, waiting at the open door as if inviting us to lead the way. I got the feeling she wasn't going to leave us alone in Allie's bedroom, but wasn't going to say anything against our being together so soon after my arrival.

After lunch, I retrieved the bird cage from the car and with Mrs. Natty's permission hung it on the veranda, where it remained for the duration of our stay.

Allie and I both changed into older clothes before walking to the barn where I became acquainted with Buster, a buckskin gelding and Midnight, a mare of about three years. Allie's whimsical half-smile, while suggesting I ride Buster made me suspicious, recalling how Gregory Peck in 'The Big Country' felt, when the ranch hands tried to get him on Old Thunder. I did my best not to let my apprehension show.

Allie mounted Midnight in the corral, while I walked Buster to the gate to open it. Once the gate swung open, Allie spurred Midnight in the flanks and started down the dirt road at a full gallop. Because of Buster's insistence on going in circles while I attempted to mount him, I finally managed to grab the saddle horn and swung up into the saddle.

By the time we reached the end of the dirt road near a small creek, the two horses were neck to neck, and we were staring at each other like two jockeys, both determined to cross the finish line first. We managed to bring the horses to a sliding stop within a safe distance of the creek, lined by a number of small willow trees. Allie quickly jumped down from Midnight, joyfully claiming to have won the race. Jokingly, I denied her claim and accused her of cheating. After tying the horses to a branch, Allie took my hand.

"Let's go for a walk. I want to show you something," Allie said pulling me forward.

We followed the creek for a short distance before coming upon what appeared to be a mound of dirt with several poles protruding from it. On the side opposite of our approach, the mound took on the appearance of what was once a house. What appeared to be a wall made of dirt, door frame, and one window stood as if challenging the destructive nature of time.

"What is it?" I asked looking at the opening from a distance.

"This was a soddie," Allie answered, as she approached the opening.

"What's a soddie?" I asked, moving nearer.

"When the white settlers first came to the plains, they made their homes of rectangular sods of grass since there weren't any trees." Pointing to the poles protruding from the mound, Allie added, "These poles were used to support the roof. Daddy said some people used the boards from their covered wagons when poles weren't available."

"Who lived here?"

"My great-great grandparents," Allie answered, smiling at my reluctance to approach the soddie. "Come on, Yogi. Look inside."

"Why did they build it here?"

"This creek was one of the few sources of water in the area," replied Allie. "This was long before the introduction of windmills to the Panhandle.

"Daddy said his grandfather told him, they used to divert the water to one side so they could dig large pits in the creek bed, which served as reservoirs in preparation for the dry seasons. After the pits were completed, the water was routed back to fill them."

As I stood looking at what had once been someone's home, I tried imagining how difficult life must have been for the early settlers of this part of the Panhandle. Having to contend with hostile Indians, outlaws, the summer heat and winter cold in addition to trying to extract a living from the land, must have taken a toll on even the hardest of individuals.

While walking the horses back toward the barn, Allie appeared anxious and talked incessantly about her family and the "old days" as if there was some purpose in my need to know or understanding her family's history. Her great-great grandfather, a Russian Mennonite immigrant, had come down from Kansas as a seventeen-year-old cowboy, with the great Charles Goodnight and started the farm with forty acres and one horse. The succeeding generations continued purchasing more land until it reached its present size of three thousand acres.

In time, Allie's confabulation turned to her brother, of whom she had never spoken except in connection with the leather jacket.

"The only horse Robert ever rode was a pinto he named Comanche," Allie added with a rueful smile. "Each year on the last day of cutting, he would saddle Comanche and ride through the open field waving his old cowboy hat high above his head and yelling like a wild Indian. Mama use to say, "Robert was the only remaining Comanche in the Panhandle.""

After recounting a story about Robert escorting her to a sixth grade Valentine dance, Allie turned away from me and gazed off into the field as if searching beyond the limits of the wheat fields. After some time, she wiped her eyes before turning to face me.

I reached for her hand.

"I miss him, Yogi," Allie stated while squeezing my hand.

Without speaking further, we mounted the horses and rode toward the barn. This time, there was no race.

Standing beside the combine when we reached the barn, was a tall man whose large stomach, hanging over his belt, was causing an obvious strain to the lower snaps of his western-style shirt. As we rode past, he lifted his broad cowboy hat and wiped the sweat band with a large handkerchief before returning it to his head. His penetrating blue eyes seemed focused on the greenhorn astride his horse, in spite of Allie's cheerful greeting to her father.

Meeting a girl's father for the first time is one of the most difficult moments a young boy has to face in life. You get the feeling he's watching your every move, sizing you up to see if you're good enough for his daughter. Are you tall enough? Or maybe you're too skinny, (which I was), or maybe you suffer from some physical defect, like your ears are too big, or your nose too long. You feel like an amoeba under a microscope, and worth about as much.

Once the horses were unsaddled and fed, the moment of truth arrived. Allie took my hand and practically dragged me toward her father for an introduction.

Mr. Henry Sailhamer's thick black hair exhibited small streaks of gray, as he habitually brushed it straight back each time his cowboy hat came off. His cowboy boots, worn and covered with dirt, seemed to have collapsed at the ankles as if his 260-plus pounds had settled on them. His raspy voice matched well his large scared hands, the result of many years of mechanical work on farm machinery.

In the world of the Zebra, a young male looking for a mate has to prove his worth by fighting the father of his chosen mare before claiming his reward. While shaking hands with Mr. Henry, his rough leathery hand, made me glad that I wasn't a young Zebra.

During supper that evening, Allie and I sat next to each other. While she held my hand under the table, I nervously thanked her parents for the Christmas gift and told them how much I appreciated the sacrifice they made in relinquishing such a treasured memento. To break the tension, Allie jokingly said, I could further show my appreciation by volunteering to help clean the kitchen. During KP duty, I tried stealing an occasional kiss as my reward for being so domesticated. With everything spotless, to the point of pleasing the most demanding Mess Sergeant, Allie suggested we take a walk. Before leaving the house, we informed her parents of our intentions, and Mrs. Natty informed me, she had laid out for me a pair of pajamas. The expression on my face brought a smile to Allie's face.

As we walked hand in hand down the same dirt road, which we had traveled by horseback earlier that afternoon, a full moon hung low over the rolling hill in the distance. On the distant hills, the lights from several farmhouses stood out as beacons of refuge across a sea of shimmering wheat. There was a unique tranquility about the evening, which made me glad I had taken the time to make this journey.

We had walked for some distance before stopping to look back toward the farmhouse, which seemed miles away. Standing in the dirt road, we embraced each other tightly, which was followed by the long passionate kiss I desired all day. A strange melancholy mood seemed to overtake Allie as she pushed away from my embrace and suggested that *We start back because her mother would be waiting up.* After giving me a slight kiss on the cheek, Allie thanked me for taking the time to visit the farm.

With my right arm around her neck and her left arm around my waist, we started walking toward the house, pretending to lean on each other. A little further down the road, we started playing this silly game where one person steps in front of his partner and then that person steps over that person's leg. We almost tripped several times along the way, and with each mishap, we stopped to reward each other with a gentle kiss.

Mrs. Natty was in the kitchen, as Allie had suspected, when we came through the screen door and entered the dining room. We both said good night to her before going upstairs.

After bathing in the old type bathtub, with claw feet, I slipped on the bottom part of the pajamas over my boxer shorts. While looking at myself in the mirror above the washstand, I wondered what my three friends back at the Base would think if they could see me in such a "get-up." Totally disgusted with the image before me, I removed Robert's old cowboy hat from the nail and placed it on the back of my head in a cocky sort of way.

The sound of the squeaky board in the hallway brought a smile to my face. I waited for the expected knock on the bedroom door.

"Howdy, Ma'am," I said with a Texas drawl, after pulling the door open.

Before me . . . stood Allie in her silk pajamas. There was something juvenile about her appearance, yet sexy in an innocent kind of way. Mrs. Natty's call from down the hall for Allie to return to her bedroom brought to a quick halt, my attempt to take her into my arms.

"In a minute . . . Mama!" Allie called back. With emphasis, she whispered, "The woman has ears like a bat."

"Now, I know why your Daddy never fixed this floor," I answered, pulling Allie close against my body.

After Allie's mother called to her once more, we kissed and said good night. Allie was almost to her room when I purposely stepped on the squeaky board to antagonize her mother.

I had trouble going to sleep, perhaps because of the different surrounds and being in a different bed. I lay there looking around the room thinking of Allie's brother and how his family had preserved his room, not wanting to let go of his memory. Perhaps losing a child is one of the most difficult things a parent has to overcome in life, and no one can judge someone's reactions to such a tragedy, until they have lived through such an unfortunate event.

Entangled, strangled, and agitated by the pajamas, I finally got up and went to the bathroom, where I sat on the back rim of the bathtub with my feet propped on the outer rim. From my perch, I tapped on the wall separating the bathroom from Allie's bedroom.

After tapping several more times, she answered from the other room.

"Yogi, is that you?"

"Yes," I answered. "I can't sleep." There was a desperate plea in my voice.

"I can't do anything about that," she replied in a whisper, so as not to attract the attention of her mother.

"Do you realize, today is Wednesday?" I asked putting my head against the wall.

"Yogi, please don't mention . . . ?" Allie's voice seemed weak.

"I miss you, Allie," I answered in a low lonely voice, putting my right hand against the wall hoping Allie would do the same.

"I miss you too, Yogi," Allie replied in an equally low tone.

At this point, I lost my balance and slid into the bathtub. Trying to brace myself, I knocked over a soap dish and a bottle of shampoo.

"Yogi, what happened?" Allie called out, as I cursed to myself.

"I'm okay," I said feeling foolish, lying on my back in the deep tub. "I fell in the damn tub."

We said good night once more, and I made my way back to the bed where I remained awake for some time, staring at Sophia Loren's picture and desiring Allie's company. After a while, I reached under the sheet, removed the pajamas bottoms, and threw them to the floor.

Chapter 16

From the grips of a deep sleep, my body slowly awakened to the sensation of a warm mellifluous kiss. Desiring to capture more fully the pleasures invoked by the aroused desires, I stirred slightly on the pillow, resisting the revivifying efforts of my olfactory nerves and taste buds to the presence of coffee. Slowly my eyes came open. Allie's beautiful face, only inches from mine, completed my waking to my first full day on the farm.

"Good morning, sleepy head," Allie whispered with a smile. "Are you ready for some coffee?"

While giving my entire body a good stretching, I smiled at Allie who was already dressed in jeans and boots. "I dreamed I already had some," I answered, folding my arms behind my head. Another quick kiss prompted me to say, "For the rest of my life, I want my first cup of coffee delivered this way each morning."

"I see you didn't sleep in the pajamas, after all," Allie said, picking them from the floor, before walking to the chest of drawers to put them away.

With an arch smile, Allie turned toward the bed and threatened to pull the covers off me if I didn't get up. Before leaving the room she informed me, her father needed my help with some farm chores. After leaving the room, the squeaky board declared her location in the hallway.

I finished the cup of coffee before getting dressed and going downstairs to a Texas-size breakfast. Allie and I sat at opposite ends of the kitchen table, secretly smiling at each other, while Mrs. Natty attempted to push upon me more hash browns, hard fried eggs, and homemade biscuits, as if attempting to correct my skinny condition in one weekend.

After breakfast, Allie and I walked to the corral where her father was filling, from the water trough, a tank on a flat bed trailer coupled behind a 1957 Farmall, Model 450. My familiarity with this tractor came as a result of a job with a farmer back home during the summer months of my high school years. Allie greeted her father with a chipper voice.

"Morning," replied Mr. Henry without looking up. "You slept okay?"

"Yes, sir," I answered assuming he was speaking to me.

"What are you doing?" Allie asked her father, while stepping up onto the trailer.

"Ah, the old windmill in the pasture done quit again," answered Mr. Henry, "and the water trough is getting low."

"Mind if I take a look at it?" My offer drew a peculiar stare from Mr. Henry.

Raising the hose from the water tank to check the level, Mr. Henry asked, "Do you know anything about windmills?"

"A little," I replied trying not to be pushy. "We had one on the sugarcane plantation where I grew up."

"That old windmill is in no condition for someone to climb," replied Mr. Henry.

"Come on, Yogi. Let's go take a look," Allie said, stepping down from the trailer and extending her hand out to me. "We're gonna take the old Ford, Daddy," yelled Allie to her father, as our pace toward the corral gate quickened.

Mr. Henry didn't answer. About midways between the corral and creek along the dusty road, we had traveled the previous day on horseback, the road veered to the right toward a large barn. Besides the barn stood a four-legged wood tower adorned with a four-foot windmill. Beyond the wheat field, the terrain appeared unimproved, almost barren, through which a small herd of cattle wandered for substance.

A quick inspection of the tower, after parking the truck near the water trough, revealed the uprights were solid, but the rungs leading to the top of the tower, as well as the support braces needed replacing. I suggested to Allie that we ride back to the other barn for the lumber and tools to accomplish the job.

The necessary hand tools, a long extension ladder, nails, 2 x 4s, and a few boards were quickly loaded into the old Ford before we returned to the windmill. While, I nailed in place the new rungs leading to the platform on top, Allie cut the 2 x 4s with a handsaw before I pulled them up with a rope. Her ability to use a handsaw surprised me.

Some two hours later, when Mr. Henry arrived with the water tank, his face telegraphed his suspicions of my sanity, as he studied the new, much larger, platform under construction. His upward glances toward me and hand gestures to Allie, however didn't deter me from my vision of what a windmill platform could be used for. Once completed, a sense of pride caused me to stand, with both fits raised above my head; I shouted forth, proclaiming my moment of victory, as the surrounding countryside opened before me with a hypnotic pull. From my lofty perch, I felt like a young lion challenging the King of pride, just to let him know I had arrived. Staring down at Mr. Henry, I felt he could sense my challenge.

From the ground, his boisterous instructions ended my short-lived, jubilant celebration. He ordered me to move the tail vane parallel to the wheel and turn the whole thing away from the breeze. In doing so, I noticed the spring on the vane was hanging free, for one of the hooks had rusted away. Replacing this spring would be a snap.

With the windmill securely tied in place, my next assigned task from Mr. Henry was the removal of the gearbox "helmet." A broken pitman arm was the obvious reason the mill wasn't pumping. Removing the broken arm amounted to the simple task of extracting two cotter pins. In the process of removing the arm, the badly worn gears driving this flat bar, caused me to believe that they contributed to the arm's demise.

After replacing the helmet, I climbed down the tower with the defective arm and spring. Mr. Henry's gratitude for the job I had done was less than enthusiastic. As I started gathering up the unused lumber and tools, he directed a question to Allie.

"Think you two could throw down some hay for the cows?"

"Sure," I answered. "How many bales will we need?"

"Fifteen should be enough," answered Mr. Henry while avoiding eye contact with me.

Allie backed the pickup truck into the hay barn after I pushed opened the big doors. The mountain of rectangular bales, giving off the refreshing smell of cured hay caused me to climb to the top, before jumping down into a pile of broken bales. Allie laughed at my childish pleasure, but cautioned her father wouldn't appreciate my destruction of more bales. After throwing the required bales into the truck, Allie asks me to follow her up a ladder to a small loft.

Upon reaching the loft, Allie pushed open two small doors, before which I sat looking over the small herd of cattle in the distant pasture. Glancing back at me with a smile, Allie walked to a corner where she pulled from among the rafters something wrapped in a burlap sack. Sitting cross-legged beside me, the familiar black book that Allie pulled from the sack brought a chagrined smile to my face.

Pretending to be ignorant, I asked, "What is it?"

Allie laughed as she wiped the dust from the cover.

"It's an Illustrated Encyclopedia on Sex. Robert ordered it when he was in the tenth grade. He hid it out here so Mama and Daddy wouldn't find it." Allie smiled as she ran her hand over the cover of the book. "I noticed he was riding Comanche out this way real often, so one day I followed him." Once more she paused, before continuing. "When he caught me spying on him, he threatened to roll my face in a pile of cow manure, if ever I told Mama about this book."

My broadening smile caused Allie to look at me with a quizzical expression.

"I ordered this same book when I was in high school," I exclaimed with a chuckle. "I thought it would be a 'how-to' book. Hell, you have to be a medical student to understand this thing."

Allie's face appeared to drop. "Did any of the girls in Louisiana appreciate your newly acquired knowledge?" she asked in a perturbed tone.

"One did." I answered with something of a boastful smile.

"You guys! You're always boasting about your conquests," Allie snapped with a piqued tone, before slamming the book closed.

"Hey! You asked," I replied trying to make light of the situation.

Allie attempted to stand with the intention of returning the book to its secret hiding place. From behind, I grabbed her ankle pulling her back down into the loose hay.

"I believe you're jealous," I said with a slight laughter while wrestling her down for a kiss.

"I am not jealous!" Allie asserted, through clinched teeth. "My daddy is still outside, Yogi."

The slamming of a truck door coupled with Mr. Henry's voice calling for Allie caused her to stand and brush the hay from her clothes and hair.

"Allie . . . you two in here?" called her father.

"Yeah, Daddy," yelled out Allie as she continued brushing the hay from her hair. "We'll be right down!"

"Well, hurry on. Need to feed those cows, before you two go into town for them windmill parts."

Before climbing down the ladder, I watched Allie wrap the book in the sack before returning it to its hiding place among the rafters.

On our way into Indian Ridge, the presence of another young couple standing near the edge of the steel bridge, looking down into the small stream, piqued my curiosity. While watching them in the side view mirror of the old Ford, my perfunctory inquiry into this "lover's gathering place" failed to bring a response from Allie.

The large brick building housing Clifford's Feed and Hardware Store on the edge of town appeared as old and tired as the other buildings on the Main Street of Indian Ridge. Backed to the loading dock, across the railroad tracks running to the side of the store were two pickup trucks, equally as old as Mr. Henry's truck. A wide set of steps, made of large flat stones led to the wooden porch, which ran the full length of the building cluttered with wheelbarrows, tires, and other necessary items for farm and ranch. On each side of the doors, long wooden benches with slick bottoms, bore scars left by numerous pocket knives.

A cowbell mounted on a flat, flexible metal band over the screen door startled me as I pushed it open for Allie. For a moment, I studied the contraption, while several men dressed in bib coveralls glanced in my direction. A mixture of odors ranging from the sweet smell of feed to the recognizable smell of leather permeated the store.

A tall, slender, elderly man wearing a blue denim apron came from behind the counter, as we entered. He and Allie hugged each other, while exchanging greetings laced with slow Texas drawls.

"Mr. Clifford, this is my friend from Amarillo," averred Allie as she moved next to me. "His name is Yogi."

"You mean like that cartoon bear?" Mr. Clifford asked mildly with a friendly smile as he extended his hand.

"Either him or Yogi Berra," I answered in an abashed voice.

"Now, that isn't a Texas accent," declared Mr. Clifford, pointing his finger at my chest. "That's south Louisiana Cajun!" Mr. Clifford patted me on the shoulder and grinned before turning to walk back to the counter. "Spent some time down there . . . in New Orleans during the war," he added while looking over his shoulder at me. "I swear . . . believe, those folks could cook an armadillo and make it taste good."

"Thanks to Colonel Ward and the New Orleans Grays who fought with Sam Houston at San Jacinto . . . the battle didn't last but eighteen minutes." Mr. Clifford laughed as he walked around the counter. "Some old timers say *dem Cajuns* wanted to get the war over with, so they could melt down the Two Sisters for a gumbo pot."

"Daddy's something of a history buff," injected a much younger man standing beside Mr. Clifford. "What can we get for you today, Allie?" he asked as he doffed his cowboy hat.

"We need some parts for Daddy's old windmill," responded Allie.

"When's Henry gonna replace those old mills with a couple of new electric pumps?" asked Mr. Clifford.

"It won't happen in his lifetime," countered Allie while placing the needed pieces on the counter.

Mr. Clifford studied the parts for a minute before looking at his son. As the younger man walked away, I wandered over to look at several saddles on display.

"You in the market for a saddle, son?" asked Mr. Clifford as he joined me.

"No, sir," I replied dully, studying the price tag. "Two thousand dollars is a bit more money than a G.I. like me can afford."

"Sooo, you're stationed out at the Air Base?" asked Mr. Clifford, while wiping the dust from one of the saddles with his big red handkerchief.

"Yes, sir," I replied while bending down for a closer look at the Texas star on the horn of one saddle.

"That's pure Mexican silver," asserted Mr. Clifford as if he was making a sales pitch.

"I'm sorry, Allie," Mr. Clifford's son said, as he returned to the counter, "we don't have any of these in stock. We could have them here by bus . . . first thing, Saturday morning."

"That's fine . . . Jimmy. We'll be back," answered Allie.

Mr. Henry's day as a farmer began long before sunrise. His expectation of the same from everyone sleeping under his roof, denied me the early morning wake-up call I desired. As usual, Mrs. Natty had a large breakfast sitting on the table as I walked into the kitchen and greeted three stoic faces. Mr. Henry said grace as soon as my bottom hit the chair.

With breakfast barely settled in my stomach, Mr. Henry and I went to the barn and loaded about fifty steel fence posts on the same trailer used the previous day to haul the water tank. Along with the posts, we brought a post driver, one role of "bob wahr" (as Mr. Henry called it), and a wire puller. I knew right off, it would be a long hard day, unlike any I had seen since joining the Air Force. My trip to the farm was turning into a working vacation. By noon, my hands were cut and bleeding, in spite of my heavy work gloves. My arms and shoulders ached with each downward thrust of the post driver. Mr. Henry was finally getting an opportunity to "grind me up to see what I was made of." I was determined not to cry, Uncle, even if he killed me.

Following KP that night, I indulged myself in a long, soaking bath. This was followed by an alcohol rubdown, administrated by the gentle hands of a caring student nurse, who understood my plight, even though she laughed at me for not being able to keep up with an old man, more than twice my age. From all this, I came to the conclusion, Mr. Henry had found a way to end the "squeaking board business" in the hallway, since my condition bespoke the unnecessary need for Allie to visit my room for a good-night kiss.

My Saturday morning began with a teasing kiss before sunrise, but once again I had to go downstairs for the coffee. My late arrival to the breakfast table produced a grunt from Mr. Henry. After greeting Allie's parents with an apologetic *good morning,* I sat beside Allie and reached for her hand under the table while Mr. Henry said grace. During breakfast, Allie's father announced he would be visiting a Mr. Pee Wee Peterson, the man who usually helped him each year during wheat cutting season.

After breakfast, Allie and I borrowed the old pickup, which I was developing a fondness for, to drive into town. When we arrived at Clifford's FeedStore, several men were sitting on the porch, which Allie said was *a favorite roost for some of the local roosters* on Saturday morning. As Allie lead the way up the steps, the roosters stood and in true Texas style touched the rims of their cowboy hats in a gesture of politeness. I quietly acknowledged their presence by saying good morning. A low growling sound mimicking a cat caused me to hesitate before opening the screen door for Allie. The cowbell above the door once more took me by surprise.

Inside the store, besides Mr. Clifford and Jimmy, was another man. He greeted Allie with a very warm smile as he removed his cowboy hat.

His face and mine turned to the cowbell above the door as the entourage from the porch entered.

Allie greeted the stranger with a hug and then turned to introduce me to him.

"Yogi, this is Earl McCurley. Earl, this is my friend Yogi, from Amarillo."

Earl was a short, stocky man, about five feet and eight inches, with light red hair that appeared freshly cut. The smell of talc was still fresh on his body. He had a nice kempt military style mustache, barely noticeable because of its light red color. His arms and face were brown from the sun, while his white forehead indicated the straw cowboy hat was a part of his daily attire. While Earl and I shook hands, I tried remembering why his name sounded familiar. After a moment or two, I remembered Allie saying he had been her boyfriend when they were in the sixth grade.

"What kind of work you're into, Mr. Yogi?" asked Earl returning the hat to his head.

"The Air Force," I replied succinctly, while taking notice of the sneering whispers directed toward Allie by two *roosters* from the porch.

"Hey . . . Allie! Aren't we good enough to be introduced to your friend," called out one of the men.

"Bubba Lee, I wouldn't introduce a dog to you," answered, Allie turning momentarily from Jimmy and the windmill parts on the counter.

"Hey . . . Bubba! Looks little Miss hot stuff done got uppity since she moved to the big city," remarked one of Bubba's friends.

"John Roy, why don't you and Bubba Lee go find something to do, besides hanging around this place, aggravating people." The flush appearance on Earl's face highlighted the bridge of freckles across his nose and cheeks.

"Hey, flyboy, I guess you think you some kind of hot stuff, too?" Bubba asked as he moved closer to me. "You know what I think?"

"I don't really care what you think." I answered back with a smirk.

"I think you got the cock and Allie's got the pit," Bubba countered with a self-satisfying grin as he moved his face closer to mine.

John Roy and Bubba Lee's other toadies jeered and offered up catcalls, as Bubba looked around for their continued support. Stepping back, I looked down at Bubba's shoes. A warm feeling crossed my back and neck as I turned in a lolling sort of way and walked away.

"You have any sledge hammers, Mr. Clifford?" I asked amid Bubba's clucking sounds.

"Yeah, look in that far right corner back there," Mr. Clifford answered, with a disappointed look on his face.

To the rear of the store among the axes, picks, cans of chains, and other items, I selected the heaviest sledge hammer in the group. Gripping the handle by the end, I started back toward the counter. Bubba stepped into the aisle before me.

A loud cry of anguish echoed throughout the feedstore as the sledge hammer came crashing down on Bubba's left tennis shoe. While he reached for his paining foot, my pummeling fist to the side of his face drove him to the floor. Earl hastily placed his cowboy hat on one of the saddles and stepped before John Roy, causing him to reconsider his intended intervention, when I stepped on Bubba's hand gripping his throbbing foot.

Leaning over Bubba, who grimaced in pain, I called Allie to come nearer, since Bubba had something to say. At first, she refused and pleaded for me to let him up. Angrily, I yelled for her to come forward. Reluctantly, she moved closer.

"Now . . . you worthless capon . . . tell Allie, you're sorry and that you have a filthy, dirty mouth," I demanded while applying more pressure to Bubba's hand.

"I won't do it!" Bubba said with a frown on his face, while still holding his foot.

In a threatening manner, I raised the sledge hammer above his foot.

"I'll break it, son-of-a-bitch, if you don't," I yelled looking down at him. My face was starting to turn as red as Earl's had been earlier.

"All right! All right!" pleaded Bubba gritting his teeth.

"All right, what?" I shouted.

"I'm sorry, Miss. Allie . . . and I have a filthy, dirty mouth," muttered Bubba.

As one last insult, I mashed Bubba's ear with my boot before slinging the sledge hammer down the aisle to the rear of the store, where it crashed into some shovels and rakes, knocking them over.

Allie and I stepped over Bubba and walked out the store. For several moments, we sat in the truck as my anger subsided. When Bubba limped out onto the porch with John Roy and the other roosters, Allie opened the glove box and took out a pistol. Not knowing what else to do, I stepped on the accelerator as Allie fired two shots into the air. Gravel and dust flew forward as the old Ford shot through the parking lot backward. When I turned onto the Main Street and started out of town, the image of Allie holding the pistol caused me to chuckle even though she maintained a somber face. After several minutes, Allie glanced toward me and smiled. At that point, I suggested that she return the pistol to the glove box. Before doing so, Allie fired another shot out the window, which caused our laughter to turn into a rapturous guffaw and yells as we blazed a trail out of town.

Since Mr. Henry had not returned from Mr. Peterson's home, Allie found the booklet for the windmill in the barn where her father stored some of the manuals for the other farm equipment. Even with the instruction book replacing the pitman arm, turned out to be more difficult than I first thought. After adjusting the mechanism for a short stroke and the new spring for the tail vane in place, the mill turned into the wind and began pumping. It took a minute or two before water started running into the trough below. On the ground, Allie expressed her approval by jumping and clapping her hands, while I did a jig on the platform.

With the wheel spinning to a clanking rhythm and a strong breeze blowing in my face, the ocean of green wheat in the distance magically transported me to the crow's nest of an ancient sailing ship. For a moment I became a mariner, perhaps Ishmael, himself, on the ill-fated Pequot. An unsuspecting white cow in the distant pasture became a part of my fantasy world, causing me to call down to Allie.

"There she blows, Mr. Starbuck! That great white devil . . . Moby Dick!"

The wind shifted. The tail vane swung around almost hitting me in the head.

"Yogi!" Allie called out. "Come down from there before you get hurt."

Later that afternoon, Allie and I went horseback riding again. This time, we followed the creek, which bordered her father's property and rode toward the iron bridge. Allie refused to ride all the way to the bridge.

Easter morning, I received a coffee-flavored kiss thirty minutes later than the previous mornings. While I sat in the bed, finishing off the cup, Allie, still dressed in her pajamas, picked from the floor the pajama bottoms I had removed during the night. Before leaving the room, she gave me a quick kiss and patted my covered legs while encouraging me, *"to get a move on, because her daddy was already dressed and ready to go."*

Thinking this would be the last such pleasure in my life for a while, I decided to finish the coffee in bed and make Mr. Henry wait. After placing the cup on the table near the bed, I slowly swaggered to the bathroom intending to shave. The large bath tub offered one last luxury unavailable on the Base, so I decided to indulge myself. With the bath over, I stood before the lavatory with a face covered with shaving cream, when I heard the bedroom door open.

"Are you decent?" Allie asked standing away from the open bathroom door, where we couldn't see each other.

"Yes." I said with something of a Cheshire cat grin, hidden behind a face covered with shaving cream.

Allie cautiously peeped around the open door. For a moment, she stood staring at me.

"Where's your GI boxers?" she asked with a jovial face, as she held one hand to her mouth.

Backing away from the lavatory with my hands spread out, I answered, "I left them at the Base where they belong. This is Sears' very best white briefs . . . three pairs for $2.19."

Allie ambled into the bathroom in a coquettish fashion in her Easter outfit and moved between me and the lavatory. I was starting to feel very uneasy thinking her 'bat-eared mother' might show up at any minute. After raking the shaving cream from around my mouth with her finger, Allie gave me a very teasing kiss, which caused a feverish sensation to course down my body.

"You had better get out of here before your mother shows up," I protested after pushing her away. I knew someday, I would regret not taking advantage of this moment.

In a more teasing move, Allie stepped behind me and began to rub my stomach with one hand, while holding me around the chest with the other arm. A wave of feverish excitement came over me as I stood frozen, trying to resist the natural impulses of my body.

"Come on, Allie!" I pleaded succinctly.

Furthering my torment, she bit me on the back of the shoulder, which brought forth a sharp "ouch" and a raised hand to the afflicted spot. I spun around and took her into my arms with the intent of rubbing the shaving cream on her face. Unaware that she still had one trick up the sleeve of her Easter outfit, she reached into the lavatory with one hand and then slapped me on the butt with her wet hand before dashing out the bathroom.

Thinking she had left the bedroom I started to shave the left side of my face. A snickering sound caused me to pause and glance toward the door.

"You have the skinniest butt I've ever seen," Allie replied with a giggle, before withdrawing her face from the doorway. The squeaky board in the hallway assured me that the early morning temptation had departed.

Some twenty minutes later as I started down the stairs, Mr. Henry blurted out in a gruff voice for *Allie, to go put some fire to that boy.*

The chastising sibilant hissing of Mrs. Natty directed at Mr. Henry caused him to express his agitation by picking up the felt cowboy hat on the table to his left and tossing it slightly forward.

Sitting at the head of the table with his back toward the stairs, Mr. Henry's brown western suit appeared tight in the shoulders, as he turned slightly to the left to greet me. His white shirt, stiff from an ample amount of starch, irritated his neck causing him to seek some relief by occasionally running his finger in the collar. A large bolo tie tightly pulled to his collar caused me to think of James.

Allie stood and pushed her chair from the table, as I walked toward her in a new Dacron uniform, I had tailored to fit a little closer than Air Force regulations permit. This was the first time Allie had seen me in uniform.

"You're very handsome, Yogi," Allie said as we walked toward each other and stood to the right of Mr. Henry. Allie's slight kiss to my cheek seemed to please her mother, but drew a rebuke from her father about my tardiness.

"And you are very beautiful," I said returning the kiss.

Mrs. Natty stood, much to Mr. Henry's dissatisfaction.

"By gosh, you two will be the best looking couple in the church," declared Mrs. Natty as she began searching through the hutch. Mr. Henry's reminder that breakfast was getting cold fell on deaf ears.

After finding a Kodak box camera, Mrs. Natty motioned for Allie and me to stand before the hutch for a picture. Another picture taken near the window became almost more than Mr. Henry could bear.

Allie and I sat beside each other as usual, holding hands under the table waiting for her father to say grace. During a longer-than-usual delay before Mr. Henry's expected offering of thanks, Allie leaned over and kissed me once more thinking that no one would notice. Mr. Henry cleared his throat causing Allie and me to glance up at his disapproving frown.

"Yogi, would you say, grace this morning?" asked Mr. Henry as we all waited for him to start.

A rush of fear shot through my body and mind. Allie released my hand.

"Dadddddy!" Allie protested dragging out the word. "Yogi's a guest in our home. You shouldn't put him on such a spot this way."

Feeling for Allie's hand under the table, I nervously touched her knee and leg several times before her hand found mine. With a reassuring grip, I looked first at her and then at Mr. Henry.

"Yeah. Sure. I don't mind," I said, trying to sound confident, even though my mind was running amuck. I felt the old zebra was again testing me. I had survived the fence-building ordeal, and done several other farm chores to prove myself, and this Baptist boy wasn't about to cave-in to a Texas Presbyterian this late in the game.

With all heads bowed, I gave Allie's hand a gentle squeeze. The only thing resembling a prayer I could conjure from my dead brain was something a Jewish Airman named Zechariah Goldman who worked in the Missile School often repeated in the Mess Hall. After clearing my throat, I began:

"Blessed are you, O Lord our God, King of the universe, who brings forth bread from the earth . . . that we might have life."

For a moment, I got confused and then remembered a line from another prayer, which Goldman often recited, so I continued:

"Blessed are you, O Lord our God, King of the universe, who created the fruit of the vine . . . that we might enjoy that life."

Having said the part about the wine, I almost stumbled not knowing how a Presbyterian like Mr. Henry would understand such a petition made unto the Almighty. I closed with a quick "Amen." For meeting the challenge, a slight kiss became my reward.

"That's a very unusual prayer . . . even for a Baptist," averred Mr. Henry as he began a methodical chopping of his eggs with a knife and fork.

"Very unusual, but very poetic," replied Mrs. Natty. I felt she was trying to throw as much support my way as possible.

"Have you ever been to a Presbyterian Church?" asked Mr. Henry as he mixed his hash browns with the shredded eggs.

"No, sir," I replied.

"Hope, Reverend Jeffers' old Geneva gown doesn't frighten you off," added Mr. Henry as he took a bite of the yellow mixture from his plate.

"Henry," interrupted Mr. Natty, "you've been fussing about that robe for years now. Why don't you and the other Elders buy a new one for the reverend?"

"We pay him plenty enough . . ." replied Mr. Henry as he took another bite and then chewed before completing his sentence . . . "he can buy his own."

There was a momentary pause in the conversation. My body gave a slight start when Allie reached under the table and rubbed the inside of my thigh. I almost chocked, causing Mr. Henry to give us a curious stare. When Mr. Henry lowered his face toward his plate, Allie whispered very softly, almost inaudibly, *I like your new shorts.*

"Clifford called last night. Said . . . you had a bit of trouble down at his place yesterday," Mr. Henry commented looking up from his plate.

"It wasn't anything . . ." I answered.

"Just Bubba Lee and a couple of his crowing rooster friends," Allie injected, coming to my defense.

"That's a problem you Elders should address," remarked Mrs. Natty, as if she still had the preacher's robe on her mind. "A disgrace . . . a man like him singing in the choir."

"Bubba . . . singing in the choir?" I asked with a surprised look.

"The man has a beautiful voice," added Mr. Henry, turning up his coffee cup and drained it. After putting it down he added. "It's a shame it has to come through his mouth."

Other than the fact that the Preacher wore a gown, I didn't notice much difference between the Presbyterian service and the Baptist church I grew up in. Since Reverend Jeffers was more boring than the spirited Baptist preachers I was accustomed to, I found myself thumbing through the hymnal. My boredom and the turning of the pages caught the attention of Mr. Henry, whose eyes sent an unspoken message to Allie, who relayed it to me by way of her right elbow.

Following the church service, Mr. Henry drove us to the diner in town, where it appeared that half the congregation showed up for dinner.

He and Mrs. Natty had the Blue Plate special, which consisted of mashed potatoes, meatloaf, peas, and corn bread. Since mashed potatoes were a staple on the Base, I decided to have a burger and small order of fries.

Upon returning to the house, Allie and I packed our suitcases while mentally preparing ourselves for the trip back to Amarillo. After neatly folding my uniform and placing it in the suitcase, I took one last look around Robert's room, feeling as if I had come to know him better, during my brief stay in what had once been his world.

With my suitcase in hand, I slowly walked toward the door wondering if my coming to the farm had made a difference in the lives of Allie's parents. I wondered if Robert's room would once more revert to a shrine to a lost son and unfulfilled dreams.

As I started down the hall, the squeaky board in the floor brought a smile to my face, just as Allie exited her room carrying her suitcase. Without speaking, I reached for her suitcase feeling she shared my desire to remain on the farm.

Mrs. Natty carried Pete's cage, as we walked to the car to say good-bye. Mr. Henry gave me a hearty handshake and expressed his appreciation for the work I had done around the place during my visit. Mrs. Natty hugged Allie for the longest time and tried to be subtle as she whispered that she *liked this boy, with the funny name.* Allie's parents assured me their home was always open, should I want to return. Before entering the car, I took one final look at the place, trying to fill my soul with a reserve of the farm's beauty.

As we pulled onto the farm road, Allie leaned over in the seat and rested her head on my shoulder. We were both quiet, feeling we were leaving behind a newly acquired relationship with each other, and a time in our lives, we would both remember for years to come.

When approaching the bridge, which we had driven across several times before, Allie sat up and spoke for the first time.

"Yogi, pull over and stop on the shoulder near the bridge."

"What for?" I asked in an uneasy voice.

"I'll tell you," Allie replied as she opened the passenger side door and got out. I was a little slow in getting out, not seeing anything special about an old bridge.

When I joined her in front of the car, she took my hand and escorted me to one side of the bridge near the steel beams.

"You have any change?" Allie asked in a somber tone, as she looked over the railing at the narrow stream below.

Reaching into my right pocket, I pulled out two quarters. Allie took one.

"You keep the other," Allie said, running slightly ahead of me.

"I've heard of toll bridges before," I called out jokingly, not even attempting to catch Allie, "but this is a little ridiculous."

"It's not so silly," replied Allie, brushing back her hair. "There's a local legend about a cowboy named Dutch and an Indian girl named Yellow Flower. They drowned here a hundred years ago, when the first bridge washed out."

"Why were they on the bridge?" I asked looking over the side thinking Dutch wasn't a very smart cowboy.

"The legend is that one day Yellow Flower was taking a bath in the river, when these four cowboys came upon her while looking for strays."

Allie walked across the bridge and pointed to a distant spot where this ancient incident supposedly happened.

"It's said they were attempting to take advantage of her, when this young cowboy named Dutch, came riding down the river bank."

Allie had a strange gaze in her eyes, as she pointed to a sandy spot in the river bed. There was something disquieting about her mood.

"The old people around here say that Dutch shot one of the cowboys in the leg before the others backed down."

"Did he and this Indian girl fall in love?" I asked, trying to draw her attention away from the river.

"It happened right here below the bridge, Yogi," Allie said with a despondent look on her face, as she now stared down into the bushes near the river's edge closer to the bridge.

Her desultory story left me confused.

"What happened here, Allie?"

Allie failed to answer. After a moment or two, I called her name once more.

"Allie! Are you all right?" I asked trying to break her frozen gaze on a spot near the bridge. After a moment or two, I touched her on the shoulder. As if awakened from a dream, she turned and looked at me.

"What did you ask, Yogi?"

"Did Dutch and the Indian girl fall in love?" I asked repeating myself.

Without answering my question, Allie walked back across the bridge, as if the other side was the proper spot to conclude her story. "The morning following a big rain storm, the Army came to take the Indians back to the reservation . . . that's why Dutch and Yellow Flower met on the bridge. They had planned to leave Texas."

"What are the quarters for?" I asked, looking at the one in my hand.

Looking down into the narrow stream below, Allie became very serious as she balanced the quarter on the tips of her fingers.

"It's said . . . if a young couple crosses the bridge without offering a gift to Dutch and Yellow Flower . . ." Allie paused for a while, and then threw her quarter over the edge. In a very somber tone, she added without looking in my direction. "It's said their love for each other will never last."

Without saying anything, I threw my quarter over the edge. A deep melancholy seemed to settle over Allie, as she continued staring into the distance. Taking Allie by the shoulders, I slowly turned her around. As our bodies came together, Allie placed her head on my shoulder. Standing together, I could feel her heart pounding as I wondered why this tragic story held such a strange power over her.

A voice from below the bridge called out, *thank-you, mister.* Allie and I pushed back from each other with surprised looks on our faces, both believing we had heard a voice from the past.

Leaned over the bridge railing, hoping to see the legendary cowboy, there stood only a young boy looking up at me. He had a metal detector in one hand and my two quarters in the other, lifted high about his head. As Allie and I walked back toward the car holding hands, I felt the avaricious nature of a young Texas entrepreneur was more fully satisfied than the demands of the legend concerning Dutch and Yellow Flower.

Chapter 17

For weeks, memories of my trip to Indian Ridge hung in my brain, like the fragrance of jasmine preventing me from concentrating on anything Air Force related. Falling asleep each night became a struggle, as my mind replayed those rendezvous with Allie in the hallway outside Robert's room. This room also plagued my memory, as its state of preservation continued to be a mystery.

Everywhere on the base, images that previously escaped my attention suddenly became reminders of the farm. Each morning as I walked to the hangar, the windsock flying above the Base Operations Control tower, reminded me of the windmill on the farm. I couldn't help but wonder if the old "cow fan," as Mr. Henry called it, was still working. My first trip with James to the coffee bar caused another flashback. Stepping on a squeaky board in the catwalk evoked a fiendish thought of Mrs. Natty's vigilance, causing me to halt a step or two beyond the devilish point. James gave me a peculiar stare, when I smilingly walked back and stepped on it a couple of times.

For the first few weeks after our return to Amarillo, Allie stayed away from the House. Secretly, I hoped the bond that developed between us during those five days on the farm was her reason. I missed the intimacy those past Wednesday evenings brought into our lives, but didn't question her. In a way, I was pleased to see she was coming to grips with her perceived need to be there. Her visits with Dr. Tully appeared to have had a positive impact on her life.

As the weather continued to improve, our social life began to revolve around bowling, riding go-carts, and horseback riding in Palo Duro Canyon. Having seen Allie ride Midnight, I didn't bother to offer any further equestrian instructions and embarrass myself.

Mother's Day fell on Sunday, May 12 that year. I surprised Allie by proposing that we drive up to Indian Ridge for the holiday. The destination was beyond the travel restrictions set by the Air Force without authorization, but my desire to return to the farm overrode my good judgment.

Since we hadn't called Allie's parents, they were both surprised when we arrived late Friday night, catching them right before bedtime. The squeaky board in the hallway between Allie and Robert's rooms offered a welcoming sound, causing me to smile as I carried my suitcase down the hall. Nothing about Robert's room had changed since my previous visit, yet its state of preservation left me feeling it too, welcomed me back. Neatly folded on the foot of the bed, as if awaiting my arrival, were the pajamas I had tossed to the floor each night in protest during my first visit. Even though the hour was late, Mrs. Natty insisted on preparing something for us to eat. Leftover meat loaf never tasted so good.

Allie and I went horseback riding early Saturday morning to see how much the wheat had grown since our last visit. The developing heads swayed gracefully in the early morning breeze beckoning me from Buster's back for a romp through the refreshing green world surrounding me. Allie's restraining hand and a story about the 'scalping' she and Robert received as children, for stomping down two acres of mature wheat one afternoon while playing cowboys and Indians, stifled for the time being, the erotic pull the dancing wheat had on my soul.

My curiosities about the old windmill on the far side of the farm lead us to ride in that direction. To my amazement, it was still pumping, but making an awful squeaking noise, which Allie said was common among windmills. After lunch, with the windmill still on my mind and hoping not to let my special project revert to its former condition, we returned to the windmill in Mr. Henry's truck with a toolbox and a can of oil.

After climbing to the platform, I removed the "helmet" of the gearbox and filled it with some heavy gear oil. As on my previous trip, I stood on the platform surveying the surrounding countryside. The vast openness of the Panhandle no longer seemed alien, and I realized for the first time how much I had come to love it. Perhaps the radiant image standing on the ground below me, with the Texas breeze gently teasing her hair, was the fuel firing my growing love for the land.

The noise of the windmill continued to decrease as the oil worked its magic. The realization that my efforts were saving a bit of Panhandle history caused a blowhard sense of pleasure to overtake me, which translated into a little jig on the platform. My stomping apparently displeased the residents of a wasp nest under the platform, for they decided to rid themselves of the human pest. One hit me on the lower lip with the precision of a dive bomber, while two others aimed for the back of the neck. In an effort to escape the overwhelming odds, I kicked the screwdriver and oil can from the platform, before executing a cannon ball jump. A mushroom of cold water leaped from the trough, cutting my breath, as I hit bottom.

Allie's hysterical laughter stopped, as I emerged from the trough. The revengeful smile on my face revealed my intentions. I soon discovered chasing someone in wet pants and soggy cowboy boots is no easy task. Out of breath, I sat on the tailgate with a lowered head, as a water puddle formed at my feet. An occasional upward glance and a smile at Allie standing several feet away, hiding her smile with one hand, soon revealed my threat of dunking her was over. Cautiously, however, she approached me. While standing between my legs, she wiped the water from my face before kissing my paining lip. My suggestion about making love in the hay barn until my clothes dried, met with a suggestion, *I go soak in the water trough until the urge passes.*

My wet clothes and sloshing boots drew a peculiar stare from Mr. Henry when we returned to the equipment shed. I felt what credibility I had achieved during my first visit, was slowly draining down my pants legs with the dripping water, as he hesitated to accept my offer to help with whatever he was doing to the combine. A displeased look came to Allie's face with Mr. Henry's acceptance.

"How long is this going to take, Daddy?" asked Allie, with a nervous quiver in her voice.

"I don't know, Daughter," answered Mr. Henry, before climbing aboard the combine. Point toward the horses, Mr. Henry added, "You need to return the horses to the corral."

With the shifting of a few levers, the header slowly raised enough for me to roll two poles under it, as per Mr. Henry's instructions. Once the header came down on the poles, I started after Allie.

"I hope you're not going to spend all your time with Daddy." Allie's voice sounded grated as we walked the horses to the corral.

"I won't," I answered, trying to be sensitive of her mercurial mood. "But right now, he needs my help."

"What about my needs?" she retorted, while throwing a saddle blanket across the top board between the two stalls, before starting out the barn in front of me.

After following Allie to the gate, I started toward the equipment shed while she walked toward the house. Just as she went through the gate into the yard, I yelled out, "I love you, even if you're jealous!"

Without turning around, Allie yelled back, "Save that for my Daddy in the hallway tonight."

Since Mr. Henry's hands were too large to fit into some of the small openings, I did most of the work of unbolting the header from the elevator. Allie stood by, silent, but perturbed. Lying on the ground beneath the combine, trying to free several rusty bolts, soon caked my wet clothes with mud, while the penetrating oil turned my hands black and nasty. Once the header was unbolted, Mr. Henry backed away the combine.

Mr. Henry continued working on the combine for approximately two more hours, during which time, the mud on my clothes dried to a hard cake. During the afternoon, Allie made several trips from the house to see what progress we were making, at least that was her version. All the while, I knew she was PO'ed, because I was spending so little time with her.

While sitting on a bench facing each other, trying to avoid the glaring light from the welding machine, Allie reversed her tactic from pouting to trying a little feminine cajoling. With a coy smile, she placed her arms around my neck and began French kissing me in a very teasing sort of way. After a short time, she bit me on the ear and offered to reconsider my earlier suggestion about going to the hay barn.

Hoping to tease her further, I answered with a sardonic whisper, "What's the use, my clothes are dry now!"

"Did you come up here to be with me or with him?" Allie shot back, as she withdrew her arms from my neck and stood.

"Well, if you're gonna be on the warpath all afternoon, you should have some war paint," I answered with a smirk while standing and making two dark marks on each side of her face with my black dirty fingers.

An expression of shock crossed Allie's face.

"You hadn't seen a warpath, yet," Allie retaliated, while storming off toward the house.

Thinking Allie's mood a feigned trick, I started after her. After catching her, I walked backward in front of her while mocking her for being a jealous little girl. Several times she tried stepping around me, but I blocked her. Thinking I could stifle her anger, I wrapped my arms around her with the intention of lifting her off the ground. For a moment, she wiggled trying to free herself. When this didn't work, she delivered a swift kick to my shin. In a sweeping motion, I picked her up and threw her over my shoulder and started toward the house while she screamed a blue streak and pounded my backside with her fist.

"Let me down, Yogi!" Allie demanded through gritted teeth, as I came through the gate into the yard leading to the house.

"Not until you say you are sorry for pouting like a child," I said while slapping her on the butt.

"Put me down, damn you!" Allie yelled. Her kicking almost caused me to drop her.

"First, say you're sorry," I demanded, trying to hold her steady.

Allie became still for a while. When Mrs. Natty's appearance on the kitchen steps, Allie spoke through clinched teeth, "Yogi, my mother is watching."

The redness of Allie's face matched her hair when I put her down. Standing before her, in a leaning position, with a grin on my face, thinking I had accomplished something to be proud of, I placed one hand on my hip and with the other, I raised two fingers behind my head as if they were feathers.

"Now, don't you feel better since you've been removed from the warpath?" I asked with a mocking smile.

From out of nowhere, a flying fist crashed into my lower lip with the precision equal to that of the wasp. My butt hit the ground with such force, every vertebra in my spinal column cracked, and I bit down my lower lip. For a minute I sat on the ground, thinking Buster had kicked me. The combined pain between my lip and butt caused me to fall backward onto the ground, with my legs fully extended in a spread cagle position.

As my senses slowly awakened, I could feel Allie's hands rubbing my face, as if trying to revive me. I attempted to sit up, but couldn't, since she was straddling my stomach.

"I'm sorry, Yogi," Allie pleaded as she continued to rub my face and occasionally kissed me on the lips, which were beginning to throb.

Doing some feigning of my own now, I asked, "Where am I?"

My facial expression must have indicated to Mrs. Natty, that I was deriving too much pleasure from the situation.

"Allie! Get off that boy!" demanded Mrs. Natty.

"What's wrong with him?" asked Mr. Henry as he approached us with an awkward stride.

In an incisive tone, Mrs. Natty answered, "Allie hit him!"

"You mean a girl knocked him out!" inquired Mr. Henry in a tone of disgust, while pulling the welding goggles from his head. "Why, yeh hit him?" he demanded of Allie.

"Because he's spending all his time with you!" Allie replied in an indignant voice, as she looked up at her father.

With a disgusted look on his face, Mr. Henry bent over and asked, "Are you gonna lie there in the dirt all afternoon or come give me a hand?"

There I was, lying in the dirt with a bleeding lip, a jealous female straddling my body and her father staring down at me with a look, which demanded I assert my masculinity.

While propped up on my right hand I pleaded, "May I go with your Daddy? He needs my help"

Leaning over me like a wild dog over its kill, Allie placed both hands on my shoulders and stared me in the eyes. "Go on . . . see if I care! Spend all day working on that stupid old combine."

Once more, my smirk caused Mrs. Natty to demand Allie get off me.

Allie stood over me and dusted off her pants before storming off toward the house. After coming to my feet, I brushed myself off before wiping my bleeding lip with the backside of my right hand.

"Your daughter has some kind of temper," I said, looking at Mr. Henry, while touching my lip once more.

"That's the German blood in her," answered Mr. Henry. After a short pause, he glanced toward his wife and added, "Her mother's side of the family, you know."

Before Allie reached the backdoor of the house, I called out to her, fully aware of the presence of her parents. "Allliie! I still love you, even though your punch is better than mine."

Mr. Henry and Mrs. Natty smiled at the twaddle.

"Kiss my butt, Yogi," Allie called back as she went through the screen door into the house.

"Allie Sailhamer! Don't you use that kind of language in this place," called Mrs. Natty, as she fanned the air with her apron and hurriedly started for the house.

Mr. Henry and I had made it almost to the equipment shed in silence before he turned to me with a grin.

"Maybe you should have thrown her in the water trough."

A moment or two passed before we both looked at each other and laughed. *It must be that time of the month,* continued Mr. Henry, with a very serious face. For a while I felt this straight-laced Presbyterian Elder wasn't so straight-laced after all, but deep down inside—a man like all other men. In that part of the male's world, where bonding occurs, nothing will cement a relationship, regardless of the age difference, better than when they agree upon the temperamental nature of women.

After a long, soaking bath and supper, I felt the only way to redeem myself was by taking Allie to a movie in town. To make the evening an authentic Texas Saturday night, we each wore jeans, a western shirt, and boots. Before leaving, Allie asked me to wait in the dining room while she ran back upstairs. A few minutes later, she returned with a bolo tie and the old cowboy hat from the nail in Robert's room. While she placed the tie around my neck, I whispered I'd wear the ridiculous thing only if I could exchange it later for a favor. She hit me on the chest and whispered that her mother was still in the kitchen. After adjusting Robert's cowboy hat in several positions to find just the right look to please her, while Mrs. Natty watched with an approving smile, we started to town in Mr. Henry's old Ford. I was feeling like a "drug store" cowboy and fearing that my path would cross that of Bubba Lee's, where no sledge hammers would be available.

On the return trip from town later that evening, I slowed down as we approached the iron bridge and pulled over. Allie became fidgety and asked why I was stopping.

"Hey, we have to pay homage to Dutch, and what's her name," I replied opening the truck door.

"Yogi, not tonight," pleaded Allie as I reached for her hand.

"Come on, Allie," I begged, sliding off the seat. "Look . . . it's a beautiful night. Full . . . moon 'n all."

"Yogi, I don't like it out here at night," Allie said locking her fingers together and placing her hands between her knees.

"Please," I begged once more from outside the truck. Feeling I had a trump card in my hand, I pushed the cowboy hat back on my head and said with a smile, "You owe me this favor for busting my lip."

After some hesitation, Allie reached out her left hand and slid across the seat. As we made our way to the center of the bridge, I was almost running while pulling her along. Upon reaching the appropriate spot, I pulled some change from my pocket and offered it to Allie. She selected a quarter. I selected a nickel before returning the rest to my pocket.

"Is it necessary to make a wish in doing this?" I asked cheerfully, looking over the railing.

"This isn't a wishing well," Allie answered while standing behind me, away from the railing.

"I'm gonna make a wish anyway," I said sarcastically, as I tossed the nickel into the stream below. After pausing at the railing to watch my coin hit the water, I turned to Allie. "Come on . . . throw yours."

With some reluctance, Allie approached the railing and threw her coin without watching where it landed. As she stepped away from the railing, I wondered if the young boy who had found my previous two coins would be back to discover these.

While taking Allie's hand, I directing her attention to the golden moon resting on a distant hill beyond the bend in the stream. As I stood there looking down at the stream, the illumination from the moon, dancing on the ripples appeared as thousands of lights below the surface. There was a magic in the night, which Allie didn't seem to share. My attempt to kiss her produced a pain in my heart and lower lip, when she turned her face from mine bumping my mouth. My reaction to the pain caused her to apologize and promise never to *slug me again.* As we embraced in a moment of reconciliation, I noticed her body trembled slightly.

"Allie, are you cold?" I asked with a chortling, almost mocking tone.

"No," she replied. "I just don't like this place at night."

As Allie dragged me back toward the truck, I teased her by asking if she was afraid of the boogieman under the bridge.

Prior to leaving the base on Friday evening, I packed my Thanksgiving "outfit," instead of my Dacron uniform as on the previous visit. Allie had told me, her mother would expect us to stay for church, since Sunday was Mother's day. Once more I came down for breakfast after everyone else, much to Mr. Henry's dissatisfaction. Much to my satisfaction, he didn't ask me to say "grace" again.

Breakfast began with Mr. Henry's ritualistic shredding of his eggs and hash browns, followed by long slurps of coffee. Mrs. Natty's mild rebuke went unheeded. During the course of the meal, the conversation turned to the health of Mr. Pee Wee Peterson, the part-time hired hand who usually helped Mr. Henry with the harvesting of the wheat crop.

Thinking this would be my opportunity to spend some additional time on the farm, I offered my assistance in this endeavor when the time should arrive. Three blank faces turned in my direction. I wiped my mouth with my napkin, thinking Mr. Henry's yellow jambalaya had mysteriously splashed on my face.

"Are you a serious boy?" asked Mr. Henry, after placing his fork across his empty plate.

"Yes, sir," I said in a confident voice. "I have a month's leave time coming . . . and besides, I can drive that old Farmall or the one-ton truck."

"There will be some long hard days," averred Mr. Henry, as if he was trying to scare me off.

"Yes sir," I replied, intending to hold my ground as, Allie watched me with a pleasing grin. "I know what it's like to do farmwork." After a pause to gauge Mr. Henry's reaction to the suggestion, I added, "This can't be much worse than picking cotton or cutting cane."

"I'll pay you for your time," answered Mr. Henry, in an assertive tone as he pushed his chair from the table.

"That won't be necessary," I insisted with a smile. "Mrs. Natty's cooking will be payment enough."

"See what it's done to me," rejoined Mr. Henry, as he rubbed his stomach with one hand, while pressing his hat down on his head with the other.

We all laughed at Mr. Henry as he walked out the dining room and into the kitchen. With her father out of the dining room, Allie gave me a kiss on the cheek and said, she would take some time off from school to be with me during cutting season. This made my suggestion even sweeter, and I felt my redemption was complete.

Our return to Amarillo about 19:00 hours, on Sunday, found us both tired and hungry. Desiring a break from burgers and pizza, I suggested that we try the Howdy Restaurant on West, 10th Street. It wasn't a very fancy place, but they served the best Barbecue sandwiches in the city.

The following evening, my friends and I had just returned to the barrack from evening chow, when an Air Police truck drove through the quadrangle with its emergency lights flashing. James was the first to notice the truck, as he and I stood at the windows of the dayroom, watching the yearlong pool saga continue between John and Paul.

"Hey, Yogi," James said tapping me on the shoulder to get my attention, "there's your favorite cop. Matt Dillon."

Through the open window, I called out to Bridgewater as he stepped out the truck.

"Welcome home Matt Dillon . . . to the land of long-legged rabbits and beautiful women."

Bridgewater reached into the truck and picked up the microphone. With the PA at full volume, he announced, "Airman Yogi! You're under arrest. Come out with your hands up."

Heads began appearing at the windows of all four barracks surrounding the quadrangle. John and Paul laid down their pool sticks, long enough to come to the window to share in my humiliation.

"Hey, Yogi," announced Bridgewater on the PA system, "come down here. I have something for you."

"Is it an arrest warrant?" called down Paul.

"No!" yelled back Bridgewater, who was now standing besides the hood of his truck.

"Come on. Let's go see what he has," James said with a grin, while heading for the door.

Arriving at the truck, we all greeted Bridgewater with a warm handshake. The few months he spent in Kansas seemed to have agreed with him, for he had put on a few pounds, but still his childlike face made me wonder if he was shaving yet.

"I brought you a souvenir from the EOD (Explosive Ordinance Disposal) unit," Bridgewater said with a grin, as he reached into the truck and removed from the dashboard an old World War II pineapple hand grenade. When offered to me, I noticed the pin was rusty.

"A hand grenade!" I replied in disbelief, while making no attempt to accept it.

"Yeah," Bridgewater said, still holding this antique bomb in his hand.

"Bridgewater, this is an Air Force Base, not an Army Post," I protested. "What I'm gonna do with a grenade?"

"Keep it for a souvenir," was his simple explanation.

"Is it alive or whatever . . . they call it?" I asked, not knowing the proper terminology for such things.

"I suppose not," replied Bridgewater, giving his shoulders a shrug. "This Warrant Officer had it in his desk for years. He told me to get rid of it, so I decided to bring it to you."

"I don't know Matt Dillon," I replied, trying not to hurt his feelings. "But . . . having a hand grenade just doesn't appeal to me."

"Hey, if Yogi doesn't want it . . . mind if I take it?" asked Paul with a wide grin.

The practical jokes that Paul had planned for such an item was too horrible to contemplate at the time, and I was hoping, Bridgewater would keep it to himself.

"I guess so," replied Bridgewater, looking disappointed as he tossed the grenade to Paul.

Paul juggled the grenade several times before dropping it. When it hit the sidewalk, the rusty pin broke, but failed to fully release the handle. Without thinking, I picked it up and hurled it toward the center of the quadrangle. My three friends were a little slower than me, in imitating a John Wayne's style of "hitting the dirt," but the sound of the grenade striking one of the painted stones at the base of Sausage Sam's oak tree brought them to varying degrees of "getting down." A second later, the grenade exploded.

As I lay on the ground, Sam's tree toppled over amid a cloud of smoke, creating the optical illusion of a giant sequoia falling to the ground in slow motion, like something from a movie. The smoke cloud appeared to rise in time with our bodies from the ground, revealing a sheared-off trunk about two feet from the ground smoldering in the evening twilight. Flying shrapnel broke several windows in the barracks surrounding the quadrangle, causing boys in various stages of dishabille to appear on the steps of each building.

Bridgewater's youthful face was ashen stone when I turned to him. With some reluctance, I began a trudge toward the fallen tree, feeling sick to my stomach. From each of the barracks, a line of boys cautiously filed toward the grassy area to inspect the fall of what had become the Squadron's icon. Their faces were somber as they marched toward the center of the quadrangle at a funeral pace of one half-step at a time.

After standing over the tree as if it were a corpse, the realization of what had transpired set in, and the crowd of curious onlookers quickly disappeared leaving the five of us to ponder how to rectify the awful mess before 07:00 hours, the following day.

"We have to find another tree," concluded John in a lifeless tone. His sigh seemed to produce a whistling sound through his diastema.

"Tonight?" asked Paul in an equally dead, quiet tone.

"We could drive out to the nursery on 287," suggested James.

"I shouldn't be involved in this," murmured Bridgewater. The color still hadn't returned to his face.

"Hey! It's because of you we're in this mess." I answered indignantly. "Bringing a live grenade on base! Matt Dillon . . . you beat everything, you know that!"

"I'm sorry, Yogi. I thought the damn thing was a dud," apologized the young Policeman with his head down. "I gotta go," Bridgewater added in a muttered tone as he turned to walk off.

"Well boys," John stated in an upbeat voice, "we have some military business to take care of tonight." In an unusual "take-charge fashion" for John, he pointed toward the parking lot and said, "To *The Iron Lung*, boys."

As we walked toward *The Lung*, the crisis lost its more serious edge and took on a humorous side, as we began to laugh and joke about Bridgewater driving around the Base with a live grenade on his dashboard. Heading toward the gate located near Highway 287, an occasional thought of Sausage Sam crossed our minds, which temporarily took the fun from the evening. To fortify our resolve, we stopped at Sarge's Place for a few beers, before continuing our quest for a replacement tree.

Since John and Paul didn't know an oak tree from turnip greens, James and I climbed the fence along the rear of the Nursery, with a couple of flashlights for a little reconnaissance work. There wasn't an oak tree in the place and nothing to make a suitable substitute.

We left the Nursery, feeling depressed and certain that we would be spending the rest of our Air Force enlistments in the Guardhouse. Before returning to the Base, we once more stopped off at Sarge's Place for additional encouragement. At 21:00 hours., we left the bar dragging our tails, licking our wounds and convinced about that we would have to face the First Sergeant before sundown the following day.

On the way back to the barrack, we drove passed the 3340th Technical School Squadron, the domain of Sergeant Sam's, chief competitor for the coveted Base Beautification Award. Looking out the window, I couldn't believe my eyes as we drove past the parking lot behind the Orderly Room.

"Stop!" I shouted at John and hit him behind the head.

"What's eating you, Yogi?" John shouted as he slammed on the brakes. The Hawaiian doll on the dashboard swayed back and forth.

"Back up! Come on, back up! Back up!" I uttered in an excited tone, while extending my upper body out of the window.

"What is it?" asked Paul, looking into the direction, in which I was leaning.

"It's a naked WAF," I answered with a cackle, thinking I had gotten one over on Paul.

"Come on, Yogi," replied John angrily. "We got problems here."

"And weeee . . . got a solution." I said with a hoot. "It's a beautiful tree."

A sense of excitement filled the car, as everyone tried looking out the windows on the driver's side to see the solution to our problem. I do believe a naked WAF could have been standing next to that tree at the time, and she would have been our second choice that evening. Upon closer inspection, we discovered the tree was about three feet taller than Sam's former tree and in a container much too large to fit into the trunk of *The Iron Lung*.

After getting back into the car and driving off, we discussed several plans on how to obtain this beauty. We had just about given up hope, when James blurted out a bit of wisdom.

"What we need is a truck."

"And where in hell are we going to find a truck at this time of night?" John asked in a foul mood.

"Air Policemen have trucks," James answered in a smooth voice.

A dead silence enveloped *The Lung*, as the idea slowly sank into our minds. A roar of laughter soon erupted.

"No way!" shouted Bridgewater, when we confronted him outside the Mess Hall. "My shift ends in about an hour, and I don't want to see you guys anymore tonight, maybe never."

"You will be seeing a lot more of us in the Guard House if that tree is not replaced before daylight," declared John in a threatening tone. "This is your fault for bringing a grenade on base!"

"Come on, Matt Dillon," I pleaded, "it won't take but a few minutes."

"You expect me to haul a stolen tree in my Police truck?" asked Bridgewater as he pointed to himself.

"It's not really stealing, Bridgewater," asserted Paul. "See, the tree actually belongs to the Air Force, and we will be planting it at one location on the Base rather than another . . . that's all." Paul held out his hands and smiled to enhance his point. "The Air Force doesn't give a damn where the tree is planted."

Paul's logic made sense. Like hungry wolves we stood around the young Air Policeman awaiting his answer, which came after a few moments of deliberation followed by a childlike smile.

"All right, but after tonight, I don't ever want to see you four clowns again."

I think all we heard was the simple little word, "all right." John accelerated *The Iron Lung* leaving Bridgewater in a cloud of smoke, which added to our cheerful mood. We escorted Bridgewater to the tree, which was quickly loaded into the back of his truck under the cover of darkness, completing the only clandestine operation of my military career. As we followed Bridgewater to the quadrangle, the sight of a stolen tree in the back of an Air Police truck raised our rapturous joy to new heights. In the excitement, Paul farted a couple of times, contributing what he could to the celebration.

After reaching its new home, it took all five of us to carry the heavy container to the stump it was to replace. Bridgewater received a radio call so he made a hasty exit from the quadrangle with flashing lights, leaving us with the chore of digging up the stump and planting its replacement. The whole process took about two hours, with the help of two guys from one of the other barracks. The new tree being taller than the old one, required some pruning with the intention of "fake out" Sausage Sam. With everything cleaned up and all the stones placed around the new tree, we decided to celebrate at the Airmen's Club across the street before it closed for the night.

With each additional beer, the thought of Bridgewater driving around the Base with a live hand grenade in his truck became more hilarious as we celebrated our accomplishment. Paul suggested that we toast "Matt Dillon, the best damn Air Policeman on Amarillo Air Force Base."

"If that young fool wishes to see his 20th birthday, he had better not take any more assignments to another EOD unit," I said, lifting a longneck in the air in honor to Matt Dillon.

Chapter 18

Watching through the Venetian blinds of my room, my three friends and I followed Sausage Sam as he walked from the parking lot toward the Headquarter Squadron. His well-starched 505 (khaki) uniform had razor-sharp creases splitting the shirt pockets and each pants leg. As always his black shoes were highly polished and his "cunt" cap with twin points sat more to the left side of his head, demonstrating a cocky mood as he strutted down the sidewalk. Whistling a little tune and swinging his arms, the First Sergeant squared each corner as if on a parade field. We sighed in relief and were confident that our ploy had worked, when he proceeded up the steps to the Orderly Room.

Sam halted before the door with his head aslant. Our breathing also stopped. Slowly he turned and stared in the direction of the tree before easing down the steps with his neck hyperextended.

"The crap is about to hit the fan, boys," Paul muttered.

Sam's pace quickened as he walked toward the tree. With his arms rigidly extended downward and his hands balled into tight fists, the First Sergeant paced around the tree, first in one direction, and then in the other. After several rounds, Sausage Sam's temper exploded into wild gesticulations coupled with Italian maledictions, called down upon everyone within hearing range. In his anger, the "cunt" cap sitting so augustly on his well-groomed black hair received a quick jerk and hit the ground just before a well-polished shoe crushed it into the grass. Like Thomson gazelles at the sign of a hungry lion, we took off for the fire escape at the far end of the bay.

At noon, when James and I approached the chow hall, he called my attention to a black wreath on the door of the Air Police Headquarters building.

John and Paul's somber faces told me that something was desperately wrong as we joined them at their table. I sat paralyzed, listening to John's explanation of how Airman Bridgewater died during the night while attempting to arrest some thieves in one of the base warehouses.

"It can't be true!" I shouted angrily at John. An uneasy hush fell across the table. "He was with us . . . just last night."

John and Paul pushed their trays forward. Attempting to hide the pain in my face caused by the suffocating feeling in my chest, I coupled my fingers together behind my neck and pulled my head down toward the table. Paul and John got up, leaving their trays on the table. James smoked a cigarette in silence, knowing I didn't feel like talking. Finally, he extinguished his cigarette by standing it in the middle of his mashed potatoes. Without speaking, we too abandoned our untouched dinner.

We left the chow hall and walked across the parking lot to the Air Police Headquarters. I asked the Desk Sergeant if he had any information about the death of Bridgewater. As usual with the military, he was unable to give out any information, since the case was under investigation. Inadvertently, he revealed Bridgewater's body was at the base morgue.

James and I went to the barrack, rather than returning to the hangar. Because the Hospital was location on the far side of the base, we took my car rather than catching the base bus. The only person in the morgue when we arrived was an Orderly, who was reluctant to let us view the body, but after some arm twisting he agreed, and took us back to a small room.

James stood against the far wall, as the Orderly unzipped the body bag. What lay before me didn't resembled the young, happy, energetic boy I had known only the night before. Looking down at the body and recalling the first bit of advice I jokingly gave Bridgewater, the pain in my heart expressed itself in an angry soliloquy: "Damn you, Matt Dillon, why couldn't you look the other way just once more?"

I couldn't return to work that afternoon. After calling St. Anthony's and leaving a message for Allie, I went to my room and fell on my bunk fully dressed in my uniform. Staring up at the ceiling, a thousand thoughts went through my mind about how short and uncertain life is, and how unfair Bridgewater's death was. Why would God allow something like this to happen to someone, who had so much to live for and who had never harmed anyone? I could feel the tears running down each side of my face as I lay there, wanting to be strong and yet wanting to grieve the loss of my friend. The lonely hours passed in silence, as I waited for Allie to call.

After work, James came by to check on me and ask if I wanted to go to the Mess Hall. I refused and went back downstairs to call St. Anthony's again. Still Allie wasn't in, so I returned to the seclusion of my room. It was getting dark when I returned to the phone booth, feeling lonely and desperate for her companionship. When the girl on the other end told me she wasn't in and the notes were still on her bed from the previous calls, I became insane with anger.

Allie where are you! Damn it! Where are you? I cried out while striking the plastic wall of the phone booth with the receiver. I rested my head against the booth wall and while clinching the receiver in my hand I softly pleading for her to call me. *I need you, Allie, please call.*

"Hey! Are you finished with the phone?" shouted someone while pounding on the door of the phone booth.

I leveled a searching glance at the intruder, before hanging up the receiver and stepping out the booth. After he closed the door, I reopened it by pushing it forward in the center.

"What day of the week is it?" I asked.

"It's Wednesday, buddy," replied the irritated Airman as he shoved closed the door.

All eyes turned in my direction, when I entered the lobby of the old Hotel and slammed the door behind me. This was the first time I had worn my uniform to the House, so my appearance was an indication that something was out of the ordinary. When Crystal saw me, she backed away from the young Airman she had pinned against the backside of a sofa with her body.

"Is Allie here?" I asked in an agitated voice while looking around.

"She's busy right now, handsome," Crystal replied while pulling my body against hers, by wrapping her arms around my waist. "Wouldn't you like to try something different tonight, Yogi?"

With both hands I forcefully removed her arms and answered, "No! Is she in room 210?"

I turned and started toward the elevator.

"She's with someone, Yogi," yelled Crystal with sharpness in her voice.

"Sam, take me upstairs," I demanded, while trying to ignore the stares generated by Crystal's outburst.

"I can't do that, Mr. Yogi," replied Sam coming to his feet. "You know you aren't allowed upstairs unless you have one of the young ladies with you."

"You can't go up there now," shouted Crystal as she walked toward me.

"The hell I can't!" I retorted.

While I ran up the stairs, Crystal screamed, "Yogi, Rose will be madder than a hatter."

When I busted through the door, a very young boy stood at the foot of the iron bed, dressed only in his boxer shorts and black GI socks. An expression of shock and fear covered his face as well as Allie's, who stood in a red negligee on the far side of the bed near the record player.

"Get out of here!" shouted Allie.

For a moment I stood frozen, as the young boy and I stared at each other. Allie's frantic yelling for me to leave awakened the jealousy within my heart I had attempted to suppress over the months and the reality of her secret world, into which I had fallen. In a blind rage, I lunged at the young Airman. With all my strength and a rush of adrenalin unknown, since my encounter with Bubba Lee, I dragged him toward the door and threw him into the hallway, while Allie franticly pleaded with me to stop.

"You can't come in here like this . . ." screamed Allie, rushing around the bed.

"What about my uniform?" asked the young Airman in a sheepish voice, as he made his way back to the open door.

After picking up his khaki uniform from the chair and rolling it into a ball, I threw it and his cap into the hallway before slamming the door.

"What are you doing?" screamed Allie. "Are you drunk or just plain mad?"

"Don't yell at me bitch!" I shouted, while raising my right hand in a threatening manner.

"Go ahead, Yogi!" Allie shouted. "Do it! Prove you're no different from Scott."

Slowly and awkwardly, I lowered my hand. Seeing the fear in Allie's eyes, I backed away and leaned against the wall near the window. Shame and guilt overtook me as I realized the promise I had made at the beginning of our relationship came close to being broken. The hurt in

Allie's face and the shame I was feeling, caused my legs to grow weak and slowly I slid down the wall to a sitting position on the floor. With my arms folded across my knees, I placed my forehead on my arms and sat in silence wishing this day had never come.

What seemed an eternity passed before Allie's hand gently touched the back of my neck.

"Why have you returned to this hell hole?" I asked without looking up.

"Yogi, what's wrong?" Allie asked while sitting on the floor beside me.

"My friend is dead," I answered in a breaking voice.

"James?" asked Allie in disbelief.

"No . . . not him . . . another boy. I never told him I was sorry for being angry . . . about the grenade."

We sat on the floor for sometime, holding on to each other without speaking, as I cried uncontrollably, no longer feeling ashamed at showing the grief I was feeling. The macho façade I felt required of me back at the base, was no longer necessary here in the seclusion of room 210, which had become a private world for Allie and me.

A din of voices drew our attention to the door just before it swung open. Anger distorted Rose's face, as she walked in looking like the goddess of Texas tornados with her long thin robe and boa streaming behind her. At her heels was the young Airman wearing his uniform cap, but still holding his rolled up uniform in his arms. Crystal and Sam followed him.

"What the hell do you mean by busting in here like some high and mighty king?" Rose shouted as she entered the room. At the foot of the bed, she stopped. Standing arms akimbo, she snarled, "What the hell's wrong with him?"

"One of his friends at the base was killed," explained Allie.

"Yeah. I heard about that on the T.V." injected Crystal, as she sidestepped the boy.

"All right," Rose said waving her arms, "everyone out of here."

"Hey, what about me?" demanded the young Airman. "I paid to have this girl."

"Well, you can have yourself another," snapped Rose. Turning to Crystal, she added, "Take this young fool to your room and give him what he paid for."

With something of a downcast look on her face, Crystal took the young boy by the arm and dragged him toward the door as if taking a child off for a scolding.

"What about my shoes?" the boy asked pulling away from Crystal's grip.

"Wellll, come in and get them!" Rose answered in an indulgent tone, looking at the shoes, to which the boy was pointing.

The boy glanced in my direction as he bent over to pick up his shoes. As Crystal dragged him from the room, Sam too left closing the door behind him. Rose stepped closer to Allie and me, still sitting on the floor. She looked back at the door and derisively said, "I remember the time when this business attracted real men. Now . . . all we get is a bunch of horny teenagers . . . like him. He should be home with his mama."

Reaching down her hands to me, Rose said, "Come on . . . get up. You'll get your uniform all dirty on that damn old floor. And, take off that tie and coat."

"I'm okay, Rose," I answered trying to sound stronger than I really was. "I'm leaving."

"No, Yogi," Allie insisted. "Please stay for a little while . . . we need to talk."

"You lie down, boy," demanded Rose as she headed for the door. "I'll have Sam bring up something to settle you down."

Rose's departure left the room in a state of tranquility, as Allie and I stood facing each other, not knowing how or where to resume the conservation interrupted by her sudden appearance. Somehow the flickering candles no longer held the same romantic appeal for me that they once did, as I stood there wondering if our relationship would ever make sense.

Without speaking, Allie moved to the bed and sat near the edge. With an enticing smile and a patting of her hand on the spread, she encouraged me to join her. After slipping off my shoes I laid down with my head in her lap, staring up at the water spot on the ceiling, while apologizing for my behavior. There was a long period of silence, during which time, she gently ran her fingers through my hair and occasionally bent over to kiss me on the forehead. After some time passed, I rolled over, facing the door.

"Why did you return to this place, Allie?" I asked in an uneasy voice. She didn't respond so I continued. "I thought after the time we shared on the farm, you would realize how much I care for you . . . and you wouldn't come here anymore."

"Yogi, I never promised you that," Allie replied, cautiously touching my head with an open hand.

"Allie, I love you," I muttered. "Is there something so wrong with me that you can't love me?"

A hiatus of several minutes passed between us, before she leaned over to kiss me. I felt a teardrop fall from her eyes onto my cheek

"There's nothing wrong with you, Yogi," Allie said reaching for my hand and squeezing it. "It's me. There's something inside of me, which prevents me from loving . . . not only you, but any man."

With this bit of her secret revealed, Allie slid down onto the bed and rolled over onto her side with her back toward me. I rolled over and pulled her body close after realizing her pain, which obviously had a long history, was greater than mine. It was sometime during this period of quiet solitude that a knock sounded on the door. It was Sam, bearing a tray with a decanter of orange juice and one glass.

"Mrs. Rose said this will cheer you up a mite, Mr. Yogi," said Sam with a grin showing his white teeth.

With a puzzled look, I graciously accepted the tray and thanked Sam. After placing the tray on the chest of drawer, I poured some of the juice into the glass and took a large swallow. The tangy unfamiliar taste, combined with the large gulp, made me cough several times. Allie sat up and looked in my direction. The flavor of the beverage had an attraction that caused me to take a couple of smaller swallows.

"What is it, Yogi?" asked Allie.

"I don't know," I answered, moving toward the bed and sitting down beside her. "Try it. It's pretty good."

After taking a sip, Allie squinched her eyes and swallowed hard.

"It's a screwdriver with lotssss of drivers," Allie answered while holding her throat. "That will do more than settle you down."

As Allie and I shared the massive screwdriver while sitting in the bed the problems, which had confronted me earlier, seemed to disappear, as the level in the decanter did the same. Under the influence of the vodka, I told Allie how I became acquainted with Bridgewater and what role I played in getting him transferred to the Air Police Squadron. As I went into this long story about the hand grenade and the destruction of Sam's oak tree, we continued sharing the orange juice. I was able to laugh as I recalled the fun we had following Bridgewater's truck with the stolen tree in the bed. As the drink slowly wasted away, the room became extremely warm, causing me to remove my shirt and throwing it to the floor. Intending to lean back in the bed to slip off my pants I failed to realize just how close I was to the edge. Allie let out a short scream when I tumbled from the bed. Trying to regain my dignity, I stood beside the bed to remove my pants while Allie giggled.

Having returned to the bed and resuming a sitting position in my boxer shorts before Allie, I accepted the glass from her and took another swig.

"Yogi, I think you've had enough," suggested Allie.

"One more," I said rising to my knees. "Here's to your mother. I know she wouldn't like us being together like this." Extending out my arm in a toast, I added with a slur, "May the ole bat, go deaf."

From the kneeling position, I looked down at Allie and once more the flickering candlelight in the room restored the magic of so many previous evenings. Coming up to her knees to meet me, our embrace led to a long passionate kiss. The effects of the orange juice caused us to become unsteady, and we fell over onto the bed.

In that moment of ecstasy, Allie whispered, "Yogi, tell me you love me?"

Taken by surprise, I managed to raise myself on one arm and looked down into her eyes. After a gentle kiss on the lips, I replied, "I love you very much and have, every since I first saw you that night in the backseat of that car."

I kissed her a couple more times and then made my own request while running my forefinger around her mouth.

"Will you ever be able to say the same to me, Allie?"

Allie demurred, as she considered her response.

"Yogi . . . what if I made you a promise instead?" Allie asked with a beautiful smile while putting her arms around my neck.

"What kind of promise?" I asked kissing her on the cheek.

"What if I promised . . . tonight would be my last night in this place," Allie stated in an uneasy tone.

I was stunned for a moment and unable to respond. When her words finally sank into my brain, I fell on her with all my weight and squeezed her with all my strength causing her to beg me to release her.

The evening that began with anger had come to an end in quiet solitude, as Allie rested her head on my chest. Feeling at peace about Bridgewater's passing and with the promise Allie had made, I lay in the old bed looking around the room, perhaps for the last time. After sometime of lying together, I suggested we get up and get dressed.

Allie left the House that evening with me.

On my way back to the base, I pulled off the road to pick up a hitchhiker. It was the young boy, who I had thrown out of the room. When he recognized me, he refused to get in. Knowing he was fresh out of Basic Training and accustomed to following orders, I commanded him to get into the car.

The coming of this unnamed boy into my life reminded me of the first time I met Bridgewater and the walk we took to Colonel O'Quinn's office. After letting the boy out near his barrack, I watched him until he disappeared around the corner. Recalling that the book of Ecclesiastes speaks of "a time to weep and a time to laugh, a time to mourn, and a time to dance," I softly whispered, *Good night . . . Matt Dillon,* and then drove off.

Chapter 19

Streaks of sunlight to my right appeared to shoot up from the belly of the earth creating in my mind, an imagery of what the first day of creation must have been like. As the city disappeared from my rearview mirror, so did the triteness my job had taken on and the agony I felt while having to escort additional young Airmen to Colonel O'Quinn's Office during the week following Bridgewater's death. Because Allie had to work, we spoke each night by phone about our upcoming trip to Indian Ridge. Several times, I attempted to apologize for my behavior at the House, but she always insisted we not discuss that part of the evening.

After coming to an elevation in the highway, sunbeams flooded my car with rays of brilliant light forcing Allie and me to shield our eyes. Allie leaned against the passenger side door while resting her head against the seat, away from the sun. Turning my head to the left, I noticed a transformation had taken place in the wheat fields along the highway. They were no longer green, but now a majestic golden brown. An unnamed opus from Tank's classical records played in my mind as I watched the heavy heads dance as so many graceful ballerinas in the morning breeze.

For almost an hour, the unending wheat fields broken by an occasional "grasshopper" oil rig bid me onward, as Allie slept on my shoulder. My musing came to an end with the appearance of a convoy of house trailers, grain trucks, and combines on flatbed trucks heading south. My letting up on the accelerator caused Allie to awaken. Fascinated by the sight of such large rigs, I watched with the enthusiasm of a kid witnessing the arrival of a circus. Allie said the convoy was the first in the annual arrival of the Custom Cutters whom she called "wheat gypsies."

We arrived at the farm just before noon since we stopped along the way to eat breakfast. Standing beside the car door, stretching and surveying the place, my body and soul seemed revivified by the beauty of the giant cottonwoods and the sight of Buster and Midnight romping in the corral. My blissful state of mind reached new heights after Allie came around to my side of the car and gave me a gentle hug. The House and city of Amarillo now seemed as distance in years as in miles.

The squeaky board in the hallway outside Robert's room welcomed my return, causing me to smile. In a way, it and the undisturbed condition of the room were comforting, given the recent loss of my friend. After unpacking, I walked to Allie's room, making sure to step on the "watchdog" in the hallway, knowing fully well, Mrs. Natty wasn't about to let Mr. Henry repair it at this stage of her daughter's life.

After lunch with her parents, Allie and I followed Mr. Henry to the equipment shed where Maude, the combine, awaited some final mechanical adjustments before cutting could begin. During our trek to the shed, I jokingly asked Allie if she planned to slug me again if I offered to help her Dad should he need my assistance. Her eyes were more loquacious than her reply.

Allie and I watched Mr. Henry, who gingerly walked around the cabless; John Deere combine with a grease gun as if stalking Maude in search of a grease zerk gone astray. The old combine was equipped with a reel, which had a row of steel tines attached to the slats running the full length of the reel. As Mr. Henry reached inside the reel to clear away some debris from around a bearing, he scraped his arm on one of the tines cutting a small gash in his forearm. His automatic reaction was to wipe the wound with his handkerchief, which he had been using as a grease rag. This brought a resounding protest from Allie.

"It's just a little cut, Daughter," explained Mr. Henry in defense of his reaction.

"Yogi, do you have a clean handkerchief?" Allie asked with a look of concern.

"Yes," I replied reaching into my back pocket.

"Here," Allie commanded her father, while handing him the handkerchief, "hold this on the arm until I get back with something to treat that cut." After taking the greasy handkerchief from her father, Allie threw it to the ground.

"The Doctor has spoken," I said sarcastically, watching for Mr. Henry's reaction while he hung the grease gun on one of the tines.

"You hush," Allie retaliated. Then turning to her father she riposted, "I suppose you think it's okay to use a grease rag to clean a laceration of this kind?" Continuing her diatribe, Allie then asked in a stern voice, "And . . . why are you limping?"

"It's nothing, Daughter," protested Mr. Henry, while temporarily removing the handkerchief to look at his arm. "I twisted my leg . . . a few days back."

"Have you been to the Doctor?" asked Allie in a more conciliatory tone.

"Not yet. Hadn't had the time . . . with cutting coming on," replied Mr. Henry in an almost submissive voice. "If it doesn't start feeling better in a day or two, I'll . . . consider seeing Dr. Adams."

"You men!"

Allie stormed off toward the house, leaving Mr. Henry and I alone to contemplate on the shortcomings of the male gender. While we awaited her return, I questioned Mr. Henry about "ole Maude." According to him, he purchased the combine for $500.00 some seven years before from a Custom Cutter who had used Maude and her pickup reel in the rice fields of south Texas. Because the engine needed overhaul, he sold it to Mr. Henry rather than hauling it back. Since Mr. Henry wasn't one to spend money on unnecessary changes, he decided to leave the pickup reel on the combine.

Allie returned to the house after dressing her father's wound. Mr. Henry and I walked to the edge of the field where he bent over and broke off one head. I watched with the curiosity of a school kid as the wheat head was placed crossways the palm of his thick, dry, calloused left hand. With his right hand placed over the head, a form of crude milling took place as he forcefully rubbed his hands together. A gentle puff, emitted by two strong lungs, separated the chaff from the kernels.

The procedure seemed simple, so I tried it, only to have the head slip from between my hands. After suffering Mr. Henry's inimical stare, I tried several more times before success came my way.

"Your hands are too soft," declared Mr. Henry in a tone, I took as belittling. Knowing we had several weeks ahead of us together, I held my tongue.

Reaching for another head of wheat and repeating the process, he then put one of the kernels in his mouth as I watched. Judging by the flexing of his jaw muscles, I could tell he was biting down on the kernel, but didn't understand why. I hesitated to inquire into the importance of this extraordinary display.

"Take one," offered Mr. Henry as he extended his hand containing several kernels. "Bite it."

My reluctance prompted Mr. Henry to insist by shoving his hand toward me.

"What's it supposed to taste like?" I asked, after biting down on the kernel cautiously placed in my mouth.

"It's not the taste you're looking for, but the hardness," replied Mr. Henry with something of a chuckle. He offered me another before standing, which brought a painful expression to his face.

While gazing over the field, Mr. Henry wiped the residual husk and kernels on his pants leg. "By tomorrow or the following day, we should be able to start cutting," he stated while shaking his head up and down slightly.

"We still have plenty of daylight left if there's something you want to do," I suggested, while trying to rid my mouth of the chewed wheat kernel, which appeared determined to cling to my tongue.

"There's a great deal to be done," replied Mr. Henry as he started back toward the equipment shed. Pointing in the direction of the three grain bins near the equipment shed, he added, "The first thing we have to do is clean out those bins."

Mr. Henry's use of the pronoun "we," I quickly learned, was used in a very loose sense, for it was I who ended up cleaning the three bins of the residual grain left from the previous year. After removing my shirt and hanging it on the small door of the bin, my handkerchief, bloody from Mr. Henry's arm, served as a dust mask, tied across my nose. With the use of a broom and grain scoop, I was able to sweep up approximately four or five wheel barrow loads of moldy wheat from each of the hot and dusty bins, before pitching it through the door onto the ground. The only reprieve I had was an occasional visit from Allie, who came to my aid with a pitcher of cold water and a warm smile.

With this chore accomplished, Mr. Henry decided that "we" should check the bearings on each auger on the grain bins, including the ones on top, while giving each zerk a shot of grease. I quickly learned Mr. Henry was a strong believer in a good grease gun. Suspecting one bearing on the ground level of going bad, "we" decided to replace it, which took about one hour, thanks to Mr. Henry's cutting torch and a fair size sledge hammer.

The sun was slowly disappearing beyond the horizon, when the clear unmistakable sound of the plantation bell near the back steps broke the evening stillness. I had long been ready for the supper, to which it was calling me. Wiping the dust and perspiration from my body with my shirt and then putting it back on, I proceeded to the house at Mr. Henry's command, leaving him to put away the cutting rig and a few hand tools.

Allie met me at the backdoor with a cup of coffee and suggested I take a bath before coming down for supper. Under my breath, I asked if she would come up and wash my back. The disapproving glance shot my way by Mrs. Natty, reminded me of her superior hearing.

Allie and I volunteered to perform the KP duty after supper, which allowed us sometime together before joining her parents in the living room. While sitting on the floor looking through several shoe boxes of family photos, Allie with an occasional remark by Mr. Henry related the story behind each member of her pioneer family, who came to Texas following the Civil War. My discovery of a picture of her wearing a majorette uniform, which was very tight, resulted in a tug-of-war that brought forth a word of caution from her mother. It was her sixth grade picture, the year she claimed she was in love with Earl McCurley. The same year, Robert Earl had taken her to the school dance. When I whispered in her ear that she looked pregnant, she pushed on my shoulder with such force I fell over onto the floor.

Because of my disparaging remarks about her picture, I received a lukewarm kiss when we said good night in the hallway. After lying in bed for some time unable to sleep, I got up, dressed only in the pajama bottoms laid out for me by Mrs. Natty, and walked toward the door. The sound of the squeaky board in the hall brought a smile to my face. Allie was startled when I pulled open the door, just as she attempted to knock on it. We both laughed quietly. The sweet fragrant of her hair blended gently with the fresh, sun dried aroma of her pajamas, as I pulled her warm soft body against mine. From down the hall, Allie's mother called for her to return to her room.

"Damn! That woman has better hearing than the Air Force's DEW (Distance Early Warning) Line," I declared while attempting to pull Allie against my body once more.

As we held each other for a final good-night kiss, the passion we shared indicated, we both desired a more intimate ending to the evening.

Reveille came at 06:00, the next morning without coffee in bed, as Mr. Henry awakened me by grasping my foot and shaking it. His only words in a very raspy voice were: *Breakfast's ready.* Peeling the sheet from my head, I managed to look up at him with swollen eyes, apparently caused by the dust of the previous day's job in the grain bins.

Trudging to the bathroom, I turned on the hot water faucet before getting a washcloth from the closet. Preoccupied with the thought of Allie sleeping in the room beyond the bathroom wall, I stuck the washcloth under the faucet. *Son-of-a-bitch,* I uttered in a restrained tone, while turning loose the washcloth and shaking my hand. Now, fully awake, I ran some cold water into the lavatory. For several minutes, I stood before the mirror holding the soothing warm cloth against my eyes, until the smell of frying bacon caused my stomach to win control of my brain.

While sitting across the kitchen table from Mr. Henry, he laid out the day's activities. Again, his use of the word "we," left me feeling tired even before the day began.

Just as we were finishing breakfast, Allie came walking into the kitchen in something of a sluggish mood. Without speaking, she gently touched the back of my neck as she walked toward the coffee pot. After pouring for herself a cup of coffee, she pushed back her hair and sat down on a chair next to me. Her smile was staid. My first impulse was to lean over and kiss her, good morning even in the presence of her parents. Instead I settled for a quiet *Good morning.*

To Allie's languid reply I responded, "I miss having my first cup of coffee in bed."

Mr. Henry cleared his throat and reminded me that we had work to do. As the backdoor slammed behind him, I hurriedly downed the final swallow of coffee. Allie stood when I did and walked me to the backdoor. While Mrs. Natty wasn't watching, we shared a quick kiss before I ran down the steps to catch Mr. Henry.

Before reaching him, I turned back toward the house; raised my right hand and offered up my secret sign to Allie as she leaned against the door frame with a cup of coffee in her hand. In return, she gave me a gentle wave as her mother stood beside her.

The first task of the day "we" had undertaken, was checking and repairing any holes in the body of the grain truck, which was an old 1½-ton Ford with a twelve-foot hydraulic lift bed. It was a simple job of cutting small squares of thin sheet metal and nailing them over suspected chinks or holes in the body.

My second job of the day was more to my liking and made me feel I was doing something worthwhile. While hooking a bush hog to the Farmall, Mr. Henry issued forth a long list of specific instructions about staying clear of the wheat and other things I was to look for, while clipping the headland around the fields and ditches. This was one job I was glad "we" decided to perform. After removing my shirt and placing it on the seat of the tractor, I began my assigned task with the enthusiasm of a green recruit.

Several hours passed before the plantation bell sounded, calling me in for lunch. Before jumping down from the tractor, which I parked near the corral, I retrieved my well-pressed shirt from the tractor seat and slipped it on. Immediately, the seriousness of my mistake in forgetting how hot the Texas sun could become at that time of the year became obvious.

Allie met me at the gate with a glass of water and a surprised expression. After peeling back my open shirt, she touched my left shoulder. It was feverish. I recoiled at her touch. The tone of her voice while instructing me to go sit on a small wooden bench near one of the Cottonwood trees indicated clearly that she was as disappointed with this member of the male gender, as she had been with her father the day before. While she returned to the house for something to treat my sunburn, I remained on the bench like an obedient child enjoying the cold glass of water.

Along with the refreshing feeling of the cool washcloth and soothing lotion, I received a stern, but loving warning about the dangers of the Texas sun. As her tender hand worked its magic on my burning back, I became almost thankful for the sunburn.

When ordered to turn around so she could *do my front,* I decided to use the occasion to change her mood by attempting to steal a kiss or two.

While facing her on the narrow bench, I moved in closer and placed my legs over hers, since we were both straddling the bench. In this new position, I was facing the backdoor of the house and noticed when Mrs. Natty opened the screen door.

Pulling Allie close to my coconut-perfumed body, I whispered in her ear, "Your mother's watching us from the backdoor."

"Allie!" called Mrs. Natty. "Lunch is ready."

"If you don't behave, my mother's going to put some saltpeter in your breakfast," Allie said teasingly. I flinched as she delivered a forceful slap to my back, before running toward the house for our lunch.

Before returning to my tractor duty, Allie told me to wait as she returned to the house once more. After a short while, she returned with Robert Earl's old cowboy hat and instructed me to wear it, even though she knew I didn't care much for such headgear. Allie adjusted the hat on my head several times until she found a position suitable to her taste. We exchanged a quick kiss before I started for the Farmall while pushing back the hat on my head, a position I preferred.

Later that afternoon when I returned to the equipment shed, I found Mr. Henry testing the wheat once more. Determined to show myself a worthy farmer, I decided to try honing my skills at the "biting technique." With some finesse, and smugness, I plucked a head and repeated Mr. Henry's milling process. I surprised myself when the first try was successful. Unfortunately, I wasn't able to distinguish a difference between this sample and the previous one.

Standing beside me, Mr. Henry looked over the field as if contemplating a major problem. Without turning in my direction, he asked, "What'd you think?"

What do I think? I thought to myself. *What the hell do I know?*

Stunned by his question, but wanting to be a part of the decision-making process, I blurted out, "I think it's ready."

"Think you're right," replied Mr. Henry turning around to face me. "Let's give it a try. We have several more hours of daylight left."

Mr. Henry made his way to Maude, favoring his right leg more than the previous day, while ordering me to bring up the grain truck from the equipment shed. The excitement of the moment temporarily made me forget the pain of my sunburn. After climbing the ladder to the driver's seat, Mr. Henry checked several levers to his right before firing up the engine. The roaring noise from the engine, which produced a belch of black smoke caused Buster and Midnight to neigh as if offering up their own excitement. As the ancient combine slowly moved into position at the headland, Mrs. Natty and Allie emerged from the backdoor. Running to the gate, Allie removed the restraining chain and allowed the gate to swing free, as she ran toward the grain truck where I was standing. A short time later Mrs. Natty joined us, nervously wiping her hands on her apron. There was a feeling of excitement and anticipation in the air, as the three of us stood watching the majestic old machine move gracefully through the standing wheat.

The turning reel plowing through the wheat field brought to my mind a scene witnessed many times while sitting on the muddy banks of the Mississippi River. As a youngster, longing from the adventures of Huck Finn, I often dreamed of taking one of the paddle-wheeled river boats to some distant destination; anywhere away from the small town in, which I lived. With the impression of the river boats locked in my mind, I blurted out, *It appears to be going backward.*

My remark brought forth a querist stare from Allie and her mother.

With apprehension I silently questioned the capabilities of the old man and his ancient machine as they entered the boundless ocean of wheat, dwarfing the tiny combine, which appeared to be no match for the challenge that lay before it. Yet, I wanted to believe their years of partnership had bounded them together as an indomitable team.

Soon, man and machine disappeared over a hill into an endless golden sea. For a moment, I thought Maude had sailed off the ends of the earth, causing me to feel, I too had waded off into an enterprise that would surely swamp me, along with them.

After an interminable period, Maude resurfaced on the far side of the field with her master still at the helm. Rising gallantly to the crown of a distant hill, as if riding the crest of an ocean wave, she continued her epic struggle, slowly, but proudly, cutting her way through the precious amber waves of grain.

Glancing over at Allie and her mother, I saw in their faces, a sense of pride and hope, that only a farm family could understand on such a day—the first day of harvest. With her apron, Mrs. Natty wiped a tear from her eyes. Up until this time, I had never given much thought to the meaning of harvest time to a farming family, even though it had been a part of my life in varying degrees. Allie moved closer to me and put her arm around my waist. Caught up in the excitement of the moment, I leaned over and gave her a slight kiss, which her mother pretended to ignore.

Upon returning to his point of origin, a rejuvenated Mr. Henry brought the combine to a rest and disembarked with the spirit of a man many years his junior. Walking in the wake of his initial pass through the field, he began to examine the ground by raking aside the straw.

"What's he doing?" I asked Allie, watching her father.

"He's checking to see how much grain is being discharged with the straw," replied Allie with a grin.

"Oh! Excuse me," I answered, feeling my ignorance was once more showing.

Allie laughed. After slapping me on the butt, she started running ahead of me to meet her father, who was still searching for a few grains among the stubble.

"How does it look, Daddy?" asked Allie upon reaching her father.

"Real good, Daughter," replied Mr. Henry as he strained to come to a standing position.

"Daddy . . . is your leg bothering you?" inquired Allie with a concerned look.

"Just a little," answered Mr. Henry, walking back toward the combine. Allie and I followed him. "Well Yogi, what you think of the ole girl?"

"I think she's beautiful," I said while glancing at Allie.

A blank expression came to Allie's face as she gave me a slight punch to the arm, knowing I wasn't speaking of Maude.

"That old machine's like this old woman, Yogi," boasted Mr. Henry as Mrs. Natty joined us and greeted him with a slight embrace. "They both seen me through some tough time . . . and we're still together."

"Henry, I believe you love that contraption more than me," replied Mrs. Natty, reaching up to kiss her husband on the cheek. With the motion of one hand she continued, "Now, you and your girlfriend get back to work."

Such a show of affection between Allie's parents caused her to smile. As she turned to follow her mother toward the house, I reached out and took her by the hand, pulling her into my arms.

"You know what I could use right about now?"

Assuming I had on my mind something other than a cup of coffee, Allie threatened me with a small "knuckle sandwich" for suggesting such a thing within hearing range of her father. With a hearty laughter, I pulled her closer and attempted to thank her for the thought with a kiss.

As Allie struggled to break my embrace, Mr. Henry growled, "Come on, boy, we have work to do."

Wishing the evocative misunderstanding could be fulfilled, I continued to hold Allie's hand as she attempted to walk away. As our fingers slowly slipped apart, her teasing smile revealed she knew the thought planted in my mind would torment me for the rest of the afternoon. Upon rejoining Mr. Henry, his suspicious glance told me he doubted my value as a farmhand.

An hour or so later, I received my cup of coffee, and that was all. The old combine continued to perform as expected and the intricacy of the machine with its many belts, chains, screens, strawwalker, and other parts continued to fascinate me. Each time the combine required unloading, Mr. Henry's hand signal beckoned me to bring forth the grain truck. Sitting on the cab, watching the cascading wheat from the unloading elevator, I began to appreciate how many grains of wheat it would take to make one loaf of bread.

Several hours later, as a fiery-orange sun rested on the distant hills, I found myself sitting once more on the truck, watching as the final bit of wheat from the grain hopper flowed into the truck body. My sunburned body was tired, and hurting, but a feeling of relief came to my spirit with the changing noise made by the screw conveyer running empty; at the same time, the plantation bell sounded in the distance.

Too hungry to bathe before supper, I followed Mr. Henry's lead and washed up at the sink on the veranda. Apparently, he wasn't as hungry as I, for he said an extra long grace in appreciation for the beginning of the harvest, thanking God for the good crop, the fine weather, my willingness to help, etc. and etc. In my impatience, I picked up my fork, ready for action if and when the "Amen" should come. Allie noticed my eagerness to get started and bumped my leg with her own while, offering up an agreeable smile when I glanced her way.

Once Allie and I cleaned the kitchen as a means of spending some time together, a long, soaking bath was in order. Stretching out in the deep tub, I submerged my whole body below the warm, relaxing water, hoping to rid myself of several pounds of Texas dust, wheat husk, and bits of straw. Following the bath, a fresh application of soothing lotion applied to my itching back by a pair of teasing hands, which reached around to my navel occasionally, couldn't arouse my physically drained body.

It seemed the night had hardly begun, before a tugging at my feet awakened me. Once more throwing back the sheet from my head, the grinding voice of Mr. Henry greeted me with the announcement *Breakfast's ready.* As he left the room, I heard him mutter something about getting a clock for my room.

During breakfast, Allie's parents and I didn't have much to talk about as I tried coming alive at 5:30 a.m. We were almost finished with the meal, when Allie came into the kitchen in her usual languorous style and poured herself a cup of coffee. In a very unorthodox move, she motioned for me to shove my chair back from the table. She sat in my lap. I gladly complied with her request. Not knowing what to do with my hands, I let them hung free by my side. My early morning pleasure came to a quick end when Mr. Henry announced, *Come on boy, there's work to be done.*

The day began with the feeding of the horses, followed by a drive to the backside of the farm, to throw out a few bales of hay to the cattle. I was amazed how Mr. Henry knew the cows by name as if they were humans, and the approximate date of their "dropping" of the calves.

The next business on the agenda was an inspection of Maude before the day's operation was to commence. While Mr. Henry pointed out each fitting on the combine, I pumped the grease gun while listening to an explanation as to the importance of this procedure, which I learned was to become a daily ritual. My familiarity with Maude took on a feeling of intimacy, when we crawled under the combine for a visual inspection and explanation of her many moving parts.

With some difficulty, Mr. Henry then climbed to the driver's seat. After starting the engine, he commenced calling off a nomenclature of parts from memory, as a pilot going through a checklist before takeoff, as I crawled back under the machine for a visual inspection. Everything appeared to be ready for the day ahead until, prompted by experience or intuition, Mr. Henry climbed down and took one more walk around the front of the machine. After explaining to me, about which lever operated the reel, told me also to stop it when signaled to do so. Mr. Henry walked back to the front of the combine as I climbed to the driver's seat.

Standing before the combine watching the reel turn at its slowest rotation, the expression on Mr. Henry's face showed his intimacy with the old machine was much deeper than I could ever hope for. Several moments passed before he signaled me to stop the reel.

After killing the engine and climbing down, Mr. Henry pointed out a small crack in the header reel shaft, which would require welding. The small fissure required about an hour to repair and then the day began in earnest. By this time the sun was high in the sky. For the rest of the day, Maude performed without a hitch and kept me on the run between the field and the grain bins having to dump the truck after every fifth emptying of the combine. I thought it was too often and expressed my thoughts on the matter, but was overruled with the logic that *in the time it takes to unload the truck, the grain tank on the combine would be ready to be emptied again when you get back.* As the morning progressed, I learned Mr. Henry was right.

Around noon, as I sat on the body of the grain truck parked alongside the combine, watching another stream of wheat flowing into the truck, the sounding horn of Mr. Henry's old pickup truck caused me to turn. Allie and I waved to each other. After parking the truck near the combine, Allie walked to the corner of the grain bed where I was sitting.

"I have your lunch," Allie said while looking up at me.

After jumping down from the truck, I greeted Allie with a kiss since Mr. Henry wasn't in sight.

"Where's Daddy?" Allie asked as we walked toward the pickup.

"Probably checking something on the other side of Maude," I said reaching for the picnic basket on the front seat.

With my boot I mashed down some stubble near the grain truck so Allie and I could sit in the shade. Sitting on the ground, we could see Mr. Henry as he walked on the other side of Maude.

"Daddy! I have your lunch!" shouted Allie.

Watching her father limp around the combine, Allie questioned him about the pain in his leg. Taking a sandwich from the picnic basket, Mr. Henry limped back to Maude to complete his midday inspection.

"Daddy, why don't you show Yogi, how to operate the combine, so you won't have to climb up and down that ladder?" Allie asked Mr. Henry when he walked back to where we were.

"Daughter, hand me one of them doughnuts," Mr. Henry said, peering down into the picnic basket.

Mr. Henry walked off with his doughnut to continue the inspection. His failure to respond to Allie's suggestion, told me he wasn't ready to trust Maude's fate to the hands of someone like me. After coming around the machine, an incredulous stare from his stoic face caused me to look at the ground.

"Daddy, did you hear me?" pleaded Allie, as her father came back around the combine for another doughnut.

"I heard you, Daughter," Mr. Henry said before biting the doughnut in half.

My education in the fundamentals of antiquated farm equipment began with a brief explanation of the levers and what they controlled. As my stay on the farm lengthened, I was to learn my scholarship in farm implementation was far from complete. Mr. Henry stood on the small ladder, giving further instructions as the transmission was engaging. His apparent reluctance to relinquish control of Maude to my hands made me feel as if I were committing adultery. As the combine slowly moved forward, Mr. Henry's long list of instructions included a warning to become familiar with the sounds of the machine, since a variation in the rhythm of the machine unusual, indicated something was wrong.

Making my first run through the field was a time of ecstasy, compatible to the tingling sensations your body experiences when kissing a girl for the first time. Your whole body responds with feelings you never knew existed, and you finally come to the realization that those feelings are what make men do crazy things and bulls walk through barbed wire fences.

From the lofty perch of the operator's seat, Maude appeared more massive than she did from the ground. For a brief magical moment, I was captain of a schooner plowing through a distant sea. A good stiff breeze blowing across the wheat brought to mind, a quote from Michener's *Tales of the South Pacific*. My imagination ran as wild as that day on the windmill. I foolishly came to my feet and with outstretched arms, as if flying, I made an attempt to quote Michener. *Waves of the great ocean formed below us and fled in the golden sunlight. There was a breeze from Australia . . .*

As the day wore on, my enthusiasm waned with the increasing heat of the sun and the swirling dust cloud surrounding the combine. I no longer cared about the breeze in distant Australia, but wished instead for a good stiff wind from Kansas to refresh my burning body.

Later in the afternoon, Mr. Henry and I swapped jobs, causing me to believe he felt his beloved Maude wasn't a place for theatrical performances. The sun was beating down on my bare back with the intensity of a cutting torch, as I worked the grain with a scoop during an unloading stop at the combine. The breeze from Kansas had temporarily stopped and the swirling dust and wheat husk confined by the sides of the trailer filled the air with a thick cloud as well as every orifice of my body.

After unloading the truck into the grain bin and desiring some relief from the heat and dust, I strolled over to the water trough in the corral. With my face almost in the water, I began to throw great scoops of water onto my back and into my face.

Something bumped me on the butt and into the water trough I plunged headlong, stirring up years of dirt and other disgusting things, Buster and Midnight might have contributed to the trough. My first thought was that Buster, in a moment of curiosity, nudged me. Rising to the top and trying to expel from my lungs a gallon of water, I hung to the side of the aluminum trough as if it were the gunwale of a fishing boat.

Once the coughing spasms were somewhat under control, I stepped out of the trough and sat on the rim. With both hands resting on my knees, and still coughing, water dripping from my hair onto my face, I could see two legs standing before me; I then realized it wasn't Buster who had done me in, but a little Texas redhead.

Remembering my last experience in a water trough and the inability to run with wet boots, I slowly removed them and placed them on the ground. Apparently reading my mind and my intentions, Allie ran for the corral gate, which she didn't reach. As I carried her back toward the water trough, kicking and screaming, she tried playing her trump card, as most women would, by threatening to never make love to me again, if I went through with what I was thinking.

"Not only, am I thinking it, but I'm going to do it!" I said standing before the trough.

A smile of sweet revenge came over my face, then with one good heave, a scream and a splash.

Struggling to the top, as I had done only moments before, Allie discharged several gulps of water and then reached for the rim of the tank. With her back against the trough and her head resting against the rim, she held onto the side with outstretched arms. Her body floated to the top as if it were a cork on a fishing line.

The urge to turn the occasion into a romantic intrigue was too great to pass up, so I jumped in with her. While she continued to cough, I took hold of the sides and pulled my body over hers and began to kiss her on the neck working my way to her mouth as the coughing subsided. At first she resisted, but slowly her response became free and eager.

When things were about to get steamy her mouth relaxed. I did the same and opened my eyes. While maintaining lip contact, I noticed her eyes were wide open. When I moved back, she let out a blood curdling scream, causing me to roll over in the water next to her. Looking up, all I could see was Buster's big head only inches away from our faces. Allie slapped him on the nose and ordered him back to the barn.

After climbing out of the trough, we started toward the house, embracing each other while leaving a wet trail in the dirt. Mrs. Natty was sitting on the back steps, with a half-whimsical smile on her face, where she had been watching the entire charade. After placing my wet boots on the ground near the bell pole, I went inside to change into something dry before returning to the field.

Desiring a drink of clean water I made a quick detour into the kitchen, while Allie sat beside her Mother on the steps leading to the dining room. While dripping a small pool of murky water on the kitchen floor and indulging myself in a tall glass of water, I became intrigued with Mrs. Natty's assessment of our foolishness.

"That boy's in love with you, Allie," averred Mrs. Natty in a very low contralto. From my place of seclusion in the kitchen, I could picture her face as serious, but approving.

Eavesdropping had never been a flaw in my character, but since I seemed to be the main topic of discussion, I took my time. With something of a devilish grin on my face, I found myself thinking this conversation could be stimulating, so I prolonged the liquid intake as the water from my wet clothes continued to puddle around my feet.

"He's not in love, Mama. He's just horny." Allie's repartee caused me to smile.

"With a man, Daughter, love, and being horny is all the same," chuckled Mrs. Natty. "Girl . . . when your Daddy was young he was like a rutting deer."

A warm feeling passed through my wet body upon learning that the old gentleman was after all a human, or at least once was.

There was a short break in their conversation as they laughed and giggled like two young school girls. Mrs. Natty drew a deep breath and in an unconventional manner asked a question, which caused me to choke, as I continued to drink from the raised glass. Water came gushing from my nostrils. I reached for a dishcloth to muffle my coughing.

"Allie, have you and Yogi been sleeping together?" Mrs. Natty dryly asked.

"Mama!" shouted Allie. "What kinda question is that to ask?"

"It's a Mama kind of question, child," replied Mrs. Natty in a soft caring voice, which expressed a quality of equanimity, which I couldn't believe a mother would possess while dealing with such a subject. "That boy can't keep his hands off you . . . and he ain't going to wait forever before trying to bed you."

"You make it sound like I'm some kind of a brood mare or something, Mama," declared Allie.

"It's not that, Daughter. But sooner or later, you will be faced with that reality." There was a short hiatus in the dialogue before Mrs. Natty spoke again. "Allie, have you told him bout your secret?"

The gentleness in Mrs. Natty's voice makes me feel guilty for having intruded into a private part of Allie's world, which I knew existed, but into which I hadn't been invited.

"I can't, Mama," replied Allie.

There was sadness in Allie's voice, which I recognized and the question about her secret prompted recollections about her strange behavior, in the drive-in movie and the motel on New Year's Eve.

"Allie, if this boy loves you, he'll understand," declared Mrs. Natty in a firm, but loving voice. "And . . . if he doesn't . . . it's best he learns the truth before you two become too serious about each other."

Thoughts of how much Allie would be hurt if my presence became known caused me to settle on the kitchen floor. Leaning against the cabinets, I struggled with my predicament and found myself not knowing how to free myself of my own secret.

"Allie, do you love this boy?" questioned Mrs. Natty.

"I can't, Mama," answered Allie in a calm voice. After several trying moments, which I felt were equally difficult for both of us, she added, "I don't know if I can love any man, Mama."

My guilt deepened. In my despair, I pulled my knees closer to my body and lowered my forehead to my folded arms.

"Mama, if I could love anyone . . . I would want it to be Yogi," continued Allie amid unmistakable sobs. "He's the gentlest boy I've ever known . . . but he deserves someone better than I."

"Now, don't you talk that way," Mrs. Natty said in a strong, gruffly, but motherly tone. "You let him be the judge of that!"

A period of silence, lasting several minutes, transpired between Allie and her mother as I sat on the floor in a small puddle of water. I wanted to run . . . I wanted to be any place but where I was at the time. Finally, a thought came to my mind. There was a way out of my dilemma.

Getting up, I made my way to the washer on the veranda where I found a pair of jeans and socks from the previous day. They reeked with stale perspiration, but given a choice they were better than what I was wearing. After changing into them, while keeping a lookout for the ladies, I made my way back into the kitchen where I nosily disturbed some dishes in the sink after mopping up the water on the floor.

Realizing how long I had been gone from the field and suspecting the grain tank on the combine would be full, and an impatient Mr. Henry would be waiting for me to return, a feeling of panic came rushing over me. Absorbed in this one thought, I exited the kitchen door and ran in the direction of the truck in my socks, causing Allie and her mother to burst forth in a heartily laughter.

"Don't you think you should take your boots . . . boy?" called out Mrs. Natty.

I stopped and looked down at my feet. Then rushed back to the bell post and picked up the boots. Without putting them on, I scampered toward the truck with the fleetness of a Texas jack rabbit.

Even at a distance, the absence of the usual dust cloud and discharge of straw at the rear of the combine told me the machine was down. I knew Mr. Henry would be madder than a hornet for the downtime I caused him, while indulging myself in a swim and soap opera session.

Upon reaching the combine, I pulled into position so the unloading elevator could reach over the bed of the truck. The look on Mr. Henry's face told me, we were about to become engaged in what would be our first extemporaneous sparring match.

"Where have you been, boy?!" he demanded, grimacing and then spat on the ground in disgust.

For some strange reason, my tongue was in motion before my brain was in gear, and I blurted out, "I had an accident."

A puzzled look came to his face as he shook his head and retorted, "Didn't I tell you there's a roll of toilet paper behind the truck seat?"

I wanted to laugh, but wasn't about to correct his misunderstanding at the time. With a polite, *yes, sir, I'll keep that in mind,* I climbed from the cab with cowboy boots in hand and sat on the ground hoping to complete the habiliment required of a true Texas farmhand.

Chapter 20

Maude continued to perform with the grace and reliability of a Swiss-made watch for the rest of the week, causing me to feel the camaraderie between Mr. Henry and his beloved old machine was indomitable. As the acres of wheat slowly gave way to this ancient farm implement, I felt for the first time in my life, I was a part of something truly important. Unlike my paper shuffling job at the Air Base, on the farm, I could stand back at the end of each day and survey the diminishing stand of wheat bending before the Panhandle breeze.

While sitting on the cab of the truck, listening to the sweet threnody of a mourning dove in the distance, I poured the final cup of coffee from the Thermos, Allie had prepared at breakfast. In the distance, I could see several combines working in a sawtooth formation on a nearby farm, as a huge almost orange-red sun sank in the western sky beyond the hills.

Mused by the beauty of the open country surrounding me, I missed Mr. Henry's hand signal beckoning me forward with the grain truck. As the distinct humming of the combine's engine died down his bellowing call across the field drew my attention in his direction. Jumping from the cab of the truck, my pants leg caught on the corner edge of the truck door, throwing me to the ground as if given a body slam by Andre the Giant.

Once the truck pulled into place, a steady flow of grain poured into the body as I stood knee-deep in wheat, attempting to move it around with a scoop. Every muscle in my upper body seemed to be on fire as I raced against the rising mound.

At last the flow subsided and the auger, now running empty, produced a recognizable sound, to which my mind and body responded by relaxing. Standing at the controls of the combine, Mr. Henry slowed the engine. I moved to the cab of the truck and sat for a few moments trying to catch my breath. During the brief period of quietness tolling the day's end, the even sweeter sound of the plantation bell caused Mr. Henry and I to turn in the direction of its pealing.

"Tarp it down, Yogi," called out Mr. Henry, from his position on the combine.

"You gonna ride to the front with me?" I called back.

"To where?" asked Mr. Henry with a puzzled look on his face.

Realizing Mr. Henry wasn't familiar with the Cajun locution presented him, I rephrased my question. "Are you going to ride to the house with me?"

"No. I'll meet you at the shed," replied Mr. Henry. "Tomorrow, I plan to start cutting on the other side of the place."

Earlier in the day, Mr. Henry asked if I would be willing to take the final load to the grain elevators in town. I agreed, thinking Allie might agree to ride with me. Mrs. Natty glanced in her husband's direction when Allie sought her approval for such a trip. Mr. Henry seemed more intent on finishing his supper before answering with a warning that it might be a long wait, and there were always truck drivers hanging around. Caving in to Allie's pleading, he signaled his approval with a nod.

Friday night was apparently a good time to go to the grain elevator because the line of trucks wasn't as long as expected, and we made it to the scales in less than three hours. Away from the prying eyes and sensitive ears of Mrs. Natty, I attempted to use the time spent in line to catch up on a little romance. Allie reclined against the passenger door with her tennis shoes on the dashboard, while I laid my head in her lap with my boots sticking out the driver's side window. Several times, the air horns on the truck behind us disrupted our quiet interlude, forcing me to sit up and drive forward.

As I pulled up to the scales, a young girl stepped into the pathway of the headlights and held up her hand commanding me to stop. Her white, almost transparent 'V' neck T-shirt clearly showed an outline of her well-developed bosom. Her provocative shorts resembling a Texas flag came just below the gluteus fold of her buttocks.

Unconsciously I blurted out, "Who the hell is that!"

"Delilah Watts," countered Allie. "And you can stop gawking!"

"Ohhh, Delilah! I could use a haircut," I murmured, watching her walk toward the truck.

A fist hit me in the ribs.

The sex goddess pulled herself up on the running board by taking hold of the brace on the west coast mirror. Every part of her voluptuous form moved within the T-shirt, putting its worn cotton fibers to a test of endurance.

"Howdy cowboy, I'm Delilah."

As her oversized bosom rested on the truck door window ledge like two large cantaloupes inflating the front of the T-shirt, I responded, "Howdy, I'm Samson."

"Drop your canvas, Cowboy so I can check you out," Delilah answered in a provocative voice as if approving of my sarcasm.

"Do what?" I asked feeling stupid.

"You have to roll back the tarp, Casanova," replied Allie, in a gruff voice before opening the truck door and getting out.

After removing the straps holding down the tarp, I followed Delilah up the ladder to the top of the scale house, while keeping my eyes on the miniature Texas flag above me. Once the load was uncovered, Delilah shoved a long sample probe down into the wheat, while giving me a coquettish grin. With the three samples extracted and dumped into a bucket, I led the way down the ladder, while admiring the little Texas flag two feet above my head.

Delilah handed the sample bucket to a young man through a small window before ordering me to pull forward slightly until the rear of the body was over a narrow grating. Before I could walk back around the truck, Delilah opened the small hatches on the rear of the body, causing a flow of wheat to cascade into a bottomless pit, like water over a waterfall. As the flow of grain slackened, a hydraulic platform slowly elevated the truck causing the remainder of the load to slide toward the small hatches. Once empty, I moved the truck to a parking spot out of the way before walking to the scale house.

The laughter of the other drivers standing around drinking coffee came to an abrupt ending, when I came through the door and paused. Among the men in the office were Bubba Lee and Earl McCurley, whom I had met at Clifford's Hardware.

While I moved to Allie's side, Bubba Lee broke the silence.

"Maybe you're afraid Delilah's gonna crash-land your flyboy," soliloquized Bubba Lee in a blusterous tone, while pointing his thumb at me. "Besides . . . I think she adds a certain appeal to this place."

"You would Bubba Lee," countered Allie in an indignant tone.

"She was hired to attract truck drivers . . . the same thing she was doing at the Wild Bull," countered Bubba, while looking at his friend for support.

"The Wild Bull is a barroom . . ." replied Allie.

"Bubba Lee, your moisture content is over 17 percent," interrupted Earl McCurley while extending a small piece of paper across the counter toward Bubba.

"Now that will cause a crash landing," I interjected.

The burst of laughter brought on by my remark died out as Bubba looked around, before walking to the counter to accept the bill of laden.

"There's no sledge hammers in this place," Bubba Lee mumbled, as he stood beside me studying the slip of paper.

"I'll see if Earl has a tack hammer someplace," was my swift repartee, which brought a few snickers from the room.

Bubba turned from the counter and glanced around the room. As if synchronizing coffee cups, went up before the changing faces staring back. Before stepping away from the counter, Bubba purposely mashed the toe of my right foot with the heel of his left boot.

"Bubba, you had better start parking your truck under a shed," said Earl, as Bubba reached the door, "or else haul your grain to Dalhart."

The dusty Venetian blinds on the door made a clanging sound, as Bubba left the scale house without replying.

Upon returning to the house, Allie and I were attempting to say good night in the hallway, when her mother came out of the bedroom shared by her and Mr. Henry. For a moment, Allie and I stood apart without speaking, while surreptitiously watching Mrs. Natty start down the stairs.

"You smell like the fields," Allie whispered, while hooking her finger in my belt buckle and pulling me back against her body, once her mother was out of sight.

"I'm sorry," I whispered, while kissing her on the neck, "maybe you could come scrub my back. While you get rid of the smell . . . I know how to get rid of this other problem I'm having . . . if you're willing to help."

Footsteps coming up the stairs caused Allie to push back.

"Tonight you'll have to handle those problems alone," Allie replied with a slight kiss before reaching for the door knob.

The voluptuous nature of Delilah Watts and her Texas flag shorts haunted me for an hour, before I fell to sleep.

In our haste to indulge ourselves in some form of uncontrolled animalistic passion, Delilah and I left a line of clothes strewn throughout the field, like so much litter along a Louisiana highway, as we joyfully violated Mr. Henry's rules about playing in the standing wheat. The eroticism and gayety associated with our frolicking soon faded as an angry combine gave chase while shredding our clothes. My boxer shorts, twisted around my right ankle, caused me to stumble headlong into the standing wheat before the demoniac combine. Staring back at Maude, I watched as she chewed up my wool blanket and spit it out as bits of rags on her way to devour me. Coming to my feet, I tried to run again, but fell once more. While sliding backward on my naked butt, I continued to kick, trying to free myself from the boxer shorts now snagged by one of Maude's steel tines.

The tugging at my feet continued, until finally I sat up and scooted to the headboard of the bed. With a wild, crazed expression on my face, I yelled out, "No! Please, stop!"

With the sheet badly twisted around my body and neck, I gasped for a breath as I stared out at Mr. Henry standing at the foot of the bed with a blank expression. After untangling the sheet from around my neck and taking several deep breaths, I relaxed before wiping the sweat from my face.

"Are you all right, boy?" asked Mr. Henry in a gruff voice.

"Yeah," I replied, still taking in deep breaths of air. "I had a nightmare."

"Breakfast is ready," replied Mr. Henry in his usual succinct manner. "Better pull up your drawers," he added, before turning for the door.

Quickly covering myself with the sheet, I let loose a blast of vulgarity in French, which drove Mr. Henry from the room.

Following our morning ritual of greasing and fueling the combine, which I approached with some consternation, we moved into a different section of the field to begin cutting. Mr. Henry "outlined" the first section of the new field, before entrusting Maude into my hands. Had he known at the time my feelings about the combine, he would have stood guard over his beloved Maude with a shotgun.

The first couple of hours in the field were pleasant as a few clouds obscured the full heat of the midmorning sun. By the time Allie arrived with our snack of coffee and doughnuts, my relationship with Maude had improved to the point that I could smile about the nightmare.

"What's so funny?" Allie asked with an elfin smile, upon noticing my comical mood.

"Nothing," I retorted, trying to hide behind the black cup from the Thermos bottle.

"Nothing! Then why are you grinning?" asked Allie, while coming up to her knees and lunging at me.

Throwing the cup of coffee aside to catch her, I fell over onto the stubble and yelled out as the stiff ends of the stalks stabbed me in the back.

While lying on top of me, Allie repeated her question with an incredulous, but nontreating face. Knowing the truth about Delilah being a part of my dream, would result in my immediate death, I decided to lie and tell her that she was in my nightmare. I enjoyed relating my misadventure to her, even in my painful position, but after sometime, the pain became more than I could stand.

"You have to let me up." I pleaded with a scowl. "I'm being stabbed to death."

A call from Mr. Henry caused Allie and me to sit up. After a quick kiss, I climbed into the grain truck and drove to the combine while Allie drove off in Mr. Henry's old pickup.

By this time, the clouds had disappeared from the sky and the full force of the sun began to beat down with a vengeance upon the wheat field and its two weary reapers. Feeling like the sun possessed fingers capable of reaching down to Indian Ridge, I glanced up briefly into the glaring brilliance, while removing Robert's cowboy hat to wipe the perspiration from my forehead. Because of the swirling dust enveloping the grain truck, I tied my handkerchief across my nose as a dust mask.

Although Mr. Henry's leg had been bothering him more than usual that morning, he didn't complain and refused to relinquish full control of the combine's operation for the easier job of running the grain truck.

After making several dumps into the grain truck, Mr. Henry climbed down from the combine for a drink of water. It was then I persuaded him to let me take over Maude for a while. The afternoon was going well, so I thought, and after several rounds in the field, I pronounced an absolution upon Maude for her transgressions of the previous evening. Remembering what I had been told about paying attention to the 'sounds' of the combine, I shortly thereafter began to detect a knocking in the front of the machine while Mr. Henry was gone to "the front" with a load of wheat. After bringing the combine to a stop, but leaving the reel and the other moving parts running, I climbed down the ladder to look around. It was then that I detected the noise coming from the cutter-bar drive case. After shutting down the machine, I sat under the combine and waited for Mr. Henry to return.

Once he arrived, I restarted the combine so he could diagnose the problem.

"Sounds like the chain is slipping on the sprocket," declared Mr. Henry, as he knelt down to put his ear closer to the gearbox. "Simple job, Yogi. Won't take long to fix," he added, while straining to stand.

With a few wrenches from the toolbox kept in the grain truck, I removed the guard under Mr. Henry's supervision, exposing what would have ordinarily been a simple job. The kicker came after Mr. Henry removed the cotter pins on the master link to remove the plate in an effort to break the chain. The plate was stuck. While using a screwdriver to pry it off, the plate popped off and disappeared into the unknown universe. Two dirty, sweaty faces, stared at each other in astonishment.

In an unbelievable outburst of Presbyterian profanity, Mr. Henry declared, "Well, kiss my butt."

I started to laugh, which soon drew a hearty laughter from Mr. Henry. After a moment or two, he regained control of himself and looked at me with a very serious face.

"You breathe a word of this to Allie or her mother, and I'll let it be known, I found you in the bed this morning with your drawers down."

Continuing to snicker, I replied while trying to look the other way, "That's not the whole truth . . . and besides . . . what you're threatening is blackmail."

Mr. Henry and I continued to laugh about his blasphemous expression, which I felt was the extent of his vocabulary in the realm of obscenity. Somehow the little exchange seemed to tear down some of the remaining walls between us.

"We had better find that plate, or we'll be down all afternoon," remarked Mr. Henry in a dry tone, as he struggled to kneel.

After joining Mr. Henry on the ground to look for the missing plate, I mumbled, "Embrasse mon cul."

"What's that, Yogi?" asked Mr. Henry while turning his head toward me.

"It's French. It's a rough equivalent to what you said a minute ago," I said with a grin. "My dad used to say that in French, when he didn't want us kids to understand what he was saying."

Our search for the missing plate continued for several minutes before Mr. Henry decided to take the chain back to the equipment shop and repair it there. Our search through fruit jars, cans, and cigar boxes, containing hundreds of items "squirreled away" over the years, still failed to produce the right size plate. Had the situation not be so critical, it would have been funny.

Deciding to give up and return to the combine to look for the missing piece, we headed back to Maude with the adjusted chain. The ride was quiet, fast, and bumpy. I kept my face turned toward my open window. After reaching the combine, we again knelt down and began a methodical search for the missing plate by combing through the straw and stubble.

I was about to give up, when Mr. Henry, sitting on his hindside, looked over at me and asked, "How do you say that in French again?"

"Why?" I asked, turning my head in his direction, while on my all fours.

"Look what I have," was his repartee, while holding up the small plate. With a smile on his face he added, "The sucker was in the cuff of my pants all the while."

Embrasse mon cul, I shouted, while standing in excitement.

Mr. Henry's attempt to curse in French caused me to laugh.

With the chain and guard replaced, cutting resumed after losing better than an hour on a job that shouldn't have taken more than just a few minutes. Mr. Henry tried to make up for the downtime by cutting well beyond sunset, with the intention of filling the truck for another run into town.

Allie decided not to ride with me on this trip. Perhaps it was a good thing for the line at the elevator was unusually long, and it was almost one thirty before I returned to the house. Before going upstairs for a bath, I went to the kitchen for something to eat. All I could find was a jar of peanut butter, so I decided on a peanut butter and jelly sandwich like my mother used to make. Taking a large scoop of peanut butter and dislodging it from the spoon with my index finger into a coffee cup, I added a scoop of jelly, using the same displacement method. To this mixture, I added a small touch of honey and vanilla. After stirring the mixture with a butter knife until it became a molten mass, I smeared it over four pieces of toast.

While indulging myself on this gourmet snack and a tall glass of milk, Allie came lumbering into the kitchen and sat on the chair next to me. While resting her elbows on the table and propping her chin in the palm of her hands, she just sat there watching me eat.

"Stop staring at me . . . you're making me nervous," I said, pushing her on the chin with my hand.

After picking up a dishcloth and wiping milk from the corner of my mouth, Allie leaned forward and gave me a kiss. She continued to watch me eat. I started to turn my back to her, but she took me by the shoulder and pulled me around.

After getting up and sitting in my lap, in a straddling position, Allie said, "I'm glad you came to the farm, Yogi."

"So am I," I said as she placed her head on my shoulder.

"You taste like peanut butter and something else," Allie said drowsily.

"It's vanilla," I replied grinning.

"I like it."

"Know what I like?" I asked, while kissing her on the side of the neck. Allie sat back and responded by shaking her head "no." "I like this little spot," I added, touching the small concaved notch at the base of her neck before kissing it.

With a chuckle Allie answered, "That's called the suprasternal notch."

Placing my right index finger through an opening between buttons on her pajama top, I touched a spot between her breasts. "This is another spot I like," I said.

"And what is that spot called?" asked Allie with a teasing smile, while holding my finger in place.

"The valley of tears," I said with a playful smile.

"Yogi! Why are you saying that?" Allie asked, with a disappointed look on her face while releasing my finger.

"Because they are crying out for some caressing," I replied. In an effort to bring some happiness to the 'valley of tears,' I buried my face in her pajamas.

Footsteps on the stairs caused Allie to quickly return to her chair. As Mrs. Natty walked into the kitchen, I was beginning to believe the "bat ear" lady was a greater nightmare than Maude.

The following morning while I ate a late breakfast, Allie prepared a Thermos of coffee and a cooler of water for her father and me. Her midmorning trip to the field would not take place this morning, since she and Mrs. Natty were going to church. Mr. Henry didn't attend church on Sundays during harvest time and justified his absence by saying, *The Lord understood the plight of the farmer, since it was he who made man a farmer.*

By the time I arrived in the field, Mr. Henry had already been cutting for sometime and was ready to empty the grain tank on the combine. After pulling the truck into position, the auger started dumping a stream of wheat kernels into the empty truck bed, producing the usual cloud of dust.

While the combine discharged its load, I took the Thermos bottle from the seat of the truck and handed it up to Mr. Henry, still seated on the combine. He poured himself a small amount of coffee into the cup, and then tossed the bottle down to me.

"You got in late last night, eh?" he called out in a loud voice, trying to overcome the sound of the engine.

"Yeah! It was after one." I yelled back.

After a few minutes, the grain tank went empty. Mr. Henry threw down the Thermos cup, which I quickly screwed in place before running around the combine to move the truck.

The morning hadn't yet started to heat up, so as Mr. Henry and Maude made their way through the wheat, I walked to the edge of the stand and broke off a piece of straw. After placing it between my teeth with the head dangling, I walked a ways through the open ground taking in the serenity of the open country, which was slowly gaining my appreciation.

Stopping for a while, I dug my bootheel into the soil. After bending over and scooping up a handful, I smelled it, before dropping it back to the ground. It wasn't black like the rich river bottom soil back home and didn't deliver the satisfaction of olfaction, I remembered as a child, walking behind my Dad, as he plowed his field with a mule.

The tranquility of the morning was broken when a noticeable drop in the sound from across the field caught my attention. The combine had stopped. Under my breath, I pronounced a curse on Maude, while removing the straw from my mouth and throwing it to the ground.

"We have a broken sickle bar," announced Mr. Henry in a brusque tone, as I pulled next to the combine in the grain truck.

Judging by the disgust on his face, I figured my questions concerning the problem would only serve to antagonize him, so I remained silent and followed his instructions.

It seemed the sun heated up right along with our frustration and aggravation, as we fought with rusty bolts and nuts trying to disconnect the reciprocating drive mechanism as well as other parts in order to remove the sickle bar. In pulling the bar free, Mr. Henry cut his hand on one of the knives. Once more, my handkerchief came in handy.

With the bar securely tied to the side of the truck, we transported it to the equipment shop. Since time was lost repairing the sickle bar, and it being out, making it easier to sharpen the knives, Mr. Henry decided to do this while the bar was in the shop.

Upon returning from church, Allie and her mother prepared for us a lunch, which we had on the tailgate of the pickup. Also Mr. Henry's hand received a medical examination and better dressing.

Three hours of cutting time were lost and my thoughts of Maude's demonic possession were beginning to resurface as we resumed cutting. The long hours of standing, while welding the sickle bar, caused Mr. Henry's leg to bother him greatly. The pain in his face caused me to insist that he rest in the grain truck, while I operate Maude for the rest of the day.

In spite of the difficulties of the day, we were able to fill the grain truck before sundown and once again I decided to drive to the elevator, knowing it would be another long night. Mr. Henry insisted I skip this nightly trip, but I was determined to go through with it, knowing that my stay was limited and his leg was going to restrict his mobility, once I returned to Amarillo.

Upon returning to the house from the elevator, I glanced at the clock on the stove. It was 1:30 a.m. Filling a glass with milk, I walked to the pantry and took out a bag of oatmeal cookies and sat on the steps leading to the kitchen. The night was quiet, except for the rustling of the leaves in the trees and the squeaky rhythmic sounds of the corral windmill. I had hoped, Allie would join me again, but my wishes went unfulfilled in spite of my tarrying.

On my way down the hall to Robert's room, I stopped at Allie's bedroom door and contemplated going in to say good night. After a second or two, knowing her mother would be manning the DEW Line down the hall, I tiptoed down the hall hoping to avoid the squeaky board. My efforts failed.

After taking a bath, I couldn't sleep for thinking of the problems encountered during the day. The bedroom became hot and the pajama bottoms were annoying me to no end. Thinking I would get some air, I walked to the window and raised the shade and then the window. Standing there taking in the night air, I noticed an amazing sight, which brought a smile to my face. *Why hadn't I seen this before?* I asked myself.

Just below the window was the roof over the downstairs bedroom. Leaning out, I noticed the roof ran well past Allie's bedroom. The fiendish thoughts that came to my mind caused me to touch my head, to see if horns were sprouting.

Stepping through the window and onto the roof, I made my way to Allie's bedroom window and lightly tapped on the window pane. After several minutes, the window shade moves slightly, revealing a sleepy, suspicious, but a very welcoming face.

"Yogi, what are you doing?" asked Allie, as she raised the window.

"I wanted to see you before turning in," I answered, stepping through the window, "and this is one way of getting around that damn board in the hall."

"If my mother catches you in here, she'll kill you," Allie said with an alluring smile, while putting her arms around my neck.

For two weeks, my whole existence had hinged upon waiting for such a moment. My heart was pounding with anticipation.

A cold chill shot down my spine when I heard the squeaky board in the hallway give forth its awful cry and a knock sounded on Robert's bedroom door. For a moment, I froze. Then, like a jack rabbit I headed for the open window and made it back to my room, via the roof, as the knocking sounded again. Standing near the open window, I breathed a sigh of relief when the board sounded in the hallway. Walking on tiptoe, I rushed into the bathroom.

With my head against the bathroom wall, I could hear Allie and her mother talking. Thinking I had better reveal my presence in the house, I flushed the commode before making a quick dash for the bed. Lying on top of the sheets for a while, I couldn't help but smile to myself, knowing that a 'cat and mouse' game was about to take place between myself and Mrs. Natty now that a new route to Allie's room had been discovered. Feeling "full of myself," as the saying goes, I remained awake for sometime before falling asleep.

My wake-up call came at 7:00 a.m. on Monday morning with the usual tugging at my feet by Mr. Henry. There was no cup of coffee and no morning kiss, only his morose face and a gruff voice announcing that breakfast was ready.

During breakfast, Allie came down and sat next to me. She was moving at a snail's pace as always, and it took most of her strength just to say "good morning." Mrs. Natty's remark about Mr. Henry's hand, now wrapped in a washcloth bound with freezer tape, caused Allie to insist on examining the cut. The expression on her face spoke volumes of displeasure with her father. The wound was red and warm to the touch. Allie and Mrs. Natty made a fuss about it and insisted he go into town to see Dr. Adams. Mr. Henry rejected the notion.

Not wanting to become involved in a family dispute, but feeling his hand needed some attention, I offered an idea.

"If Allie could handle the grain truck until you get back . . . then I'll take over the combine . . ." I paused to judge Mr. Henry's reaction before continuing. "Besides you need to see the Doctor about that limp."

A pallid complexion transformed the old man's face. I couldn't tell if it was from the thought of me having complete control over Maude or the fact that I hadn't sided with him in his dispute with Allie and Mrs. Natty.

"Why, she can't handle that truck," declared Mr. Henry, while shifting around in his chair, thinking he had found a way out of what he perceived as a dilemma.

"You think just because I'm a girl I can't drive a truck?"

There was a hiatus in the conversation for several moments before Mr. Henry looked at me.

"She wrecks my truck, I'm holding you responsible."

Trying to lighten up the tension in the kitchen, I agreed with the assertion, "Okay. If she destroys anything, you can take the damages out of my wages."

Mr. Henry gave me a blank stare for several seconds before we all laughed. Since my wages were nonexistent.

Allie made a hasty retreat upstairs. Several minutes later, she came down wearing Robert's high school baseball cap, a pair of jeans, boots, and a western shirt tied in a big knot at the waist. I hadn't seen her do this since the past summer, when we went riding in Palo Duro Canyon. As she stood in the doorway between the dining room and kitchen "reporting for duty," I thought she was at least the most beautiful truck driver in Indian Ridge, if not the most experienced.

After going through the morning ritual of greasing and fueling the combine, I gave the decrepit old machine, a tongue lashing in French just to show her who was boss and running the operation for the day. Allie stood beside the combine, laughing with her hand over her mouth. It must have worked, for the morning went well, and Maude performed magnificently. Allie also surprised me by pulling the truck up to the combine, in the proper position, and on time, each time I signaled her to do so.

However, her first trip to the grain bins didn't go so well.

She backed the truck too close to the unloading chute. When she opened the hatches, the grain began spilling onto the ground. In a panic, she forgot to close the hatches before pulling the truck forward, thus spilling even more on the ground. Finally, she got the hatches closed and then drove back to the field to get me. The anger she tried to disguise while relating her tale of woe, caused me to take her into my arms to keep from laughing.

In exchange for a kiss and a smile, I showed her how to back the truck into the right position and promised not to tell her father about the spillage. After all, if black mail wasn't below the dignity of a Presbyterian Elder, it surely wasn't beyond the capabilities of a lowly Airman. Allie and I scooped up the spilled grain, the best we could, and fed it to Buster and Midnight.

Following Dr. Adams' advice, Mr. Henry decided to stay off his leg a couple of days, even though he had Allie drive him to the field each morning to witness the ritual greasing of Maude.

"Looks like some of these knives could use changing, Yogi," said Mr. Henry, as he hobbled in front of the combine on a walking stick.

"Maybe tomorrow night I'll change them, rather than making a trip to the elevators," I answered.

"Daddy, you should get off your leg, now," implored Allie.

"I'm coming, Daughter," answered Mr. Henry. "I'll dig out that manual so you can read it tonight," continued Mr. Henry, as he started toward the pickup.

While Allie drove her father to the house, I finished Maude's morning greasing with a blessing in French, which included a threatened shot of Louisiana Red Hot Sauce in her grease, if her knives didn't hold out until Wednesday evening.

The following evening, I decided to skip supper in order to get an early start on changing the knives. Mr. Henry had given me instructions enough to overhaul Maude from bow to stern before returning to the house with Allie. He had wanted to stay in the field to supervise the job, but Mrs. Natty insisted he should attend the wake for Mr. Pee Wee Peterson, the hired man whose place I had taken during harvest time. Allie had supper with her parents that evening and then stayed home to clean the kitchen, while they went to town.

Using the headlights of the grain truck to illuminate the job, the work went better than expected and I enjoyed the solitude of the evening, as well as the satisfaction of accomplishing the task on my own. The stillness in the field after dark, reminded me of my nights on guard duty during the Cuban crisis, and I chuckled to myself as thoughts of Hopper came to my mind. The lights of the farmhouse in the distance, reminded me that Allie and I were spending our only evening alone on the place, separated by an ocean of wheat, an old machine named Maude, and dirty dishes.

A few hours later, while picking up the tools, the headlights of a vehicle traveling through the field caught my attention. I was busy cleaning my hands with Go-Jo when Allie pulled up near the grain truck in the old pickup.

"Brought you some fresh coffee, Yogi," Allie called out after getting out the car.

"Thanks. I could use it."

After wiping my hands with a clean rag, I embraced Allie with both arms before kissing her.

"How much longer will you be?" Allie asked, after breaking away to pour some coffee into the Thermos cup while standing before the grain truck.

"You're starting to sound like your mother," I said with a chuckle. While lifting the toolbox and walking to the passenger side of the truck I added, "Ah . . . just a few more minutes. Things went better than I expected."

As I walked back to the front of the truck, Allie offered me the coffee cup. I thanked her with another kiss.

"You mind shutting off the truck and turning out the lights?" I asked, before taking a drink of coffee.

"I have supper on the stove . . . any time you're ready," added Allie in a raised voice from the truck cab.

When Allie rejoined me in front of the truck, I finished off the coffee before slinging the cup dry and placing it on the hood. For a moment, I felt we could read each other's thoughts, as I pulled her body against mine for a more passionate kiss.

"Why don't we take this canvas into the wheat and roll down about five acres?" I whispered, while kissing her on the lower part of the neck. "I'll kiss all my favorite spots, while exploring them."

"Have you forgotten about my father's rule?" Allie asks with some alacrity.

"Right now, I'm more concerned with Maude watching us, than your father," I responded, recalling the role Maude played in my nightmare. "Maybe I'll flatten her tires so she can't get after us."

Allie's momentary laughter led me to believe she agreed with my suggestion. Grabbing the canvas with one hand and Allie by the other, I started running toward the standing wheat while pulling Allie along. For almost three hundred yards, we romped through the swaying heads, before falling to the ground with a roar of laughter.

"Aren't you too tired for this?" Allie asked, trying to catch her breath.

"Yeah, but it's a good kind of tired," I said, looking down into her smiling face. "I believe I'm starting to love being a farmer, the Panhandle, and even that damn old combine," I said with a sense of affability.

"What about the trees of Louisiana?" asked Allie with a giggle. "Have you forgotten how much you love them?"

"A man learns to love different things at different times in his life, Allie, and right now, I've found something . . . and someone else to love."

"Please don't say those things, Yogi," Allie murmured, while avoiding eye contact with me.

Rising to one elbow, I asked, "Allie, why are you afraid of being loved and sharing your love?"

"Yogi, I told you once before, I don't want you to fall in love with me."

"I am in love with you, Allie," I said, sitting up while attempting to bring some order to the canvas.

"I'm not worthy of your love, Yogi," Allie answered in a morose tone, while looking away.

"That's not true," I replied, gingerly while stretching out beside her.

"Yogi, maybe if we had met before . . ." Allie said softly and then stopping.

"Before what?" I asked.

"Before a lot of things," replied Allie, turning her face from me.

For some time, Allie and I lay on the canvas both looking up at the nebulous shrouded moon, as I wondered how many more times must I express my love for her before the veil covering her mind and heart, would be removed. I felt her hand grasp mine, before asking a question in a soft tone.

"Yogi . . . let's pretend this is our first time."

"What?" I asked, rolling my face toward hers.

"Let's pretend this is our first time," Allie said, while rolling onto her side and placing her hand on my chest. My blank expression caused her to request that I look the other way while she undressed.

With our backs toward each other, we undressed and placed our clothes in two orderly piles on separate sides of the canvas. Devoid of all clothing except for my boxer shorts and dog tags, I sat on the canvas, until Allie told me to turn around. She was lying beside me with only her panties on and her arms folded across her breast. The soft moonlight against her body made her more desirable than ever, and I thought this must have been what Adam and Eve experienced the first time they made love in the Garden.

As I bend over to kiss her, my dog tags fell against her body.

"Remove them, Yogi," Allie whispered without moving.

"Why?" I asked, giving her a slight kiss, "I thought you liked the way they feel against your body."

"I want to make love to you . . . this time, Yogi. Not some GI, and you won't need a condom."

"Are you sure, Allie?" I asked in a quiet doubting voice.

Allie responded by moving her head in the affirmative.

After removing the dog tags and putting them inside my boot, I threw the condom on the canvas next to the boots. When I turned back to Allie, her eyes avoided mine, as I slowly lifted her arms from across her breast and placed them to her side. Propping myself on my extended left arm, I looked down at Allie, whose eyes seemed to concentrate on the stars. My right hand softly cupped her left breast as I leaned forward to kiss the other.

The tenseness in Allie's body and the lack of enthusiasm demonstrated by her left me with the impression that in her mind, this was her first time. As my passion increased, my right hand sought to explore an area forbidden to my touch by the House rules. Pulling my hand back from this forbidden zone, Allie pleaded for me not to touch her in this most personal area.

The tone of Allie's plea and the frigidness I could feel in her body caused my hands to never again venture into this forbidden area of her body. Allie's willingness to make love to me away from the House was an indication she was attempting to overcome her fears, which denied us such moments before. Yet, the lingering fear in Allie's mind restricted her passion and freedom in our lovemaking.

After the less-than-passionate *affaire d'amour* had concluded, we laid side by side holding hands, while looking up at the moon. However, the feelings between us left no room for shame from our nakedness and no thoughts for tomorrow or its consequences. We were young and had shared a once-in-a-lifetime experience. That was all that mattered. Tomorrow would have to take care of itself.

For the longest time as Allie and I lay there, she talked about many things, yet her thoughts seem jumbled, as if there was something she wanted to say, but couldn't. As a gentle breeze blew across the standing wheat, Allie became quiet before rolling onto her side to face me.

"We have to go, Yogi," Allie said softly before giving me a kiss on the cheek.

Allie and I dressed without looking at each other before returning to the house. After her parents had gone to bed, we met on the roof outside my bedroom window. While sitting on a throw rug taken from Robert's room, Allie sat between my legs, while leaning against my chest. Sitting there on the roof like two night owls, just listening to the sounds of the night, I finally realized how much I had come to love the farm and of course, Allie. I didn't want this night and this summer to even end.

The night ended with the usual tugging at my feet by Mr. Henry announcing that breakfast was ready. Ignoring Dr. Adams' orders, he decided to return to the combine while using a cane to get around. No amount of pleading from Mrs. Natty and Allie, was going to change his mind. Thanks to Maude's good behavior, the day went well. It was extremely hot that morning, so when Allie came to the field with our midmorning snack, she convinced her father into taking a small break while, she ran the truck, and I resumed operating the combine.

Later in the afternoon, Mr. Henry returned to the field, cane in hand, and insisted he take control of the combine. The day's cutting was slowly taking us closer to the area where Allie and I had spent our time together the previous evening, something I hadn't counted on, especially with Mr. Henry at the controls of the combine. I knew the trampled wheat would attract his attention and raise a question that I wouldn't be able to answer.

The afternoon dragged on, and the levels of my anxiety heightened to a state of paroxysm.

Upon returning from the grain bin, I noticed the combine parked near the spot where Allie and I had made love the evening before. A cold chill ran down my back as I drove through the cutover field and stopped at a respectable distance from Mr. Henry. In view of his gloomy face, I decided to remain unflappable.

"What's wrong?" I asked, pretending to be ignorant of the reason for the mashed wheat.

Reaching out his hand, Mr. Henry offered me the condom I had forgotten in the field.

"Is this yours?" he grimaced, while shifting his weight to the walking stick.

A sickening feeling came to my stomach. With a downcast look, I reluctantly took the condom in silence, knowing I was about to experience another nightmare.

"Well is it!" shouted Mr. Henry, as he stepped forward and delivered a solid blow to my left upper arm with his walking cane.

"Yes!" I shouted back.

"Is this the way you repay my hospitality, boy?" shouted Mr. Henry as he attempted to strike me again. When I grabbed the walking cane, he stood frozen, staring at me until I released the cane.

Mr. Henry turned and limped toward the combine.

"I took you into my home . . . I thought I could trust you with my daughter." He pounded the tire with the walking stick before turning to face me. "There was a time, boy . . . I was hoping you could become the son I lost . . . the one I never knew."

Assuming Mr. Henry was speaking of Robert, I yelled back, "I can't replace Robert! He's dead! Such a thing would only dishonor his memory."

"What do you know about honor?" shouted Mr. Henry. Once more with a contortion of his face, he added, "What you have done, boy, has disgraced me, . . . my wife, and my daughter, . . . and . . . and yourself." Pointing the walking stick toward me, Mr. Henry shouted, "I want you off this place . . . *Now!*"

His words fell upon me like a great weight, for I realized they were true. I stood motionless for an interminable amount of time. Instinct or shame forced me to crush the condom pack in my hand before pushing it deep into the pocket of my jeans.

As I walked back toward the truck, Mr. Henry called out while pointing his cane at me. "You walk to the house. I'll need the truck to unload the combine."

"I'm just getting my shirt!" I shouted angrily without turning to face Mr. Henry.

After retrieving my shirt, I walked back toward the combine and stopped several feet from Mr. Henry. With all the humility I could muster at the time, I said, "I'm sorry, . . . you found out about Allie and me this way."

"I want to know if you forced my daughter," Mr. Henry asked.

His question went through me like a sharp knife bringing to an end, my attempt to button up my shirt.

"I would never do such a thing to Allie." I could feel my temper beginning to rise, so pausing to take a few deep breaths and trying to relax, I finally answered, "I love her too much to even think of such a thing. What happened between Allie and me out here was an act of love between two people who freely shared their love with one another. Maybe it wasn't in keeping with your moral standards, or even mine, as that goes, but it doesn't mean I love her any less because of it. And if, some day she will have me, I plan to marry her with or without your blessing."

"That doesn't change anything," Mr. Henry answered before starting back around the machine.

Trying to get him to change his mind about my dismissal, I pleaded, "Mr. Henry? Let me stay to finish out the crop. You need my help . . . with your bad leg 'n all. And . . . I swear . . . I'll keep my distance from Allie while I'm on the place."

"You heard my ultimatum. Now get!" he answered in a gruff voice as he proceeded around the combine. I remained where I was, as he climbed aboard the combine with some difficulty. After sitting in the driver's seat, Mr. Henry called down, "Tell Allie to come out here . . . she'll have to drive the truck from now on."

The loud roar produced by the combine starting up, filling me with a degree of anguish I had not known before. In my shame and hurt, I started running down the dusty road toward the house. My lungs, starving for oxygen, burned deep within my chest, while my leg muscles started to cramp until they could no longer sustain the stride I had set for myself. Exhausted, I fell to the ground and rolled in the dust gasping for a breath. As I lay there looking up into the bright afternoon sun for some strange reason, the words of an Old Testament prophet came to my mind. *I will scatter you as chaff driven away by the wind . . . throw your shirt up over your face that your shame may be exposed . . . and show the lewdness of you harlotry on the hills in the field.* I don't know why I thought of these things, or when was the last time I had read them.

Chapter 21

The unenthusiastic good-bye wave that Allie gave me in response to my hand sign expressing my love for her as I backed out the driveway left me feeling I was deserting her at a time when she needed me most. Yet, I felt it best to leave after what had transpired between Mr. Henry and me. As the miles separating me from the farm grew lonelier through a state of musing about our future together, the sense of shame I had felt only hours before, began to fade with the thought that our time together in the field that evening was much too wonderful to regret.

Upon my arrival at the Base I found the barrack almost deserted, except for a couple of boys watching television in the dayroom. In a way, I was glad my friends weren't there, for, I didn't feel like answering any questions about my early return. After spending three weeks in the Sailhamer's large spacious home, my room in the barrack seemed extremely small, and I felt claustrophobic. Pete and Rosella however appeared to be happy and expressed their delight by breaking into a chirping competition.

The revitalizing power of a relaxing shower washed away some of the weariness brought on by the trip and the events of the day. After dressing with the intention of walking to the Airmen's Club for a burger and beer, I decided to give Allie a call.

The sound of Mrs. Natty's voice caused me to hesitate before speaking.

"Mrs. Natty," I responded in something of a mild tone. "This is Yogi. Is Allie home?"

"She's still out with her father."

"Are they still cutting at this hour?" I asked, feeling guilty.

"No, Yogi," Mrs. Natty replied in a soft voice, indicating she recognized my concern. "Seems something broke on the old combine, and Henry's been trying to fix it all afternoon."

"I'm sorry to hear that," I answered trying to imagine what else could have gone wrong with Maude. "Would you please tell her, I called?"

"Sure, Yogi," she answered. "Should she call you back?"

"No, it's not necessary," I answered in a somewhat despondent voice. "Just tell her, I'm sorry . . . about what happened."

There was a moment of silence on the other end before Mrs. Natty spoke again.

"Whatever happened between you and Henry will be forgotten after he cools off. Henry's a good man, Yogi, but he can be hard at times."

I felt Mrs. Natty hadn't yet learned the reason behind my abrupt departure. Recalling the conversation between Allie and her mother on the back steps, the day I sat on the kitchen floor dripping with water, I felt perhaps an explanation from Allie would be less painful, if she were to learn the truth.

Approaching the large open doors of Hangar 4000, the following morning, the soft threnody of a mourning dove from the open field beyond the tarmac caught my attention. Walking past the rear section of the hangar used by the Aircraft Accident Investigation Team, I made my way to the edge of the pavement in search of the elusive bird, which lifted my spirit with a stirring memory of the farm. Several more calls from the bird drew me close to the tall grass beyond the hangar. Standing at the edge of the pavement in the quietness of the early morning hour, I could see a shadowy outline of the city and the rising of steam from some industrial plant far beyond the airport. I stood there sometime, before turning to walk toward the hangar.

While removing my jacket, a large stack of revisions to the Jet Engine Technical Orders sitting on the floor next to my desk, caught my attention. As the office came alive with the arrival of others, who welcomed me back, I settled down in my swivel chair behind a mountain of paperwork, longing for Maude's contrariness, which at the time seemed desirable.

The only way I could possibly catch up on the backlog of work, was to stay beyond normal office hours. This I did, after calling the Air Police Headquarters and reporting that I would be working late in the Hangar office. About at 20:00 hours, I decided to call it a day and walked to the Chow Hall for something to eat, before going to the barrack. John and Paul, more so than James, gave me a hard time about my Gung Ho attitude when I came into the dayroom. After several minutes of their "warm approbations," James told me, someone had pinned a note on my door about a phone call from Allie.

My attempts to reach the Sailhamer's home were unsuccessful until my last attempt around 22:00 hours. Hearing Allie's voice took away what little energy existed in my spirit and for a moment, the reason, for her call became lost in a quiet mutual exchange of apologies.

"Yogi, my father had an accident."

"What happened?" I asked.

"He slipped on the top step of the combine and fell to the ground." There was a faltering sound in her voice. "He broke his ankle."

"Is it the same leg which has been hurting him?" I asked.

"Yes," replied Allie, still struggling to speak.

"What about the crop? What's going to happen now?" I asked.

"I don't know, Yogi."

"What if I came back to the farm? I still have some leave time," I said, trying to sound confident.

"Mom and I tried to talk to Daddy about that, but he wouldn't even discuss it," Allie responded with a worried sound in her voice.

"He'll just have to accept it, if I can get the balance of my leave time," I said resolutely.

"Yogi, with just the two of us, it will take more than one week to finish out the crop," replied Allie.

There was a moment of silence between us, as an idea began to take shape in my mind.

"Yogi, you're still there?" asked Allie.

"Yeah," I retorted. "Allie, I'll get back with you tomorrow night, okay! Everything will be okay. I promise."

After hanging up the receiver, I made a dash for the door of the barracks while checking my wallet. When I entered the dayroom, James was perched on the back of a chair watching the nightly pool contest between John and Paul.

"How would you guys like to go for a beer . . . on me," I solicited, trying to catch a breath.

The unusual offer caused three blank faces to turn toward me. Abandoning his position on the back of the chair, James spoke first.

"You're offering to buy us a beer?"

"Yeah."

"So, what's the catch? Are you and what's her name getting married?" asked Paul with a full grin on his face.

"There's no catch. It's been a while since I saw you guys . . . and I just thought you would like a beer . . . while we discuss an idea I have."

"I knew there was a catch!" declared Paul.

"We ain't planting anymore trees," John demanded while sliding the pool cue onto the table.

With a Cheshire cat grin, I asked, "How would you guys like to spend a week on a wheat farm?"

"On a what?" asked Paul with a disappointed expression. "Are you out of your mind?"

"Just one week. That's all I'm asking," I pleaded.

"Thanks for the offer of a beer, but no thanks to the offer," answered Paul, as he headed out the door. "I grew up on a damn wheat farm, and my ass still remembers the beatings I took because of a damn combine."

"Look! I'm planning to go back to help finish up the crop, since Allie's father broke his ankle, and I'll need some help."

"How can we help?" asked John, while stepping aside to allow a couple of boys to go up the stairs. "I don't know anything about driving farm machines."

"You can drive a truck, can't you?" I countered rather quickly. "And Paul . . . you probably know how to drive a combine."

"What kind of combine does this man own?" asked Paul, leading the way to the door.

"An old John Deere."

"My old man had a Cockshutt, so I don't know if I would be of any help to you," replied Paul, while looking back at me. "But, I'm still gonna drink the beer."

"There can't be that much difference between the machines, Paul," I pleaded, hoping to counter his argument. "The only other thing I could promise you guys is lots of hardwork, long hours, and some of the best home cooking in Texas."

"Would that include fried chicken?" asked James.

"That's right. Home-style fried chicken, like you wouldn't believe," I answered, as we left the barracks.

"If," stated James with a pause. "I'm just saying, if we agree to this hair brain scheme, how are all of us going to get a leave at the same time?"

"That's minor crap, you little Red Neck," answered John, while pushing James off the sidewalk. "What I want to know . . . is there any other kind of fried chicken in that hick town, or is it just farmers and pigs?"

John's inquiry into the subject having predominance always in his mind, quickly turned the conversation away from wheat fields and combines. However, like the idea about the squadron oak tree, I hoped time and beers would fertilize the thought planted in their minds.

Upon arriving at the office the following Monday, my first phone call of the day was to Airman Zuccarello at the Orderly Room, requesting an appointment with Captain Ford. By chow time at noon, I hadn't heard from him, which worked in my favor, for by then, the idea of such a trip had started to generate some enthusiasm. Paul's interest in Maude's capabilities versus his father's Cockshutt began to work its magic. His usual languorous spirit was giving way to a different side of his personality, I hadn't seen before and without pushing the issue, I allowed his curiosity to ensnare James and John.

The phone call I had waited for didn't come until Wednesday morning. By that time, Paul's enthusiasm had generated a full head of steam, which enveloped James and John in spite of his concerns about a hick town populated by only farmers and pigs.

Standing at attention before the Captain's desk later that afternoon, awaiting his return salute, we held our position, until he looked up and acknowledged our presence.

"How may I help you gentlemen?" asked Captain Ford while lifting his loose shirt collar with his left index finger.

"Sir," I began trying to sound as courteous as possible. "I know . . . that is, Sir . . . we know . . . of a local farmer who is having some difficulty in bringing in his wheat crop because of an injury . . ."

"How does that concern you . . . gentlemen?" interrupted the Captain.

"Well, Sir," I continued in a confident tone. "We were thinking it would be good PR for the Base if we could help this man. I mean, since Paul and I both know how to operate a combine, and James and John can drive a truck."

"Didn't you just return from a leave, Airman?" asked the Captain while glancing down at a folder before him.

"Yes, Sir. But, I still have one week coming."

"How much leave time will you need?"

"Each one week, Sir." I answered trying to hold back a smile.

After tugging at his loose collar, Captain Ford made a note on a tablet before looking up. "I'll let you know something by tomorrow."

"Sir, there is one other thing," I answered after hesitating for a moment. "Would it be possible for us to leave the Base on Friday morning rather than waiting until Monday? We'll need the extra time."

"You want a three-day pass in addition to a leave?"

"If you don't mind . . . Sir, the farm is located beyond travel . . ."

"Is it safe to assume, this farmer has four daughters?"

"Just one, Sir," I said with a quick glance at my friends.

"As I said, I'll let you know by tomorrow." answered Captain Ford before leaning back in his chair and tossing his pen on the desk.

After a snappy salute, we made a quick exit from the office. Before returning to the Hangar, I stopped by the phone booth in front of the barracks and called Allie to let her know what was in the works.

James and I pulled into the yard a few minutes before John and Paul roared past the house in *The Iron Lung*. Realizing he had passed up the driveway, John slammed on the breaks, bringing *The Lung* to a squealing stop before backing down the road and into the yard.

"You weren't lying about this place," said James walking around the front of the car. The merriment of his voice drew my attention away from *The Lung*, now enveloped in a thin vale of dust.

The screen door to the kitchen swung open with force as Allie rushed down the steps into the yard. Her appearance left me impaired for a moment before starting in her direction. Our embrace filled with a euphoric outburst of laughter, and repeated kisses lasted several minutes, before a harrumphing sound ended the sweet reunion.

"Are we invisible?" asked John, which brought forth a chuckle from Paul and James.

"No. But I wish we were." Was my reply with a rueful stare, "Allie, you remember the guys, don't you?"

"Yes, of course," she answered and then greeted them with a handshake.

While proceeding toward the house with suitcases in tow, James continued to brag on the beauty of the farm, while Paul questioned Allie about how much of the crop remained in the field. Mrs. Natty exited the kitchen door and joined us at a point between the cars and house. During a round of formal introduction, Mrs. Natty's eyes seemed focused on James, causing Allie and I to glance at each other.

"We have one bedroom downstairs . . ." began Mrs. Natty, while gesturing to James to lead the way toward the steps. "Two of you can stay down there . . ."

"Mama, since Yogi is accustomed to Robert's room . . . he and James can share that room," injected Allie.

"Looks like John and . . . what's your name again, son?" Mrs. Natty asked turning to Paul as we entered the dining room.

"Paul."

"Well, then Paul and John can share the bedroom down here."

"I hope you have twin beds," answered Paul with a wide grin. "I'm not sleeping with this horny bast . . ."

Paul's voice seemed to echo through my brain as we all stared at him with deadpan expressions. Before leaving the Base, I had pleaded with the three of them to be on their best behavior, especially Paul. There were to be *No* dirty jokes, *No* demonstrations of his flatulent capabilities, and *No* eating before Mr. Henry said grace.

I didn't inhale, until Mrs. Natty responded with a chuckle and a hardy slap to Paul's back.

"You can relax, boy," Mrs. Natty said to Paul, who was blushing. "I've heard the word before."

"I still ain't sleeping with him," replied Paul, with some emphasis.

Mrs. Natty assured Paul, she would provide him with a pallet. While leading them into the downstairs bedroom, Allie gestured to James to lead the way up the stairs.

Allie and I both laughed when the squeaky board in the hallway caused James to step aside as he approached the door to Robert's room. Nothing had changed about the room since my last visit, except for several cardboard boxes stacked against the far wall, which immediately caught my attention. The empty closet and chest of drawers gave me some clue as to their contents. Although I wanted to, I didn't question Allie about them in the presence of James. As he and I unpacked, Allie sat on the bed watching our every move.

"Who's the guy in the picture?" James asked Allie, while putting away some of his things into the top drawer of the chest.

"My brother," answered Allie while standing, before walking over to the chest. "Yogi said he thought the two of you look alike."

"Is you father in his room?" I asked in an unsteady voice, after putting my suitcase in the closet.

"Yes," answered Allie while returning the picture to the chest. "You know he was against this . . . I mean you and your friends coming here," added Allie, while giving James an uneasy glance.

"Well, with a broken leg he can't very well kick us out," I answered, before giving Allie a slight kiss.

"Hey Yogi," James interrupted, "maybe I'll wait downstairs."

After James left the room, Allie and I embraced for several minutes before leaving the room. As I walked down the hall toward Mr. Henry's room, Allie leaned against the door facing to Robert's room, offering what visual support she could.

The journey down the hallway was one of the longest walks I have ever taken. I knew this had to be done, if my self-respect was to be regained and the difference between Mr. Henry and I put to rest.

The Air Force had taught me how to enter an Officer's office, so I treated this situation the same and gave the bedroom door a good firm knock. I didn't reach for the door knob until a reply from within granted such permission.

When I entered the bedroom, Mr. Henry was sitting in a high back damask chair near a window with his leg resting on a hassock. After a quiet "Hello," I walked over to him and extended my hand in friendship, which he accepted reluctantly before turning back toward the window. His appearance was gaunt and his complexion pale.

"I was sorry to hear about your accident, sir," I said in an apologetic tone.

"You've wasted your time coming back here," replied Mr. Henry in a gruff voice.

During the trip to the farm, between James' many questions, I had rehearsed in my mind some of the things I planned to say once Mr. Henry and I faced each other. Now that the moment had arrived, all I had prepared seemed to slip my mind. I was determined to be magnanimous, but I wasn't going to be "walked on" or falsely accused of taking advantage of Allie.

"I'm back because of the commitment I made some months ago, to help you with the crop," I answered in a courteous tone, while attempting to look him in the face.

"You're no longer under that obligation," murmured Mr. Henry rubbing his face. "Besides I told you . . . I didn't want to see you around this place anymore. And . . . I've already made arrangements for a custom cutter to come in and finish up the crop. He'll bring it in for $3.75 in the bin."

"Why pay someone to do this, when my friends and I can do it for nothing?" My tone was harsher than I had anticipated.

"You think I'm going to trust my equipment and crop to a bunch of young boys? I saw how that one boy backed into the yard." shouted Mr. Henry, as he turned to face me.

"These 'young boys,' as you call them, took a week of their annual leave to come up here to help you! You're just being pigheaded, and you know it!"

"You got no right to come in here and lecture me, boy!" shouted Mr. Henry.

Realizing I had done the very thing that I swore wouldn't happen caused me to walk over to the other window. Holding back the lace curtains, I spoke in a more conciliatory tone after a few moments of silence.

"That day . . . when I asked you to let me stay, I promised to keep my distance from Allie." I paused once more, for what seemed an interminable time before continuing. "I give you my word again . . . and . . . I'm asking you to accept my apology."

After a couple of minutes and Mr. Henry failed to respond, I turned and started toward the door. "I'm here and I'm staying," I declared before reaching the door.

"You think . . . ?"

Mr. Henry's uncompleted question caused me to stop at the door.

"Are these young men up to the job?" continued Mr. Henry while, turning his head slightly toward me. "It'll take a full week, maybe more, if Maude continues to cooperate."

"I think so. Or we'll give it the devil trying," I replied. "There's no need to worry about Maude. One of the boys, who came with me, grew up on a wheat farm, up north . . . some place, and he's familiar with combines. As for the hot-rodder, I'll watch him."

Once more a moment of silence filled the room as I waited for Mr. Henry to respond.

"Well, if I'm gonna be stuck with these young men for a week, I guess I'd better make my way downstairs to meet them," answered Mr.

Henry, as he turned around as if searching for something. "Reach me that crutch, if you would."

In assisting Mr. Henry to his feet, he didn't appear as large and threatening as I remembered the first time we met. In a way he appeared old, frail, and vulnerable. The story of the young zebra challenging the father of the mare he hoped to mate, no longer held for me the fear that it once did.

As I watched Mr. Henry hobble on his crutches toward the bedroom door, I wondered how many more times must I admit my error, before he would accept my apology? While Mr. Henry made his way down the hall, I followed close behind, while stealing a glance at Allie still standing in the hall. I felt the expression on my face told her things between her father and I hadn't gone so well.

Throwing my shoulders back, I hurried down the hall and offered to assist Mr. Henry down the stairs while Allie carried his crutches. With his arm around my neck, we cautiously made our way down the stairs into the dining room, where my three friends stood before the window in military style formation, according to height, as if awaiting uniform inspection.

Beginning with James, the shortest, I introduced them in order ending with John, the tallest. Standing before them with a very serious face, Mr. Henry repeated their names a couple of times as if trying to get a feel for these common names.

I was beginning to believe Texans were unaccustomed to the names, James, Paul, and John.

"Sounds like the three Apostles," declared Mr. Henry without smiling, while shifting around on his crutches.

"I don't think you'll want to confuse these guys with the Apostles," I quickly added, attempting to break the uneasiness in the room.

"You . . . speak for yourself," injected Paul with a snicker. "You ain't exactly a Pope."

Paul's jovial personality took the stillness off the impromptu reception, which prompted Mrs. Natty to invite us to sit down, while she and Allie prepared for us something to eat. Once Mr. Henry settled in his chair, he began questioning Paul about his father's combine. I got the impression there was more behind the questions than Paul's knowledge of combines. In a very uncharacteristic way, Paul's seriousness left the three of us glancing at each other, knowing that the "mouse" was playing with the "cat."

With lunch completed, Paul suggested we take a look at the combine. After thanking Mrs. Natty for the lunch, our noisy troop made its way out the dining room and into the yard, while Allie's parents stood in the doorway. Mr. Henry's face reflected his concern for Maude. Mrs. Natty offered him some assurance by placing her arm around his waist.

The sight of Maude standing motionless in the field stirred a warm feeling within my body, causing me for the first time to understand Mr. Henry's love for the old machine. Paul jumped from the pickup truck before it came to a complete stop and ran to the combine. After climbing aboard, he studied the levers to the right of the driver's seat for a minute or two, before reaching for the ignition key. The engine gave an obstreperous beginning, causing my heart to skip several beats, while I stood on the ladder leading to the driver's seat. Finally, a belch of black smoke exited the tail pile and the engine fired up, bringing forth an unforgettable broad grin to Paul's boyish face and a round of applause from the three spectators on the ground.

The noise of Maude's engine and the clanking of her many moving parts seemed to transform the ex-delinquent farm boy, into the man I imagined Paul's father wanted him to be. Among Paul's many characteristics, his spirit of lethargy ranked higher than his "gas capabilities," but somehow, on this day, his energy seemed contagious.

"Paul! Keep in mind this old machine is all this man has and so help me, if you wreck it, I'll put something on you . . . your old man never even thought of."

"Relax, Yogi," Paul shouted back with his usually broad grin, "you're looking at the best damn Cutter my old man ever stomped the hell out of."

"Paul, I'm serious as all hell . . . you hear!" I shouted.

"You remember what the DIs (Drill Instructors) said in Basic Training, Yogi?" Paul yelled back with a grin, while pushing forward, the throttle. "I'm the lawnmower and your ass is grass. And, today I'm gonna mow some grass!"

Before I could clear the steps of the combine, Maude was in motion almost throwing me to the ground. A queasy feeling came to my stomach as I stood there, watching Maude spew out a trail of straw in a cloud of dust. While Allie drove James and John back to the equipment shed to get the grain truck, I stayed behind to watch over Paul during his maiden voyage through the field. The afternoon sun beating down on me, quickly resurrected in my mind some of the difficulties Mr. Henry and I had had with Maude, and I began questioning my decision to involve my friends in this endeavor.

By the time the grain tank needed dumping, a thick layer of dust covered Paul's body except for the lower part of his face, protected by his handkerchief used as a bandanna. Feeling confident enough to leave him alone, Allie and I rode back to the grain bins in the pickup truck while, John and James followed in the grain truck. After several such trips, their skill in backing the truck to the unloading station at the bins began to improve. I started feeling better about our purpose for coming to the farm.

Darkness and not the lack of enthusiasm forced us to abandon the cutting that first evening. After unloading the grain truck for the final time, the four of us walked toward the house, amid a hubbub of laughter and jokes about Paul's dusty experience. The adrenaline fueling our spirits was more inebriating than any drinks we ever found at the Pink Elephant. The camaraderie we shared that evening, I hoped would transcend the week. Feeling tired, but intoxicated with laughter and joy for having taken hold of a challenge many would have said was beyond our abilities as young men, we blew through the kitchen door with the force of a hurricane coming ashore in south Louisiana.

The aroma from the kitchen assaulted our olfactory senses, causing the Three Apostles to stop momentarily before the stove. Our high spirits and approving guttural sounds seemed pleasing to Mrs. Natty, who jokingly threatened to drive the ravenous beasts from her kitchen with a large wooden spoon.

After washing up, we joined Mr. Henry already sitting at the head of the table. His stoic composure did not have much impact on our noisy scramble for sitting places nor the "ohs and ahs" generated by the feast awaiting us on the table.

After Allie and Mrs. Natty joined us, Paul and James without waiting for Mr. Henry to say grace, began to serve themselves. Paul stabbed a piece of roast beef with his fork and transferred it to his plate, while James moved the large bowl of mashed potatoes to a more accessible position before his plate. A swift kick to Paul's shin coupled with the tightening of my jaw muscles, caused him to give me a peculiar stare while the slight tilting of my head toward Mr. Henry, caused James to return the large scoop of mashed potatoes to the bowl.

Mr. Henry's seemingly unending grace had a calming effect on the atmosphere surrounding the table, until he questioned Paul about his assessment of Maud's performance.

"It's a good machine, but it can't compare to my old man's Cockshutt," answered Paul. "I was thinking we could install some lights on the combine . . ."

"Lights . . . on a combine!" exclaimed Mr. Henry. "That's ridiculous."

"I can do it if you have a welding machine," Paul fired back. "We'll have to start earlier and cut later in the evening, if we hope to finish on time."

"How you gonna deal with the moisture problem if you start earlier?" Mr. Henry asked.

With a Cheshire cat smile, Paul answered, "That's the easy part. The Texas sun will take care of that." Mr. Henry didn't smile, indicating he didn't appreciate Paul's sarcasm. "How many tarps do you have around the place?"

"Three or four large ones," answered Mr. Henry with a puzzled expression.

"Tomorrow we'll inspect them," Paul answered nonchalantly, as if ignoring Mr. Henry's concern. "Also, tomorrow Allie can go into town and pick up four headlights, fifty feet of wire and a toggle switch." In between bites, Paul added, "I'll need about ten old inner tubes."

"Sounds like you got things all figured out," declared Mr. Henry in a gruff voice.

"All except for how he's gonna deal with the dust," James injected, which brought a roar of laughter from everyone except Allie's parents.

While holding his forefingers and thumbs about three inches apart before his face, forming an imaginary rectangle, Paul's old personality momentarily slipped back into his body, causing his mouth to move while his brain was still in neutral.

"I thought I could make a dust mask with a Kotex to . . ."

The sounds of choking coughs arrested Paul's thoughts. James attempted to restrain his laughter with a mouth full of mashed potatoes, which spewed across the table onto John's face. Mrs. Natty gasped aloud, while Allie's face turned blood red. Mr. Henry's face took on the appearance of Mt. Rushmore, while his fork remained frozen midway between his plate and mouth. With my boot, I landed a sharp blow to Paul's shin.

"That's a great idea, Paul!" declared John angrily. After wiping his face with a napkin, he threw it at Paul. "Maybe you should write the

Texas Farm Bureau and tell them about this great dust mask you've thought of."

The equanimity, with, which Paul took the ribbing, which followed, was part of his good nature. While we tried finishing the meal with some semblance of good manners, an occasional snicker punctuated the tension felt around the table.

Following supper, the Three Apostles suggested we pull KP in appreciation for the fine meal. Mrs. Natty appeared a bit nervous, having so many boys in her kitchen. But she finally relinquished her domain to the younger generation, with Allie acting as Mess Sergeant. The ruckus emanating from the kitchen during our attempt to clean up brought Mrs. Natty from the front porch several times before she came in to say good night and announce that our pajamas awaited us on the foot of our beds. Since I hadn't shared with my friends this part of my experience while on the farm, their facial expressions caused Allie and me to force back a snicker until her mother left the kitchen.

Once James was sleeping peacefully, I got up and quietly raised the bedroom window and stepped out onto the roof over the downstairs bedroom. With the small rug from the floor before the bed, I made my way down the roof to Allie's bedroom window and tapped on the pane. After a moment or so, she joined me outside. Our liaison on the roof was quiet, but romantic, as Allie sat between my legs with her head resting on my chest. For several hours we just talked, mostly about nothing of importance, for words seemed unnecessary to express our feelings.

After returning to the bed, I found James still sleeping in the same position as when I left him. With my arms folded behind my head, staring up at the ceiling, I felt good that the first day on the farm with my friends had gone so well. There were a few rough spots, such as Paul's remarks about the dust mask, but other than that, I thought everything went well, and I was starting to feel good about having returned, even though my attempts at reconciliation with Mr. Henry had been a "one-way street." However through the experience I learned apologies are often a "one-way street" and how others respond to your efforts can be "their blessing or their grief."

Chapter 22

From below, we watched as James climbed to the rafters of the equipment shed to throw down the three tarps stored away many years earlier by Mr. Henry. Without a warning, the first tarp dropped, hit one handle of a wheelbarrow, flipping it over in front of John. Amid his lambasting of James, the other two tarps dropped in rapid succession, creating a dust cloud, which drove everyone from the building.

"What the hell we gonna do with these things?" John demanded of Paul angrily as we waited for the dust cloud to settle.

"Everything we cut before 10:00 a.m., will be dumped onto the tarps and allowed to dry in the sun," answered Paul, walking away from John toward one of the tarps.

"Then what?" John asked sourly, giving Allie and me a quick glance, before starting toward the building after Paul.

"Then we'll haul it to the bins," Paul answered, sounding exasperated.

"Are you out of your damn mind?" John grimaced, while stooping over to assist Paul in lifting one tarp into the wheelbarrow. "How are we supposed to get the grain from the tarps to that screw . . . contraption that goes up to the top of those tanks?"

With a Cheshire cat grin, Paul coolly pointed at the wheelbarrow. "The Mexican dump truck, that's how!"

"Do you know how many tons of grain you're talking about?" asked James with a dejected look, as he brushed the dust from his jeans.

"And I guess driving the Mexican dump truck," interrupted John in an agitated tone, "will become the job of the little Red Neck and me . . . right?"

"Yeah! Since you can't operate the combine," Paul retorted.

I could see, John wasn't very receptive to Paul's newly assumed position as boss or the menial labor to be involved in carrying out this untested plan. I felt the idea was feasible and given a chance, it might work, if everyone, including Maude cooperated.

"Hey! Come on, guys!" I injected after leaving Allie's side to join Paul and John. "We'll all take turns on the wheelbarrow . . . okay!" Turning to John, I added, "Since Paul can drive the combine, it's obvious he will have to do most of the cutting . . . and when I relieve him, then he will do some duty on the wheelbarrow."

"I liked the little gung-ho bastard more when he was burning farts," snarled John.

"I think y'all should kiss and make up since you're sleeping together," injected James.

Everyone laughed except John.

"John . . . you take the first shift on the grain truck," I suggested, hoping to soothe his wounded feelings. "There's something else I need to do in the meantime."

Following Maude's morning ritual of fueling and greasing, our second day on the farm, although begun with a minor personality clash, left me hoping if there were to be any mechanical problems, they too would be as easily resolved. Once James and I returned to the grain bins, we laid out a second tarp before driving to the other side of the farm to check on Mr. Henry's cattle. After throwing out a few bales of hay for the cows, we drove to the old windmill to check the water level in the trough. To my surprise the mill was still pumping, a bit squeaky as it slowly turned in the morning breeze.

By 11:00 a.m., a pile of wheat two feet deep lay drying in the morning sun. As James and I continued working it with garden rakes to ensure that it dried evenly, Mr. Henry occasionally appeared at the backdoor monitoring our efforts. The remaining loads of the day were unloaded directly into the grain bins. At first, the job seemed insurmountable and daunting, but with the aid of an ear-splitting radio hooked up to an extension cord, which was James' doing, since he said he couldn't work without music, we continued raking the pile under the watchful eyes of Mr. Henry.

Around noon, while James and I devoured two sandwiches and a pitcher of ice tea in the shade of the equipment shed, Allie took a sample of wheat to the elevators for a moisture test to pacify her father.

When Allie returned from town an hour later with a new wheelbarrow and an "okay test on the wheat," she relieved John on the grain truck so he could join us at the wheat pile. John became annoyed with the new assignment, but after sulking for a few minutes, he settled down to his new job as "Mexican dump truck driver." James took advantage of the opportunity to taunt him once more and mockingly told him the *new job paid more.*

Working in the blistering sun without shirts, the pile of wheat seemed to diminish with the speed of a snail, as James irritated John and me with his crooning to the music from the radio. By midafternoon, the pile of wheat no longer existed, and we swept the tarps clean before rolling them up. Because we had faced the devil of doubt and beaten him back, our spirits were frenetically wild as we headed toward the corral to rinse the dust from our bodies. In John's usual way of harassing James, he threatened to throw the "little Red Neck" into the trough, which ended up in a chase around the corral several times before James climbed the gate and ran toward the house. Their playful mood proved how quickly the body and spirit of the young recover.

Mr. Henry was standing in the kitchen talking to James through the screen door, when John and I walked up to the back steps.

"How long it's been, Yogi since you check on Maude?" asked Mr. Henry from inside the kitchen?

"I think they're all right, or Paul would have gotten word to me," I answered, without turning toward the screen door.

"We could give you a ride to the field if you'd like," suggested James.

"The man has a broken leg, you little Red Neck peckerwood," rebutted John. "How's he gonna ride in a truck?"

"It's simple you damn Yankee," James snapped back. "We could put him a chair in the bed of the truck."

James' idea generated an outburst of negative responses before we realized its feasibility. Mrs. Natty was very much opposed to such *"foolishness"* as we kicked around the suggestion with various ideas of how to get Mr. Henry into the truck.

"If you boys back the pickup to the steps," suggested Mr. Henry while opening the screen door, "then you could help me in."

"Henry!" protested Mrs. Natty with a mild shout. "You'll end up falling and breaking your fool neck."

"Let's give it a try," suggested John with some enthusiasm. "For once, the little peckerwood showed some smarts."

"Stop calling me a peckerwood you damn Yankee," shouted James as he stood to confront John.

Stepping between them, I said, "Come on John! Stop agitating James and go get the pickup."

While John ran back to the equipment shed for the pickup, James and I moved a large wicker chair from the front porch to the back steps.

Once John backed the truck to the kitchen steps, James and I loaded the chair into the bed before assisting Mr. Henry into the truck by allowing him to put his arms across our shoulders.

As the truck pulled away from the steps, James pounded on the cab and ordered John to stop.

"What the hell do you need now Red Neck?" John shouted from the cab as James jumped from the truck and ran toward the picnic table in the yard.

"The man will need some shade," answered James with a grin while removing the large umbrella from the center of the table. After James planted the umbrella pole into the bed-steak pocket immediately behind the cab, John accelerated through the yard before stopping on the other side of the gate to wait for James.

Riding toward the field, Mr. Henry bounced around in the chair, while James and I pounded on the cab warning John to take it easy. Upon our arrival in the field, I relieved Paul of combine duty for the rest of the day, so he and Allie could drive into town for the necessary materials needed to rig Maude with lights later that evening. Mr. Henry sat in the back of the pickup truck in the shade of the large umbrella like some master of a Louisiana plantation, making sure that his field hands were discharging their duties with the utmost diligence. After a few hours, James drove Mr. Henry home when John made a trip to the bins so the two of them could help him out of the truck.

The first step in Maude's four-hour transformation after supper began with the mounting of two braces bolted to the frame before the driver's seat over an inch or so of rubber, cut from old inner tubes to absorb the vibration. Welded to these braces was a piece of angle iron measuring about eight feet above the header. Four small frames equally spaced along the angle iron and well cushioned with rubber served, as the mounting brackets for the headlights set at slightly different angles.

As the project took shape, my appreciation of Paul's hidden talents slowly pushed from my mind the image of the indolent boy I knew at the Base. My contribution to the project consisted of 'holding' or 'fetching' certain things to facilitate Paul's efforts, which was more than that of James and John who fell to sleep on the pile of tarps. As the image in Paul's mind took shape with each weld, Allie and I sat on a small bench with our backs turned to the blinding light.

Picking up a small clump of dirt from the ground, I threw it at John hitting him on the side of the face, which wasn't my intended target. He just brushed his face and continued to sleep.

"Don't Yogi," scolded Allie, as she elbowed me in the ribs. "Let him sleep . . . they're both tired."

"Think we should leave the Chicken Man and the Red Neck here for the night?" I called out to Paul on the other side of the header.

After raising his welding helmet, Paul's face, covered with soot, perspiration, and specks of flux chippings appeared to have a metallic appearance.

"I have a way to get them up," Paul replied, wiping his face with a handkerchief. The lustrous sheen from the perspiration on his dirty face caused his teeth to appear much whiter than before. "Reconnect the battery cables, Yogi."

As I connected the battery cables, Paul climbed to the driver seat of the combine. When I gave him the signal, he flipped the newly installed toggle switch, illuminating all four headlights. A flood of brilliant light washed over the sleeping Apostles, who sat up in a state of confusion while shielding their faces with both hands.

With sundown the following evening came the big event of the day, as Maude's lights illuminated the Texas night. It was a historic moment. Mr. Henry, sitting in his wicker chair in the rear of the old Ford, bore a sulky appearance, which expressed his opposition to this new idea. Mrs. Natty however, expressed her delight with Maude's transformation, as she sat on the tailgate next to Allie.

"How much longer are you planning to cut, Yogi?" asked Mr. Henry, in a gruff tone, while looking at me.

"Until we fill the truck," I answered, stepping away from Allie's side. After adjusting my cowboy hat to the back of my head in a jaunty kind of way, I glanced at my watch before answering, "John and I are planning to take this load to the elevators."

"This night air will be getting damp . . . soon." Mr. Henry's voice had a touch of defiance in it.

"I think we can hold off a little longer." I quipped, repositioning the cowboy hat once more. Allie stood and reached for my hand in a show of support as we moved around the truck to where James and John were standing.

"'Pears you young boys got things under control," sighed Mrs. Natty as she stepped down from the tailgate, "when you boys are ready for supper come on to the house. Jim . . . how about you drive us to the house." Calling to Allie, Mrs. Natty added, "Come on daughter, you'll have to help us unload this old man."

"Go on," I whispered to Allie, after leaning over to give her a kiss. "We won't be much longer."

It was almost 1:00 a.m., when I pulled up to the scales at the elevator. While waiting in line, John and I managed to get a nap between each incremental move toward the scales. When Delilah Watts stepped in front of the truck wearing her Texas flag shorts, John hastily sat up to look out the windshield and bumped his head on the rearview mirror.

"Who the hell is that piece of chicken?" John asked, rubbing his head before checking his hand for a sign of blood.

Delilah pulled herself upon the running board by grabbing the brace of the outside mirror. Once more as she leaned forward against the door, her large breasts appeared as if they were going to pop out of her shirt.

"Haaaay, I know you," Delilah said giving me an ogle. "You're Allie's friend. Where have you been . . . hadn't seen you for a spell."

"Had to return to Amarillo for a while," I answered.

"Who's the cowboy riding shotgun?" asked Delilah, smiling at John.

"John's the name, Miss," John hastily answered, while extending his hand in front of me to reach Delilah's.

"Welcome to Indian Ridge, Big John," replied Delilah with a flirtatious pumping of John's hand. "It's always good to have a new rooster in the barnyard."

"Ma'am, I'm the rooster who can crow the longest."

"I bet you can," replied Delilah with a smile, before jumping from the running board.

Paul and James took over the early morning cutting, since John and I continued into town each night with the final load of the day. John's friendliness with Delilah each night left no doubt in my mind he was seeking a new "chicken to fry." The rueful smile on his face told me my explanation for our being in Indian Ridge was words falling on deaf ears.

Each day's routine was much the same as the previous day, and Maude's performance was beginning to impress me, since we had gone four days without a mechanical failure. Still, I kept my fingers crossed as Mr. Henry and I sat in the back of the pickup truck watching the combine discharge its load into the grain truck.

"Seems that boy, Paul, knows what he's doing," said Mr. Henry.

"They're all good men," I answered in a blasé way, biting down on a straw. "A little rough around the edges, but they're all right." After a moment of silence, I removed the straw from my mouth and tossed it to the ground. "I've been thinking Mr. Henry . . . we may need to hire someone to haul some of the wheat to the elevators," I stated while standing in the bed of the truck.

"Why's that?"

"With the longer hours, we're putting in, we can't make but one load at night . . . and the bins . . . here on the place are starting to fill up."

"Let that big boy . . . what's his name? . . . John. Let him make another load tonight. And tomorrow, I'll give Earl a call to see if he can help us out," answered Mr. Henry.

Against my better judgment, the grain truck was loaded and parked in the yard with the intention of letting John make a trip into town alone. As the four of us walked toward the house to wash up, John attempted to change my mind about discontinuing the nightly runs by arguing they were necessary, if we hoped to accomplish our goal. His enthusiasm for continuing the nightly runs left even James and Paul suspicious of his motives.

"Since when you became so gung ho about our goal and this hick town with its pig farmers?" asked Paul as he turned sideways to look at John.

"Since the last couple of nights," added James with a wiggle of his hips as we approached the steps to the dining room. "There's chicken to be fried in this pig town."

"Hey, you guys watch your language," I cautioned in a whisper, as we climbed the steps.

"Come on, Yogi," pleaded Paul with a snicker, "the man loves his fried chicken."

"Fried chicken!" exclaimed Mrs. Natty in a high-sounding voice, as she entered the dining room from the kitchen. "I don't know of any place in Indian Ridge that serves fried chicken this late at night."

"If you boys wanted some fried chicken," injected Mr. Henry from the far end of the table, "Natty and Allie will be glad to fix up some tomorrow night."

The Three Apostles and I glanced at each other before taking our places at the table. As Allie and I reached for each other's hands under the table, John and I glanced up at each other, knowing that his Aesopian terminology had gone undeciphered for the time being by Allie's parents.

After supper, while James, Paul, and I pushed back from the table and started helping Allie clear the dishes from the table, John walked out the dining room door heading for the grain truck. Putting down the plates I had in my hands, I left the dining room and ran after him.

"John!" I called to him.

"I know what you're going to say, Yogi," John answered while continuing to walk toward the truck.

"*And,* I know what you were thinking when you were sweet talking Delilah last night! If you have any intentions of enjoying a chicken dinner, you had better not do it in Mr. Henry's truck."

"What about on top of the truck?" John asked, with a smirk while running his pocket comb through his hair.

"You just remember why we're here!" I answered, before turning to walk toward the house.

John gave the air horns several long blasts as the truck pulled onto the farm road. I felt he was attempting to irritate me. I just shook my head and kicked the ground with the heel of my boot before starting toward the house.

After James fell asleep, I was able to sneak out the window to spend a little quiet time with Allie on the roof for the first time in three nights. It seemed our time together was much less than we both desired, and these few moments were the only time we had together. Once I returned to bed, I dozed off for a while before having to get up for a latrine call around 2:00 a.m. While up, I decided to go downstairs to see if John had made it home.

Finding John's bed empty, I decided to have a few cookies and a glass of milk in the kitchen while waiting for him. Stopping for a moment at the hutch in the dining room, I removed a pair of scissors and cut the legs off my pajamas above the knees.

Sitting alone in the dark caused me to remember how my mother used to wait up at night for me during my high school days. A sense of guilt came over me as I realized for the first time, all the hours of sleep she missed because of my youthful thoughtlessness. Sometime later, Allie came down and joined me making my wait less anxious as she sat in my lap and placed her head on my shoulder. For a while she drifted off into a restless sleep; my legs also went to sleep and tingled with a million needles. Not wanting to disturb her, I endured the uncomfortable sensation before dozing off.

The familiar sound of the grain truck's engine caused me to stir. The sound of the slamming truck door awakened me fully. After shaking Allie, I asked her to stand before we walked toward the screen door. The two shadowy figures leaning against the front bumper of the truck shared a drink from a beer bottle amid giggles, while attempting to shush each other. As they walked toward the house holding on to each other, I quietly asked Allie to return in the kitchen.

"John!" I whispered, as he and Delilah came through the door.

"Yoogggi, ole pal. You want a beer?" John asked, while lifting the bottle in my direction. "I've needed one since we came to this pig farm," said John with a slur. Delilah let out a short burst of giggles before taking the bottle from John, once she noticed I wasn't going to accept it. "What are you doing up, Yogi?" asked John, as he pulled Delilah close to his side.

"Waiting on you," I answered in an unpleasant tone. "What are you doing . . . bringing a beer in this house . . . and her?"

"Be cool, Man, or you'll wake up the whole house," answered John with a gesture involving both hands as if intending to push me back.

"Have you forgotten the talk we had earlier?" I asked, clenching my teeth.

"Nope," replied John with a slur, while tickling Delilah in the side. "You said I couldn't do anything in the old man's truck."

"Get the hell out of here, John, and take her with you!" I shouted in an indignant tone, while pointing toward them. "Take her to a motel . . . or out to the barn. But get this bitch . . . the hell out of this house!"

"Who are you calling a bitch . . . bastard!?" Delilah swore, while stepping away from John.

"You! That's who!" I exploded. "Get her out of here, John, before Mr. Henry wakes up!"

"What makes you so high and mighty these days?" yelled John, staggering past Delilah toward me. "I guess you don't remember where you found that little bitch you've been banging for over a year! Well, do you?"

An ashen expression came to John's face when Allie stepped into the doorway from the kitchen. For a moment, he and Allie looked at each other, before he pushed Delilah toward the open screen door.

"John! You had better be back here tomorrow morning by 9:00 a.m., or carry your ass back to Amarillo," I yelled to him from the back steps, as he and Delilah walked toward *The Iron Lung*. "I mean it! You hear?"

A cloud of white dust filled the yard as *The Iron Lung* cut a doughnut around the grain truck and sped from the yard. The loud squealing noise produced by the rear tires signaled John's anger.

My anger caused me to slam the screen door, before sitting on the steps and pulling my head toward my knees with interlocked fingers to the back of my neck. Like gasses within a volcano, my anger continued to build, until I lifted my head hoping to relieve the fury by yelling out. My throat and tongue paralyzed by the intense anger, failed to generate the outcry I needed. Sitting there, I wished I had never returned to the farm or involved my friends in this idiotic dream of mine.

I had forgotten about Allie, until her hand softly touched my tightly locked fingers. After sitting, her left arm caressed my neck as she pulled my head against her own, burying my face in a perfumed refuge of tenderness. After several minutes, I pulled away and stared into the darkness. I swallowed hard, before speaking in a faulting voice.

"I'm sorry . . . you . . . heard . . . what John said."

Taking my hands and clasping them in hers, Allie gently kissed my finger's tip. As I turned in her direction, she responded in a very soft, loving voice.

"I'm sorry you had to suffer this pain because of me, Yogi." The muscles in Allie's face were tightening as she struggled to hold back the tears welling up in her eyes.

With a gentle embrace, Allie pulled my body close to hers and rested her face against my naked back. The warmth of her tears trailing down my scapula caused an unexplained numbness to overcome me.

While sitting in the darkness without speaking for an undetermined duration, Allie ran her fingers up and down the runnel of my back while kissing me on the shoulder blade, as if trying to comfort me in some primitive way. Finally, she pulled my face toward hers and kissed me on the cheek.

"Come on, Yogi," she said, "it's time you go back to bed."

Shaking my head, I answered, "No. You go. I'm not sleepy now."

Allie stood and opened the screen door. Before stepping inside, she leaned over and kissed me on the back of the neck.

"Thank-you, Yogi. For being the one good thing to come into my life," Allie murmured, before stepping inside leaving me alone.

Knowing I wouldn't be able to sleep, I went to the veranda and retrieved a pair of dirty jeans from the hamper and slipped them on over my cutoff pajamas. The first pair of socks I picked up from the floor were not my own, this I knew by the holes in the heels, but I carried them, my boots and a shirt to the back steps. After putting on my boots, I ran toward the grain truck while slipping on the shirt.

The silhouette of Maude sitting in the moonlit field seemed to me as a forgotten paramour, as I drove toward her in my hour of madness. After climbing aboard, I started the engine, flipped on the headlights and put the combine in motion, almost unaware of my actions. All around me, both physically and emotionally, darkness prevailed and the forlornness tearing at my insides, indicated all I had hoped to accomplish during the week was coming unraveled.

Alone in the moonlit night, befriended only by the sound of Maude's engine and the rhythmic sounds transmitted by her many moving parts, I was able to find a respite of peace for my troubled spirit, as I lost myself in my imagination. Once more pretending to be an ancient mariner, I imagined myself sailing through the night at the helm of an ancient vessel, plowing through the Indian Ocean or the South China Sea taking myself far away from my current troubles. How long this nocturnal madness continued I couldn't tell before fatigue replaced my maniacal desire to escape the present reality of life.

Chapter 23

"He's here!"

The shout of James' voice, caused me to move under the tarp, in which I had wrapped myself during the night. Looking up from within the body of the grain truck, I could see him grinning down at me as I sat up from my bed of wheat. With one hand held before my eyes to block the morning sun, I folded back the tarp while attempting to sort through the night's events. Soon Paul's face appeared over the side of the truck body. His broad boyish smile was reassuring, but his wasn't the face I wanted most to see.

Very slowly a crown of light red hair emerged between Paul and James, as Allie struggled to pull herself up onto the truck body to look over at me. The early morning sun seemed to radiate the hue in her hair, giving her an angelic appearance as she smiled down at me.

And then . . . a peculiar stare came to Allie's face, while letting out a terrifying scream. While clinging to the body of the truck with both hands, Paul and James flipped her over into the truck body causing her to land next to me in a sitting position.

Paul and James laughed uncontrollably as Allie turned around and feigned her displeasure with their action, by shaking her fist at them.

The passion of our first kiss of the day coupled with the healing properties of the morning sun and the laughter of my two friends, were sufficient to drive away some of the ill effects the night had brought into my life.

"You had us worried to death," Allie said as she quickly kissed me once more. "We looked everywhere for you."

"Hey! You two better climb out of there, or you'll be covered with wheat in a little bit," Paul yelled down at us, before he and James jumped from the truck bed.

Allie and I drove back to the house in the pickup truck, while Paul and James began fueling and greasing Maude. After changing my clothes and eating breakfast, while getting some peculiar stares from Mr. Henry, I went to the grain bins and prepared for the morning ritual, which included hooking up the radio. Being shorthanded, Allie took over the grain truck after James dumped the first load, so he could join me for tarp duty.

Approximately two hours later, *The Iron Lung* pulled into the yard, much slower than its departure the previous night. James and I looked at each other as John got out and started for the gate.

Sashaying toward us in his usual disjoined manner, John clapped his hands and yowled at Buster and Midnight, causing them to kick and romp around the corral.

"Looks like the Chicken Man has flown the coupe," James said under his breath, as John drew near us.

"Sorry boys. I overslept," John said in a nonchalant tone, as he approached us.

John's blasé attitude, combined with his sarcastic grin, so irritated me I didn't answer.

"What you want me to do this morning, Yogi?" John asked, stepping closer to me. After I failed to answer, John responded in a more chipper tone, "The Little Red Neck and me . . . can do this . . . if you want to drive the truck?"

"Allie's driving the truck!" I answered roughly. "What the hell were you thinking last night?" I demanded, while throwing down my grain scoop.

"Hey!" John replied with a smirk, holding both arms away from his body. "I was half drunk, okay! I'm sorry."

"And that's another thing . . . lover boy," I shouted back, pointing my finger in his face. "You shouldn't be drinking while driving Mr. Henry's truck."

"I'm sorry, Yogi! Ooookay . . . I wasn't thinking!" John replied with a more serious tone.

"That's your trouble, John, you don't ever think . . . except with that thing between your legs!" I responded, pointing at his crotch.

John's face turned red. Before I could raise my arm to protect myself, his fist landed a solid blow to my left cheekbone, causing me to fall backward onto the pile of wheat. Scrambling to my feet, I charged him. As we fell onto the wheat, I managed to get in one blow to his face, before James grabbed my leg and pulled me off.

"Cut it out you two or I'll clobber you both," James shouted, as he picked up one of the grain scoops and held it up as if it was a giant-fly swatter. "I swear I'll do it if you two don't stop!"

With a twisted face I looked at John and said, "You son-of-a-bitch don't you ever say anything about Allie again! You hear!" Grabbing a hand full of wheat kernels, I threw it in his face.

"How many times I gotta say I'm sorry, before you believe me?" shouted John, while wiping the kernels from his face.

"Hey, Yogi! There's someone coming," said James, looking toward the house.

For a moment I forgot about John, while watching a short middle-aged man wearing a short sleeve white shirt, eye glasses, and bowtie fumble with his clipboard and camera, while attempting to loop the chain back through the gate to secure it.

"I guess you know . . . you damn little Cajun, I'm gonna have a shiner," John said, while touching his eye, before pulling the seat of his pants away from his buttocks and giving it a little shake. "Damn it, boy! I believe I have some of them wheat things caught in the crack of my butt."

"Well, don't shake them . . . back into the pile," chuckled James, "or some poor fool will have some crappy tasting bread in a few months."

"Howdy, boys," the stranger said with a slight nod of his head, as he paused at the edge of the wheat pile, as if wondering, which one of us he should address. "You boys having a little dispute?" he asked looking at John.

"Yeah!" answered John brashly while giving his pants another shake. "His scoop is bigger than mine, and I don't like it."

Caught off guard by John's sarcasm, the stranger extended his hand toward James who was standing closest to him.

"Emanuel Dubbs . . . of the Indian Ridge Weekly."

"What's that . . . a newspaper?" asked James with a smile.

"Yes. It's a local . . . weekly paper," replied Mr. Dubbs, as if disappointed we hadn't heard of his paper. "I understand you boys put some lights on Henry's old combine. I was wondering if you would like to share with the readers how you accomplished this."

"It wasn't us who did the work," answered John, glancing toward me. "It was this other guy, Paul."

Since Paul deserved the credit for the lights on Maude, I felt he should be the one interviewed for the article, and I offered to drive Mr.

Dubbs to the field. Before leaving, Mr. Dubbs requested the three of us stand beside the wheat pile for a picture. Since he felt his readers would be offended by *our nakedness*, Mr. Dubbs requested James and me to put on our shirts before taking the picture.

At lunch time, because John and I were the only two around the place, Mrs. Natty called us in to eat at the kitchen table. Mr. Henry informed me that Earl's truck wouldn't be available for several more days, which caused John to suggest he could make another run into town with the last load of the day. Mr. Henry didn't understand my objection and insisted that John make another run.

The tension between John and me eased somewhat, as the afternoon wore on, and we continued working on the grain pile without speaking. Later in the evening, I relieved Paul on the combine, while John took over the grain truck. Around 9:00 p.m., after the last bit of grain spilled into the truck, we trapped down the load without speaking, before riding to the house in the grain truck.

At the equipment shed, James and Paul jumped on the running boards of the truck and rode into the yard with us. As we walked toward the house, the festive spirit, which filled our first evening on the farm reasserted itself with the thought that we would enjoy a few moments of notoriety with the publication of the next issue of the Indian Ridge Weekly. Upon approaching the steps leading to the kitchen, the aroma of fried chicken overpowered our olfactory senses bringing to a temporary end, our joyous raucousness before rushing into the kitchen.

"You boys go on and wash up before coming to the table," laughed Mrs. Natty, as she stood before the store.

Paul pretended to reach for a piece of chicken on the platter next to the stove, only to have Mrs. Natty slap at his hand with a large wooden spoon. When I attempted to steal a quick kiss from Allie, who was leaning against the kitchen sink, Mrs. Natty pointed the spoon at me and demanded I too wash up for supper. Her gentle, but serious command caused a scramble to break out for the sink on the veranda. In a hurry to get to the feast awaiting us, James and Paul wiped their hands on their dirty shirts while John and I, not fully reconciled, wrestled for the one towel at the sink.

Because the bruises were beginning to show on our faces, Mr. Henry gave John and me a peculiar, but silent stare, as we came to the table and sat across from each other. After clearing his throat to call the table to order, Mr. Henry began his usual long blessing, while Allie and I reached for each other's hands under the table.

Mealtime became a symphony of sounds, as the crackling of crispy fried chicken skin blended with slurping sounds and the tintinnabulation of flatware against china. Massive bowls of potato salad, butter beans, hominy, and mounds of homemade bread began to disappear with the approving smiles of Mrs. Natty.

Following the meal, the Three Apostles and I remained at the table with Mr. Henry, while Allie and her mother returned to the kitchen for the coffee and lemon pie awaiting us. Pointing first toward my face and then John's, Mr. Henry asked in a stern tone, "You two having some kind of problems?"

"Not anymore," John answered soberly. I didn't respond.

Paul in his never-ending buffoonery let out a hardy belch, just as Mrs. Natty reentered the dining room with the dessert. Amid our verbal chastisement of Paul, Mrs. Natty blushingly thanked him for the complement. John excused himself, saying he didn't care for any pie. Without saying anything else, he walked out the door and started for the grain truck.

"Catch him, Yogi," demanded Mrs. Natty, while rushing back toward the kitchen, "I have something for him."

After calling for John through the dining room screen door, I waited for Mrs. Natty before starting out to the truck with the brown paper bag she handed me.

"I think Allie's mother fixed you some fried chicken for later," I said with a serious face, upon meeting John at the truck.

"Tell her thanks," John said as he opened the truck door and climbed in. "It'll be enough to hold me through the night."

"John! If it's not . . ." I said with a slight wave, "I'll see you tomorrow at 9:00 a.m."

I watched the truck until it pulled onto the farm road, before starting back toward the house. John sounded the air horns several times as the truck straightened out and accelerated into the night.

At breakfast the following morning, Mr. Henry attributed Maude's good behavior since the arrival of the Three Apostles to the fact that *two Catholics, two Baptists, and three Presbyterians were praying for her.*

Having settled Paul and James in their respective positions as operator and truck driver, I returned to "the front" to set up the tarps for the first load of wheat. Around ten, John came walking toward me, while I signaled James into position over the tarp. Watching John in the rearview mirror, James knocked the truck out of gear and accelerated the engine causing John to jump out the way.

"You little red neck where'd you learn how to drive!?" shouted John as he picked up a grain scoop and slammed it against the truck body.

"Didn't your mama teach you not to walk behind a moving truck?" James shouted, while watching us in the rearview mirror.

When the truck came to a stop, Paul jumped out on the passenger side and walked to where John and I were standing.

"What are you doing up here, Paul?" I asked, opening one of the port holes on the rear of the truck bed.

"We have a problem," replied Paul, lifting another of the porthole gates. "I think the threshing cylinder is plugged," added Paul, stepping back from the cascading wheat pouring at our feet.

"How bad is that?" I inquired, moving away from the truck bed as it began to rise.

"It's like a bad case of constipation."

Paul's intonation made Maude's condition sound funny, but at the time I wasn't in a laughing mood.

"Come on, Paul," I solicited in a raised voiced. "How serious is this?"

"I've seen it happen to my ole man's Cockshutt . . . and we had to take off the header and feeder conveyor to unplug it."

The seriousness on Paul's face caused me to swear.

"John, how about you get the pickup and bring it to the back steps," I said in an agitated tone, "we'll have to drive Mr. Henry to the back."

After assisting Mr. Henry into the bed of the pickup truck, Paul explained to him what he thought was Maude's problem. Once in the field, James parked the truck beside Maude, before assisting John and me in helping Mr. Henry from his chair and onto the ground.

Upon Mr. Henry's signal, Paul started the combine and engaged all the parts except the feeder and header. Because of his many years with the old machine, and his familiarity with Maude's many sounds, he quickly diagnosed the problem.

"Open this shroud here, Yogi," demanded Mr. Henry while he moved away from the combine on his crutches. "I believe you'll find the drive belt to the threshing cylinder is busted."

After opening the large shroud, Mr. Henry's suspicions proved right.

"How long will it take to fix this?" asked James, as Mr. Henry gave the broken belt, a slight angry tug.

"Replacing the belt won't take long," he replied, turning on the crutches and walking toward the header. Using one crutch as a pointer, Mr. Henry added, "You'll have to break lose the feeder conveyor where it joins the combine."

"Can we do it out here?" I asked, moving beside him.

"Yeah," Mr. Henry answered gruffly. "But we'll need the cutting rig from the shed in case we run into some rusty bolts," answered Mr. Henry, as he leaned against the header to brace himself. "First, you'll have to back Maude away from the standing wheat, or we'll set the whole field on fire."

"Paul, why don't you and James drive to the front and get the cutting rig . . ."

"We'll need two crossties to set the header on," Mr. Henry said, cutting me off. "And go to the house and fetch Allie, she'll have to run into town."

Once I backed Maude away from the standing wheat, James and Paul removed the wicker chair and umbrella from the truck before starting to the equipment shed. John hoisted the wicker chair above his head and moved it to a spot nearer the combine. After he planted the umbrella in the ground, Mr. Henry hobbled to the chair and sat down before using one crutch as a prop to rest his leg.

With a few hand wrenches from the toolbox kept in the grain truck, John and I started loosening the bolts around the feeder conveyor. Most of the bolts connecting the feeder to the combine gave way to our hand tools, but as always a few resisted our efforts, so we left them for the cutting rig, which arrived approximately twenty minutes later.

"See if you can find a number on that belt, Yogi!" yelled Mr. Henry from his chair, as James drove up pulling the cutting rig behind the pickup.

"How long is all this going to take, Yogi?" asked Allie with a concerned look, as she walked around the front of the truck to join me.

"I don't know," I answered with a shrug, as we started around the combine. "You'll have to run into town for a new belt while we attempt to unplug the feeder."

"Hey Yogi," called Paul from the operator's seat, "you two out the way? I need to lift the header."

"Yeah. Go ahead," I yelled out, before Allie and I stepped away from the combine.

As the header came up, John pulled one of the crossties from the pickup and walked toward the header with it cradled in his arms.

"Boy you gonna bust a gut packing that thing by yourself," chuckled Mr. Henry as he lowered his leg from the crutch.

"Where do you want it?" asked John, standing there as the Colossal of Rhodes.

"Just drop it on the ground," stated Mr. Henry, "and roll it under the header . . . about two feet from the end."

With a thump the crosstie hit the ground, stirring up a small dust cloud and a roar of laughter.

"Missing that fried chicken dinner in town last night restored your strength," Paul shouted from the operator's seat.

"How about you climb down here and help the little Red Neck roll that tie under the header," retaliated John in a boisterous voice, before walking back to the truck.

Allie and I walked back to the broken belt to look for the number, while the Three Apostles continued working on preparing the header for its removal.

"What's this joke, you guys have about fried chicken?" Allie asked, as we moved behind the open shroud.

"It's nothing," I answered with a smile, before giving the belt a slight tug, "just something John says about girls."

"John doesn't think very much of women, does he?" asked Allie while leaning against the combine.

"That's because he doesn't think much of himself," I replied. Turning loose, the belt, I moved before Allie and placed one hand on each side of her head. Before leaning forward for a kiss, I said, "If ever he finds a piece of chicken as beautiful as you, he'll stop trying everything in the hen house."

"Just pull the belt out, Yogi and bring it here," shouted Mr. Henry from the other side of the combine.

Responding to her father's call, Allie turned her face away from mine. "Not now, Yogi," Allie said as she pushed me back a little. "Daddy sounds agitated."

"Let him be agitated," I answered, attempting another kiss. "We haven't spent three full hours together this week."

"Yogi, just bring the belt here!" shouted Mr. Henry once more.

Feeling piqued by what was happening; I stepped away from Allie and gave the belt a hard jerk. When the belt gave way, my knuckles slammed against the shroud. Allie laughed as I swore under my breath, while dragging the long belt toward Mr. Henry.

Once Paul finished cutting the bolts holding the feeder to the combine, I backed it away from the header so Mr. Henry could inspect the cylinder. As we watched, he attempted to pull free some of the embedded straw.

"It's badly plugged," scowled Mr. Henry, as he shifted around on his crutches. Pausing for a moment he looked at us with a dejected frown before grumbling, "Go on . . . get started . . . you'll have to dig it out."

"We'll be here for a while," I said, attempting to soften the impact Mr. Henry's words had on our spirits as he hobbled back toward his chair. "Allie . . . maybe you should drive back to the house and call

Clifford's to see if they have a belt in stock. James, if you would . . . go with her and take the water cooler, it needs to be refilled."

While Allie and James were gone, Paul, John, and I worked at rotating intervals digging out the cylinder. The job was hot, dusty, and difficult, but we tried to make the best of it, under the watchful supervision of Mr. Henry. Several times during the process Paul taunted John and me by describing how wonderful a cool beer would taste at a time like this. Mr. Henry's stoic expression indicated he didn't appreciate Paul's suggestion, and I cautioned Paul to watch himself.

When James returned to the field, a rush broke out for the truck, which led to a posturing for first chance at the water cooler. Being stronger and bigger, John managed to push Paul and me away from the cooler, which caused Mr. Henry to smile for the first time since coming to the field.

"Grown men should drink before children," said John with a strain, while pushing Paul away once more, before unhooking the homemade tin can dipper from the handle of the cooler.

While John delivered the dipper of water to Mr. Henry, James removed a dirty metal tumbler from the dashboard of the pickup and pitched it to Paul.

After indulging in two helpings of water, Paul passed the tumbler to me. For some unexplained reason, Paul climbed on the feeder housing against Mr. Henry's advice and gave out a Tarzan call, while beating on his hairless chest. While mocking Paul's poor imitation, John splashed him in the face with a full dipper of water. The shock from the cold water caused Paul to step back, losing his balance as the header rocked under his shifting weight. Attempting to regain his balance, Paul spun around and fell toward the header. A mixture of shouts and expletives erupted from our group as we came to our feet. In some miraculous way, Paul landed upright on the ground, but in the process his left hand landed on an upright tine impaling it to the header. For a moment or two, numbness swept over us as we stood motionless. When Paul's knees gave way, John threw down the dipper and ran to his aid.

John lifted Paul from the ground. The sight of the steel spike piercing his hand made me a little nauseous, as I slowly lifted it from the tine. After John laid Paul on the tailgate of the pickup truck, I washed his hand with some water from the cooler before John wrapped it with a shirt, James retrieved from the header.

The only thought to come to our befuddled minds amid the confusion, was to get Paul to the house and into town as quickly as possible. Grasping the side of the truck bed, John leaped in and pulled Paul against his chest in a sitting position. James ran round the driver's side of the truck and got in behind the steering wheel, while I climbed in on the passenger side. We were off toward the house leaving behind a trail of dust . . . and Mr. Henry sitting in his wicker chair.

By the time we arrived at the house, Paul had come to and was able to get into my car, which Allie used to drive him to town. John insisted that he ride with them, so James and I returned to the field where we found a very disgruntled Mr. Henry sitting under the shade of his umbrella. James and I quickly resumed the work of freeing Maude of her problem, while Mr. Henry's face expressed his displeasure over being left in the field.

After digging at the impacted straw for about three hours with screwdrivers or any other tools available, we finally cleared the threshing cylinder. Work then began on freeing the feeder conveyor. Taking Mr. Henry's suggestion, we used a large pipe wrench and cheater pipe to turn the conveyor. After a few strenuous pulls on the main drive shaft, the conveyor began to move, freeing itself of the entangled straw.

Once reunited to the feeder conveyor, I backed Maude from the crossties, which James and I struggled to load into the pickup truck, along with the wicker chair and Mr. Henry. The better part of a full day had been lost and still Maude wasn't back into operation. As I drove around the combine heading back toward the equipment shed with the cutting rig in tow, Maude seemed as exhausted as my body felt.

James and I had a late lunch on the picnic table in the yard, before resuming the task of scooping up the one load of wheat left on the tarp since morning.

Around 3:00 p.m., Allie drove into the yard, announcing their arrival with several blasts of the horn. James and I abandoned the wheelbarrows and grain scoops, retrieved our shirts from the door of the pickup and ran toward the house to greet Tarzan "the fallen" Ape Man.

Paul was greeted with slaps on the back and acclamations befitting a war hero and proudly displayed his bandaged hand, as if worthy of a Purple Heart. Amid all the panegyrizing, Allie offered up a sardonic smile while dangling before me a new belt for Maude.

At 8:30 p.m., I decided to call it a day. While standing on top of the combine watching the last of the grain cascade into the grain truck, I mockingly called out to James to *put some muscle into it* as he frantically tried to level out the load with a scoop. The rattling noise of the auger running empty brought a smile to his face as his pace slowed before collapsing backward onto the soft bed of kernels.

Knowing Paul's accident would incapacitate him for the remainder of our stay, a change in our work strategy was in order. I decided Maude's daily greasing and refueling in preparation for the next day, would take place at the end of the day's cutting. This would allow me to sleep a little later, since operating the combine all day would become my job. For the time being, John would continue his nightly "fried chicken" runs to the grain elevator, and Allie would continue to fill in on the grain truck when needed.

With this new strategy in mind, after supper, I returned to the equipment shed to fill the fuel drum before driving back to the field. I wasn't expecting any company during this late night duty, but was glad when Allie came to the equipment shed and asked if she could ride to the field with me. I knew having her with me in the field under a canopy of a billion stars would distract me from the task at hand.

Lying beneath Maude on the canvas next to me, Allie held the flashlight while I pumped two shots of grease into each zerk.

"How many more of those things are there?" Allie asked sounding tired.

"Just a few more minutes," I answered shifting around. "Move the light over here, there should be a fitting here. If you're tired I could drive you back to the house."

"No, I'm okay. How many more days of cutting do you have?" asked Allie sitting up and leaning against me as I reached for another grease zerk.

"If Maude cooperates, we should finish up around noon tomorrow." With a chortle, I added, "I know the Three Apostles will be glad to get back to Amarillo." Letting the grease gun rest on the ground, I turned to Allie and said, "That's the last one, we're done."

After crawling from under the combine, I helped Allie up before stretching to work the stiffness out my back.

"I like it out here at night," I said, walking toward the pickup. "The openness of the Panhandle doesn't seem as desolate at night since you can see the lights of the houses in the distance."

Allie walked away from the combine while I began gathering up my tools. For a moment, I watched as she stood gazing across the standing wheat.

"Yogi, bring that canvas."

Taken by surprise with Allie's request, I stood frozen for a moment before throwing the grease gun into the bed of the truck.

Remembering the consequence of our last rendezvous in the field, a part of me cautioned against such a liaison. Yet within me, a reckless, youthful desire was willing to take the chance once more. The desires of the flesh won over common sense.

"Hey, wait a minute!" I yelled out, as Allie began running into the standing wheat.

With the canvas in tow, I started across the field while attempting to pull my shirt free at the waist. As I approached the spot where Allie was standing, she glanced back toward me before running deeper into the field. For a moment I stopped before resuming the chase. Upon catching Allie, I attempted to throw the canvas over her shoulder. In the process, our feet became tangled and amid a din of screams and laughter, we tumbled to the ground on to a bed of crushed wheat.

"If you keep running from me," I said gasping for a breath, while looking into her eyes, "I won't have enough energy . . ."

The solemnness of Allie's expression caused me to pause.

"Are you . . . sure you want to do . . . this? If you father catches us, he'll likely shoot me this time."

With an abashed voice and gentle touch of her hand to my shoulder, Allie sat up before replying, "That's not why I came out here, Yogi."

My face must have shown my disappointment, for Allie leaned forward and kissed me softly on the mouth. The kiss lacked the passion and hunger I had anticipated and desperately needed, but somehow it conveyed the mellifluousness of a first time experience. Without speaking, Allie attempted to spread out the canvas in a more orderly fashion over the small patch of trampled wheat before assuming her favorite Oriental position, as she had done so many times before at the House.

"Yogi, about the other night . . . what transpired between you and John . . ."

I interrupted her without thinking.

"Hey, look," I pleaded while reaching out for her hands, which she withdrew. "Don't concern yourself about that. John and I . . . that's been settled." I paused and tried to offer up an indulgent smile. "I should have told you, he apologized."

"He . . . also apologized to me," Allie said with a downcast glance. "I'm sorry I didn't tell you, Yogi, but we haven't had much time together this week."

"And that's my fault," I answered leaning toward her, hoping another kiss would ignite in her, the passion I was feeling. "I'm willing to make up for lost time now . . . if you're willing."

After Allie turned her face from me, I sat back and asked in disgust, "What? You brought me out here to talk about John?"

"No! I don't want to talk about him," snapped Allie, as she turned to the side and stared off into the night. After a hiatus of silence, Allie nervously wrung her hands together before looking down toward the canvas and speaking in a soft tone. "Your friends think a great deal of you, Yogi . . . enough . . . to be truthful . . . which I haven't been."

"Come on, Allie," I said with something of a chuckle while gently touching the upper part of her arm. "What are you talking about?"

After pushing away my hand, Allie turned and gazed into the night. The stillness was finally broken when she swallowed hard and tried to speak with a trembling voice.

"About the way my brother died, for starters," Allie said, while wiping her eyes with her index finger, "and . . . some other things."

The movement of her facial muscles and the tightening of her lips were uncontrollable expressions of extreme pain, even though she managed to hold back the full flow of tears.

"Allie, you don't have to talk about this now," I said moving closer to her. She wrapped her arms around her chest as if trying to avoid my affection.

"He did die on a Friday night after a football game, as I said. That part is true." Allie continued, as if she had not heard my plea. "He and I were coming home from a football game . . . when this car came up beside us and forced us off the road . . . near the old bridge . . . you know the one . . ."

Allie's voice trembled, as she attempted to continue.

"These three boys . . . were drinking and one had a pistol. They made us get out the car and forced us down the river bank below the bridge. There was a lot of shouting and cursing, and this one boy kept touching me and pulling at my blouse, until Robert slugged him." With both hands Allie covered her face while gasping for her breath amid a strange mixture of crying and moans.

"Please, Allie. Don't do this to yourself," I begged, taking her into my arms.

"No, Yogi," Allie said lowering her hands before lifting her face toward the night sky. "I promised you . . . that someday I would tell you . . . about my fears and that place . . . ."

"It's no longer important. Believe me . . . Allie. It's not important." I answered, while trying to caress her face in my hands.

"But, it is!" Allie insisted.

Realizing her response was louder and perhaps sharper than she had intended, she begged my forgiveness before continuing.

"One of the boys stabbed Robert in the stomach several times with a switchblade knife. And . . . they threw me on the ground beside him." Allie leaned forward with her head almost touching her knees, as she continued to speak. "Over and over again, they raped me, while Robert lay dying beside me on the ground."

Allie's tears, no longer restrained by fear or shame flowed freely amid loud sobs of ululations, in a strange almost nonhuman fashion, as her whole body moved with great jerks. After taking her into my arms, the sobbing slowly came to an end before she fell over onto the canvas. For the longest time I sat beside her, as she avoided my face.

"I can still hear him begging me to forgive him for not being able to protect me." With this, Allie rolled away from me and pulled her knees close to her body in a fetal position.

Loss in my inability to understand her pain, all I could do was to gently lie beside her and hold her trembling body against mine. After several minutes, Allie began to speak again, revealing to me the most private part of her personal tragedy.

"When those bastards were finished with me . . . one of them broke a beer bottle . . . and began to cut me." Allie hesitated for a while, as I continued to hold her. "I almost died Yogi and there were many days after I came out of the coma, I wished I had. After I came home from the hospital in Dallas, my father didn't speak to me for weeks. Then one day he disappeared. I thought he blamed me for Robert's death. Then one day, after about two months, he returned without letting me or mother know where he had gone."

Again Allie paused for several minutes, before rolling onto her back and looking at me.

"Yogi, you remember that day in Rose's apartment, when you asked me to take a bath with you? I wanted to so badly . . . because of the kindness you showed me that weekend. But, I was afraid. Afraid you would see my scars. Yogi . . . I'm so ugly . . . I'm so ugly . . . down there." As if speaking to herself, Allie mumbled, "Heather, the young girl who died that weekend after being raped was lucky she didn't survive."

"Allie, no part of you is ugly," I answered with a faltering voice while pulling her closer to my side. "You're very beautiful. I love you very much. And someday, I hope you will love me as much as I love you."

"I can't Yogi," Allie answered with a sob while moving slightly away from me, "those bastards destroyed more than my body . . . they destroyed something inside of me . . . that prevents me from loving any man . . . even someone . . . as kind as you."

After pulling Allie back into my arms, we lay in silence for an undetermined period, listening to the sounds of the night and each other's heart. After giving me a gentle kiss on the lips, Allie stood.

"We had better go back to the house," Allie said, before turning to walk off.

"Allie?" I called to her while standing. She stopped but didn't turn to face me. After picking up the canvas I walked to within a few feet behind her, before asking, "I don't understand . . . I mean about the House?"

"Dr. Tully, the Psychiatrist at the Hospital, says subconsciously I'm attempting to get some revenge by selling damaged merchandise to those who will pay." Allie paused for a while before turning to face me. "That's what I am, Yogi, damaged merchandise."

"Allie, don't ever think of yourself that way, because I don't. You're a wonderful, sweet person, who just happened to have an awful thing happen to her."

As Allie walked off without responding, a slight breeze blew across the wheat field bring to an end our second, but most painful, rendezvous in a Texas wheat field.

When we returned to the house, everyone had gone to bed so after having a glass of milk and several cookies; I went to the front porch where I removed my boots before stretching out on the hammock. In the field I had managed to restrain my feelings, but alone as I lay there in the silence of the night, the emotions over came me and my tears flowed freely down each side of my face as I stared up at the ceiling.

Somehow, the peace of mind, I had imagined for myself by discovering what troubled Allie during those many months of our courtship, didn't materialize, but instead, more confusion and pain were added to my heart by learning the truth.

After lying there for some time, Allie came through the screen door and stood in silence beside me. I tried to hide my sniffles and wiped my eyes. I moved over on the hammock, and she lay down with me and rested her head on my chest while placing her left leg across my lower body. For some time, I brushed her hair with my hand until she went to sleep. I lay there for what seemed hours before I dozed off.

That was the only night Allie and I slept together. It was a night absent of sex, but not absent of love.

Chapter 24

The distant crowing of a rooster announcing the arrival of another day awakened my mind to pleasant subconscious images of my childhood home in Louisiana. A competing champion from another farm responding to his call caused my eyes to slowly come open to the reality that Allie was still lying next to me in the same position, in which she had fallen asleep. The light bedspread draped over us became a temporary curiosity as I lifted it, thinking Mrs. Natty must have placed it there. For a moment I wondered why she hadn't protested our being together in such an intimate fashion. Knowing the pleasures of these moments wouldn't last, I softly brushed Allie's hair while rehearsing in my mind, her painful confession of the previous evening.

The smell of frying bacon temporarily gained mastery of my attention, and I gave Allie a gentle kiss to awaken her. An exquisite smile beamed forth from her face as if surprised to learn where she had spent the night. In a move, which both surprised and pleased me, she pulled the bedspread over our heads. Under the not so secluded, protection, Allie began teasing me with multiple kisses all over my face, which I found enjoyable until Paul jerked the spread off us and announced breakfast was ready *if we were interested.*

During our drive toward the field later that morning, the sun appeared to rest over Maude, and for me it took on a majestic appearance as I realized this tiny machine, once dwarfed by the massy wheat field, had conquered the challenge before it, and now stood silently waiting to complete its annual mission. For the first time, I began to understand the relationship Mr. Henry enjoyed with the antiquated machine, and I recalled how I once jokingly thought the two appeared indomitable as a team. Now, I saw Maude as more than just a simple farm implement, but a complex network of gears, chains, and many other parts, which gave her life and character, thus making her worthy of a name. Indeed a lady of the Plains, Maude stood, a little weather beaten and worn, and perhaps tired, but like so many Pioneer women who had gone before her, she too had made a contribution to the Panhandle's history. Now, so close to our goal of finishing the crop, the Three Apostles and I also shared in that distinction.

As the morning sun moved across the sky, I stood at the steering wheel to get a better look at the rapidly disappearing field of golden wheat. A sense of heightened excitement dominated my spirit as the realization that my promise to help Mr. Henry bring in the crop was nearing completion. Lost in my own thoughts, I didn't pay much attention to the grain truck creeping beside the combine, until James laid on the horn while holding a Thermos bottle through the open window. After looking back into the grain tank, I signaled him to meet me at the end of the field where I would stop to unload.

After bringing Maude to a stop, I watched the small team of "Airmen turned farmers" toasting me with raised coffee cups. While letting Maude run for a while before starting the auger to transfer her load to the grain truck, I noticed Paul approaching the header while unzipping his pants.

"We brought you some coffee and doughnuts," Paul yelled while urinating on the tine he suspected of piercing his hand.

"Paul! Damn it boy . . . are you drunk?" I shouted from atop Maude.

"Not as drunk as I'm gonna get when I return to Amarillo," slurred Paul.

"John? Are you responsible for this?" I shouted, before starting down the ladder.

"I had nothing to do with this, Yogi," answered John with a slight chuckle. "The little fart-burner had it stashed in his suitcase all this time."

"Well . . . since this is our last day," I said, gazing at John, "maybe . . . a celebration is in order."

Sitting on the ground in the shade of the grain truck, we celebrated the occasion with coffee and doughnuts listening to some of Paul's more scintillating tales, until the old Ford pickup heading across the open field with Mr. Henry riding in the back, brought us back to the reality of our mission.

By 11:00 a.m., the final pass was made in the field bringing to an end a monthlong struggle for me and a week of hard labor for the Three Apostles. During the final unloading of Maude, I remained at the driver's seat, watching the level of the grain tank drop as the Three Apostles celebrated the event with more coffee and an occasional toast to Mr. Henry sitting in the shade of his umbrella. After pouring the final bit of coffee into a cup, Paul handed it to Allie's father with the suggestion he toast his crew. My hand signal to dissuade Paul from attempting such a move caught Mr. Henry's attention.

After paying a tribute to his crew, Mr. Henry downed the coffee with one gulp. The absence of a frown on his face told me the old man was onto the chicanery of the Apostles. Pitching the cup back to Paul, Mr. Henry suggested we head to the grain bins.

As our small caravan slowly made its way across the open field, stirring up a small dust cloud, the thought that I had met a man-sized challenge and won, coupled with the knowledge I had proven myself before Mr. Henry and my friends, caused a euphoric feeling to sweep over my entire being. While standing behind the steering wheel with both fists raised high in the air, I began to whoop in exultation; declaring to the world what I perceived as my arrival into manhood.

As James and John topped off the grain truck from one of the bins, I hosed down Maude making sure every inch of her complex system was free of dust and straw, before returning her to the equipment shed for a period of hibernation, which would last until the next season. As I drove the combine under the shed, Mr. Henry carefully watched my every move, making sure Maude would spend her days of rest in the proper spot. After shutting down the engine for the final time, I pushed back in the seat for a few moments, before blowing out a long, slow breath. Looking down at Mr. Henry, I couldn't help but wonder how many more seasons he and Maude would enjoy together, before time would relegate them to a place of obscurity. And, I wondered if I too would be back for another season.

During lunch, the Three Apostles announced they would return to Amarillo after cleaning up and packing. Allie's parents attempted to get them to stay one more night by promising them a steak supper in town, but I could sense the celebration temporarily interrupted by the call of duty in the field still needed to be completed. I, on the other hand, decided to stay on until Sunday morning, which would allow me time enough to make at least two more trips to the grain elevator. And of course, I wanted to spend some additional time with Allie.

While the Three Apostles prepared to leave, I finished loading the grain truck and 'tarped' it down before starting toward the house. In passing the corral, I recalled how Allie once said her brother would celebrate the final day of cutting by riding his pony Comanche through the open field, which was for so many months of the year off-limits. I decided to saddle Buster and Midnight so the Three Apostles could participate in this tradition before leaving.

After leading the horses toward the house, I tied them to the gate and went upstairs to say a private good-bye to James. I wanted to express to him my appreciation for all the work he had done, without one word of complaint. He was just getting ready to leave the room when I arrived. The moment was awkward for both of us so I quickly thanked him for his efforts before picking up his suitcase and carrying it downstairs.

The mood in the dining room was vapid, as Allie's parents said good-bye to the Three Apostles. Mrs. Natty gave each of them a hardy hug while repeatedly wiping her eyes with her apron. Mr. Henry's face was solemn, and while trying to maintain his balance on one crutch, he gave each of them a firm handshake. Allie thanked each of them with a slight hug.

"Hey, come on," I announced, leading the group toward the dining room screen door. "There's one thing you guys have to do before leaving. Allie told me her brother would always celebrate the end of the harvest by riding his horse across the open field."

"That's right," laughed Mrs. Natty. "Henry would never let the kids walk in the wheat field, so Robert would always ride across the field on the last day of harvest. That boy was like a wild Comanche . . . a riding and a whooping . . ."

For a moment Mrs. Natty paused, before raising her apron to her mouth as if restraining herself from speaking further.

"Hell! I'm for it," said Paul, with a quick glance at John and James before dropping his suitcase to the ground.

Before Allie and I could say anything about Buster's customary spinning habit to dissuade would-be riders, two other suitcases hit the ground and a three-man scramble for the horses broke forth, leaving us standing in a wake of dust. Even with his arm in a sling Paul arrived at Midnight's side first, which caused James and John to both try for Buster. In the excitement caused by two riders attempting to mount him, Buster's whirling hindquarters delivered a solid blow to Paul, knocking him from the stirrup and into the fence. Mrs. Natty gasped while holding her apron to her mouth. James abandoned the struggle with John for the excitable Buster and quickly mounted Midnight.

Racing through the open field as if riding for the Pony Express, James and John did their best to honor Robert's memory by raising a wild raucous, which could be heard all the way back to the house. They made a wide circle across the top of a distant ridge before heading back toward the equipment shed and then toward the yard. Buster and

Midnight were neck to neck in a full gallop when they rounded the corner by the equipment shed and started toward the yard.

As they approached the yard, James pulled back on the reins to slow Midnight, but John held Buster to a gallop until midway the yard. Allie, Mrs. Natty, and I scattered like scared chicken as Buster came to a sliding stop before the steps. His hind hoofs plowed two deep rivulets into the ground, creating a cloud of dust, which quickly enveloped Mr. Henry.

Swinging down from the saddle in true cowboy fashion, John offered the reins to me. With a smirk on his face he said, "Let's see you top that."

Buster, now sufficiently agitated as a result of John's "rough landing," made my attempt to mount him more difficult as he whirled with more resolution. Finally, after swinging up into the saddle by grabbing the horn, I helped Buster find his bearings and tried to catch Midnight, now past the equipment shed.

Using Robert's cowboy hat on Buster's rump as a form of encouragement, I caught Paul before he made it to the crown of the distant hill, where we turned and circled back toward the house. Rounding the corner at the equipment shed, I edged Paul off the road causing him to lose control of Midnight and veering off into the open field away from the house.

Buster was brought into the yard at a slowed pace, as I waited for Paul to recover and rejoin me. Losing the race didn't dampen Paul's usual jovial spirit and after dismounting, he kissed Midnight on the nose and declared she was the *prettiest female he had kissed all week.*

Having honored, to the best of our ability, the tradition begun many years before by Allie's brother, the laughter over the race died down and the deadpan faces of good-bye reappeared. With some trepidation, Mrs. Natty, Allie, and I accompanied the Three Apostles to *The Iron Lung*, where we watched in silence as they each tossed their suitcases into the trunk. During the final hugs and handshakes to say good-bye, I realized a magical time in our young lives was coming to an end. I sensed the Three Apostles were feeling the same way.

The Iron Lung rocked from side to side as John accelerated onto the farm road, leaving behind a trail of blue smoke. A hubbub of yells and screams came from the car, as three arms extended above the roof, each giving me the finger.

Allie agreed to return the horses to the stable since I needed to leave for the elevators. During my trip into town, I had time to consider the events of the previous evening. Allie's heart breaking confession replayed itself repeatedly in my mind, while waiting in line to unload. It was then I realized Allie's rape, in some small way was also an assault against my life, for it was denying me the love of the girl, whom I wanted very much to become more in my life, than just a friend. In the solitude of the truck, I came to realize the healing process for both of us would be long and painful.

The alarm clock on the small table beside my bed went off at 4:00 a.m. After turning it off, I lay in the bed for a few moments thinking that my three friends were probably still sleeping, after a Saturday night of partying at the Pink Elephant or some other honky-tonk back in Amarillo. Looking toward the bathroom wall that separated Allie's bedroom from mine, I thought about climbing out the window and making my way to her room by way of the roof, a route I had used less often than desired during this trip to the farm. My better judgment prevailed this time. I got up and shaved. But the thought of what lay beyond the wall never left my mind.

After shaving, I packed my clothes, except for a pair of jeans, western shirt, and cowboy boots that I planned to wear on the trip back to Amarillo. As I made up my bed, the aroma of fresh brewed coffee filtering through the house was beckoning me downstairs. Why, I made up the bed . . . I don't know. I had not done this before while on the farm. Perhaps, it was an entrenched response learned during Basic Training, which was manifesting itself in order to prepare me for a return to a military life. As I started to leave the room, I removed Robert's cowboy hat from the nail near the door and shoved it down on my head. Once

I entered the hallway, the squeaky floorboard that had so many times before been an adversary, brought a smile on my face.

Mrs. Natty greeted me with a cheerful "morning" as I walked into the kitchen. After pouring myself a cup of coffee, I stepped out onto the back steps and sat down. While sipping the coffee, a desire to see the farm once more before leaving came over me. I quickly drained the cup and set it on the step.

"Mrs. Natty," I said while turning to face the screen door, "I'm going for a ride."

"I'll ring the bell when breakfast's ready!" Mrs. Natty called from the backdoor, as I skipped toward the gate on my way to the equipment shed.

My immediate destination was the windmill on the far side of the farm, for this had become my favorite spot, perhaps because it was the sight of my first triumph on the place. After climbing to the platform and letting my feet dangle over the edge, I watched as the morning sky toward the east, slowly evolved into a suffusion of colors, as if a mighty, capable hand was painting the universe. I wondered if this majestic portrait of the heavens, a reenactment of its birth, was for my benefit as a going away gift.

The whole area appeared more open than before, yet I saw a beauty in the land I hadn't seen before. Perhaps, this new found beauty came from the remaining stubble, which offered a silent testimony to its fruitfulness and the realization that I had had a small part in bringing forth its bounty. The land had yielded its annual crop of the golden grain and like ole Maude, it too was now resting. It asks nothing of us, except we respect it, as a living thing, and in return, it would continue to give us life through the power bestowed upon it by its Creator. Considering this new found fondness for the open plains, I smiled as I remembered how, upon my arrival in Amarillo, I hated the vastness of the area, for to me, it was an alien land devoid of trees, as the ones of Louisiana, which, at the time, was the only measure of beauty I was capable of seeing.

The threnody of a mourning dove interrupted my daydreaming, causing me to turn my head toward the creek bordering the farm. For several minutes, I sat looking in that direction. The crumbling old soddie caught my attention, causing me to wonder how many more years this tired old sentry, of a bygone era, would stand before giving way to time. With a gust of wind, the windmill moved around and offered up a squeaky sound as it began to turn. While standing to move the tail vane to the side and turning the mill away from the wind, I noticed my car traveling across the open field. Knowing it was Allie, I watched until she pulled up beside the pickup truck.

"Come on up!" I gestured with a slight wave, as Allie stepped out the car.

"What are you doing?"

"Nothing," I yelled down, leaning over the edge to look down at her, "just enjoying the view. Come on up!"

"No thanks." Was the reply with a return wave. "I have acrophobia."

"What?" I yelled back down.

"I'm scared of heights!"

"You're just chicken!" I yelled back. "Come on . . . chicken." I started taunting Allie by placing my thumbs under my armpits and flapping my elbows and clucking like a chicken.

The teasing finally got the better of Allie, and she slowly made her way up the ladder as I hung my head through the opening in the platform, encouraging her to continue without looking down. Once she reached the top of the platform, she slowly crawled through the opening and quickly wrapped both arms around my neck. While struggling for a breath, Allie pleaded with me to not let her go. Several times I reassured her that I wouldn't let her fall, and for a while I thought she was going to faint as her complexion took on a pale color.

"Is this your first time up here?" I asked with a chuckle, while struggling to pry her arms from around my neck.

She just nodded her head in the affirmative and tightened her grip around my neck.

"Okay, look," I said, pulling her arms from around my neck with both hands. "I'm not going to let you fall, but you have to let me breathe." I gave her a slight, reassuring kiss. "Now, I'm going to move against the frame, and you can sit between my legs . . . okay."

"Do it, slow." Her voice had a quiver in it.

With a great deal of caution, I slid back against the frame below the windmill and pulled my knees up as high as I could. Allie sat between my legs and wrapped her arms around my knees while leaning back against my chest. I could feel her body move with each breath. I kissed her several times on the back of the neck and encouraged her to take slow, deep breaths, which she did. After several minutes, her breathing became more normal, and I could feel her body relax.

"What are you doing up here?" Allie asked nervously, while pushed back against my body.

"Nothing," I replied, relaxing my arms around her shoulders. "I just decided to take one last look at the place before leaving."

"What time are you leaving?" Allie asked, pulling my arms back to their former position.

"After breakfast. I'm already packed."

"Why so early, Yogi?" Allie asked, pulling her knees near her body and wrapping her arms around my still-raised knees.

"I have a bunch of stuff to do back at the Base," I answered, removing my arms from around her shoulders. Our vapid conversation seemed to have a calming effect on Allie, for her breathing was steady, and her voice became stronger.

"What about you?" I asked, pulling her head back against my shoulder. "How long before you return to Amarillo?"

"A month . . . I guess," Allie answered, looking up at the clouds. Then she turned her face toward mine. "I'll have to call the Hospital to be sure." Allie paused as if considering if she should continue. "It's possible . . . I'll have to wait until September."

"September!" I replied in almost a shout. "Allie! I'll be crazy . . . if I can't see you until September. I remember what my life was like when you were gone for the Christmas holidays. And that was just a few weeks."

Allie must have felt a little confident, for she turned slightly to the right and tucked one leg under her body and put one arm around my neck. With an alluring smile, which I knew was intended to taunt me she asked:

"How did you survive before we met?"

"My life was a blur before that night we met at the Double Dip," I answered with a slight kiss to the bridge of her nose. "And I hope there will never be a time again in my life when you're not a part of it."

Allie turned away from me and softly said, "Yogi, let's not speak of tomorrow."

I recognized the change in her demeanor as an expression of her often reoccurring melancholy moods. I tried to embrace her as before, but she moved slightly away from the protective enclosure of my raised knees. We remained silent for some time.

"If you keep moving away from me, you'll fall into the water trough," I said, softly touching her shoulder.

After what appeared to be a lifetime of waiting, Allie slowly moved back closer to me and rested her chin on her raised knees. For a long time, we sat there without speaking as I continued to rub her back hoping to change her mood. I thought of jumping off the tower into the water trough to cheer her up, but decided against that, since all my other clothes were packed. I had to do something to snap her out of the mood she was in.

With a long "Yahooooo," I sent Robert's cowboy hat sailing into the air. Allie was startled and sat erect. The hat floated toward the ground, and for a moment I thought it was going to land in the water trough. Instead it landed near the pickup.

"I believe there are moments when you are a little mad, Yogi," Allie said with an exquisite smile while looking at me.

"I am a little mad," I answered, laughing while leaning back against the structure of the windmill. "Madly in love . . . with my life for the first time . . . ever . . . and madly in love with this place!"

We both laughed uncontrollably for a while, until our eyes met in a moment of quietness.

"Allie . . . if you don't kiss me so that I'll remember this moment for the rest of my life . . . I'll stand and madly scream my love . . . for you . . . so loud the whole Panhandle will hear it."

Allie turned and placed her legs around my hips. I assumed the same position and drew her body close to mine. What began as a soft warm mellifluous kiss, quickly turned to a passionate devouring fire, a fire held in check since the night of our rendezvous in the wheat field.

The faint ringing sound of a distant bell caused Allie's lips to pull away from mine. I attempted to pull her face back toward mine not wanting to disrupt the current of passion raging deep within my body.

"Breakfast is ready, Yogi," Allie said, putting her fingers to my lips.

"I prefer the breakfast I'm having," I replied, while removing her hand.

"Come on, Yogi. We had better get back." Allie said, glancing toward the opening at the ladder.

Pulling her face toward mine once more I said, "Hey, promise me, you'll never climb this windmill with anyone else. Okay?"

A moment of silence transpired between us, as Allie remained sitting on my lap facing me. After pulling my face to hers with both hands, I received a less passionate kiss than before as the answer to my request.

Before making our way down the ladder, I moved the tail vane back into position and the windmill swung in the direction of the wind and resumed its squeaky greeting to the morning.

Mr. Henry and Mrs. Natty were both sitting at the dining room table when Allie and I came walking through the screen door. We quickly took our places beside each other, holding hands under the table, while waiting for Mr. Henry to say grace.

On the table, only inches away from my plate, laid a white envelope, bearing my name, hastily scribbled with a pencil. Mr. Henry's blessing was extra long and my curiosity got the better of me, so I opened one eye to look at the envelope. Allie caught me. We grinned at each other.

"You leaving this morning?" asked Mr. Henry, as he reached for his fork and knife immediately after closing the blessing. His question sounded as if coupled with the "Amen."

"Yes, sir," I answered, "I have some things to catch up on once I return."

"Henry and I appreciate very much what you and your friends did this week," added Mrs. Natty. Reaching across the corner of the table, she touched her husband's hand as if reminding him of something.

"You and your friends did a first rate job," added Mr. Henry quickly, as he commenced chopping his eggs and hash browns into a yellow mixture. "Sorry, your friend . . . Paul . . ." he stopped long enough to take a sip of coffee before continuing, " . . . got hurt. But, he's young. He'll be fine."

"I'm sorry I wasn't able to haul more of the grain to the elevator," I added reluctantly, while taking a bite.

"Earl's sending out his trucks this coming week," Mr. Henry countered resolutely. Then, pointing to the envelope with his fork, he added, "He brought me a check this week. That's for you and your friends."

My hesitation to pick up the envelope caused Allie to nudge me with her elbow.

"Go on Yogi. Open it."

The envelope wasn't sealed. Pulling the flap open I took hold of the money with my thumb and index finger and carefully extracted four fifty-dollar bills that fell on the table, almost in my plate. My heart did a couple of fast palpitations, for that was the most money I had ever seen at one time in my life. Had I not received such a sexual arousing kiss on the windmill earlier, this moment would have been the crowning event of my final day on the farm.

"Mr. Henry, this is way too much," I said, picking up the money from the table.

"Divide it up with your friends. As you see fit," declared Mr. Henry, pointing his fork in my direction.

In a way, I was glad he didn't agree with my polite, insincere suggestion.

"Thank-you, sir," I replied with a glow on my face, as I proudly reached for my wallet.

"Thank-you, Yogi," Allie said, as she rewarded me with a slight kiss on the cheek.

"Oh! I have something for you and your friends," said Mrs. Natty, as she got up from the table and walked over to the hutch.

Returning to the table with what appeared to be several newspapers in her hands, she added, "I got five copies, just in case you needed an extra one."

Holding up one copy of the Indian Ridge Weekly, a broad smile came to my face as I looked at the front page. There we were . . . bigger than life . . . enjoying our five minutes of fame. A moment of exuberant passion overcame me and with my tongue in motion and my brain in neutral I said, "Man, wait until the Three Apostles see this, they're going to crap!"

My remark wasn't as crass as Paul's remark about the Kotex, but it drew the same response from Mr. Henry. I could feel my face turning red and a feverish feeling washed over my entire body. Allie giggled and from under the table she reached for my hand and gave me a reassuring squeeze. Mrs. Natty, feeling my embarrassment, at long last came to my rescue.

"Well, thank goodness, Paul wasn't here. He would have said something a little more colorful."

With breakfast over, Allie and I slowly made our way upstairs while holding hands, to retrieve my suitcase from Robert's room. I squeezed her hand in mine and worked my fingers between her knuckles as if playing a piano trying to get her to smile. Knowing this would be my last visit to the farm and to this room, in particular, for an unspecified period of time, I wasn't in a great hurry to leave, even though I knew the trip ahead of me was long.

Allie and I sat on the bed beside each other, both dreading the moment of my departure. Robert's room had become as much a part of my life as it had been a part of his, and I couldn't bring myself to just grab my suitcase and leave. Allie rested her face on my back as I leaned forward, resting my elbows on my legs, while nervously playing with Robert's old cowboy hat. A lonely silence filled the room. Finally, Allie reached out and pulled my body upright with a gentle tug and placed her arms around my neck. The cowboy hat, which had occupied my hands, fell to the floor as I turned to take Allie into my arms. After a few minutes,

I could feel her tears soaking through my shirt. Several minutes passed before she spoke. Her voice was dry and broken.

"You call me tonight . . . okay." Allie wiped her eyes with the palm of her hands.

"I will . . . promise," I said, kissing the remaining salty tears from her face. "Allie, please don't wait until September before returning to Amarillo."

"Maybe, you can come back up here in the meantime," Allie said, trying to sound hopeful. Patting the bed with her hand, she added, "Your bed will always be available."

"If you promise to meet me out on the roof, I'll come back." I said taking her hands in mine.

"Maybe we'll try out the hammock again," Allie replied with an enticing smile.

I grinned and replied. "Make that a promise and I'll go AWOL next weekend."

"I said, 'maybe,' Yogi," Allie quickly countered with a giggle.

We both looked at each other and somehow knew that the palaver between us had run its course. I bent forward and picked up the cowboy hat from the floor. After standing, I took my suitcase from the bed and started for the door. My hand seemed to refuse to let go of Robert's hat, as I hung it on the nail beside the mirror. I felt the use of his bedroom and hat and Allie's revelation of his death had formed a kinship between Robert and me. After releasing the cowboy hat, I turned to his picture on the wall and gave it a slight salute.

"Thanks, pal for the use of your bed and hat."

Allie smiled. Perhaps she was thinking once more that I was experiencing a moment of madness similar to that on the windmill.

"I wish you could have known him, Yogi," Allie said with some sadness in her voice. Momentarily, she bit down on her bottom lip, fighting back the tears. "I think the two of you would have liked each other."

Chapter 25

My arrival at the Air Base in the early afternoon found the place almost deserted, except for a few boys sunbathing on blankets in the quadrangle. Carrying my suitcase and birdcage past them, I had to fight back a chortle, as my mind flashed back to my first sunburn on the farm.

The usual Sunday afternoon's ghostly silence of the barracks seemed to amplify my footsteps as I rushed up the stairs, hoping to find James in his room. After dropping off my suitcase and bird cage near the door of my room, I walked down the hall to his room. He wasn't in. Upon returning to my room, I found everything in place just as I left it. No surprises from the Three Apostles.

After raising the windows to air out the room, the arduous task of unpacking began. The fresh clean scent of my sun-dried laundry caused me to hold one of the shirts to my face. Mental images of Allie and the farm caused me to smile. While stripping the bunk with the intention of washing the sheets, I realized my Sunday afternoon ritual of laundry, room cleaning, and letter writing was reasserting itself.

With my laundry going, I walked over to the Orderly Room to sign in, while wearing a pair of shower thongs, jeans, and a white T-shirt. The expression on the CQ's face indicated he didn't appreciate my appearance, but said nothing. With his permission, I left a copy of the Indian Ridge Weekly on Captain Ford's desk.

Upon returning to the barracks, I checked James's room once again. He still wasn't in. For a little while I watched television alone in the Dayroom, before deciding to go for a walk. In front of the Base Theater, I paused to study the placard. I decided against spending the twenty-five cents to see "Thunder in Carolina" with Rory Calhoun, and started walking, again with no destination in mind. The loneliness of the Sunday afternoon brought upon me a sense of forlornness equal to the night I spent on Maude, after fighting with John. In a strange way, I desired to be alone, yet longed of Allie's presence, something I had grown accustomed to. Upon returning to the barracks, I called Allie as promised. Neither of us was very talkative and the silence between us after she stated her father's leg was bothering him more than usual, left me feeling her afternoon had been as lonely as mine.

Because James was a late sleeper, I didn't bother waking him for breakfast the following morning. Upon returning to the barrack, I found him in the latrine preparing to shave. It was my intention to leave for the office earlier than usual and asked if he would join me in Paul and John's room for a minute or two. After presenting each of them with a copy of the Indian Ridge Weekly, Paul declared his approval with a simple, '*Holy Shit! Would you look at this?*' While the three of them settled on the bunks to read the article, I opened the envelope given me by Mr. Henry and offered each of them a crisp new fifty-dollar bill. A brief period of silence filled the room as three dumbfounded faces studied the largest bills they had ever seen. Once assured the bills were real, the room erupted into the most euphoric mood the barracks had ever witnessed on a Monday morning.

Returning to my desk job in the hangar office seemed paltry, after the challenges faced each day with Maude. About midmorning, Airman Zuccarello called from the Orderly Room with a message from Captain Ford who had read the article in the Indian Ridge Weekly. The good Captain was placing a letter of commendation in each of our personnel files.

Each evening, during that first week, I called Allie to check on Mr. Henry and to see if she had called St. Anthony's about resuming her classes. I felt my life was slipping into a period of stagnation with her so far away. Attempting to fill the void in my life, I became a regular bar denizen as did my three friends, now that we had more money than we could drink up.

It was almost noon on the second Saturday morning after returning to the Base, that a loud military style knock sounded at my door.

"You're Airman Yogi?" asked a young Airman Third Class, cowardly poking his head through the partially opened door.

"Yeah," I answered, rolling over in my bunk.

"You have a phone call downstairs," said the stranger before disappearing down the hall.

Wearing only my boxer shorts and flip-flops I rushed down to the phone booth. The sweet soft voice, responding with a giggle, to my hastily spoken 'Hello' caused a wave of tranquility to wash over me. The reality that my life source had indeed returned to the city, left me speechless for a moment, before a barrage of questions came flooding from my mouth.

"Hold on, Yogi," Allie said with a slight chuckle. "I'm not back in school yet. And, I'm not working at the Hospital."

"I don't care about neither, right now," I said, in a state of heightened excitement. "Please, Allie, can we get together tonight?"

The phone went silent for a moment. Longing to hear her voice I chortled. "Hey, are you still there?"

"Yes." Allie's voice sounded grim and faltering. "Yogi, I'm here with my Dad. He was admitted a couple of days ago."

"A couple of days ago?" I repeated, as if asking a question. "Why didn't you call me?"

"I did, Yogi!" There was a short pause. "Some guy said he would give you the message." There was a tremor in Allie's voice, followed by a sniffle.

"Allie, are you okay?" I asked leaning against the wall of the phone booth. When Allie failed to respond, I asked, "Is it his leg? Did he break it again?"

"Daddy . . . has bone cancer . . . . Yogi," answered Allie in a chilling tone.

I could hear Allie softly crying, as the silence between us dragged on for a minute or two.

"Allie, are you there?" I asked, after sometime.

"Yes," she answered. Her words seemed to come in jerks as she continued to speak. "Yogi, could you . . . please come . . . sit with . . . me?"

"Sure," I answered, "I'll be there just as soon as I can get dressed. Allie . . . don't worry . . . okay . . . everything will be fine. You'll see . . . promise."

Walking down the hall toward Mr. Henry's room, I noticed Allie leaning against the wall in the hallway. Standing there in a pair of jeans and a white shirt tied in a knot at the waist caused my mind to flash back to the afternoon we spent horseback riding in Palo Duro Canyon. In my mind, she was still as beautiful as I thought that afternoon. Until that moment, I couldn't believe how just a few days of separation had affected me. As Allie turned in my direction, a beautiful smile transformed her solemn face as she pushed away from the wall. As she started walking in my direction, my pace quickened until we came together in an enveloping embrace.

I felt alive again and squeezed her several times with excessive force, which brought forth a gentle plea. In the excitement of the moment, I almost forgot my reason for being at the hospital.

"You want to look in on Daddy?" asked Allie, while trying to pull away from my arms. After letting up on my embrace, she continued with a dolorous glance toward the door. "They have him on morphine and several other medications, so he may not wake up."

In silence I stood in the darkened room, gripping the rounded metal foot railing of the unshaven patient's bed. After a few moments I turned briefly toward Allie standing slightly behind me. As if reading my thoughts, Allie moved beside me and wrapped both arms around my waist. Staring down at the frail, gaunt patient propped up by several pillows, my mind rejected the idea that this was the same virile man I once knew and feared. Recalling how my sluggish morning began on the farm, with a violent shaking of my foot, I gently reached out and touched his toes as if to arouse him to that moment in time.

"Is that you, Yogi?" With this weak inquiry, his usual stoic face produced a gentle smile.

"Yes sir," I replied, coming to a more erect stance at the foot railing.

With a barely audible voice, Mr. Henry answered, "Good." He attempted to raise his right hand as if extending it to me.

For a while his lips continued to move, producing only a whisper. Allie's arms around my waist tightened as she turned her face away from her father. Frozen in silence, I watched as this once powerful man struggled against the overpowering medication. Within a few seconds he was sleeping again. For several painful minutes, Allie and I stood at the foot of the bed before the ordeal became too great for her. Without speaking I turned and led her out of the room.

Since Mrs. Natty wasn't able to make the trip to Amarillo, I felt compelled to stay all day with Allie, in spite of the long depressing hours. We lounged around the room most of the morning. For a while, Allie sat in my lap with her legs across the arm of the high back leather chair, while resting her head on my shoulder. By the late afternoon, I was suffering from claustrophobia and needed to get away. After some cajoling, I was able to talk Allie into riding down the Polk Street to the

Double Dip for something to eat. The parking lot as usual was a miasma of exhaust fumes, hilarity, and honking horns. The sights, sounds, and even the smell of burgers and fries, which filled the air, took my mind back to that first night Allie and I met. So much had transpired since that night; it now seemed like decades rather than little more than a year.

Allie was standing in the hall the following afternoon as I rounded the corner near the nurses' station. We greeted each other with a slight kiss, but a long embrace.

"How's your father doing?" I asked looking toward Mr. Henry's door.

"He's awake," Allie said in an upbeat tone. "Against the wishes of Mama and me, he told the Doctors, he wants off all medication except for the morphine."

"Is your mother in town?" I asked.

"She and Earl McCurley came in early this morning, and they left about an hour ago," answered Allie taking me by the hand. "Come on . . . Daddy's been asking for you."

Mr. Henry was sitting in the bed as we entered the room. My mind temporarily flashed back to those occasions on the farm, when he sat in the back of the old Ford pickup truck under the umbrella. No longer under the influence of the heavy medication, he resembled the man I knew back then. He was clean shaven and wearing a western style shirt over his hospital gown that caused me to grin. Allie didn't appreciate my smile or her father's garb.

"Daddddddy!" Allie's voice sounded almost disparaging, as she dragged out the word. "You have to take off that shirt!"

"It's cold in here, Daughter." Mr. Henry's voice was stern and raspy as he folded his arms across his chest; pertinaciously demonstrating the shirt wasn't coming off. I couldn't help but smile, for the father and daughter tug-of-war seen so many times on the farm hadn't subsided.

Mr. Henry and I greeted each other with a handshake. The massive hand that once enveloped mine seemed to exist no longer, as Mr. Henry continued gripping my hand during the usual inquiries concerning his condition. A hiatus lasting several minutes followed, while Allie adjusted her father's pillows, checked his IV and adjusted the blanket and sheet on his bed, which seemed to annoy him. I moved away from the bed and sat in a nearby chair.

"Would you sit still, Allie?" demanded Mr. Henry in a gruff voice. "And stop fussing over me. You're like an old mother hen."

I figured the pain in Mr. Henry's leg was making him more petulant than usual. Allie walked over to me and started to sit in my lap, when Mr. Henry spoke again. His voice was now more conciliatory.

"Daughter, you mind stepping out for a few minutes?"

Allie and I, both baffled by Mr. Henry's request, glanced at each other.

Allie turned to her father with a look of resentment before glancing down at me, hoping to be rescued from her ouster. I shrugged my shoulders.

"Well, I guess it's time the women folks and little children leave the room, so the men can discuss how you plan to fight off the Comanches." The intonation of Allie's voice sounded as if she was mimicking some starlet from an old John Wayne western. Her face was red and taut. With her hands on her hips, she concluded, "This isn't Texas of the 1800s . . . if you two are interested!"

With my elbow propped on the arm of the chair, I held my left index fingers across my lips hoping to disguise my smile.

"I know what year it is girl," replied Mr. Henry. His voice sounded husky. "But I have something to say to Yogi, and you don't need to hear it."

Allie stormed out the room.

"I think she's upset," said Mr. Henry looking my way.

"I think she's PO'ed." I countered, while coming to my feet.

We both laughed. Mr. Henry grimaced while pushing back on the pillows. Reaching for his leg, as if trying to mitigate the pain, he clenched his teeth.

"You're okay, sir?" I asked, moving to the foot of the bed. "Want me to call Allie back in?"

"No," sighed Mr. Henry, tightening his lips. After a few minutes, his face relaxed enough for him to add, "'Pears ole Maude and me done seen our last harvest, Yogi."

Trying to sound optimistic I gave forth a small chuckle. "I don't believe that, Mr. Henry. The Doctors here will have you up and about in no time."

"It's nice of you to say that, Yogi, but what's ailing me, can't be fixed by any Doctor." His face became stolid as he appeared to be staring at a corner of the ceiling.

"You can't . . . just give up, sir," I pleaded. "Maybe you should agree to get back on your medication."

"I ain't giving up. I'm just facing life as it is." He paused for a while and turned his face away from me. As he spoke again, his voice was vapid. "Somewhere in the Bible, it says there is appointed a time to be born and a time to die." There was a brief hiatus in his thoughts, before he continued with a sigh. "It 'pears . . . my time has come."

"That's in the book of Ecclesiastes." I answered, not knowing if my reference was correct or not.

Mr. Henry looked back at me as if surprised to hear my response.

"You're familiar with the scripture, Yogi?"

"At one time I was," I answered, while briefly looking away. "I guess somewhere along the way I got sidetracked."

"We all get sidetracked at some point or another in our lives, Yogi," answered Mr. Henry, as if he was reading my mind. He paused for several moments. After taking several deep breaths he continued while looking away from me. "When a man's facing something like what's facing me, Yogi . . . he realizes it's time to gets things right with his Creator and his fellow man."

I stood patiently by the bed and watched this once robust man, who once had the physical strength to accomplish almost any task on the farm, struggle for the words to convey his innermost thoughts.

"You're a young man, Yogi . . . and . . . you showed me up!" Mr. Henry sighed once. "Your apology . . . and the work you did that last week on the farm. It took a man of real character to do what you did. I wasn't able to say I was wrong . . . as you did." Mr. Henry cleared his throat before continuing. "If . . . you can find it in your heart to forgive this pigheaded old man, I would appreciate it."

The reconciliation I had long desired came at last, but under the circumstances it now seemed unnecessary as I extended my hand to him.

"There's no need to apologize, Mr. Henry . . ."

With a loud harrumph from deep down in his throat, Mr. Henry broke my trend of thought as he tried shifting around to a more comfortable position on the pillows. I tried to assist him by adjusting some of the pillows behind his head.

Mr. Henry coughed several more times before speaking again. "Yogi . . . that day in the field, you know when . . ."

"The day you wanted to stomp my skinny ass in the ground," I asked in a joking tone.

"Yeah . . . that day," chuckled Mr. Henry. He frowned and rubbed his thigh before speaking again. Pointing his finger at me, he continued with a grin, "I could have done it, too. You know that, don't you?"

"Yes sir." My answer was laconic and humble.

"You said then that . . . you love Allie . . . and would like to marry her some day." Mr. Henry's memory of that day caught me by surprise.

"Well, something to that effect, sir." As I recalled it, my words had more defiance to them.

"Allie's a good girl, Yogi, but she has some problems, which I'm sure you're aware of. The man, who would marry her, would come into three thousand acres of the best farm land in the Pan . . . handle." Once more Mr. Henry grimaced from the pain in his leg and clinched his teeth together.

"Sir," I didn't mean to cut him off, but my tongue just started moving. "If Allie would have me, I'd marry her, if all you had were three acres of the worst land in Texas. But, that decision will be hers . . . not ours."

"Well, what I'm saying, Yogi, is that if you still feel that way about Allie . . . I'd be pleased to have you for a son-in-law."

"Thank-you, sir." I replied with a grin. "But, any such plans will have to be some years in the future, since I'm still obligated to Uncle Sam for several more years."

"Bah," replied Mr. Henry with the wave of his hand. "You're young boy, and that little bit of time will fly by."

Thinking back to what Allie had said before leaving the room, I felt as if we were living in Texas of the 1800s, and I had just traded a dozen horses for a squaw and three thousand acres of land.

I turned to leave the room.

"Yogi, hold up one minute." Mr. Henry's face was pale, as I turned back to face him. "There's something else about that day you need to know."

"That's not necessary, Mr. Henry . . ." I answered, with a constriction in my throat realizing the emotional pain he was enduring.

"It's necessary, Yogi," answered Mr. Henry. There was a short respite in his struggle, before he continued. "About my anger . . . that morning . . . in the field." Mr. Henry's voice dropped as he stretched his neck, as if dislodging something in his throat. He paused and pointed an accusing finger at me and then swallowed hard. "I just want you to know that it wasn't totally the result of what you did. Mind you, I don't approve of what you and Allie did." Once more Mr. Henry swallowed hard.

"When I was seventeen . . . I left home and went up into Kansas to work as a bindlestiff in the wheat fields." A sanguine color rushed across Mr. Henry's face causing me to feel uncomfortable. "Anyway, I . . . I met this girl . . . and we too . . . made love in a wheat field. Put near a year and a half later, my father received a letter from her father saying that she had given birth to a baby boy and . . . and that I was the father."

Visibly shaken by his recollection, Mr. Henry struggled to continue. "My old man, a real martinet, took me out to the barn and tied my hands to one of the joists. He stripped me down naked and commenced to flog the hell out of me with a razor strop."

Mr. Henry rested a while before speaking again. "After Robert's death, and Allie so long in the hospital, there was a terrible emptiness in my life. I tried filling it by locating this boy. I left home for two months without telling Natty where I was going. My trip wasn't successful so one day I just drove back into the yard and walked to the equipment shed as if I had been gone just an hour. Natty never asked any questions, and I never tried to explain. To have a son some place that you will never know and never see is an awful burden to live with."

Mr. Henry paused to wipe the tears and dolorous gaze from his eyes. "That day in the field . . . I saw myself in you and that's why I was so angry. I didn't want that kind of pain to be a part of your life or Allie's. God knows, she has suffered so much already."

Mr. Henry pressed his head back on the pillows, as if trying to bury the shame on his face. His facial muscles tightened from the physical and emotional pain he attempted to hold back with tightly closed eyelids. I took this as a cue and quietly left the room.

Allie was leaning against the wall near the door when I exited the room. The expression on her face telegraphed, she was still peeved about having to leave. Thinking I would cheer her up, I moved before her and placing one hand on each side of her head before leaning forward to meet her mouth. Her response seemed renunciatory.

"Well, did you men take care of all your business?" Allie asked with a belittling tone, after our lips parted.

"Yeah!" I answered insouciantly while twisting my mouth to the side.

"Come on, Yogi," Allie pleaded, "what did he want that's so secretive?"

"It's no secret," I said with a grin and leaned forward once more to kiss her. After pushing back, but still resting my weight on my outstretched arms, I stared into her eyes. "He apologized for not accepting my apology. And, he said some other things, which I can't discuss right now."

"Is that all?" Allie asked with a surly tone.

"No." I responded with a grin.

"What then?" Allie asked with a quizzical look.

"In a nut shell . . . he offered me three thousand acres of wheat land and an old combine to become his son-in-law."

Allie's face lost all expression. She turned pale. Standing away from the wall, Allie placed both hands on my chest and pushed me backward. After standing there for a few moments, she turned and started walking down the hall toward the nurses' station. I stood petrified for a few seconds before starting after her.

Allie was wiping her eyes as I approached her near the elevator. Several visitors exiting the elevator looked first at Allie and then me, as if detecting something was wrong. A flash of lighting drew our attention toward the windows. Allie turned and walked toward the window while wrapping her arms tightly around her body, as if seeking solitude within her own arms.

"I like the rain," I said, moving to a position close behind her. "It rains a lot in Louisiana." As I watched her reflection in the window, I tried putting my arms around her, but she moved forward nearer the window.

"Come on Allie! What's wrong?" I asked, looking at her reflection in the window.

"This crazy idea . . . is what's wrong!" Allie's voice seemed tart as she reached forward with one finger and dragged it down the window pane following a streak of water. "Why are you doing this to me, Yogi?" Allie continued while gently touching the window with her forehead.

"I'm not doing anything to you! I'm not trying to hurt you!" My voice was far from friendly, but not effusive. "I realize we can't get married until my tour in the Air Force is up and by then you'll be finished with Nursing school . . . and maybe then. As things stand now, we still have several more years to get to know each other better."

"A couple more years won't do it, Yogi. A hundred more years won't change the person I am," answered Allie, as she stood back from the window. "Maybe, Rose is right. Girls like me and others, at that place, aren't meant to fall in love and get married."

"Rose is full of crap," I snapped back in a cruel tone. "Is that what's bothering you . . . your past?"

After glancing toward me briefly, Allie asked in a melancholy mood, "Have I ever told you what Robert said about the rain?" Turning back toward the window, Allie began tracing the streaks of water running down the window while waiting for my answer, which didn't come.

"When I was a little girl, Robert told me the rain drops were angel tears being shed for those who can't love. That's why they're crying today, Yogi . . . because . . . as I told you that night in the field, I can't love you . . . not with my heart, the way a woman should love a man."

Several agonizing moments passed before Allie stopped tracing the window pane and turned to me once more. Slowly her arms reached out and pulled my body against hers. We clung to each other for several minutes twisting from side to side, as if performing a primordial dance, oblivious to the world around us.

The following morning, around 10:00 hours, I received a phone call from the Orderly Room. Airman Zuccarello informed me that Captain Ford wanted to see me and my three friends in his office at 14:00 hours.

As we stood at attention before the Captain's desk, our faces were sullen. The Indian Ridge Weekly I had placed on his desk now rested to his right.

"At ease, Gentlemen," said the Captain, as he sat back in his high back chair and dragged the paper to the center of his desk. "Well Gentlemen," the Captain began by locking his hands behind his head, "I have some good news for you. Your story will be reprinted in the Jet Journal next week."

We all looked at each other and smiled. Paul gave the Captain a "thumbs-up."

"As you all know," continued Captain Ford, "this Flight was authorized only two stripes this go around." He adjusted his tie, which couldn't get any tighter since his collar was too large as always. "However, I was able to persuade the Colonel to make an allowance this time, considering the work you Airmen did by setting an example for each of us to follow in service to our community." The Captain stood and extended his hand first to John. "Congratulations Gentlemen, you'll receive the official notification of your promotions tomorrow."

After a brief moment of sharing smiles, we all came to attention and saluted. We were in the process of doing a right face to exit the office, when Captain Ford picked up a group of papers from his desk.

"Gentlemen," he said stopping us in our tracks. "I have some additional good news for one of you."

We all stood still, as the Captain extended his hand and offered the papers to me.

As I accepted the papers, Captain Ford said, "Congratulations, Airman. You're being transferred to Japan."

Dumbfounded, I stared at the Orders. My name and the word "Japan" seemed three-dimensional on the paper. I wanted to find some reason to be happy about this new assignment, since this was my reason for joining the Air Force. 'See the world' was what the recruiting posters had promised. So far, all I had seen was Texas, and now that I was starting to like the place, they wanted me to leave.

The news about my transfer, and the discussion between Allie and me the evening before, weighed heavy on my mind during the rest of the day. Recalling the passionate good-bye, we shared on the windmill the Sunday morning I left the farm and my concern about Allie not returned to Amarillo until September now seemed so trivial.

My three friends wanted to go out that evening to celebrate our promotions, so I agreed to join them after calling Allie and explaining why I couldn't make it to the Hospital.

Our celebration at Serge's Place went well past midnight. I tried flushing the word "Japan" from my mind, which took more than my usual two beers.

At work the next morning, my head was splitting while my stomach continued to defy its normal function of sending its contents down rather than up. James and I must have made thirty trips to the coffee bar that morning. Adding to my problems was the thought of Allie and the way I had upset her by joking about her father's desire for a son-in-law. By noon, the agony of not knowing how she was coping was more than I could bear. My finger seemed to resist the commands of my brain as I dialed the Hospital's number from the phone on my desk.

Mrs. Natty answered the phone. She said Allie needed a break from the Hospital and had gone over to Crystal's house for a little while.

The words, "Crystal" and "House" reverberated through my pounding head like the noise of crashing cymbals. My body rippled in fear with the thought that possibly my foolishness had driven her back to the House. I made up some lame excuse for leaving the office early.

When I arrived at the House, wearing my Dacron uniform, most of the girls were lounging around the lobby watching television, filing their nails, or applying additional mascara and makeup to their already heavily covered faces. Crystal, who was wearing a hot pink negligee with matching heels, stood to greet me as I walked in her direction.

"You're in town early today, aren't you?" asked Crystal, vigorously working her chewing gum, which made a popping sound.

"Is Allie here?" I quietly asked Crystal while trying to ignore some of the provocative replies offered by the other girls about my uniform.

"Yeah," Crystal answered, working her chewing gum with more rapidity. "She's up in my room. Come on. I'll take you up."

I felt strange going upstairs alone with Crystal, almost as if I was cheating on Allie. We quietly stood on opposite sides of the elevator looking at each other, as the smell of cheap perfume assailed my nose. Crystal began manipulating her large breast up and down in a coquettish way that caused me to smile briefly before lowering my head. Her tempting smile and gentler chewing of the gum caused me to believe she was taunting me like a house cat, playing with a dead mouse.

Before entering the room, Crystal knocked lightly on the door and without waiting for an answer from within, she walked in. I stood in the doorway for a while not knowing if I should enter or not.

"Allie," said Crystal in a cautious voice, as she stood near the open door, "there's someone here to see you."

With some hesitation, I moved further into the room and stood beside Crystal. Allie was standing near the window, looking through the partially opened Venetian blinds, through which the only light in the room filtered. She was wearing a simple cotton dress and a pair of flat shoes, which caused her from the back to look like a simple farm girl. For several moments, an uneasy silence filled the room, before Allie turned to face me. I could scarcely move, except for the nervous fidgeting with my military cap.

"Hi . . . Yogi." Allie's voice was soft and seemed to tremble as she at last acknowledged my presence.

"Allie." I answered in an equally soft tone, while bending my military cap with both hands giving it the ole "forty missions' look."

Allie gestured with her hand as if pointing toward me. "You wore your uniform to town again."

I couldn't tell if she was making a statement or asking a question.

"Yeah," I replied with a forced chuckle. My mind was running in a tangent.

"You're very handsome. Just like that Easter morning . . . when you first came to the farm," Allie said in a low tone, as she advanced a few steps toward me. With her right arm almost fully extended, she reached out and slowly dragged her finger tips down the shirt and stopped at a point near my heart, which was now racing.

Feeling abash, I glanced briefly at Crystal who blushed and without speaking, exited the room, leaving the door open. Allie removed her hand from my chest and faltered with it for a moment or two, as if not knowing how to reclaim it.

Hoping to ease the tension in the room, I pointed to the new chevrons on my upper sleeve. With a hubris spirit and a broad smile, I asked, "Have you noticed? I got another stripe."

"Congratulations, Yogi," Allie said, before moving closer to kiss me on the left cheek.

With this, Allie turned and walked back to the window. As she opened the Venetian blinds slightly, more light entered the room.

Facing her back, my arms ached with a longing to take her into my arms. I just stood motionless, as if frozen to the floor, still fidgeting with my cap. Beads of sweat were starting to form on my forehead. My mouth was starting to dry out, and my throat was swelling, closed, assuring me that speaking would be more difficult the longer I demurred. My neck muscles tautened as I tried to swallow what saliva remained in my mouth before speaking.

"Allie . . . what are you doing here?" I asked.

"I had to get away from the Hospital for a while, Yogi," she replied. "I needed a place to think."

"Allie . . . I'm sorry about the other night." The words came out, but they seemed stolid. "I did the very thing you've always asked me not to do. I guess I was being pushy and . . . I now realize it wasn't a very romantic way to ask a girl to get married. I mean . . . with your Dad in the hospital 'n all." My pleading amounted to desultory rambling. Almost out of breath, I paused for a while. Not meaning to, I blurted out, "Allie, please look at me!"

"It won't work, Yogi," she softly said before turning from the window. Her head was down. I took several steps toward her and then stopped.

"Allie, if you would, please give me another chance . . ." I demurred and continued to fidget with my cap, bending it with both hands.

"Your proposal was as romantic as any girl would want." Allie hesitated for a while and wiped her eyes with the back of her hands. "It's just that this thing between us has gone too far and this proposal finally made me realize that." Her voice seemed vapid, almost cold. "Remember . . . when we started seeing each other . . . we both agreed we would just be friends . . . and that was all." Once more she demurred for a few seconds. "It's best if we end it now." Again Allie stopped and turned toward the window. "We had some good times, Yogi . . ." She paused once more. When she spoke again, her voice changed to a higher pitch that caused me to believe, she was putting on a good front for my benefit. "Now . . . well, it's time you find another girl, Yogi . . . a decent one . . . who would be worthy of your offer."

Without wanting it, my tone was more peevish than desired, when I replied, "Hell, Allie, after all these months together, I just can't put my feelings in abeyance like a torn parachute! Allie, please . . . you know how deeply I care for you, and I've told you before I can live with the knowledge of your past life. Now that I know the reason . . . it makes it even more forgivable . . . for me anyway."

"Yogi, you know the problems I have and why I can't love you in the normal way a woman should love a man. Besides . . . in a few years, should we get married, how will you feel then, knowing that your wife was a whore? Could you live with it then? And besides that, there will always be men like John . . . who will come along someday and remind us of that fact. I don't want you to be hurt that way again. I . . . I don't want to be hurt like that again!"

"I don't care what John thinks!" I snapped back. "Besides . . . every girl he dates is turned into a whore five minutes after they're in a drive-in movie. For the price of a ticket and a bag of popcorn, they prostitute themselves on the backseat of *The Lung*." After pausing for a moment, I asked in a more gentle tone, "Allie, I have to know if you are going to honor the comment you made about leaving this place. You promised me that . . . the night we had that orange juice together. And . . . what about all the time we spent together on the farm? Doesn't that count for something?"

My pleading seemed pointless, as I searched for reasons to prevent her from returning to her old life in the House. I moved close enough to put my arms around her waist. Her body recoiled with my touch. My tone softened. "Allie, if you return to this place . . . you will never bring to an end your problems, and you will always be the victim of those guys who raped you."

Allie stood motionless as I pulled her body against mine. I buried my face in her hair near her ear. Her body trembled as I continued to hold her. The refreshing smell of her hair evoked many wonderful memories in my mind. I knew a desire for this captivating fragrance would hold my mind prisoner for many months to come, once I left Amarillo.

"Allie, I love you. I can live with the knowledge of who you were. A part of loving someone is learning to forgive them." Reaching around to her face, I kissed her on the cheek. "Besides, we were all something else, before we became what we are," I said with a chuckle. I pushed back the hair on her neck and kissed her several times on the lower part of her neck. "Besides," I added with a snicker, "this place has been as much a part of my life as yours."

"This place doesn't carry the same stigma for a man that it does for a woman," replied Allie, moving away from me. Trying to be nonchalant, Allie rubbed her hands together while putting on a fake smile and repeating herself. "We had some good times together, Yogi. That's all we promised each other. The other night at the Hospital you . . . and my father . . . cooked up a fantasy that isn't meant to be."

"Allie, there's something I need to ask you." Beginning this way seemed crass, but I knew of no other way. "I'm leaving Amarillo . . . the first part of next week for a Base in Japan." I almost choked on the words. After clearing my throat, I tried to continue while fidgeting with my cap. "I was thinking maybe you and I could spend sometime next week on the farm before I leave."

"My Dad may be going home this weekend," answered Allie in a low voice, as if she hadn't heard my question, "and I should be with him."

"That's perfect," I countered quickly. "I could look after your father's cattle and do some other chores around the place while there. I don't have to report to Travis Air Force Base for two weeks."

"Shouldn't you go back to Louisiana and see your family before leaving for Japan?"

"I would rather spend the time with you, Allie," I answered, hugging her from behind. Trying once more to cheer her up, I added, "Hey, we could go for a midnight swim in the water trough like you and Robert used to do as kids."

"Yogi, please don't do this to me," Allie pleaded in a breaking voice, while holding her hands up to her face as if breathing through her fingers.

"Please, Allie. I want to spend my last weekend in Amarillo with you." My voice sounded desperate. "I want to make love to you once more before I leave."

"It's over for us Yogi," Allie added with an abashed voice while looking out the window. "So please . . . just leave." After turning from the window, Allie feigned a smile and said, "When you get to Japan, you'll have yourself one of those little Josans within six weeks, and you'll be bragging to all your buddies over there about your little Texas whore back in Amarillo."

"I'll never speak of you that way, Allie," I answered almost choking.

"Yogi! Please leave," Allie said turning back toward the window.

Her request caused a lurching in my heart, as I realized my world was crumbling before my very eyes. Broken in body and spirit, I couldn't believe all the months we had spent together were being set aside as so much dirty laundry. Still hoping to hang onto what possible love there may have been in her heart for me, I made one last request before leaving the room.

"Allie, if I write . . . will you answer my letters?"

"Please, don't." Allie replied through a choking voice. "I don't know if I'll have time to answer."

"May I ask you to promise me something?" My throat almost closed before I could complete the request. My breathing became difficult.

"It depends," she replied succinctly without turning to face me.

"Allie, promise me that you won't return to this place." I had to stop and take several deep breaths. "Please go back to school and make something of yourself, by putting this life and this place behind you. Maybe some day after you learn to forgive yourself . . . you'll start loving yourself and others again. You're a beautiful person . . . Allie." I lost my breath and stopped for a moment or two to inhale. "You have much to offer if only you would allow yourself to be loved."

"You're a beautiful person too, Yogi," replied Allie as she turned around to face me. With both hands she touched my face. After pulling me closer to her face, she gently kissed me on the lips and began to cry.

Taking her in my arms, I gently pulled her trembling body against mine. Once more in a union of overwhelming emotions as our hearts pounded against each other's chest, our souls seemed to merge into an oneness unknown since that night in the wheat field. For several minutes we stood there in silence, both trying to control the emotions crushing our spirits.

After releasing her, I reached up and held her moist face in my hands and kissed her on the forehead and whispered in French, *Je te mets dans les mains de Dieu.* (I put you in the hands of God.)

"Yogi," Allie called as I turned to walk away, "thanks . . . for being the best friend I've ever had. I'll always . . . always remember your kindness."

Without turning to face her I replied, "Adieu, (farewell) Allie. I'll always remember you, as well. And, someday I'll come back to Amarillo."

Chapter 26

The shifting of my body in the large comfortable seat of the commercial jet transmitted a message to my brain that the plane was beginning its decent. The soft beeping of the warning light in the cabin confirmed that message, as I awakened from the best sleep I had had in days. Somewhat groggy, I brought the seat to an upright position as requested by the flight attendant and looked out the small window. A strange sensation tugged at my heart.

Through the small oval window, the terrestrial world below appeared dry and lifeless as the plane made its approach to Amarillo Air Terminal. The sparsely spaced trees and wide open expanses of the Panhandle stood in stark contrast to the green mountainous woodlands of northern Japan, where I had spent three winters in Wakkanai. Adrenalin surged through my body along with a mixture of emotions, ranging from a heightened sense of hilarity to a burning ardor. For a moment, the imaginary smell of dust in the air and the odor of the stockyards brought an elfin smile to my lips, as Wakkanai reentered my mind. "*How appropriate*," I thought, "*Japan, the smell of fish and Texas, the smell of cattle.*"

I visualized a wisp of smoke trailing from the tires, as the plane touched down with a slight bounce and the sound of the tires coming into contact with the runway. Mesmerized by the sight of the B52s parked in the far distance at the SAC Base, I began to question my decision to leave the Air Force. I also questioned my reason for returning to Amarillo, even though I had promised Allie, someday I would.

As the plane came to a stop, I pushed back in the seat after unbuckling the belt. While the rest of the passengers rushed for the aisles and overhead luggage compartments, I remained seated staring out the window. *I'm home,* I thought, *or what I once considered as my home.* Interlocking my fingers, I stretched out my hands and cracked my knuckles, releasing some nervous energy.

My early morning arrival at Amarillo found me suffering from jet lag, but determined to satisfy the longing tugging at my soul since leaving Amarillo. While seated in a rented car facing Route 66, my brain wrestled with my heart over the sanity of my quest. After a few minutes of sitting still, a few honking horns forced me to pull onto Route 66, heading toward Amarillo. The drive toward town became a trip back in time causing a feeling of happiness to overtake me, as several familiar places came into sight. Seeing the Pink Elephant club, brought James' face to my mind, as I recalled how he ended up in Oklahoma by getting into a car similar to mine, with the intention of sleeping off a bad head.

St Anthony's soon came into view, well before making the turn onto the Polk Street. A warm sensation rushed across my body as I anticipated seeing once more the long flight of steps and buttresses that had consumed so many evenings of my life. Somehow, the hospital seemed larger than I remembered.

The drive down the Polk Street was as if I hadn't left at all. The years I spent in Japan seemed to vanish within a few moments, as the rented car rebounded across the railroad tracks, which my friends and I crossed so many times before, as we dragged up and down Polk Street between the Double Dip and St. Anthony's. Approaching the House caused a tidal wave of memories to serge back into my mind. Still feeling apprehensive about my mission, I cautiously pulled into the parking lot, feeling somewhat embarrassed, as if this was my first visit to the location. After getting out of the car, an interminable period of time passed, as I stared at a top floor window where I last saw Allie.

My anxiety increased to a state of near trepidation as each step brought me closer to the old Hotel. This strange feeling caused me to remember how this same old building had once been a welcoming sight to a younger boy . . . I no longer knew.

Realizing it was much too early for a "House call," for even the streets of the downtown area was dead, except for an occasional passing car. I knew the Devil himself would have to be confronted if Rose was still running the House, but I had traveled this far and was now determined not to let the old bat frighten me off. I inhaled a deep breath and blew it out with force as I stood before the door, peering through the lace curtain. I thought to myself that *a good cup of strong New Orleans chicory-flavored café noir would go good right about now.*

Following a loud harrumph, I spat on the sidewalk and threw back my shoulders. A heightened surge of testosterone and adrenalin shot through my body as I stared at the door bell.

Armed with a devilish smile and an ample supply of fiendish pleasure, knowing these hard working girls would all be sleeping, I pressed the door bell and held it down for a second or two. The deep rich tone of the bell assured me it was working. After a few minutes and no one appeared at the door, my finger again pressed the door bell with delight. At long last, after the fourth time, I heard a voice growling from inside and recognized it as that of Rose's. Knowing this early morning visit would renew the feud between Rose and I, in spite of my years of absence, brought a heightened sense of pleasure to my tired body.

Through the lace curtains, I could see Rose as she trudged through the lobby. From inside, a surly voice yelled out, "We're not open!"

"Open the door, you damned old wench!" My gruff response made it almost impossible to maintain a straight face, a subterfuge I hoped would hold out a few minutes more.

"Go on back to the Base and take a cold shower," Rose answered in an agitated tone.

"Rose! Open the damn door!" I answered in a boisterous voice trying even harder to hold back my laughter.

"Hey! Dimwit! Don't you understand English, or are you drunk? We're not open yet! Now, leave or I'll call the cops."

Through the lace curtain, I saw Rose turned from the door. "Rose, after all these years you still hasn't bought yourself any decent clothes to cover your sagging old butt," I yelled.

Rose paused for a moment, before turning and walking back toward the door. In preparation for a frontal assault, I pulled my uniform cap down a little lower over my eyes to obscure my face. In her long gossamer nightgown and robe, Rose stood before me with her hands firmly planted on her hips, sullen face, and uncombed hair, ready to do battle with this intruder of her domain. There was a minute or two of silence. I could scarcely keep from bursting out in a roar of laughter. I stood motionless as Rose reaching out and slowly lifted the cap from my head.

"Is that you, Yogi?" Rose asked. "Well, son-of-a-bitch, if it ain't."

Before I could reply, Rose pulled me through the door by the arm. I almost tripped on the threshold.

"Damn, boy . . . if you ain't a sight for sore eyes!" Rose replied, while trying to bring some order to her hair. "You done put on some weight," Rose said, standing back to take a look at me.

"Yeah," I lamented with a shrug. "I finally made it up to 170 pounds."

"Yeah . . . but you still got that skinny little butt," Rose said, looking at my backside. "You look good, Boy." I received a hardy slap on the back. "I always did like a boy with some meat on his bones." Taking time to rake her fingers through her hair once more, Rose continued, "Although, you were always good looking . . . even thin."

As Rose and I continued exchanging niceties, Carrie, Dixie, and Angel, all came downstairs to see what the commotion was all about.

Or, perhaps they were looking for some early morning business. After a few hugs and a few more comments about my weight, which they all agreed looked good, Rose sensed my visit wasn't business related.

"Are you back at the Air Base?" Rose asked with a starkly stare, while lighting up a cigarette now inserted into a long plastic holder.

"Rose would like to have you for a customer again," Dixie added, cutting in before I could answer.

"Yeah . . . the business dropped off ten percent, while you've been gallivanting all over the world," added Carrie, while sashaying around in a small circle. Her antics brought forth a round of laughter from everyone.

"No. I'm not . . . back at the Base," I answered, with a chuckle and a nervous movement of my head. "I'm just passing through." My eyes and voice seemed to fall to the floor.

"You're here looking for Allie," solicited Angel in a quiet tone, "aren't you?"

Angel's question seemed to steal the ebullient spirit from the moment.

In an almost apologetic voice I answered, "Yes, I am."

"She left Amarillo the same week you shipped out," Rose answered in a tart tone, while pulling her gossamer robe closed, as if she would rather change the subject. After tying it closed, she took a long drag on her cigarette and blew the smoke in my face. "I always did say, you would be the cause of me loosing the prettiest girl in the place."

Rose's words had a ring of familiarity about them from the "cold war" days, when she and I often disagreed over the relationship between Allie and me.

"Lighten up Rose," Carrie snapped back in my defense. "They were in love."

"Yogi, we don't know where she is now." added Dixie. "But," she paused as if thinking. "Hey, Crystal would know. They call each other from time to time."

"Yeah . . . Rose. Call her down," Angel added with a plea in her voice.

Rose appeared to hesitate for a minute or two and then picked up the phone and dialed a number. As the girls and I made small talk, Rose asked Crystal to come to the lobby.

I wasn't sure if my heart could take the strain of seeing another beautiful American girl so skimpily clothed at such an early hour, but I was willing to take the chance.

Crystal wasn't fully awake when she entered the lobby. She pushed back her hair with one hand and then gathered, closed her robe with the other, hiding her voluptuous form showing through her hot pink negligee. She hesitated at a distance and looked at me with a questionable stare.

Dixie's high pitch voice broke the silence that seemed to permeate the room.

"Hey, Crystal, look who's here to see us."

We stood looking at each other for a short while before I spoke.

"Good morning, Crystal."

Stillness enveloped the room as Crystal studied this person who so rudely interrupted her sleep. Then she asked in a soft demure tone, "Yogi, is that you?" She appeared confused and groggy, as she held the front of her robe closed with one hand.

"Of course, it is," Angel answered for me.

"Yeah. Yogi's here, so it must be Wednesday," Carrie added with a slight giggle.

We all laughed. Rose was more subdued. After Crystal and I hugged each other, she too made a remark about my weight. I was starting to feel self-conscious and thought I should consider going on a diet.

"He's looking for Allie," Rose announced in a sarcastic tone.

Looking disappointed, Crystal demurred before answering. She nervously ran her fingers through her hair and then said, "Yogi, she moved back to her father's farm."

"When?" I asked.

"Shortly, after you left Amarillo," she said and then looked down toward the floor. "The same week . . . I believe."

I was relieved when Crystal confirmed Rose's statement about Allie leaving Amarillo soon after I had and for the first time, I realized she had kept her promise to me, that the House would not become a part of her life after I was gone. I wondered if she had managed to finish nursing school at some other College. Crystal's demeanor conveyed the impression she was reluctant to say more.

"What is it?" I asked in almost a sharp tone.

"Yogi," Crystal started to say and then stopped for a second or two, while she tied her robe close. "Allie's married."

Crystal's words rumbled through my head like thunder. For a moment, I suffered the illusion of teetering, as five feminine faces watched over me. I wanted to scream out in disbelief, but somehow suspected as much, or so I tried telling myself. Deep down inside, I knew she would someday find someone she could love. A number of reasons flashed through my mind, as to why she hadn't waited for me, knowing how much I had loved her. The downcast expression on my face caused Crystal to speak again, breaking the silence that had once again fallen upon the room.

"After you left town, Yogi, her father died of cancer," Crystal added, "and Allie moved back to the farm to be with her mother."

"Is Mrs. Natty still living?" I asked.

"She died just a few months ago . . . that's what we heard," answered Rose stoically.

"Who did Allie marry?" I asked looking at Crystal.

"Some guy from back home," Crystal answered, in a somewhat reluctant voice. "I believe, he was her high school boyfriend."

"Ain't that the way it always happens?" injected Dixie in a loud squeaky voice.

"Dixieeee!" Crystal said in a sharp response, as if to negate the remark.

"Maybe, you should go back to Lubbock, Dixie and try to get back with your old high school boyfriend," Angel added to the chastisement of Dixie.

"I hope that bastard dies from a slow-eating cancer," Dixie snapped back. "He's the one who got me into this lousy business. He thought I was his personal whore during high school and then dropped me for some society debutante during college."

I wasn't ready for Dixie's apologia, but remembering Allie's situation, I wondered how many of these girls had a similar story.

"You got time for breakfast, Yogi?" Rose asked rising from her chair. "Old Sam should have it ready."

"I could use a cup of coffee," I answered glancing around at the girls.

Crystal's face beamed with a smile as she said, "Yogi, you go with Rose and the girls while I run back upstairs. I have something for you."

After greeting Sam with a handshake, I settled down to the best breakfast I've had in several years. My desire for a strong cup of New

Orleans café noir almost came to fruition with Rose's deep black ropy coffee. The girls kept the conversation during breakfast on a ribald level, Paul would have enjoyed, by questioning me about their counterparts in Japan. Rose had her usual complaint about life in general, men in particular and the girls, now ten in attendance, all offered their rebuttals to her woes.

Crystal soon walked into the kitchen and placed a shoebox on the table next to me.

"These are yours, Yogi," Crystal said taking a chair next to me.

"What's this?" I asked with a chuckle. "A pair of shoes?"

"No, silly," Crystal responded with a soft smile. "It's your letters." She quickly added, before I could open the box. "And, I didn't open them, either."

"My . . . letters?" I asked, removing the ribbon around the box timidly before the staring faces watching me. Carefully, I removed the box top and laid it aside. In silence, I thumbed through the envelopes. A constriction gripped my throat, as I recalled the heartache and pain associated with each of them. There were so many.

"Why did you keep them?" I asked not looking up, trying to hide my feelings from the faces surrounding me.

"I knew . . . someday you would come back," Crystal answered with a degree of empathy that I found startling, for I had not imagined girls such as she and the other sitting at the table were capable of such kindness. "Yogi, I called Allie several times about the letters but she didn't want me to mail them to her."

"Why did you send your letters here?" asked a pretty blonde in her early twenties who I didn't know.

"Because . . . I was a fool," I said with a tremor in my voice. "I didn't have the faith in her to trust . . . that she would make the right decision about her own life."

"Look, Yogi, why don't you forget about trying to see her right now?" asked Crystal as her hand touched mine. She's married now. She's no longer the girl you once knew, Yogi."

"I know. But, I must see her once more before returning home." I answered dryly.

I enjoyed two more cups of coffee, which I felt sure would leave a dark brown stain on my teeth, as the one on the carafe, before being escorted to the front door by a fine entourage of pretty American girls.

After a round of hugs and farewells Rose, in a gesture of friendship offered, "Yogi, if you ever come this way again . . . stop by. The first trip upstairs will be on the House."

"Rose," I answered with an askance look, "I do believe you're getting soft in your old age." With a smirk on my face, I added, "And, if I should come back this way, I hope, by then you'll have a thicker robe. You're starting to sag a little in the derriere."

"Someday, buddy boy; you will sag in a place, you won't find so damn funny!" yelled Rose before I reached the door.

As I made my way down the sidewalk, I could hear the girls laughing at Rose. She had managed to get the final words in on our 'cold war' as it was coming to a close. Before getting into the car, I stood and took one last look at the House. Looking up at, what I assumed was still room 210; I thought I saw someone standing at the window. Perhaps it was a ghost. Still, I raised my hand and offered up the International sign for "I love you."

Before starting the car, I hesitated, considering once more, my intended destination, after placing the shoebox on top of the leather coat Allie had given me for Christmas.

Pulling onto Polk Street, I noticed the traffic had picked up. Amarillo was awakening to another beautiful summer day.

Chapter 27

The longing for the vast openness of the Texas Panhandle and the golden heads of wheat dancing in the breeze had become an unquenchable thirst to my soul during my tour in Japan. Now, the maturing wheat lining each side of the highway began to fulfill that thirst as my eyes scanned the horizons. My years of absence caused the memories of the long hot days in the field with Mr. Henry and Maude to appear, as if they were from some other person's life, until the old iron bridge came into view. After slowing down, I drove across at a more moderate speed, while searching the horizon for the large trees in the Sailhamer's yard. Since leaving Wakkanai, they and the girl who treated my sunburned back beneath their boughs, had been my intended destination.

Slowly, I turned into the driveway and stopped a short distance from the house. Stepping out of the car, ever so slowly, I stood timidly behind the open door and surveyed the place, as if reconciling the present reality with my memory. The warmth of the filtered sunlight through the trees enhanced the stillness about the farm, as my face, momentarily turned upward to the gentle rustling leaves.

My fascination with the dancing broad leaves of the cottonwood trees was broken by the musical whinnying of two horses in the corral. Their romping caused an ebullient rush to wash across my body, until I realized the two horses were not Buster and Midnight.

Very little had changed except, the addition of a recent coat of paint to the house and a child's swing set in the yard near one of the large trees. Looking at the porch, I noticed the hammock was gone.

The noise created by a small boy pulling a red wagon from around the back corner of the house abruptly ended my reminiscing. His youthful adventure came to a stand still when he spotted me. He appeared to be about four years old. His coarse black hair was straight and *a little long for a boy,* I thought. Wearing only a pair of short pants, his skinny upper body and legs at first gave me the impression he was malnourished.

After studying each other for a short time, the boy allowed the wagon tongue to fall to the ground, before slowly walking in my direction. I stood still, intimidated by his stare.

With his eyes squinched, the boy looked up at me and asked, "Are you an Army man?"

Kneeing before him on one knee, both to answer his question, and to get a better look at his tiny dirty face, I gazed into his dark brown eyes as they appeared to see through me. Supposing him to be Allie's son, an unexplained desire to take him into my arms tugged at my soul. His long hair needed brushing back from his face, but something restrained my hand.

"No. I'm not an army man. I'm in the Air Force, and we're called 'Airmen,'" I answered after clearing my throat.

"Air Men?" he asked with a puzzled expression that caused his little face to contort. For a moment his expression reminded me of a young Japanese boy I had befriended at an orphanage in Wakkanai, whom I named "Ringo," because his reddish face look like an apple.

"What's your name?" I asked, lightly touching his left shoulder.

"Robert Earl," he answered. With a movement of his shoulder, he dislodged my hand.

Remembering how much Allie loved her brother, I thought it only fitting that she would name her son after him.

"Is your mother home?" I asked, as tightness gripped my throat. My heart palpitated within my chest at the sound of my own words.

"Uh-huh," the boy replied, as he turned and pointed toward the house. "Mommy's inside."

"Are you strong enough to ring that old bell near the steps?" I asked standing.

Once more Robert answered, "Uh-huh."

"Go ring it. Let's see if Mommy will come outside."

I watched for a moment as Robert ran ahead of me as fast as his skinny legs could carry him. His tromping through the flower bed surrounding the bell pole brought a smile to my face. The vigor, with which he began pulling the rope, told me this wasn't his first time. With each clear peeling of the bell, some magical force pulled me closer to the back steps leading to the kitchen entrance.

From within the kitchen, a woman's voice called out, "Robert, stop ringing that bell!"

Robert continued looking in my direction, as he pulled even harder on the rope.

The kitchen screen door came partially open.

"Yogi!" shouted the woman looking at the boy from the top step. "Stop ringing that bell! And, get out of my flower bed!"

Letting go of the rope, Robert pointed at me and said, "He told me to Mommy."

When Allie turned in my direction, my heart vaulted within my chest. We both stared at each other in disbelief. For an infinitesimal moment, the hands of time moved back to a summer, lost in time.

"Yogi! Is it you?" Allie asked in quiet disbelief, as she eased down the steps.

Allie's voice caused a temporary paralysis to take control of my feet and mind. As she walked toward me, it seemed the doldrums of a four-yearlong nightmare was coming to an end. For several moments, we stood facing each other, before we embraced with an outburst of laughter and hilarity. Our ecstatic happiness brought a smile to Robert's face as he moved to Allie's side.

Allie gently pushed away from my arms after a while and stood back, as if taking a grander view of me. A smile parted her lips.

"You've put on some weight," Allie said, holding her right hand up to her mouth.

"So have you," I sniggered while looking down at her stomach. Without intending the crass gesture that immediately embarrassed me, I pointed and asked, "Are you . . . ?"

"Yes, I am. Four months," Allie replied with a blush. With both hands Allie raised her apron, revealing more clearly her condition. "Well, do you think motherhood is becoming to this one time . . . ?"

The question hung in the air incomplete, as Allie lowered her head slowly as an abashed expression came to her face.

"It's very becoming to the student nurse I knew some years ago," I answered, lifting her chin with one hand. After kissing her lightly on the cheek, as a show of approbation, I whispered, "Allie, that place no longer exists for either of us."

"Thanks, Yogi," Allie said, as she wiped her eyes with the edge of her apron.

"Mommy, how come you're crying?" asked Robert looking at Allie with a puzzled expression.

"Because . . . Mommy's happy," answered Allie, bending over to pick up the boy. "Robert, this is Mommy's very good friend from a long time ago."

I offered my hand to Robert. He responded by offering his small, soft, dirty hand.

"I'm pleased to meet you, Robert," I said, looking once more into his dark brown eyes and then at Allie. "Does Mommy call you Yogi, at times other than when she's upset?"

I apparently held the boy's hand longer than he felt comfortable with and after a time he pulled his hand away from mine.

"When he was born . . . Mama gave him that name," answered Allie, as she lowered Robert to the ground.

Standing before Allie with her son at her side caused a multitude of questions to enter my mind, most of which, I knew would never be answered. A deep dryness came into my throat and for a moment I turned away pretending to look over the farm.

"This place hasn't changed much. It's still as beautiful as ever." Without thinking I blurted out, "Just as you . . . are."

"You're just being kind, Yogi," Allie said, placing her hand on my shoulder. With a laughter that seemed contrived, Allie added, "I'm as big as a blimp and as country now as my mother used to be. I've even let my hair grow out."

"I like it," I answered desiring to touch it.

Turning to watch Robert as he resumed pulling the noisy wagon, Allie said in a chipper voice, "Let's not stand here in the sun, Yogi. Do you still like coffee?" asked Allie taking me by the hand and leading me toward the steps.

"Yes. Of course," I answered following Allie's lead. "To be truthful, I drink too much."

Being in the kitchen reminded me of the nights the Three Apostles and I, along with Allie, pulled KP duty, as an expression of our appreciation for the fine suppers prepared by Mrs. Natty.

"The guys and I really enjoyed your Mom's cooking," I said looking around. With a chuckle, I added, "I swear . . . I believe she was trying to fatten up the four of us in one week."

"I'm sorry you won't get a chance to see Earl," Allie apologized, while filling the coffee pot with water. "He had to go into Amarillo for a meeting with the Wheat Growers Association."

"Earl McCurley?" I asked. The doubt in my voice caused Allie to pause with her back toward me.

"I married him . . . eighteen months ago, Yogi," answered Allie, putting down the coffee pot without turning.

"Eighteen months ago," I repeated. Looking out the screen door toward Robert, I asked, "Then whose Robert's . . . ?"

My unfinished question brought a long silence to the kitchen as Allie stood with her back toward me. Her hand trembled when she attempted to plug in the coffee pot.

"Robert Earl is your son, Yogi," answered Allie, while resting her weight on both hands spread out on the counter.

For several minutes I stood frozen, staring at Allie's back as the noise of Robert's wagon reverberated through the stillness of the house with increasing loudness. Finally my rumination came to an end, as Robert came running through the dining room door.

"I gotta go pee, Mommy," announced Robert scrambling toward the stairs.

"Don't forget to wash your hands," yelled Allie. As we both laughed Allie apologized. "I'm sorry Yogi, but he's one-hundred-percent boy."

Several moments of silence passed while Allie and I looked at each other not knowing if we should resume the conversation.

"Was he conceived that night . . . ?" Glancing down at the floor, my question went unfinished. When Allie turned toward me, I saw the answer in her eyes. Still for some strange reason, its importance demanded a verbal response.

"Yes, he was . . . Yogi," Allie answered with some reluctance. After reaching for two coffee cups in the cabinet to the left of the sink, Allie stood motionless with her head down.

"You haven't told Earl about that night, I hope?" I asked, with an upbeat tone in my voice, trying to cheer her up.

"Of course not, Yogi," Allie answered turning to face me. "That will always be our secret, our . . . most special moment." Allie walked toward me. I didn't know what to expect. "Let's go sit in the dining room, Yogi, while the coffee is brewing."

Like the kitchen, the dining room hadn't changed, except for a few new pictures and a different color of paint on the walls. Seeing Mr. Henry's chair at the head of the table and the revelation that I had fathered a son caused a whirlwind of thoughts to traverse my mind, as Mr. Henry's painful confession in the hospital came flooding into my brain. Not knowing what to ask or say I stood looking toward the staircase.

"Is the squeaky board still pulling guard duty?"

Allie gave an imperceptible grin. "Yes, it is." Rubbing her stomach, she added, "If this is a girl, it'll remain on guard duty for many years to come."

Feeling restless, I moved about the room hoping Robert Earl would come back down the stairs. My aimless wandering brought me within a foot of Allie.

Looking down into her eyes, I quietly remarked, "Sounds like you're anticipating another young Airman visiting the farm some day."

"I wouldn't mind, Yogi . . . if he's as nice as the one I once knew," Allie said, staring into my eyes for a moment before looking away.

The slamming of an upstairs bedroom door caused Allie and me to look toward the stairs.

"I'm hungry, Mommy," pleaded Robert as he came running down the stairs.

"In just a minute, Honey," Allie answered looking at me, as I watched Robert walk toward the kitchen. "Yogi, get a couple of cookies and go play for a little longer while Mr. Yogi and I talk."

"Is your name Yogi?" interrupted Robert, as he stared up at me. A couple of furrows developed in his small forehead.

"Yes, it is," I replied while studying his face. "Just like yours." He smiled as if pleased.

Allie and I remained quiet as Robert pushed a chair across the kitchen floor so he could reach the cookie jar on the counter. His exit through the kitchen screen door was announced with a loud slamming sound that drew Allie and me back into the kitchen.

"Is Earl still running old Maude?" I asked, as Allie filled one cup with coffee.

"Maude's in a museum, Yogi," Allie answered gaily, offering me the cup of coffee. "Some little town in Kansas bought her for their museum the year after Daddy died."

"That's great," I said with a chuckle, while walking back into the dining room. In a raised voice I said, "I know your Daddy would be pleased."

When Allie entered the dining room carrying her cup of coffee, I pulled a chair from the table for her. With a quiet "thank-you," Allie sat down. After running her hand across the table as if sweeping away some invisible crumbs, Allie said with a smile, "God, I still remember the joy and laughter, which filled this old house the week you and the Three Apostles were here."

"I remember the expression on your father's face when Paul suggested a new type of dusk mask," I countered with a chuckle.

"I remember the happiness the four of you brought to my mother's heart, as y'all gobbled up that pile of fried chicken." Allie stopped and inhaled a deep breath as she placed her cup on the table. The old melancholy spirit that I had seen take possession of Allie so many times reasserted itself as she paused with her head down. "I want that feeling someday, Yogi. I want to watch my sons . . . grow up in this old house . . . and around this big old table."

The sadness expressed in Allie's voice was now apparent in her eyes. I took her hand in mine, and trying to sound upbeat, I suggested, "Maybe if you have three more boys, you could name them after The Three Apostles."

With a slight giggle Allie said, "I would like that, Yogi."

"You'll have a job refining their personalities."

Allie and I enjoyed a brief moment of laughter, before a silence enveloped the room. The ease, with which we once shared out thoughts, had been eroded with the passing years. Without finishing the coffee, I stood and kissed Allie on the cheek.

"I have to be going. Come out to the car . . . I have something for you."

We walked to the car without speaking. After opening the car door, I retrieved the shoebox and offered it to Allie.

"What's this?" Allie asked with a slight laughter. She removed the ribbon and opened the box revealing its contents. A smile parted her lips. "What are these, Yogi?"

"The letters I wrote you from Japan," I said with a shrug.

"Where did you find them?" Allie asked, not looking up at me as she thumbed through the letters as if counting them.

"Crystal saved them." I answered.

"When did you see her?" Allie asked looking up from the box.

"This morning . . . before leaving Amarillo," I replied with a smile. "I stopped there briefly, to see if she knew where you were living."

"There are so many . . ." Allie softly answered, as she resumed counting the letters. Her hands began to tremble.

I reached out and touched her arm.

"Writing these letters became a substitute for the time we used to spend together each Wednesday." I paused to clear the lump in my throat. "Each Wednesday, Allie, around 5:00 p.m., I would think of that special time we shared and before going to the Mess Hall, I would sit down and write to you." I paused for an even longer time before continuing. "Allie . . . do you remember how special our Wednesday evenings were?"

"Yes, Yogi," Allie answered, looking down. "I remember. They were very special."

"Allie, you'll never know how much I missed you during those first few months in Japan," I said, turning my head downward a little trying to see her face.

"Yogi, you know I never felt worthy of your love," Allie said, as her voice began to break. "You deserve someone better than a . . . a girl . . . from that place." She paused for a second or two, while looking at the letters. "You knew I could never love you the way a woman should love a man . . . I'm still not capable of that kind of love, Yogi."

"What about Earl, do you love him?" I asked with a touch of anger in my voice.

For several moments, Allie paused before answering. Her eyes diverted away from my face.

"No. I don't Yogi," she answered softly with a slight movement of her head. "But, I remember the feelings I had for him as a child . . . and for now that's good enough. That may not make much sense to you, Yogi, but it's all I have to hang onto. Earl's a good man and a good father to little Yogi. He knows, Robert is your son . . . and he loves him as if he was his own." Allie paused once more in her desultory speech and wrung her hands together. "Maybe . . . in time, Yogi, I'll learn to love Earl as a man and as a husband."

Realizing Allie was still suffering from the same emotional problems after so many years, I asked, "Are you still going to counseling?"

"No," Allie said with a slight movement of her head. "I took the advice of a very caring friend . . . and got out of the life I was living and started making it on my own." Handing the shoe box back to me, Allie said, "Yogi, I can't accept these, it wouldn't be right."

"Is it because of Earl?" I asked, accepting the box.

"Yes. He's my husband now."

Without saying anything else, I retied the ribbon around the shoebox. After placing it on the front seat, the leather coat was then taken up.

Offering the coat to Allie, I said apologetically, "It's a little worn now, but I want you to have this back." I swallowed hard. "It rightly belongs to your family."

"Yogi, it was a gift," Allie pleaded.

"Yeah, I know," I answered with a shrug. "It was a beautiful gift and served me well during those cold winter months in Japan. But, I want you to save it for Yogi. Some day he'll grow into it." As I held out the coat, I added, "Some day if you like . . . tell him the story behind this gift."

Trying to hide the pain that must have been showing in my face, I turned my attention toward the boy now playing on the swing set.

"Allie, will you ever be able to love him?"

"Because of him . . . Yogi, I'm starting to have some feelings of love in my heart again. Maybe it's just maternal," she answered, again lowering her head. "There's in him . . . a part of the only two boys . . . who were ever important in my life . . . you and my brother." Allie looked into my face as the tears began to stream down her cheeks and said, "Yogi, if I could have ever loved any man in a normal way . . . I would have wanted it to be you. Perhaps someday, through little Yogi, that hope, which I keep deep down inside, will come true."

Allie moved close to me and once more we embraced. I felt her pain and sadness as her body trembled. From deep down within my being, I wished the power was mine to turn back the hands of time for her, to the days before the incident, which changed her life forever. For the first time, I found myself hating the boys who had destroyed the capacity of this beautiful girl to love, not only me, but all men who would become a part of her life. I thought of what Dixie had said earlier that morning about her High School boyfriend, and wondered how many other girls had had their lives destroyed by uncaring and unloving boys.

"Allie, when Robert's old enough to understand, tell him about me . . . please make him understand, I love him and would have been here for him, had I known."

Fighting back the tears, Allie shook her head up and down.

"I'll tell him Yogi. I'll tell him what a wonderful and kind father he has." Allie wiped a tear from her eyes with the corner of her apron. "I hope someday he'll grow up to be as gentle and loving a man as you are."

"Could I say good-bye to Yogi?" I asked wiping my eyes.

Allie wiped her face and called Robert away from his wagon. When he reached Allie's side, she picked him up and held him in her arms.

"Mr. Yogi is leaving Robert, and he would like to say good-bye to you."

"Good-bye, Mr. Yogi," said young Robert with a big smile.

"Good-bye, Yogi," I responded with a forced smile. After pausing for a moment, I pinched his bare chest and asked, "Yogi, will you do a big favor for me?"

"Yep," the child answered with another grin.

"Promise me," I began, "you'll always love your Mama for me." I paused for a while to allow the constriction in my throat to clear, and then continued the best I could. "Please . . . grow up to be a good boy . . ." I had to stop at this point.

Taking him into my arms, I held him as tight as I could. Tears ran down my face, and I wasn't ashamed that as a man, I was capable of crying. Placing my head close to his, I whispered, "I love you, Yogi."

I held Robert until he began moving around in my arms, as if the intimacy was uncomfortable for him. Reluctantly, I stooped to place him on the ground, and he immediately leaned against Allie's legs as if seeking shelter.

Standing I gave Allie what was to be our final kiss. It was soft, gentle, and very brief. The tears flowed freely down her face as I pulled away and her arms tightened around the leather jacket she was holding.

"Allie." My mouth became extremely dry and my tongue stopped moving. Then I continued with the same words spoken so many times before, for they were the only thing I could think of. "I've loved you since the first moment I saw you in the backseat of that car . . . the night you and your friends picked me up at the Double Dip. I'll always love you . . . even until the day I die."

Allie pulled my body against her own and placed her head on my shoulder. With a whisper, she said, "Yogi, I've loved you since that night."

We stood there holding on to each other and crying with equally broken hearts. The world at that moment was of no importance to us, as we leaned on each other for the final time. Allie had finally declared her love for me, yet deep down inside, I knew she was saying what my heart wanted to hear. I accepted it as the truth, because I knew it was all she was capable of doing.

"Good-bye, Allie," I said in a demure tone. She remained silent and pulled Robert's head against her legs.

Gently I pulled the car door closed.

As I pulled onto the black top road, I glanced back for the final time at the girl and the place, which had changed my life. Allie remained motionless with her face buried in the leather coat, while little Yogi clung to her legs.

Driving down the narrow country road, the wheat fields on each side swayed in the gentle panhandle breeze, as if waving to me a final farewell. Once more my eyes burned with the tears I tried holding back. Driving on, the presence of the shoebox on the passenger side of the seat, pulled relentlessly at my heart, until I picked it up and held it against my chest.

The old iron bridge soon came into sight once more. After pulling the car onto the shoulder near the bridge I got out, taking with me the shoebox. I walked to the center of the bridge and stared down into the small stream thinking of Dutch and Yellow Flower. After several agonizing minutes, I gave the shoebox a gently toss. I watched as it floated down stream for a ways before becoming entangled in a snag. As the top of the box disappeared below the water surface, I knew this chapter of my life was over and that Allie and little Yogi would never again be a part of my world.

I stood on the bridge for some time without moving, just looking down into the water, trying to understand why life had dealt Allie and me such a hand. I wondered if this was God's way of punishing her and me for the sins of our youth. Like the Prodigal Son, that I had become, I knew the journey back home would be long, both geographically and spiritually and like the wayward son in Luke's gospel, I also knew welcoming arms would be awaiting me, in spite of the secret ignominious ending to this era of my life. Before leaving the bridge, in a breaking voice and with a broken heart, I expressed for the last time, my love for the beautiful Texas girl who had come into my life, like the rush of the panhandle wind blowing across the amber waves of grain.

The End

Get Published, Inc!
Thorofare, NJ 08086
08 March, 2010
BA2010067